About the Author

In addition to writing novels, Olivia Isaac-Henry is a crime drama lover, occasional keyboard player, and backing vocalist ... and The Protaganist. She grew up in Worcestershire ... lives in London, where she loves the theatres, food ... and festivals.

Other titles by Olivia Isaac-Henry:

Someone You Know

THE
VERDICT

OLIVIA ISAAC-HENRY

OneMoreChapter

Published by ONE MORE CHAPTER
A division of HarperCollins*Publishers* Ltd
1 London Bridge Street
London SE1 9GF

www.harpercollins.co.uk

A Paperback Original 2019

A catalogue copy of this book is available from the British Library.

ISBN: 978-0-00-831777-5

Typeset in Birka by Palimpsest Book Production Limited, Falkirk, Stirlingshire
Printed and bound in UK by CPI Group (UK) Ltd, Croydon CR0 4YY

MIX
Paper from
responsible sources
FSC C007454
www.fsc.org

This book is produced from independently certified FSC™ paper to ensure
responsible forest management.

For more information visit: www.harpercollins.co.uk/green

For Keith

Prologue

Stumbling down the hill, filthy and too exhausted to even lift the shovels dragging behind them, they looked up to see a red glow starting to stretch along the ridge above. Dawn was breaking.

'Hurry up,' he said.

At the bottom of the hill, she managed to haul herself over the stile, only to tumble down the slope on the other side and fall face down in the road, her fingernails bloodstained, her mouth and nose clogged with dirt. She could have fallen asleep there and then, not caring if she were seen.

A hand reached under her armpit and hauled her to her feet.

'Keep moving.'

What was the point in moving or any attempt at concealment? He wouldn't lie buried for ever. Someday, maybe tomorrow, maybe next week or next year, someone would find him.

Chapter 1

It feels like centuries since I was young. I look around my office; Miranda is scrolling through Tinder while drinking a coffee. Her lithe body falls across a hard-backed wooden chair as if it were a hammock.

Paulo wears mustard-coloured jeans, his feet up on the desk, the soles of his boots splayed towards me. The urge to kick them off becomes so great, I have to look away.

'Yeah, I know, yeah,' he drones into his phone, too loud and irritating to tune out.

What right do they have to youth? They do not value it. They will waste it, as I did mine, and one day wake up, middle-aged, in an office full of people who believe them to be obsolete, an irrelevance. They will stare at the calendar and not believe the year – how did we reach 2017 so quickly? And then the day, Wednesday – how many hours until the weekend?

I used to wonder what these millennials thought about me, then I realised, I'm invisible, they don't think about me. On the first day Miranda made some polite enquiries. I tried to ignore her lisp as she asked, 'Are you married, single?'

1

'Separated,' I say.

'So, what you gonna do about it?' she asked.

'About what?'

'Being single?'

'Nothing,' I told her.

She gave me an odd look.

'Well, Jonathan's going to be on the desk next to you,' she said. 'It's easier if you're together.'

Easier because we're around the same age? I'm sure Jonathan would balk at the idea. He wears slim-fit maroon trousers and goes sockless in slip-on shoes, believing he's not so different from the kids around us. At least I'm not suffering under that delusion.

Since that first day, Miranda's barely spoken to me. And whenever I ask what she and other members of the team are laughing about in the corner, she says, *nothing*, and slopes off, like a kid caught cutting class.

She chats to Jonathan, despite his age, but then he is her boss. Today she's telling him about her cousin's upcoming trip to Vietnam.

'My son was there in his gap year – loved it,' Jonathan says. 'But Cambodia's more interesting. Took a trip out there a few years ago – Angkor Wat – amazing.'

Bless Jonathan. If you've been to the moon, he's been there twice.

'My cousin's going to be working, not just travelling,' Miranda says.

'I suppose your son's at that age now, Julia,' Jonathan says.

He catches me off guard. I'm unused to being included in conversations.

'Sam's only seventeen, still doing A levels – not sure what he wants to do afterwards,' I say.

'Uni, gap year?'

'Still undecided.'

'You need to look into it now,' Jonathan says. 'At least a year in advance. Have a chat with him. Are you close?'

You're a whore. I hate you.

'He's growing up. Doesn't need his mum so much these days.'

'You always need your mum,' Miranda says. 'I'm twenty-five and I still talk to mine every day.'

I wish you were dead.

'I think you need some independence, before you become close again,' I say.

'That's difficult these days,' Miranda says. 'Because no one can afford to leave home. I only managed it because I found this property guardian job.'

Jonathan turns the conversation back to his son and the flat he's helping him to buy. I make a coffee and slip out of the door. No one notices.

Outside, it's a bright day, with only a hint of rain in the air. A man in a padded jacket enters the Sensuous Bean next door, my co-workers' preferred coffee shop. Sometimes they take their laptops and work in there. My café is the green in the square of Georgian houses behind the main road. A small patch of grass with benches provides fresh air and somewhere to sit and drink. The tall poplars surrounding it are turning to rust in the early October chill. Their leaves swirl around the square, hugging its corners and clogging its drains. A toddler jumps into a great pile of them, kicking whorls into the air and giggling with glee. He reminds me of Sam at that age, in his red jacket with the hood falling back from his head.

Loitering by the bin is a man dressed entirely in khaki. He's constantly hanging about the square, a roll-up wedged between his forefingers. I've always suspected he's a drug dealer. People come and stand and talk to him for half a minute or so, money changes hands, and the people wander off. It all seems very friendly, not how I imagined the trade to be carried out, with knives and Rottweilers. I've spent so many coffee breaks here, khaki man and I are now on nodding terms.

Today, a few workmen, in thick boots and high-vis jackets, are sitting around chatting and drinking tea from polystyrene cups. One of them, who hasn't bothered to take off his hard hat, is chatting to a man in mustard-coloured jeans. I do a double take and realise it's Paulo from the office. He turns and sees me, gives me a nervous smile and looks a little embarrassed. Is the man in the hard hat Paulo's bit of rough? *Not everything's about sex*, my mother, Audrey, always tells me. She's right, not everything, but it's what most things boil down to. That and greed.

A bleep from my phone distracts me. I check straight away, in case it's Sam.

Jules, we're back! Come over tomorrow and we'll talk. XXX

My oldest friend, Pearl, is the only person I can forgive for not being Sam, but I wish he'd contact me. Missing him has become a physical ache. I'll text her back later.

I'm walking to the next free bench when my phone beeps

again. An unknown number this time, probably informing me I've been mis-sold PPI – whatever that is.

I open the message. I must have misread it. I stare at the phone and force my eyes to focus. I read it again.

It's a photo link to a news website, a picture of lush, rolling hills, dotted with clumps of beech trees. Clouds cross a bright sky, casting shadows over the dells and copses. Above the photo is a headline: *Surrey University Students Discover Body Buried on North Downs*.

My throat constricts. Black spots start to float in front of my eyes. The square, its leaves, its inhabitants disappear. I drop the coffee.

Chapter 2

1994 – Guildford

Julia stood outside Guildford train station, twisting a flimsy A–Z in her hands and trying to orientate herself towards the six locations, ringed in red biro, where she'd arranged viewings. Her two criteria were that the room must be clean and close to the train station. Guildford was to be a place of work only, the room she sought somewhere to rest her head. Her life would be in London. At weekends, she'd stay over at Pearl's, and catch the late train back on weeknights.

After a couple of wrong turns, Julia found the first place. What the advert had described as a charming cottage was, in fact, a tiny terrace house. The landlord was waiting outside. Rotund, and in his late fifties or early sixties, he was more of a yokel than the Surrey stockbroker type she'd expected.

'Jeff,' the man said and stuck his hand into hers.

'Julia,' she replied.

'You're the first to see it. If you like, you can help choose the other tenants.'

So far, so good.

Jeff wrenched open the rusted gate into a small front garden, overrun with weeds. Inside, the house was empty, except for a thick-pile beige carpet on the floor.

'I've ordered new furniture,' the landlord said once inside.

A sofa and coffee table may have helped to hide some of the stains or distracted from the thick dust on the skirting boards.

'Did the last tenants wreck it?' Julia asked.

'Who?'

'The previous tenants, it doesn't look like they took care of the place.'

The man scowled. 'My wife's always been a stickler for housework,' he said. 'If it's a little dusty, it's because we moved out a couple of weeks ago and there's been no chance to run a cloth over it.'

Julia eyed the sticky mug ring on the mantelpiece and caught a whiff of dog hair rising from the carpet.

'What do you think?' Jeff asked, after giving her a tour.

'The bedroom's a bit small,' she said.

The second room on her list was in a similar Victorian terrace to the first. Two male PhD students, from Surrey University, were already living there. It annoyed Julia that she hoped at least one of them was good-looking and single. The first hope was wiped out as she entered the house, and she never got around to asking about the second.

Ewan, twenty-six and reading physics, showed her the room, which was large and had its own sink. Promising. And while the place couldn't exactly be called clean, it wasn't filthy, and the location was convenient.

Ewan sat her down in the kitchen and made her a cup of tea.

'This is Simon,' he said. 'He'll be your other housemate.'

Simon sat at the other end of the table to Julia, his face hidden behind some academic tome.

'Hi,' Julia said.

Simon lowered the book, peered over the top, but didn't respond.

'So, what do you do?' Ewan asked.

'I'm about to start as a ...' Simon distracted her by putting down his book, placing his elbows on the table, his head in his hands and devoting all his energy to glaring at her. 'As a software developer at Morgan Boyd Consulting.'

Had she done something wrong? She looked directly at Simon and smiled. He continued to glare. Ewan appeared unaware of his housemate's open intimidation.

'We're kind of quiet in the week, but go out on Friday and Saturday,' he said.

Simon's expression remained fixed and hostile. A mild panic ran through her. Was this a trap? Did these men lure young women in with the offer of a room, do away with them and stash their corpses under the floorboards? Perhaps her tea was drugged. Perhaps Simon kept his dead mother mummified in the basement. She'd seen *Psycho*.

Julia put down the mug. 'You know, it's lovely but ... er ... too far from the station.'

'It's a three-minute walk,' Ewan said.

'Thanks.'

Simon was still staring at her. Julia picked up her bag and ran out down the hall, towards the door.

'Is it the mess? We're thinking of getting a cleaner,' Ewan called from the kitchen.

Julia slammed the door behind her and ran to the end of

the road before turning back. She almost expected to see Simon racing from the house to hunt her down. The front door stayed shut. She walked around the corner and out of sight before stopping to catch her breath. As soon as her breathing had slowed down, she laughed out loud. *Psycho* – she was being ridiculous. People aren't murdered in cosy commuter towns. Perhaps all Simon had wanted was to keep Ewan to himself. Perhaps he'd end up murdering Ewan in a fit of jealous rage. Again, Julia laughed. Her mother, Audrey, always told her she had an overactive imagination and it was possible that, for once, she was right.

Three more places were left on the list. One turned out to be more of a cupboard than a room, the other was next to an MOT servicing garage, open six days a week. By the time Julia headed towards the last potential room, she had scratched 'clean' and 'near the station' from her list. As long as there was no heavy machinery next door and it was free from homicidal maniacs, she'd take it.

Downs Avenue was a steep, winding road on the edge of town, further from the train station than was ideal. On one side of the road, houses of varying styles and sizes stood at the bottom of sharply sloped drives. On the other lay the open hillside of the Downs.

Julia had not seen them before, the low-rolling hills, covered with meadow flowers interrupted by clumps of trees, lusher and more inviting than the hills at home.

On reaching number 72, she thought she had made a mistake and rechecked the address. Downsview Villa, 72 Downs Avenue – it was the right place. The house was in a modern style, with a nod to Georgian, detached, double-fronted and set over three storeys. Far grander than anything she'd expected. Julia rang the bell and waited a moment before swathes of fabric floated across the frosted glass of the front door. A slender woman of medium height opened it. A classical beauty, with high rounded cheekbones and long curled eyelashes. Around Audrey's age, Júlia thought, fifty or so, but her mother would never dress like this. A printed silk scarf was wrapped around the woman's head and fashioned into a turban and she wore a matching dress, long and flowing. Was she on the way to a fancy-dress party, or perhaps rehearsing for a play? Julia waited for her to speak, but the woman remained bolt upright at the door, one arm stretched across its frame.

'Hi. I'm Julia. I've come about the room,' she said, when it was clear the woman wasn't going to speak first.

The woman's spine relaxed a fraction and she looked Julia up and down for some moments before saying, 'Julia? You don't look like a Julia. My name is Genevieve.'

The retort, *You don't look like a Genevieve*, would have been ill-applied. No one could look more like a Genevieve. Julia would have been very disappointed if she were named Mildred.

Unsure how to respond, Julia stayed silent, half expecting the woman to turn her away, but she said, 'Come in,' stepped back and flung her arm out to usher Julia inside 72 Downs Avenue.

Chapter 3

The Georgian square I'm standing in, the small green, the autumn leaves, all feel distant. Someone is screaming at me.

'You dozy cow! Look what you've done.'

I stare transfixed at the photo link on my phone.

'It's all over him. He could be scarred for life.'

I recognise those hills and those beech trees on my screen. Someone grabs my arm and yanks me backwards.

'Are you on drugs or something? I said you've scalded my son.'

A woman wearing a puffer jacket thrusts her face into mine. I pull away and look down. It's the toddler from earlier, his red coat stained and dripping with coffee.

'I ... I'm sorry,' I say.

'Sorry isn't good enough.'

She still has hold of my arm.

'I don't think he's hurt.' It's Paulo. He gently detaches me from the woman's grip.

'What – are you a doctor?' she says.

Paulo kneels down to the boy. 'Are you hurt, pal?' he asks.

'Wet,' the boy says.

'See, he's just wet. No harm done, eh?' Paulo says.

'No thanks to her.' She glowers at me. 'Look – she doesn't even care – high as a kite at eleven o'clock in the morning.'

'Let me deal with this,' Paulo says.

He picks up my coffee cup from the ground and pulls me onto the nearest bench. Some survival instinct impels me to place the phone face down on my lap. I sit there, shaking.

'Bad news?' Paulo asks.

He glances at the phone. I keep the screen downwards.

'Yes. I mean no. It's nothing.'

'Anything I can do?'

'Thank you. I'll just sit for a moment.'

'Sure.' He looks concerned. 'I'll be over there if you need me.' He points to his friend.

The mother's still glaring at me, after he leaves. I think she's going to come over, but the boy is pulling at her sleeve and pointing at a squirrel running up a tree and she turns away.

I flip the phone over in my lap and press on the link. It takes me to a news website.

Environmental Science students from the University of Surrey have discovered human remains while taking soil samples on the North Downs, just outside Guildford. Police have confirmed that the death is being treated as suspicious but refuse to speculate further.

No further information is being circulated at this time.

I knew this day would come. I always thought I'd face it with grim resolve and a rational, cool pragmatism. It feels like I've been hit by a train. My lungs won't draw air, my limbs are weak and shaky.

I need to act normally. I've already been foolish. Paulo

might remember this. Tactfully, he's turned away from me and is talking to his friend. I have to pull myself together. I steady my hand, go to the phone settings and delete the message and browsing history.

Once I've managed to stop shaking and am able to breathe, I put the phone in my pocket and walk over to Paulo. He looks up as I approach.

'Everything all right now?' he asks.

'Fine. Sorry about all the drama. Some family trouble, I over-reacted. It's all good now.'

'Great,' he says. 'See you back at the office.'

A light drizzle has started. Drops slide down my neck. I shiver and turn up my collar. The man I saw outside the Sensuous Bean slips into the nearest newsagent. I'm alert to him now. Is it a coincidence he arrived at the same time as the text? It doesn't matter. I must act normally – whatever that is.

I have to calm down and think. The shock of the news, the picture of the Downs bathed in golden light, the shaded dells hinting at the darkness, the tightness in my gut – all this has stopped me from asking the most important question. Who sent the text?

Chapter 4

Stepping past Genevieve and into Downsview Villa for the first time, Julia was struck by its sense of space. The entrance hall was double-heighted, stretching to the roof and opening up the whole house. A window spanning both floors flooded the room with light. It was as far from her friends' poky dives in North London as Audrey's was from the dog hair and coffee-mug rings of the *charming cottage* she'd viewed earlier.

'And where have you come from today?' Genevieve asked.

'Flaxley, Worcestershire. You won't have heard of it. It's a tiny place just south of Birmingham.'

Genevieve's face expressed a mixture of horror and pity.

'Oh dear, never mind, you're here now and you'll very much like it – so much greenery.'

'There's greenery in the Midlands too.'

Julia suddenly missed the fields and woods in which she'd played, growing up.

'I thought it was all factories,' Genevieve said. 'Queen Victoria used to insist the curtains of her railway carriage were lowered when travelling through Birmingham. Like me,

14

she was unable to tolerate ugliness. I've never been north of Cheltenham, except for Norway, but that's something quite different. Have you ever been?'

Julia was unsure if Genevieve was referring to Cheltenham or Norway. But as she'd visited neither, she simply said, 'No.'

'You're young, there's still time,' Genevieve said.

Perhaps the first house hadn't been so bad. The mug stain could be cleaned and the dog smell Shake n' Vac'd from the carpet.

'Can I see the room?' Julia asked.

'First, you must see the rest of the house.'

Genevieve skipped around her and opened the door on the other side of the hall.

'This is the kitchen,' she said. 'My lodgers are free to use this room. The lounge and dining room are for my personal use, but the kitchen is large enough for you all to socialise in. And there's a television if that interests you. Can't bear the dratted thing myself.'

The room was large, its mahogany cabinets outdated but not unpleasant. Patio doors opened onto a terrace with steps leading down to a well-maintained garden. At the far end, a woman in a burgundy body warmer pottered about clipping at plants and placing discarded stems into a bucket. Another woman, Julia's age or a little older, twenty-five perhaps, was sitting at a wooden table in front of the doors, eating a cheese sandwich. Her mouth was full, and she merely lifted a hand in greeting.

'This is Lucy,' Genevieve said.

'Hi, I'm Julia.'

'You can ignore her,' Genevieve said curtly. 'She's leaving us.'

15

Lucy shrugged and smiled.

'I'll show you the room now.'

For a woman in her fifties, Genevieve was light on her feet, as if she'd been a dancer. She floated up the stairs and Julia had trouble keeping pace. The staircase was in two flights. The first led to a landing running along the large window at the front, before going up another flight to the first floor. A separate staircase led to the attic.

'My rooms are on the top floor and the bathroom is at the back of the house,' Genevieve said. 'And this one will be yours.'

The bedroom was on the far side of the staircase. Genevieve opened the door and allowed Julia to enter before her. The room was small, with a single bed and a double wardrobe. The walls were magnolia, the carpet beige, and pine-scented furniture polish hung in the air. It was neat and orderly, too bland to be objectionable. It would do.

Julia walked to the window. A green bank rose sharply above the hedge on the opposite side of the road. She couldn't see the tops of the hills but was aware of their presence and how abruptly the town ended and gave way to open countryside. Genevieve followed her gaze.

'The Downs,' she said. 'I told you, I can't tolerate ugliness. It's wonderful to wake every morning to this beauty, the pure blue colour of the sky you only get here. I grew up just down the road. I don't suppose many people appreciate it as I do. Even when I lived in the Alps, I longed for the Downs, to lie on the grass on a summer's day and look up at the clouds blowing across the sky.'

It was a performance, Genevieve's lines rehearsed and repeated many times before, an impression reinforced by her switch to a pragmatic tone when the discussion turned to business.

'It's two hundred and eighty-five pounds a month including bills,' she said. 'Payment sharp on the first of every month and two months' rent in advance.'

Julia was tired. And if Genevieve was a little annoying, at least the place was clean, and she wouldn't be sharing with Norman Bates.

'I'll take it,' she said.

'Wonderful,' Genevieve said. 'Come downstairs and we'll sort it all out.'

They returned to the kitchen.

'I'll need the deposit now. Make the cheque out to Genevieve D'Auncey,' she said. 'I'll just pop to the lounge and get my receipt book and you can sign the contract.'

Julia took her chequebook from her bag and sat at the table, as Lucy was finishing her sandwich.

'So why are you leaving?' Julia asked.

'Moving in with my boyfriend.'

A shard of pain sliced across Julia's chest. Until two months ago she'd used the same casual tone as Lucy to say, 'I'm moving in with my boyfriend.' As if it were the most normal thing in the world. Instead, here she was with strangers, two hundred miles away.

Julia realised Lucy was looking at her and expecting her to speak.

'What's it like here?' she asked.

'OK,' Lucy said. 'Genevieve's a bit ...'

'Theatrical?'

'I suppose,' Lucy said. 'That as well.'

'As well as what?' Julia asked.

17

'She's fond of—'

Light footsteps, scampering across the hall, signalled Genevieve's return.

'Ah Lucy,' Genevieve said as she entered the room. 'Haven't you anything to do?'

By way of reply, Lucy stood up and took her plate to the dishwasher.

'Who else lives here?' Julia asked.

'Well, there's Alan,' Genevieve said. 'Been here five years – a fixture you could say – though he's not in much. And the other three rooms will be free once Lucy's left. You'll be taking one of them, of course. I wasn't sure when you first came to the door, but now I can see you'll be perfect. I have a good sense about people. It's a ... a ...' She wound her hand in a circular motion from the wrist but didn't finish her sentence. Out of the corner of her eye, Julia saw Lucy smirking. 'Yes, you'll do very well,' Genevieve concluded.

Julia finished writing out the cheque and handed it to Genevieve, who folded it and slipped it under her silk turban.

'I'll see you in two weeks,' she said.

Chapter 5

2017 – Central London

On returning from the park, I go back to my desk. All I can think about is the text, concentrating on work is impossible. Without leaving a cyber trail, I have to find a full news report about the body unearthed on the Downs. I've already been careless with Paulo and using my phone. I'm itching to leave but I must not arouse suspicion by any unusual behaviour. *Why did you leave work early on 4th October?*

Only two people on the planet could have sent that text, and both know not to contact me. We agreed, twenty-three years ago, how to behave if it ever came out: no phone calls, no unusual activity, no change in routine. Few people had mobile phones back then, and we made no specific stipulation regarding texts, but the principle remains. And it's difficult to believe either of them could be so stupid.

Sitting at my desk becomes intolerable. I stare at the laptop, then remove my glasses and rub my eyes. The screen blurs into streaks of black and white. I replace the glasses and reread my current e-mail. It makes no more sense in focus.

How can I find out more, without using my phone or laptop? We were careful to leave no trace at the time. I can still smell the acrid fumes as we found every photograph and negative we'd ever taken in that place and burnt them. I must not be careless now, but I have to find out more. Do they have a name? Do they have suspects?

A pay as you go from a phone shop would accept cash, but they would probably have CCTV, and all mobiles have serial numbers so that each handset has an individual identification. How do criminals go about it? I think of the khaki-wearing drug dealer. He must be in constant communication with buyers and suppliers. I need to go and see him. I start to invent fake emergencies – burst pipes, a family death – just to get out of the office. I get lucky when Jonathan snaps his laptop shut.

'Got a meeting with Ulrich,' he announces.

He should be gone for a couple of hours at least.

I wait a minute in case he returns for his keys or wallet then leave the office. I check behind me as I pass the Sensuous Bean. The man in the padded jacket has gone. Probably, he was just someone passing through, another face in the crowd.

It's raining hard now and the square is clear of visitors except for the man I'm looking for. He's sitting on a bench, the glow of his roll-up just visible under a large golfing umbrella.

I cross the green to reach him. He looks up and smiles in recognition.

'More coffee already?' he says.

'No. I came to see you,' I say.

'I see. And what can I do for you?'

He shuffles along the bench and pats the space next to him. The wood is dry beneath the umbrella and I sit down. He stinks of weed. I try not to wrinkle my nose.

'Tell me,' he says.

'I was wondering.' I'm suddenly aware of the formality in my voice, the clear and precise enunciation of my mother ordering a slice of Victoria sponge. 'I need to get hold of a phone.'

His face splits into a broad smile.

'Do you now – and what made you think I could help?'

'I don't know.' I can't admit to watching his drug sales. 'I just thought you might.'

He gives the faintest nod. 'You come here to drink coffee, one of those tech lot, been here a few months.'

No one in London notices other people's comings and goings. One of the things I love about it. My mind returns to that feeling of being observed. I make a move to stand up. He places a hand on my forearm. It's not a menacing gesture, it's even comforting in some way.

'Don't worry, love. I'm not a stalker. Got to watch people in my game – keep an eye out – know what I mean? I'm Garrick, by the way. Everyone knows me around here.'

He extends his hand and I take it.

'Garrick, like the theatre?' I say.

'My mother was a hoofer back in the Sixties. Tells me I was conceived there.' He smiles. 'And your name is?'

'Audrey,' I say.

I don't know why I've given my mother's name, perhaps because I'm speaking like her.

'And what is it for, this phone, Audrey – up to a spot of adultery?'

I don't answer. Garrick grins.

'Not a problem, Audrey. No information required. It's not as though you're going to be moving in on my patch, are you

21

now?' He laughs at his own joke. 'How about you go to the cashpoint up near the station, withdraw two hundred pounds, go for a little walk and by the time you come back I may have a phone for you.'

'Two hundred?'

'That's the price.'

Two hundred pounds – I'll be living off boiled rice for the rest of the month.

'It needs to be a smartphone,' I say.

'Are you sure? Some people prefer the old-style ones, harder to trace.'

'No. It has to be a smartphone.'

'As you desire, milady.'

He takes a shallow bow and withdraws the umbrella, so that it no longer shields me from the rain.

'I'll be seeing you, Audrey.'

I stand and walk towards the Tube and the nearest cash-point.

Garrick won't want to speak to the police any more than I do. I look at the road behind me as I cross. A man in a dark-coloured padded jacket is standing at the corner of the street, under the newsagent's awning. The same man as before? The rain leaves his face and figure indistinct. He could be anyone.

Once I've taken the money from my bank account, £14.38 is all that's left before it hits my overdraft limit. God knows what I'm going to do for money. I can't ask Audrey for any more. I could borrow from the petty cash until my next payday but knowing my luck I'd be found out and get dismissed, which is all I need. I stuff the money into my bra for safe-keeping and turn around. A few people are milling about in the rain, but the man in the padded jacket is gone. I still can't get over the feeling of being watched.

Garrick's gone when I return. I walk across the square and back to the main road but still can't see him. I've started to circle back when I hear a whistle. I turn around. Garrick's slouched in the doorway of one of the Georgian houses. As I walk towards him, he forks two fingers, peers down them and scans the road.

'Sometimes I choose to stay out of sight,' he says.

Considering the stench of weed, he's remarkably lucid.

'Do you have it?' I ask.

'If you've got the money.'

I pull the money from my bra, which raises a smile from Garrick. After I count the twenties into his hand, he raises the notes to his mouth, kisses them, leers at me and says, 'I'll treasure these.'

I step back, having visions of being dragged into the house.

'I've brought the exact money and nothing more,' I say.

Garrick looks amused.

'No need to worry. I never harm paying clients – wouldn't stay in business if I did.'

He disappears into the house and returns only a few seconds later with the phone. It's an old Samsung Galaxy, badly scuffed, but I'm hardly going to have it on display.

'I've turned the Wi-Fi off for you – no point to an untraceable phone if all your searches come up through your router. You'll need to set a PIN. And there's twenty pounds on it. If you want more, go to FoneFirst down the road. They're very discreet.'

'Thanks,' I say.

'Anything else, just ask.'

I'm about to turn away, hoping to God I'm never this desperate again, when I have a thought.

'You know how you said you keep an eye out for people in the area?'

'Necessity of the trade,' he says.

'You've not seen anyone new around?'

'There's always someone new.'

'I think a man is following me.'

He leans back on the wall and lights a spliff.

'Is that so?' he says.

'Have you seen anyone?'

'That first time you spoke to me a fella was watching. Just being nosy, I think. Not police – I can always spot them.'

'Can you describe him?'

'He didn't come close enough to have a good look. All I noticed was that he was older, had grey hair and wore a dark jacket.'

'A padded jacket?'

'Couldn't say.'

His eyes have moved beyond me, looking for his next trade.

I race back to the office and head straight for the toilet and lock the door. I take out Garrick's phone and open the web browser. *Body found on North Downs* – is the headline on the BBC South East webpage. Underneath is a video link. I turn the phone's volume to low and press play. The familiar rolling landscape comes into view. The journalist is wearing a green wax jacket and corduroy trousers, as if he were interrupting walking his gun dogs to give this report. Behind him stands a beech copse and behind that, a radio mast on a distant hill. Through the trees white tents are visible and people of indeterminate gender move about in plastics suits.

A body was discovered today by a student from the Environmental Science Faculty at the University of Surrey.

The journalist's voice takes on a false gravitas. He wants to be the next John Simpson, reporting on international conflicts, not bypass protests and increased drunkenness in the town centre.

Police have confirmed that the remains are human. There's been no comment on the cause of death, but it has been confirmed that it is being treated as suspicious.

Police refuse to speculate on whether this could be Hayley Walsh – the teenager who went missing in Crawley three weeks ago.

The shot changes to a man in late middle age, wearing a grey suit. At the bottom of the screen the caption reads: *Detective Inspector Frederick Warren.*

DI: *We're making inquiries into all missing people in the area.*

Reporter: *Is this a recent death?*

DI: *We're not jumping to any conclusions right now.*

Cut back to the reporter standing in front of the copse.

And that's all we have to tell you at the moment. We'll be keeping you up to date as and when we have more information.

The clip ends.

I remember that hill. It's a little different now, perhaps the beeches have grown, but the copse stands on the route we used to take to the pub. On cloudy nights the only light was the streetlamps from the town reflecting against the sky – a lonely, dark, isolated spot.

I watch two more clips from different sites. Their reports

are much the same. No clue as to the identity. But on a local newspaper site, one word differs from all the other reports.

It's believed the remains indicate a violent death.

Violent. A lonely, violent death.

Someone bangs on the door.

'You've been in there ages. Are you ill?' Miranda's voice.

'I'm fine.'

I leave the cubicle and scuttle back to my desk. Jonathan's back and, fortunately, hasn't registered my absence.

I shift in my chair and look at the clock on the wall. The hands appear to be ticking backwards. I really have to go but Jonathan expects long hours. Miraculously, at six o'clock, Miranda becomes my unlikely saviour.

'Anyone fancy a drink? I'm going to the Huntsman.'

She pronounces it 'Huntsthman'. Jonathan looks up.

'I've been here till ten, the last two nights,' Miranda says defensively.

I expect Jonathan to roll his eyes, but he says, 'Could do with a drink myself.'

I never socialise with work. Instead, I stay late to create elaborate charts that will go unread, and no one presses me to join their trip to the pub. I wait for the office to empty before pulling on my coat.

The sky's a smudgy grey, and the drizzle diffuses what little light there is into a yellow haze. To the left I can see the fuzzy profile of two smokers standing outside the Huntsman. One of them looks like Paulo, though it's impossible to be sure through the mist, and I turn in the opposite direction, towards the Tube.

A man stares out of the Sensuous Bean's window. He lowers his head to his coffee cup as I pass. A padded jacket is thrown over the arm of his chair. Is it the same man as earlier, the one Garrick saw, or am I being paranoid?

I reach the entrance to the Tube and I'm about to pull out my Oyster card when my phone bleeps in my pocket.

The unknown number.

IT'S HIM.

Chapter 6

1994 – Archway, London

Two hours after leaving Genevieve and Downsview Villa, Julia arrived at Archway Underground station, North London. The surrounding streets, noisy and litter-strewn, stood in contrast to the bourgeois avenues of Guildford. Pearl shared the same draughty house with the same seven people as in her final year at university. Despite all having jobs now, they continued to live off junk food and alcohol, as evidenced by the polystyrene cartons and beer bottles scattered about the place. It was a long way from the immaculate rooms of Downsview Villa, where the carpets might be dated, but at least they weren't covered in fag burns and stained with chilli sauce. Strangely, some part of Julia envied Pearl's overspilling bin and rattling windows. It symbolised city living, youth, vibrancy and independence. In going to Guildford, she couldn't help thinking she'd swapped one dull backwater for another, with a different middle-aged woman hovering over her instead of Audrey.

Audrey, ever present and ever critical – Julia never thought of her as 'Mum'. 'Mum' was used by daughters capable of pleasing. Whose mothers didn't tell them being dumped by their boyfriend was their own fault, who didn't always take the side of step-siblings over flesh and blood, because wasn't it their father, not hers, paying for everything? Why was she so difficult and contrary? Why did she have to study computer science instead of something feminine, French perhaps? Couldn't she have nice friends instead of misfits like Pearl and Andre? No, in her mind, Audrey would never be 'Mum'.

A housemate let Julia in, and she made her way up to the room on the top floor, where Andre was already sprawled on the bed, a bottle of Holsten Pils in his hand. Pearl was sitting in front of the mirror, getting ready for their night out. She had shaken off the remains of parochial teenage misfit in the last couple of years and now smoked roll-ups and drank German lager, instead of the Consulate menthol and Diamond White she'd preferred in sixth form. Her hair had changed from a short, jet-black crop to a choppy, dirty-blonde shoulder-length bob.

'We used to call that cut a shag,' Audrey said when she first saw it.

Pearl had turned to Julia and smirked.

'Well, it does get me laid,' she'd said.

Today, Pearl was wearing a powder blue baby doll dress and enormous black boots. She leant towards the glass to smudge her eyeliner and muss her hair. An enviable look Julia couldn't pull off. Dishevelled, she looked more like a librarian gone to seed than a hard-partying rock chick. Half of her longed to be forty, when the tailored dresses and slender-heeled shoes, which actually suited her, would be more acceptable. As it was, she had twisted her hair into two long plaits and wore a loose vest top, jeans and new blue suede Converse, and hoped a little of Pearl's don't-give-a-fuck cool rubbed off on her.

'I want to meet her,' Pearl said, when Julia told her about Genevieve's eccentricities.

'Me too,' Andre said. 'She sounds like a hippy version of Audrey.'

'Please don't compare that woman to my mother. At least not in front of her. Can you imagine Audrey in a turban?'

'She'd look adorable,' Andre cooed.

'She'd have an aneurism,' Julia said.

'Who else is going to be living there – any guys?' Pearl asked.

'Someone called Alan, but he wasn't in.'

'A pity. Never date someone you're sharing with, but he might have friends.'

'I'm not looking,' Julia said.

'Well, you should be.'

'Pearl's gone all Cupid's arrow because she's got some news herself, haven't you, Pearlie?' Andre said.

'No,' she said and scowled.

'What?' Julia said.

'Nothing,' Pearl said.

'Are you seeing someone?' Julia asked.

Pearl and Andre glanced at each other.

'Not exactly,' Pearl said.

'He's called Rudi,' Andre said. 'They're inseparable.'

'Not inseparable. I'm not with him now, am I?'

Pearl smeared lipstick across her mouth, with no attempt to stay inside the lip line.

'You see him most nights,' Andre added.

Julia felt suddenly jealous that Andre knew all about Rudi

and she didn't. She and Pearl had always been the closest of the trio, perhaps because they were both girls, or perhaps because Pearl was an only child, and Julia had been too, until the age of nine, whereas Andre was one of four. Now, it seemed, their physical distance had resulted in an emotional one. Pearl used to tell her everything. It would get back that way, once Julia moved nearer.

'How long has it been with this guy, Pearl?' Julia asked.

'Not sure.'

'Two months,' Andre said. 'She's only pretending not to remember.'

'Two months!' Julia said. 'That's a marriage for you, isn't it, Pearl?'

Andre laughed, and Julia was about to, when she checked herself. Although Pearl was smiling, something in her expression made Julia think she'd been offended.

'You really like him, don't you?' Julia said.

Andre stopped laughing too. 'Do you?' he asked.

Pearl shrugged and turned back to the mirror without replying. Andre threw Julia a confused look.

'What is it?' she mouthed.

'I don't know,' Andre mouthed back.

'Er ... guys, I can see you in the mirror,' Pearl said.

'So, what's going on, Pearl?' Julia asked.

'I didn't want to say anything. It's really bad timing, me getting a boyfriend so soon after you and Christian split up. I didn't want to upset you.'

Julia felt sick. She couldn't lose Pearl to coupledom. Not just now.

'Nothing's going to change,' Pearl said. 'We didn't stop hanging out together because of Christian.'

That was different, Julia wanted to say. They still lived with their parents and Christian used to come out as part of their group.

'No one would ever put you three together as friends,' he'd said.

He was right. At school, their bond had been that none of them fitted in. Before Pearl was effortlessly cool and desirable, she had been weird-looking. Tall and spidery thin, with hands and feet too large for even her height, her domed forehead, large wide-set eyes, narrow chin and small mouth gave her an odd and unnerving appearance. Craig Carter, the school bully, said she looked like an alien. 'E.T.', he had called her, and it stuck.

Only at sixteen did her features start to make sense – ethereal rather than alien, her figure willowy not lanky. *Jolie laide*, Audrey called it, that peculiar, off-beat beauty, androgynous and without symmetry, beloved of avant-garde fashion shoots.

Andre always preferred hanging out with girls and was taunted for being a 'poofter' long before he realised he was, in fact, gay. At which point, he embraced his sexuality, modelled his clothing on Quentin Crisp and any boy taunting him was met with, 'You weren't saying that in the bushes last Saturday night, were you, darlin'?'

Unlike her two friends, Julia felt she had yet to blossom. Awkward and shy changed to slightly less awkward and slightly less shy.

'We'll find you someone tonight,' Pearl said. 'Or I'll introduce you to one of Rudi's friends. We could go on double dates.'

'I told you, I'm not interested,' Julia said.

'Well, whatever, nothing's going to change. When are you moving to this new place?' Pearl asked.

'The beginning of June,' Julia said.

'Yay! The old gang back together every weekend,' Andre said. 'And without Craig Carter hanging around.'

Julia looked at Pearl. Would she be with Rudi every weekend? She tested the water.

'I can't crash at Pearl's all the time.'

'Of course, you can,' Pearl said.

'And if not, you can stay at mine,' Andre offered.

Andre shared a dank basement flat in Finsbury Park. Julia had once come across a slug on the bathroom floor.

'She's staying at mine, aren't you, Jules?' Pearl said.

She really did love Pearl.

Chapter 7

2017 – Archway, London

It's nearly seven o'clock and the Tube is still busy when I get off the Northern Line at Archway station. My thin jacket's insufficient against the chill. I pull it tight around me and turn the collar up, while casting an envious eye over the woman in front of me wrapped in a cashmere scarf.

I loiter at the exit and check no one's followed me. Perhaps Audrey was right, I shouldn't have moved back to this area. Too many memories. It's only two streets down from the house I shared when I first came to London. The area's supposed to be gentrifying, which just means the prices have gone up, otherwise it's not changed since I left, with Turkish kebab houses, Greek cafés and Irish pubs. Lorries spew their fumes into the cold night air as they rumble up the A1 towards Suicide Bridge, a soon to be obsolete sobriquet for the vast iron structure that spans the Great North Road, as an anti-jumping fence is to be erected.

After a couple of minutes I'm shivering and, certain no one has followed me onto the Tube, I head home. Even if my pursuer is imaginary, the texts are real. Turning into my road, I half expect to see a police car, but the street is empty, apart from a few people like me, hurrying to get home, out of the cold and dark.

My flat is on the top two floors of a tall Victorian property. The lounge and kitchen are on the lower floor, the bedroom and bathroom in the attic. I can only afford it because it belongs to friends of Andre, who had nightmare tenants and were willing to take a considerably lower rent from someone who didn't get raided by the police for growing cannabis. There are still holes in the ceiling where they hung the lights.

Once back inside, I fetch a half-empty bottle of Californian white wine from the back of the fridge. In the local saver shop you can buy it for £3.49. Chilled to nearly freezing, it has no taste.

I sit at the kitchen table, unscrew the cap, fill my glass and stare out of the window at the blurred City skyline in the distance. I finish it quickly and pour another. Many years ago, I set myself a limit, no more than two glasses of wine on a work night. This rule, I've broken three times: when my husband discovered my infidelity; when my son called me a whore; and again today, when an unidentified body of someone who died a violent death is discovered on the Downs outside Guildford.

IT'S HIM.

Not *her*, not the missing schoolgirl, Hayley Walsh – *him*.

The landline rings. My head's a little fuzzy from the wine. I go to the lounge, lift the receiver and wait for a low voice, to repeat the menace of the text.

'Hello, darling.'

It's Audrey. I should have known. She's the only person who calls me on the landline.

'Hi, Mum.'

'How are things with you?' she asks.

'Fine.'

'You don't sound fine.'

'You always say that,' I reply.

'I can't help worrying about you, Julia. Neither can your father.' Robert Hathersley is *not* my father. 'I know you made your bed, as they say, but it doesn't mean I don't care.'

I ignore the implied criticism.

'Did you ring for a reason?'

'Do I need a reason to ring my daughter?'

I wait.

'I spoke to your husband today. Am I still allowed to call him that?' she says.

'How did he seem?' I ask.

'He's not happy.'

'But did he sound upset, anxious?'

'I imagine he's all of those things after the way you've treated him.'

My husband could never stand my mother. Only since our separation have they started having cosy chats together. To him, Audrey's just another weapon to use against me. Not that she sees it like that.

'I made myself clear I'm one hundred per cent on his side in this matter,' she says.

'Your support is always valued.'

'Well, I can hardly condone your behaviour, Julia. I'm old-fashioned enough to believe fidelity in marriage is important. And it's just as well I did take that line, because he let me talk to Sam.'

My heart jumps. 'How is he?'

'How do you think? Angry, confused – he's a teenage boy.

36

I had one of those once and they're like that at the best of times. Not just boys either – you and your sister were moody little madams.'

I hate being lumped together with my step-siblings and try to get her back to the point in hand.

'Mum – Sam.'

'Oh yes. Well, he said he's OK. Studying hard for his A levels. We didn't talk about you know what, but I know he misses you. I'm sure if you called him, or wrote to him ...'

You're a whore. I hate you. I wish you were dead.

'I'll think about it.'

'Which means no.'

I walk back to the kitchen and top up my glass. 'It's too soon. I need to give him time.'

'Oh well, it's up to you. But if he were my son ...'

'I've got to go, Mum.'

'Wait a moment, Julia. Before you do, I was thinking, I mean asking, if I could come and stay tomorrow night.'

'You hate London. And you know it's only a one-bed flat.'

'There's an exhibition on at the Tate Modern and Vanessa Miller – you know, my old friend, we used to work together at Rackhams – said she was going.'

'You hate modern art more than you hate London.'

'I do not hate modern art. You're always telling me what I do and do not like. I'm open to all kinds of art.' As long as it predates 1900. 'And don't worry about the sleeping arrangements. I can take the sofa.'

Audrey Hathersley would as soon sleep on a park bench as a sofa.

I can't think of a good excuse for putting her off and she did lend me the deposit for the flat, which she had to lie about to Robert to get hold of. Besides, having company might do me good – stop me rattling around in my own head.

'Have my bed. When are you coming?' I ask.

'Vanessa and I are going to the midday viewing then having a spot of lunch. I'll be there by five. I can let myself in.'

After I've hung up, I return to the kitchen and ferret around for something to eat. There's half a packet of crackers left and a little cheese in the fridge. I eat them with the remains of my wine. I'm just finishing the glass and thinking about going to bed when the landline rings again. I pick it up, expecting Audrey's forgotten something.

'Hello,' I say.

Silence.

'Hello.'

Sharp breaths hiss at me through the receiver. I'm about to put the phone down, when a voice whispers, 'Better get your story straight.'

A low, rasping voice. An unnatural voice, not the caller's own. Not a text to my mobile phone, a call to my landline – a link, a specific location. Whoever's making contact knows where I live. It's intimate and menacing. I want to ask who it is, but the words won't escape my mouth. The line goes dead.

I rush to the window and look outside. A black and white cat is scratching at the door of the house opposite, desperate to escape the damp chill of an October night. Headlights swing from the main road and onto our street, briefly spotlighting the cat, which ceases its scratching as if ashamed to be caught in so undignified an act. The lights power past and it's left yowling for its absent owners. Nothing else moves. I look at my mobile then the landline, waiting for it to ring again. It doesn't.

I reread the text from earlier. It's still there, it's real, I'm not losing my mind. I need a plan. It can only be a matter of time before this person states their intention or someone joins the dots.

Chapter 8

1995 – Archway, London

Ghosts do not exist. It was Julia's imagination that heard the tread of heavy workmen's boots behind her as she walked down the dimly lit streets of North London. Paranoia caused her to spin around to find a deserted pavement. Since escaping Guildford, she sensed a pressure on the edge of her bed that woke her in the night and made her turn on the light, expecting to see Genevieve sitting there, tearful and confessional.

'I knew Dominic would come back,' she had said. 'I hadn't understood the form.'

Maybe Genevieve was right, maybe they all came back in one form or another.

But recently the footsteps behind her hadn't been heavy. And when she spun around the street wasn't empty. A man would pull his head under the hood of a winter jacket and duck into a doorway.

There had been no contact between her, Gideon and Alan, a blessing mostly. But a tiny part of her wanted to speak to them. Did they hear the dull thump of Brandon's boots behind them when they crossed a street? Did they catch the scent of beer and sweat as they opened their eyes in the morning? She wanted to ask them, does knowing you're going insane mean that, actually, you're not?

Julia had finished work late that night. The pub, just off Goodge Street, had been busier than usual and it had taken forever to empty the drip trays, wash down the bar and hoover the floor. By the time she emerged from Archway Tube station, with sore feet and an aching back, it was gone twelve. The entrance hall funnelled the wind. Discarded crisp packets and flyers spiralled above her, in mockery of autumn leaves. Julia pulled her collar up against the cold and bent her head to the wind as she crossed Junction Road and descended the hill.

When Pearl had moved in with Rudi, she suggested Julia took over her room in the shared house on Fairbridge Road. Julia had accepted. The last of Pearl's housemates had moved out the following month. The new ones were strangers. Julia liked it that way – they left her alone.

Pearl often phoned and even came to the house. If she hadn't been busy decorating her new place in Maida Vale, she would have been more persistent in her calls, which Julia failed to return. Like Audrey, Pearl saw too much.

Andre had moved back home to live with his parents while he studied for a Master's in business administration. He could rarely afford trips to London.

Working two jobs kept Julia busy, stilled her mind and gave her an excuse to avoid all of them. The new exciting careers she'd dreamt of when living in Guildford had turned into working as a receptionist by day and a barmaid by night. She hardly spoke to her customers at the pub and had only the most functional conversations on the reception desk.

Perhaps ghosts were only the mind pushing out loneliness.

On her infrequent days off, she would walk for miles and miles, up Highgate Hill or the Great North Road underneath the Hornsey Lane Bridge – *Suicide Bridge* they called it – a popular spot for self-destruction. Julia would end up in Hampstead or Alexandra Palace and carry on walking to exhaustion and beyond. Only when physically drained would her body allow her to sleep. Pills terrified her. How easy it would be one night to decide that she couldn't face the next day and be found by one of her housemates, her face contorted, a paper envelope in her hand.

As she approached her house, she saw a man waiting on the pavement outside. It wasn't Gideon or Alan – wrong build. She felt sick. Could it be Brandon's father? No, this man wasn't old enough. He was mid-thirties, wore corduroy trousers and a blue parka.

Julia walked past and opened the gate, without acknowledging him. She was halfway up the path when he said, 'Ms Winter.'

'Yes,' she said automatically.

'My name's Mike Lancaster. I'd like to ask you a few questions.'

'Why?'

'I'm trying to find someone. A Mr Brandon Wells. His parents haven't heard from him in fourteen months. They're extremely concerned and have hired me to try to find him. I thought I'd start by speaking to everyone who shared his house in Guildford. See if he's been in touch. You lived there at the same time I believe.'

'The police already asked me about this, back in Guildford. He stole some money.'

'The family aren't convinced by that version of events, especially as they've heard nothing from him.'

'Then they should contact the police. I can't help you, Mr Lancaster. Now please, I've been on my feet since seven this morning.'

Lancaster came through the gate and held out a card.

'Here,' he said. 'My contact details, in case you do remember anything.'

Julia took the card without a word and walked to the door, pausing as she placed her key in the lock. Lancaster was still waiting, watching her. She turned to him.

'Have you been following me?' she asked.

'No.'

'You have – for the last month, at least.'

He responded with a cough that suppressed a laugh.

'Ms Winter, I was paid to find you and ask about Brandon. The Wells' budget doesn't stretch to long-term surveillance. Would I find something out if it did?'

'Goodnight, Mr Lancaster.'

Julia shut the door behind her. Through the spyhole she watched his distorted image move away under the glow of orange streetlamps. His size and gait were not that of her pursuer. Ghosts don't exist. If Mike Lancaster hadn't been following her, who had?

Chapter 9

1994 – Guildford

It would have been difficult to find two women of the same age who contrasted more than Julia's mother and Genevieve. Despite driving two hundred miles to Guildford in an over-stuffed car on a hot day, Audrey's navy blue suit remained crease-free, and she only needed a hat to look as if she were going to church. With her neatly curled crop, a splash of Rive Gauche and discreet gold stud clip-ons – Audrey considered pierced ears to be vulgar – she could have stepped straight out of the 1950s.

For Genevieve, the 1970s were an unending inspiration. She answered the door in loose silk trousers and a kimono-style top, the fabric impregnated with the scent of lemon and cinnamon. Julia was relieved she'd at least dispensed with the turban. Instead, enormous gold and jade earrings swung to her shoulders. Her hair was pulled away from her face and a single long plait, which Julia assumed to be a hairpiece, hung to her waist.

'You must be Julia's mother. Delighted.' Genevieve tilted her head and flicked her eyes upwards, in an almost flirta-tious manner. 'Do come in,' she cooed, oblivious to Audrey's incredulous look. 'May I offer you a cup of tea, Mrs Winter?'

'It's Hathersley. And no thank you,' Audrey replied in an icy tone.

As before, Genevieve behaved like a theatre director giving a backstage tour.

'The bathroom,' she said with a dramatic sweep of the arm as if it were Sir Laurence Olivier's dressing room, leaving Audrey's eyebrows disappearing under her hairline.

'Does she smoke marijuana?' she asked Julia when they were unpacking together in the bedroom.

'How should I know?'

'She looks the sort. If there's anything like that going on, you move out straight away. Go to a hotel. I'll send you the money.'

'It'll be fine. I don't need looking after, Mum. I'm twenty-three. You were married with a kid at my age.'

'That doesn't stop me worrying. Things are different now. Twenty-three is young. I've still no idea why you had to move so far. If it was to get away from Christian, you could just as easily have gone to Birmingham or Worcester, not the other end of the country. I can't see how it's any easier to find someone new down here than at home – probably harder, they're not so friendly, unless they're like your landlady, which is not the sort of company you want to keep.'

Audrey gave the door the disapproving look she'd like to have given Genevieve.

'Finding someone new? That's the last thing I want.'

'Now, Julia, you don't want to end up like your Aunt Rena.'

'I'd love to be Aunt Rena.'

'Julia, no!'

For Audrey, Aunt Rena was a sad example of what could

45

befall a woman who didn't secure a man young enough in life. In her fifties, single and childless, Rena was to be pitied. 'I'd feel a little more sympathy for her if it wasn't all her own fault. If she had just made an effort with any of her men, I'm sure one of them would have married her.' The fact that Aunt Rena seemed perfectly content, had travelled the globe, published several bestselling travel memoirs, and was currently residing in Buenos Aires with a younger man called Norberto was scant consolation to Audrey. And any attempt to persuade her Rena could be happy was met with utter incredulity.

'I just mean, I don't want to end up with someone on the rebound,' Julia said. 'I need to give it some time.'

'Not too much time,' Audrey said.

Arguing was pointless. Audrey's opinions were as inflexible as her spine, and Audrey Hathersley never slouched.

Julia stood back and let her mother organise her clothes, alphabetise her books and move the bed to use the available space more efficiently. Only as Audrey was leaving did Julia realise she didn't want her to go. They had never been apart for any significant length of time. Aunt Rena told her that Audrey had suffered several miscarriages and, before Julia arrived, Audrey had believed she was unable to carry a baby to full term.

'Even after you were born, she hovered over your cot. Convinced you were about to stop breathing,' Rena said.

And fourteen months later, Julia's father died. She couldn't mourn a man she'd never known, but it must have devastated Audrey, though she never spoke about this period in her life. The wrench at their separation must have afflicted Audrey as much as Julia. But displays of emotion weren't Audrey's way. She considered them as vulgar as pierced ears. Julia could think of no reason for asking her to stay longer, and as she had said earlier, she was twenty-three, an adult, not in need of her mother.

'I better go, it's a long drive,' Audrey said. 'Give me a hug.'

Julia gave her a longer squeeze than usual and was engulfed by the scent of Rive Gauche. Audrey handed her fifty pounds in cash, 'for emergencies', then went out to the car. Julia followed her and watched as the little blue Fiesta chugged to the end of the road.

Genevieve had gone out to meet a gentleman friend and the house stood empty. Julia returned to her room, sat on the bed and looked out of the window. Audrey would be getting onto the motorway by now. In a couple of hours, she'd be hundreds of miles away.

What was she doing here? Escape to overcome heartbreak should have meant adventure – not a corporate job at a medium-sized firm in the Home Counties. She should have gone to France, lived in Paris, the Latin Quarter, had an affair with a handsome artist called Emile, who lived in a small flat above a café. They'd stay in bed till noon, making love and smoking Gauloises. Later, they'd amble downstairs to the café, share a bottle of wine with friends and talk politics and philosophy until the late evening, before falling back into bed.

Instead she was fetching an iron from the utility room to press the clothes for her new job at Morgan Boyd next week. She took the iron and ironing board to her room and allowed it to heat up as she fetched coat hangers from the wardrobe and pulled her work blouses from her case.

Her escape didn't have to be France. She could head south

to Portugal or Spain, work in a bar and send a postcard to Christian – *Wish you were here?*

Mechanically, she pressed the blouses, the steam having little effect on the deep creases. She could leave now. Repack and catch a train to London. Pearl would let her crash on her floor until she found a job. She stopped ironing. London was no more likely than France. It wasn't lack of language skills stopping her. It was cowardice. Julia craved safety and certainty, a proper job with steady money. Adventure was for other people.

She hung the blouses in the wardrobe, returned the iron and board, then sat on the bed and pushed her back to the wall. The elation she'd felt at leaving home, the hope of catching up on exciting life experiences, evaporated. She no longer felt the thrill of sticking two fingers up at Christian and his new girlfriend, Ellie – *See, I don't care, I've got a new life*. Christian and Ellie would be glad she was gone. They could carry on their perfect lives without the anxiety of running into Julia at unexpected moments, prodding their consciences, a reminder of their lies and broken promises.

It was Saturday night and Julia was alone, in a house and in a town where she knew no one. She was the only one suffering for her choice. Tears bubbled up and she couldn't stop herself sobbing. What on earth had possessed her to come to this place? She wished she'd gone back with Audrey. She wished she'd gone home.

Chapter 10

2017 – Archway, London

Better get your story straight.

The caller has been careless and left their number, a mobile. I could ring it back. Not from my phone and not from Garrick's phone – I don't want to provide any link between it and me. I consider the payphone on St John's Way. It's a bit of a walk and it's dark and if I am being followed ... Part of me doesn't want to know who this is. Can it be the same person who's sending the texts, and are they warning or threatening me? I shouldn't have started drinking. I need a clear head. I try to think of a scenario in which the texts are the result of some hideous coincidence but there's no wriggle room. Someone knows. The best thing to do is nothing, to wait and see, though that hardly constitutes a plan.

I feel so alone, even my husband would be a comfort. I remember now why I married him.

Upstairs, I go through the motions of going to bed: wash my face, clean my teeth, comb my hair. I put on Radio 4, hoping to find friendly, familiar voices to soothe me. Tonight, all voices serve as an irritant and I switch it off. I look at Garrick's phone again. A new article has appeared. The investigation has moved on. Hayley Walsh has turned up in France with her schoolteacher. Suitably lurid headlines accompany this discovery, which is of more shock value than the corpse. Given the state the body must be in, the police can't have believed it was a recent death. And despite knowing little about forensic science, I'm pretty sure it couldn't have been mistaken for a fifteen-year-old girl, even on a superficial examination.

I scroll down the other search results – more mentions of Hayley – then I see it in a local Surrey paper, *Speculation Growing About Body on the Downs*. The first mention of a name.

The opening paragraphs tell me what I already know, and the article is padded out by an interview with the student whose soil sample resulted in the body's discovery. Althea Gregory says she 'couldn't believe it', and there's a picture of her looking pleased with herself and her fifteen minutes of fame.

Only the latter part contains anything of interest.

Speculation is growing that the body is that of missing back-packer Brandon Wells, last seen in August 1994. Sources within the investigation have confirmed that this is a viable line of inquiry and they are currently in touch with police in his home country of New Zealand.

I scroll down to see further results. BBC South East has a clip.

The same journalist as before stands on the same spot on the Downs. Behind him, the ridge of the hill glows yellow. The shot pans down to a small copse. Yellow tape flutters at the edge of the trees and, just visible through the trunks, is a white tent.

Police have refused to rule out that the body found is that of missing backpacker Brandon Wells, last seen in 1994. Locals may remember his parents coming over from New Zealand and putting pressure on the police to launch an investigation. However, it must be emphasised that these are early stages in the investigation and DNA tests will be required before continuing this line of inquiry.

I put down the phone.

Nineteen ninety-four. Twenty-three years ago. Brandon Wells. Guildford.

It won't be long now.

It's him. Better get your story straight.

Chapter 11

1994 – Guildford

Julia spent the entire weekend in Guildford, alone. Genevieve had disappeared with a man, whom she briefly introduced to Julia as Edward. The elusive Alan was yet to return, and Lucy would be working in the Netherlands for the next fortnight.

Monday morning's seven o'clock alarm came as a blessing. Julia was better suited to work than solitude.

With only one cup of coffee inside her and wearing a new suit and crisply pressed blouse, Julia headed out of the house, her desire for company overcoming her first-day nerves.

'A word please, Julia,' Genevieve called, as she was halfway through the front door.

Dressed in emerald silk pyjamas and with a full face of make-up, she struck an incongruous figure in the grey morning light.

'It's my first day, Genevieve. I don't want to be late.'

'I shan't keep you a moment,' she said. 'I don't mind today, but in future could you use the side door – the silver key on the fob I gave you. It takes you through the garage and into the kitchen. The hallway gets so mucky with all you young people coming in and out.'

'You want me to use the tradesmen's entrance?'

'The *side door*,' Genevieve said. 'Alan and Lucy don't mind.'

She gave a little tinkling laugh, which sounded false and forced. Was she drunk? It was eight in the morning. Julia remembered Lucy's wry smile when she'd said, 'She's fond of—' Booze, was that what she had been going to say? Audrey had accused Genevieve of being a pothead, but it seemed she was just a common or garden lush. Julia didn't have the time to argue.

'Fine. I'll use the *side door*,' she said.

Genevieve came out onto the step as Julia walked up the drive.

'Do enjoy your day,' she said brightly.

The position at Morgan Boyd Consulting had been a sideways move. Julia had more experience than her manager expected, and she handled her workload with ease. The other two graduates, Bee and Fraser, asked her advice on several points, and later invited her out for drinks at a wine bar in the town centre, where they shared a meat platter, downed a couple of bottles of wine and filled her in on the office gossip.

Fraser then started mimicking their boss Jim's obscenity-ridden outbursts. To the office in general, 'What did I fucking do to deserve having to work with such a bunch of fucking incompetent fucks?' To his PA, Penelope, when she forgot his wife's birthday, 'I should just sack you and get some useless tart from Office Angels – at least she'd be easy on the eye.'

'How does she put up with it?' Julia asked.

'Fraser reckons she's in love with Jim,' Bee said.

'No way.'

'Jim's an ugly tosser, but who else has she got to fantasise about? Middle-aged, divorced, her kids have left home.' Fraser counted off Penelope's deficiencies on his fingers. 'She probably hasn't had it in years. It's sad, the way she's always angling for invitations to the pub.'

'Maybe she's just lonely,' Julia said.

'Then she should find people her own age to hang out with,' Fraser said. 'What would we have to talk about – knitting, *Songs of Praise*?'

'You know who you really should seduce, Fraser, and do us all a favour?' Bee said. 'Jim's wife. I'm sure she had her eye on you at the Christmas party. A toy boy would keep her happy, which would keep Jim happy, which would get him off our backs.'

'Suddenly Penelope's not such a bad prospect,' Fraser said. 'What about you, Julia – do you have a boyfriend, girlfriend, crush?'

'No,' she said. 'No one.'

'There must be somebody,' Bee said.

Julia thought of Christian. Most likely he was wrapped in Ellie's arms right at that very moment. She downed her wine and made her excuses.

She stumbled back to Downsview Villa at around eleven. Remembering to use the side door, and without turning on the light, she crept through the garage and into the kitchen and hall where the streetlamps provided just enough illumination to see the stairs. As she neared the top, a shard of light fell across the landing. A door opened, and a man stood silhouetted in its frame. Genevieve came out and pulled it shut behind her. The landing fell dark again. She turned and started to ascend the stairs to the attic rooms, then stopped.

'Who's that?'

'It's only me,' Julia said.

'Who?'

'Julia, Genevieve. It's Julia.'

She continued to the landing and switched on the light. Genevieve's face was wet with tears.

'What's happened?' Julia asked.

Genevieve moved towards her, holding her arms straight out in front, as if bracing for a fall. At the last moment she wrapped them around Julia, placed her head on Julia's shoulder and started to sob.

'Genevieve?'

She made no response. Julia looked to the door, from which Genevieve had come. It was only a few feet away. The occupant must be able to hear her crying. A little drunk and unsure what to do, Julia decided it best to lead Genevieve to her bedroom and sit her on the bed.

'Has something happened, Genevieve?'

'No. Nothing. I know people think I'm ...'

Her voice was weak and fractured.

'Think you're ...?' Julia prompted.

'Alan was quite horrible. He doesn't understand.'

'Understand what?'

'Is it so bad for a woman my age to enjoy the company of younger men?'

Julia's thoughts were fuzzy. She wished she'd said no to the second bottle of wine.

'I ... err ... you mean ...'

'It's not sexual,' Genevieve said.

'No?'

'It's their vitality, their beauty, their strength.' It sounded sexual. 'And now Dominic isn't here ... I was an actress, you know. I was in a Polanski film. My agent said I had Hollywood potential. I gave up all ambition for Dominic. He was everything to me. I miss him every day.'

'Dominic – your husband?' Julia asked.

'My son,' Genevieve said.

Did women really value their sons for their vitality, beauty and strength? Audrey would never describe Julia's stepbrother in that way. She'd describe him as a sweet and clever boy, a catch for some lucky girl when he got older.

'Is Dominic coming back soon?' Julia asked.

Genevieve frowned.

'Is he at university?'

'No,' Genevieve said. 'He's in Switzerland.'

Genevieve's voice had hardened, the confessional tone gone, discouraging further questions, which, in any case, Julia was too tired to ask.

'Why don't you give him a call, if you miss him?' Julia said.

'Hmm.'

Genevieve remained seated on her bed. Julia wasn't sure what to say. Perhaps she still wanted to talk about Alan.

'The thing is ...' Julia said. 'I mean, if you go into someone's room at night, they might think ...'

'I'm sorry,' Genevieve said. She stood up. 'You have work tomorrow, and I'm keeping you awake.'

'It's not a problem,' Julia said.

'I've been so silly.'

'It doesn't matter, Genevieve. Really, any time.'

Genevieve dabbed at her eyes with her sleeve. 'Goodnight then,' she said.

Julia waited for Genevieve's footsteps to disappear up the

stairs to the attic before going to the bathroom. The landing light had been turned off, but she caught the flash of white gloss on Alan's doorframe glinting in the streetlight, before the soft shunt of wood on wood.

She was too tired and too drunk to care if he'd overheard her conversation with Genevieve. Julia hadn't said anything she shouldn't.

After washing her face and cleaning her teeth, she returned to her room, slipped into bed and lay back with the blinds open, watching the night sky.

Poor Genevieve, she must have been a beauty in her youth, captivating men, not seeking them out in the dead of night, to be rebuffed and humiliated. Not dissimilar to Penelope at work. But Genevieve did not long occupy her mind as wine and exhaustion tugged at her eyelids.

Julia wasn't concerned with the fading of youth. Middle age seemed as far away as the moon above her. A place to which other people travel but she would never venture herself.

Chapter 12

There's a moment when I wake, still cosy and warm under my duvet, that I forget, and all that lies ahead of me is the Tube and a laptop screen. As I roll over to switch off the alarm, I remember the missing backpacker Brandon Wells, the texts and the phone call.

It's him.

Better get your story straight.

A warning or a threat? Again, I can't think of anyone who *could* have sent the text, who *would* have sent the text, nor who would have called me. My mind starts whirring – the last thing I need is Audrey coming to stay, but it's too late to put her off now.

I'm stuck in a meeting all day with Jonathan and Ulrich, who were at university together and are old friends. The only words I speak are an introduction, my name and role in the project. Then I just sit there as they run through figures and statistics. Occasionally, Jonathan asks, 'Isn't that right, Julia?' and I nod without registering the question. My phone lies still and silent. I'm starting to hate the sound of these men's voices, their charts, deadlines, projections and the occasional aside about uni days – *Wasn't Jonathan a lad, eh?*

All I can think about is Garrick's phone. I'm continually aware of its weight in my pocket, as if it's calling to me. Has anything new arisen? Will I leave this office to find police officers waiting for me? My fingers tingle with frustration, and still Jonathan and Ulrich go on and on about leverage, bandwidth and accountability.

Eventually, they even bore themselves and decide to dedicate the rest of the day to swapping tales of their riotous youth.

'We're going for a quick drink,' Jonathan says. He looks at me, slightly nervous. 'You don't want to come, Julia, do you?'

I'm tempted to say yes just to annoy him. Instead, I tell him I have work to do.

The second they leave I head straight to the toilets.

As always with such torturous waits, they're in vain – no new information has been reported from Guildford. I'm disappointed, though I should be relieved. I'm becoming over reliant on Garrick's phone, I won't be able to keep it for ever. And I worry about my own phone. How would a stranger interpret the anonymous texts? What assumptions would be made about their being sent to me? At some point I'll have to dump the phones as I did Brandon's lump of a Nokia, over twenty years ago.

I wonder what happened to it. For how long are phone records kept? Has the Nokia been smashed to pieces or is it fifty feet deep in some Kentish landfill? Does it hold a trace of me, a hair, a fragment of fingernail?

My phone rings. Another false alarm.

'Hi, hon,' Pearl says. 'You didn't reply to my text. Are you coming round tonight?'

'Audrey's coming to stay.'

'Tomorrow then.'

'Rudi won't mind?'

''Course not. Come for dinner. We need to catch up with all your shit.'

Pearl thinks my shit is the end of my marriage. She's been in the States for the past three months. She wanted me to go over there and stay with her when she heard about my separation, but I had to be nearby in case Sam needed me. Which he hasn't.

'I won't be able to get there until eight.'

'You work too hard – and the girls will be in bed by then.'

'I can't get out of it,' I say, 'but I need to see you.'

'I'll keep a plate of something warm.'

Audrey's small blue case is in the lounge when I get home. It's the one she's had for as long as I can remember. Her efficient packing means that she could easily be staying one night or one month.

She comes in from the kitchen and hugs me. I catch the scent of Rive Gauche. It doesn't matter how much she irritates me, the waft of perfume and the hug always gives me a moment of inner calm. A memory from childhood, when a mother's love and home-baked biscuits could shoo away the world's ills.

'I'll take your bag up to the bedroom,' I say.

'I really can take the sofa, you know,' she says.

'Don't be silly.'

I put the bag down next to the bed and check Garrick's phone. Nothing new.

When I come down, Audrey's poking around in the lounge then follows me into the kitchen.

'This flat's much nicer than I thought it would be. I remember that awful place you rented in Archway before,' she says, looking out of the window. 'This has a fantastic view. It's not very big, but you don't need much space and I suppose it's only temporary.'

'Tea?' I say. 'How was the exhibition?'

'Oh, very good, very interesting,' she says distractedly.

I knew she'd hate it. The trip isn't about broadening her tastes in art. She's down here to see me. The first visit since my separation.

'We've got pasta for dinner. Is that OK?'

'Lovely,' she says. 'I suppose this is what they call a bachelor pad – spinster pad doesn't have the same ring, does it?'

'No.'

'Though technically, you're not a spinster.'

'Divorcee pad doesn't sound any better.'

'You're not divorced. There's still time to make it up. Sam might be close to adulthood, but he still needs his mother. This flat's nice but wouldn't you rather be home?'

'It's not an option.'

The kettle boils. I pour a little into the mug for Audrey's tea and the rest into a pan for the linguine.

'Have you spoken to Sam yet?' she asks.

I see his face twisted in disgust. *You're a whore. I hate you.*

'I think he needs more time, Mum.'

'Patching things up with your husband would be a good start.'

'I've told you, that's not going to happen.'

I filch the tea bag from Audrey's mug, put the milk in and hand it to her. Her nose wrinkles a fraction.

'I don't have a teapot, Mum,' I say.

She says nothing, takes the tea, rests it on her lap and tips her head to one side. I know what's coming.

'I still don't know what you were thinking, Julia?'

'Don't start,' I say.

I plunge the linguine into the water and start slicing some tomatoes.

'If you said you're sorry – that it was a mistake ...'

'I'm not sorry. It wasn't worth it because it's made Sam hate me. I told you, my marriage was over years ago.'

'And what about him – this Hugh person – did you think about him and his wife? How do you think she felt?'

In truth it wasn't until Hugh's wife confronted me in the lobby at work – *What sort of woman was I? Did I really think I could break up their marriage, fifteen years and three children?* – that I remember crying similar tears years ago over Christian, when he betrayed me. Her face showed anger, but also fear that her husband would leave. I'd forgotten that some women love their husbands. That not all marriages are a slow tussle of one person imposing their will on another, seeing how much the other can bear. This woman loved Hugh. Only then did I feel ashamed.

'You could start over, afresh. I'm sure he'd take you back. Say that you were feeling neglected, you wanted to make sure you're still desirable,' Audrey says. 'All women feel like that at your age. We just don't ...'

She raises her eyes to the ceiling and searches for the words. I decide to help.

'Just don't shag your son's rugby coach,' I say.

'Have affairs,' she says firmly. 'You think you're being very modern, don't you, Julia? When ninety-nine per cent of your marital problems are down to your attitude. If your husband was neglectful, it's because you made it clear you don't need him. You're so masculine.'

'Remind me to shave my beard off.'

'And sarcastic.'

'You're feminine, Mum, always let Robert rule the roost. How did that work out for you? Is he still changing secretaries every few years?'

She ignores my dig.

'What I'm saying is, all marriages go through rough patches. Often much more serious than yours. You can both get through this.'

'Neither of us want to get through this. We've not been happy for years, and anyway he's found someone else.'

'Who?'

'Plain Jane.'

'Well you're definitely in with a chance of getting him back. You've still got your looks. My genes, no need to thank me. Though a little make-up wouldn't go amiss. You should be making more effort now you're separated, not less.'

I smile. 'Jane's not really plain,' I say. 'I just call her that because she's so boring. I think they were seeing each other before.'

'Maybe you should try being a little more boring. It's all very well being a career girl—'

'No one's used that expression since 1979. In the same way that no one says "lady doctor".'

'So what am I supposed to call female doctors?'

'Doctors?'

'You've got an answer for everything, haven't you, Julia? I don't know why you always have to be so hard on me.'

'Not as hard as you are on me. *Sam's going to grow up hardly knowing who you are, the amount you work. Is it any wonder your husband's had enough? I'm not taking your side in all this.*'

'They're called home truths,' she says. 'And I may be hard on you but at least I don't sneer.'

'I—'

Audrey raises a hand.

'Don't deny it. Poor Mum, the little woman at home in the kitchen who gets into a tizzy if her husband's dinner's not warm enough and worries that her windows aren't as clean as next door's.'

'That's not true,' I say.

'And it's not just the words I use or being a housewife. It's everything. Oh, she reads Joanna Trollope and Maeve Binchy, while you're reading something with no plot that's won a prize, thinking it makes you clever.'

'I like those books.'

'Well I like Maeve Binchy and Joanna Trollope. There's nothing wrong with them.'

'I never said there was.'

'No, but I see you smirking every time I pick one up. It's the same with television or even the curtains. If I was clever and educated, I'd like better television and have better curtains. Well, where's your cleverness got you? Halfway to a divorce and relying on a handout from your stepfather to put a roof over your head. And you look down at me for not being independent.'

'Touché.'

'And why haven't you got any money after all your years working?'

'Sam has to stay in the house, and I have to help pay for it and Sam's upkeep.'

'No savings?'

'Sam's starting university soon.'

'He can't cost that much. I know you're at fault ...'

'Yeah, we covered that.'

'But you should be able to live decently. What would you have done if I hadn't been able to lend you the money for the deposit?'

'You did, and I'm doing OK.'

I go to the stove. The pasta's turned to mush. I hold up the soggy mess. Audrey shakes her head. Another example of my domestic ineptitude.

Audrey looks out of the window. It's clear tonight and the lights of the City outline its buildings against the inky sky.

'I suppose when Sam does leave home, you'll get your share of the house,' she says.

'Hmm,' I say.

After dinner we go to the lounge and watch Audrey's favourite television programme. It's about an English couple renovating a French château. There's about a hundred episodes. After the first advert break I sneak off to the bathroom and check the phone. Nothing new pops up.

I come back to the lounge and slip the phone down the side of the sofa. After three episodes of the château programme Audrey says, 'I'll go up and read. It's been a long day. I'm leaving early tomorrow. I'll ring you when I get back.'

'I'll be at Pearl's tomorrow,' I say.

'Friday then, when you're free.'

I kiss her goodnight. When she's gone, I retrieve the bottle of vino cheapo lurking at the back of the fridge and pour myself a glass.

I'm a third of the way down when the buzzer goes.

It must be for the previous occupants – no one ever calls for me. I decide to leave it. It buzzes again.

'Hi,' I say. 'Rex and Sol have gone.'

'Is that Ms Winter, Julia Winter?' a male voice says.

'Who's this?'

'I'm Detective Inspector Warren and I'm with Detective Constable Akande of Surrey Police.'

The intercom crackles.

'What's this about?' I ask.

'Perhaps we could come up and speak to you?'

'It's getting late,' I say.

'It is rather urgent, Ms Winter.' Another voice, female – this must be Akande.

'Can you tell me what it's about?' I ask again, though I know what they're going to say.

'We're here to talk to you about Brandon Wells.'

Chapter 13

1994 – Guildford

Julia didn't get to meet Alan until Wednesday at breakfast. She had a spoonful of Fruit 'n Fibre in her mouth when he sauntered into the kitchen, still in the process of doing up his tie. He was much as his silhouette had suggested, of average height and a little too thin. He must have been older than he looked because, in grey trousers and a white shirt, he had the appearance of an overgrown schoolboy.

'Hi,' he said and was out of the door before Julia could respond.

She ran into him again that evening, when she came in from work. He was sitting at the kitchen table, watching television.

'Hello, again,' Julia said.

He turned slowly from the TV and scanned Julia, as if seeing her for the first time.

'Hello,' he said and turned back to the TV.

Maybe he was shy, and she should be the one to instigate conversation.

'I'm Julia, by the way,' she said.

'I know,' he said without looking at her.

'And you're Alan, right?'

'Well deduced.'

His eyes remained fixed on the television. Julia was sure he wasn't actually watching the soap opera that droned on in the background. She tried again.

'Is there much to do around here? Do you go out much?'

This time he did make the effort to look at her.

'You've got to be joking,' he said. 'I'm glad I've got a girl-friend back home. All the girls round here are right slags and the guys are no better.'

His expression made it clear Julia was included in this derision.

The prospect of sitting alone in her room all evening wasn't great, but it was better than being with Alan.

She was about to leave when he switched off the TV and swung his leg over to sit astride the bench. She automatically turned to face him.

'What do you think of Genevieve then?' he said.

Julia was sure whatever her opinion, he would deem it contemptible.

'She seems nice,' she said neutrally.

Alan pulled a disappointed face, as if this was exactly the sort of wishy-washy comment he'd expected of someone so dull-witted.

'I saw Genevieve leaving your room the other night,' he said.

Julia remembered his sly closing of the door as she went to the bathroom.

'She didn't try it on with you, did she?' he asked.

The question shocked Julia. She knew that was exactly what Alan had intended and managed to feign nonchalance.

'Why would you think that?' she said.

He tipped his head to one side. 'No reason. I thought she might swing both ways. She seems the sort and she certainly can't resist young flesh.'

He smiled and stood up as if to leave. Julia didn't want to give him the satisfaction of riling her but couldn't hide her irritation.

'If Genevieve's behaviour bothers you, why are you still here?' she asked.

Alan stopped and looked at her, a sneer twitching at the corner of his lips.

'Who said it bothers me?'

'I wouldn't like it, someone coming into my room at night.'

Alan raised himself up and looked more superior than ever. 'Ah, but she *did* come into your room at night.'

'Not for that reason,' Julia said.

He laughed. 'If you say so. And anyway, as far as I'm concerned, Genevieve can drop in any time she likes. She's hardly going to overpower me, is she?'

'What are you talking about – she's just missing her son,' Julia said.

'And what exactly do you know about her son?'

'He's in Switzerland.'

'*In* Switzerland. Technically accurate, I suppose,' Alan said.

God, he was infuriating.

'What do you mean – is he in jail or something?' Julia asked.

'It's a bit more permanent than that.' Alan slowed down his speech as if waiting for her clunking brain to catch up. 'He's dead.'

This time Julia couldn't hide her shock.

'Why didn't she say?'

'Hello.' Alan waved his hand in front of Julia's face. 'This is Genevieve. She and reality have never been the best of friends, y'know. And Valium and vodka aren't helping the situation.'

Julia had thought Genevieve affected and melodramatic. It hadn't occurred to her that she might be grieving.

'What happened to him?'

'He was on a climbing expedition in the Alps. There was an avalanche. The body was never recovered, which is why she can kid herself he's coming back.'

'There's no chance?'

'No one survived.' His tone was matter-of-fact. 'It was six years ago. You'd think she'd have moved on.'

Julia thought of Audrey's miscarriages. The absent children, never spoken of.

'She lost her son,' she said.

'And how is pretending he's still alive helping her?' Alan said. 'You know she keeps his room exactly how it was, buys him birthday and Christmas presents for when he comes back?'

'What about Dominic's father?' Julia asked.

'Never on the scene, as far as I can tell. Genevieve was cuckoo long before the whole thing with Dominic. You know she changed her surname to D'Auncey by deed poll. That's Dominic's father's name. He never married her, already had a wife and he wasn't going to leave her. And who could blame him?'

'Poor Genevieve,' Julia said.

'Ah yes, the poor Genevieve narrative,' Alan said. 'The script she wants us all to stick to. Well, you can if you like. I've better things to do with my time.'

He ended the conversation by turning from her and exiting the room, leaving Julia unsure what to believe.

Chapter 14

I hunch next to the door and listen as two sets of footsteps ascend the stairs, one a dull thud, the other a light, barely audible tap. The last time I'd been interviewed by the police, over twenty years ago, I had the arrogance of youth on my side. Now, my heart's pounding and my palms are clammy.

As they come closer, I can hear panting and pauses. Finally, I open the door to a man in late middle age, with a heightened complexion and moist brow, his gut spilling over his trousers. The other is young, slim and slight. Barely out of breath, she's obviously been slowed down by her boss. They introduce themselves again.

Warren has a northern twang, too soft to identify any specific location. Akande is a South Londoner, trying to sound Home Counties. She has eyes the shape of a cat's, sharp and sly. The dislike is instant and mutual. My instinct is to slam the door in their faces, but I have little choice other than to invite them in.

'Can I get you a cup of tea?' I ask.

Warren looks at my glass of wine. It's late on a Friday night. He can't normally work these hours. A glass of wine would

71

be his preferred option, or perhaps a pint of bitter. He sees me watching him.

'Just water, thanks,' he says.

'Nothing for me,' Akande says.

'Take a seat,' I say as I head to the kitchen.

I watch the detectives' reflections in the window above the sink. Neither has sat down. Warren is standing where I left him and Akande is moving about the room, looking at my small collection of books, then at my phone on the table. She looks at Warren expressively. He doesn't react. Perhaps he'd be more interested if she found the one stuffed down the side of the sofa, a poor choice of hiding place. They have no right to take it, no warrant has been produced. But other than love cheats, who needs a secret phone?

I've been away from them too long. I fill the glass and return to the lounge.

'So, you're from Surrey,' I say on my return. 'How can I help?'

My voice sounds strained, my words contrived.

I should have been bold and said, 'I suppose you're here about Brandon,' or, 'If you hadn't contacted me, I'd have contacted you.' My breezy manner won't fool them. They deal with liars every day.

'I don't know if you follow the news,' Warren says. He's still a little breathless from climbing the stairs. 'And perhaps you don't get the Surrey news up in London, but I understand you used to live in Guildford.'

'A long time ago,' I say.

'At 72 Downs Avenue, owned by a Mrs Jennifer Pike.' He observes my confusion. 'Perhaps you knew her as Genevieve D'Auncey.'

A swish of silk. The scent of lemon and cinnamon.

'Yes, of course. It was very sad.'

Again, my words sound forced, like lines learnt and repeated.

'You shared the house with four other lodgers. Gideon Risborough, Alan Johns, Lucy Moretti and ...' He pauses. 'Brandon Wells.'

'That's right.'

'What do you remember about Brandon?'

'It was a long time ago.'

'Anything?'

'He left suddenly. Genevieve's sister thought he'd stolen some money.'

'Are you aware that, in 1995, his parents contacted the police and reported him as a missing person – his last known address being Downs Avenue?'

'You know, I'd forgotten until you mentioned it,' I say. 'But, yes, a man did come and speak to me. I can't remember his name.'

'Lancaster,' Akande says. 'Michael Lancaster.'

'It could have been.'

Corduroy trousers, blue parka; he waited outside my house, not two streets from here.

'Do you recall what you told him?' Akande asks.

'I don't know if I had anything to tell. Brandon's leaving, well it was all overshadowed by the whole thing with Genevieve.'

'Brandon never told you he was going, even though you were close?'

'Who said that? We weren't close. Not at all.'

'He told a friend he was seeing a girl in the house. Her description matched yours.'

I don't reply straight away. Akande waits.

'I don't recall Brandon having any friends. I can't remember meeting any. He just hung around with people in the house.'

'So, when you say you weren't close at all ...' Akande says.

'I wouldn't have expected him to remain in contact after he left, even if he hadn't stolen that money.'

'You hadn't argued.'

'We had nothing to argue about.'

Warren looks unconvinced. 'There were no conflicts – what about the male occupants of the house?' He refers to his notebook. 'Alan Johns and Gideon Risborough – did Brandon argue with them?'

'I really can't remember. Why are you asking me all of this?'

Warren looks to Akande.

'A body's been found on the Downs, less than a quarter of a mile from the house you shared. We believe it to be Brandon Wells.'

A dull thud lands in my guts. However much I expected this, it's a shock, hearing the words from a policeman. The identity of the body is no longer confined to website supposition and all hope that the past week was some surreal nightmare is erased.

'It can't be him,' I say.

'Forensics are sending DNA confirmation, but we're pretty certain that the body discovered is Brandon Wells.'

I place my hands on the back of the sofa to support my weight. What else will Forensics find?

'Do you know how? I mean, what happened to him?' I ask.

Warren looks at me hard, trying to gauge my reaction. 'We're undoubtedly looking at a homicide, though we're not releasing further details at the moment. But you can see why

74

we need to talk to all the people Brandon knew from that time,' he says.

'Have you spoken to the others?'

'Both Mr Risborough and Mr Johns are on holiday in Italy, with their families.' Does either of them notice me wince? 'But we've spoken to Lucy Moretti. Was there anyone else living in the house back then?'

'Only Genevieve.'

'We're also trying to find any photographs from that time,' he says. 'I don't suppose you have any?'

My nose burns in memory of the acrid smoke from the small bonfire we made, fulfilling our pact to destroy all records of the time. The thought of current social media existing back then makes me shudder. Whenever I saw Sam posting on Facebook or whatever the hell kids use these days, I used to say, 'You're only seventeen. You don't know when you'll want that information to disappear.'

He'd laugh at me. 'Why would I want it to disappear?'

'Ms Winter?'

Warren asked me a question – what was it?

'Sorry ... I ...'

'I asked if you had any photographs from that time,' he says.

'No. I didn't own a camera,' I say.

'Unfortunate.'

'Do you recall exactly when Brandon left?' Akande asks.

'You know what happened to Genevieve?' I ask.

Akande nods.

'There were so many people coming and going,' I say. 'Everything was muddled. I was working hard, seeing friends, trying to find somewhere else to live. I can't be sure when he

75

moved out. I think it was Genevieve's sister who noticed he'd gone.'

Akande glances towards Warren. He runs his fingers around his collar and takes a deep breath. 'A friend in London heard from Brandon in the fourth week of August,' he says. 'Brandon was going to move into his place over the bank holiday weekend, but never turned up. The friend didn't think anything of it at the time, thought Brandon had changed his mind. We've worked out this was Saturday 27th August 1994, the last definite contact we have from Brandon. Twenty-three years later his body is found buried on the hillside opposite Downsview Villa.'

Warren continues to study me.

'I still can't believe it's him,' I say. 'No one wished him harm. And if they had, he was a big lad – he could take care of himself.'

The detectives exchange glances. I'm being played. I must stay calm.

The stairs creak and I realise Audrey's awake.

'Excuse me,' I say to the detectives.

I leave the lounge and meet her on the small landing. She's wrapped in my dressing gown, which is far too big for her. I rarely see her like this, without the armour of tailored clothes, her face free from powder and lipstick. She looks small and vulnerable.

'I thought I heard voices,' she says. 'Is anything the matter?'

'It's nothing, Mum. Just some trouble across the road – kids. Go back to bed.'

'Really, I don't like you living here, Julia. It's dangerous.'

'Please, Mum, it's not a big deal. Get some sleep.'

When I return, Warren and Akande are whispering to one another. They stop when I re-enter the room.

76

'I wasn't aware you lived with your mother,' Warren says.

'She's just staying over,' I say.

Something about her presence has made him uncomfortable. Perhaps he's reminded of his own mother, because his tone's almost apologetic as he explains, 'You see the significance of where he was buried – not four hundred yards from where he lived. It's unlikely he left then somehow ended up back there.'

'I suppose so,' I say.

'It's more probable he was killed while still living there,' Warren says.

'But what happened to his stuff?' I ask.

'That's what we're trying to find out.'

'And he took that money.'

'Someone took the money,' Akande says.

'You see where this leaves us?' Warren says.

'Not really.'

'Brandon was killed while he lived at 72 Downs Avenue by someone who had access to his room.' Warren pauses. 'And perhaps Mrs Pike's money.'

'Which suggests someone living in the house,' Akande says. She allows the words to hang between us.

'That's not possible,' I say. 'Someone would have noticed.'

'You'd think,' she says.

'You said yourself, the house was in confusion,' Warren says. 'All sorts of people coming and going.'

'No one in the house would have wanted to harm him,' I say.

'Who else had the opportunity to clear out his room?' Akande says. 'We really do need to get to the bottom of any disagreements.'

'Honestly, I can't remember any.'

'Three boys and two girls living in a house and there were no conflicts, no jealousies?' Warren says.

'Nothing major.'

'What about minor?'

'I ...'

'Don't remember?' Akande crosses her arms.

'It was over twenty years ago. What can you remember from back then – were you even at primary school?'

Akande opens her mouth to reply, but Warren gets in there first. 'Did you know, Ms Winter, that Mrs Pike had been giving Brandon money?'

I tear my gaze from Akande's sneering face and back to Warren.

'She let him off the rent, because he wasn't working,' I reply. 'She took a shine to him.'

'Was there any resentment about it?'

'Not from me.'

'Ms Moretti recalls a good deal of resentment,' Warren says.

'Memories vary.'

'They certainly do,' Akande says under her breath.

'One more thing,' Warren says. 'You left Guildford in September that year. Not just the house but your job too – why was that?'

How did they discover so much in such a short space of time?

'The whole thing with Genevieve shook me up. I just wanted to get away and forget about everything.'

Akande raises her eyebrows.

'You know, it's getting late,' I say. 'And I'm not sure how much more I can tell you.'

'We're pretty much done,' Warren says. 'Just one more thing – your phone.'

'What about it?' I say too quickly.

Akande notices and looks at my mobile sitting on the table. They can't know about the other one, though it's less than three feet away.

'Can we get your number please?'

I breathe again. 'Of course,' I say and recite my number.

Does my voice tremble? Do they notice?

'Thank you,' Warren says. 'We'll be in touch.'

I don't close my door until I've heard them descend all the stairs and the front door shuts.

I knew the police would contact me. I should have been better prepared.

My landline starts ringing. I dive to answer it.

'Hello.'

Nothing.

'Hello,' I say again.

The line goes dead.

Chapter 15

Pearl's presence lingered in the room Julia had taken over from her after leaving Guildford. Her Magritte print still hung on the wall and used gig tickets were tucked behind the mirror. Julia missed her and Andre. But not enough to risk meeting them.

She closed the door and wedged it shut with a chair. Not that anyone was likely to come in. She removed her shoes and a couple of large bags, lifted the wardrobe floor and removed the envelope. She took it over to the lamp and pulled out its contents.

A clever place to conceal something. Brandon had only betrayed his hiding spot through carelessness. She would never have found it without the backpack strap trapped in the gap.

There was a knock on her door. No one ever visited her in Archway.

'Who is it?'

Silence. The knock sounded real. Not a ghost. Not an echo amplified by her mind. A solid knock, the door vibrating slightly against the frame. She knew that knock. She stood, staring at the door, half expecting it to fly open. Another knock.

'Who is it?'

'Me.'

She knew that voice.

'Just a moment.'

She hurriedly replaced the envelope and its contents and put the shoes and bag back on top of it. Sliding the chair from under the handle, she opened the door. It was the first time she'd seen Gideon since Guildford.

'We agreed no contact,' she said. 'Ever.'

'I need to see you.' He stepped into the room and shut the door behind him. 'There's a private detective—'

'I know.'

'You've seen him?'

'Yes. How did you find me?'

'I had your home number from Genevieve's address book. Your mother told me.'

Bloody Audrey.

'What did you tell Lancaster?' Gideon asked. His jaw was tense.

'Nothing,' Julia said.

'You're sure?'

'Why would I talk to him?'

Gideon seemed to relax. He took a moment to look around the room.

'Why are you living in this dump?'

'It's cheap,' Julia said.

'But you've got ... I mean ...' His brow creased in confusion. 'What have you done with it?'

She looked away from him and didn't answer. Just moments ago she had it in her hands.

'You can't leave it lying around,' he said.

81

'I can't spend it,' she said.

'Guilt won't turn back the clock. Nor will grand gestures. Alan and I invested it in the business.'

'Alan? We weren't to have any contact.'

'Let's just say he's not coping too well. I thought if he worked for me, I could help him out.'

'Keep an eye on him.'

'Support him. You could work for me, if you like.'

'No, thank you.'

'I could pay you enough to live somewhere better than this.'

He spread his arms to indicate the small room, its tiny ineffectual radiator emitting more noise than heat, the worn carpet and sagging, single bed.

'I don't know how you can live in that town,' Julia said. 'I don't know how you can just carry on. It's getting worse. I hear him. I smell him. Don't you?'

Fear flashed across Gideon's face. 'I think you're unwell, Julia.'

'And what about his parents? They're looking for him. We could still go to the police, say it was an accident.'

Gideon moved so fast, Julia had no time to react. He thrust her against the wardrobe door. Her head banged onto the wood. His face was so close she could feel his breath on her cheek.

'But it wasn't an accident, was it, Julia?' he said.

She wanted to push him off but was afraid what her struggling would provoke.

'You don't talk about this to anyone,' he said. His eyes drilled into her. 'We were protecting ourselves. We were protecting *you*. What would have happened if Alan and I hadn't turned up?'

82

'Everything all right up there?' someone called from the bottom of the stairs.

'You'd better go,' Julia said.

'Hey, is everything all right?'

'Thanks, Mica. Gideon's leaving,' Julia shouted.

Gideon let her go and glanced at the wardrobe behind her.

'You need to be careful,' he hissed, then turned and left.

Mica came up the stairs and put his head around the door. 'Are you OK?'

'I'm fine. Thanks.'

'Is he your boyfriend?' Mica asked.

'No,' Julia said. 'He's no one.'

Mica nodded and left.

Julia closed the door behind him and went to the wardrobe, removed the envelope once more, then took out a pen and paper. She retrieved Michael Lancaster's contact card from her coat pocket and started to write the letter she knew she must write.

Dear Mr and Mrs Wells

Chapter 16

1994 – Guildford

Over the next couple of weeks in Guildford, there was no repeat of Genevieve's coming into Julia's room and crying on her shoulder. And if Alan received any more nocturnal visits, Julia was unaware. His tales of Genevieve's seduction attempts rang hollow. She had no lack of attention from men her own age, several of whom used to call at the house. Genevieve would provide them tea then hurry them away. Edward, never Eddie or Ted, was the only one who came regularly and sometimes stayed the night, though no one was allowed to call him her boyfriend, and not just because he was in his fifties.

When there were none of her gentlemen to entertain, Genevieve spent much of her time with the gardener, a dumpy woman with a downturned mouth that made her look permanently disappointed as she plodded about, moving soil back and forth in an ancient wheelbarrow. Julia was surprised to learn she was Genevieve's sister, Ruth. They were so unalike – one exotic, the other almost invisible, lumbering around, trowel in hand.

Lucy came back from the Netherlands and turned out to

be far more sociable than Alan. She'd broken up with her boyfriend and would be staying after all. She and Julia started chatting in the kitchen and meeting for after-work drinks. Alan had been no friendlier and far less communicative than the first time they'd met. That Tuesday evening, as Julia was reheating the remains of her previous evening's macaroni, he sat down and switched on the TV without saying a word, or even acknowledging her.

Moments later Genevieve burst into the kitchen.

She stopped and clasped her hands together. 'Well, I know you'll all be so glad. You've got a new housemate,' she said.

'We're ecstatic,' Alan said.

For a moment, Genevieve looked disconcerted, but her features quickly settled back into serenity.

'He's one of our New Zealand cousins,' she said. 'Or their friend's son, or something. Anyway, Ronald – he's my first cousin, I haven't seen him since we were both at school – he says Brandon—'

'Brandon?' Alan spluttered. 'What sort of name is Brandon?'

'If you must know, I think it's a beautiful name,' Genevieve said. 'Brave and manly.'

'Yes, *Alan*, a *manly* name,' Julia couldn't resist saying.

Alan looked like he wanted to punch both of them.

'As I was saying, Ronald tells me Brandon is lovely. He's a carpenter. He's had to leave his room in London in a hurry, so he's coming here tonight. My sister's not keen, but I told her, Ruth, family is family.'

'He's not family,' Alan said.

'Sorry?'

'A friend of your cousin doesn't count as a relation.'

'As good as.' Genevieve waved her hand to dismiss Alan's

comment. 'You're as bad as Ruth. Anyway, he'll be here tonight. He's about your age. You must show him around.'

Alan muttered something that Julia was sure involved the word 'tradesman'. If Genevieve heard, she ignored it.

'Lovely,' she said. 'He'll be here at eight.'

Julia hurried to put her plate away and get out of the kitchen and back to her room, to avoid the inevitable snide comments from Alan.

An hour or so later, a taxi pulled up outside.

Julia peered through the window. A man squeezed himself out of the car and threw a backpack over his shoulder. A black baseball cap covered his face, but Julia could see that he was tall and bulky and wore dark baggy trousers. Genevieve ran up the drive to meet him. Julia returned to reading the Iain Banks book Pearl had lent her, until Genevieve knocked on her door.

She entered the room, more flushed and agitated than Julia had seen her before.

'You must come downstairs and meet Brandon, Julia. He's simply wonderful.'

Julia wasn't sure how wonderful the scruffy mess she'd spotted emerging from the car could be.

'I'm reading, Genevieve,' she said.

'Julia, you simply must come and meet him. I insist.'

Being told how wonderful he was prepared Julia to dislike him, and she wasn't disappointed. When she first came into the kitchen, he made no disguise of looking her up and down like a farmer assessing a prize heifer.

'Which one are you?' he asked.

'Julia,' she replied coolly.

'Fantastic,' he said.

Alan was sitting at the table, his habitual sneer hardened to a scowl.

'Are you staying long, Brandon?' Julia asked.

'Dunno. I'll see how it pans out.'

Julia examined Brandon more closely. He was broad, bordering on chunky, and had a square jaw and heavy brow. Not bad-looking, but no film star.

'Why are you in Guildford?' she asked.

'I thought I could find work here. And Ronald said I should look up Jenny. I mean Genevieve.'

All the time Genevieve was watching him, her eyes wide and glistening, an expression of rapt wonder on her face.

'I want to get to know the area,' Brandon said. 'Know any good bars?'

The question was directed at Alan, and Julia was expecting a curt reply. Instead he said, 'The Grape's good, more of a country pub.'

'Girls?' Brandon asked.

Julia braced for a comment about 'slags'.

'You're better off in town. Bar Midi, or somewhere like that.'

'Great. Up for a quick drink?'

'Sure,' Alan said.

Julia looked at Alan, in utter amazement. He carefully avoided her eye. She thought back to her first impression of Alan, as a thin schoolboy. Perhaps he'd been one of the frail and effete ones, bullied as a child and forever desperate to be accepted as one of the lads.

'Do you want to come?' Brandon asked Julia as an afterthought.

'I'll leave you two *lads* to it,' she said.

Alan was still avoiding her eye.

'Enjoy yourselves,' she added.

The boys left around nine. Julia watched their easy lope up the drive before they disappeared behind a hedge, only to reappear further down the road. Alan was nodding along as Brandon talked, his obvious discomfort amusing her. He'd have to spend the evening listening to Brandon and pretending to be interested in sport and the girls from town. Would he tell Brandon about his girlfriend? Julia had yet to meet her. She imagined a timid girl, with zero personality, who would consider Alan as clever as he thought himself.

Genevieve interrupted her speculation by knocking at the door and entering without waiting for a reply. She appeared dreamy, her eyes glistening as before, and she was carrying a photograph. She sat on the bed without asking and held the photo face down in her lap.

'And what do you think of Brandon? Isn't he just as I said?' Her voice was low and languid.

'Yes, he's er ...' Julia glanced down at the photograph. It had May 1985 written on the back. 'He's very nice.'

'I know people think I'm delusional. I'm sure Alan's said something.' Fortunately, Genevieve wasn't expecting a reply. 'But I've always known Dominic would come back.'

'He's been found?' Julia asked.

'I'm not religious,' Genevieve said. 'But I do believe in something. A force, I mean, something powerful at work in the universe. I just knew Dominic would return. Stupidly I thought that one day he would walk back through the door. But it doesn't work like that. Things aren't always as you imagine they're going to be. Look.'

Genevieve peeled the photograph from her thigh. It revealed

a faded print of a lanky teenage boy, looking away from the camera lens.

'You see?' she said.

'Is this Dominic?' Julia asked.

'Yes. But don't you see?'

Julia studied the picture. It had been snapped in the back garden at Downsview Villa. She recognised the terrace and bushes, which had grown several feet since the photograph was taken. For the first time it struck her how strange it was that there were no pictures of Genevieve's son about the house. Perhaps she kept them in her bedroom or the lounge, which was off-limits to the lodgers.

'You must be able to see it.'

Julia wasn't sure what was required of her. Genevieve looked on, willing her to understand the picture's significance.

'See?' Genevieve said again.

The awkwardness was becoming tangible.

'I'm not sure,' Julia said. What was Genevieve talking about?

'They're so alike.'

'Who are?' Julia asked.

'Dominic and Brandon.'

Julia studied the photograph again. They were both male and, had Dominic lived, they would be about the same age. The similarities ended there.

'Is that why you like Brandon so much?' Julia asked.

'It's some sort of miracle. I don't believe in them in the religious way. But my astrologer—'

'Your astrologer?'

Alan's irritation with this woman was becoming more forgivable.

'My astrologer said I would find solace for Dominic's loss. He has come back. Not in the way I thought. But he has come back.'

Julia examined her face to find traces of acting but Genevieve appeared completely sincere. Perhaps she'd been playing the role for so long she'd forgotten who she was. Forever Genevieve and never Jenny.

'And you think Brandon is Dominic?'

'Not exactly, but in essence they are the same. I'm letting him have Dominic's room – you know, the one overlooking the garden – rather than the downstairs one directly below yours. It feels fitting.'

Neither Valium nor vodka could produce this. Genevieve needed help.

'Have you told your sister any of this?' Julia asked.

Genevieve sat upright and looked a little panicked. 'Ruth? No. She wouldn't understand, and you mustn't mention it to her. Or to Alan.'

At least on some level she must realise how far-fetched her claims sounded.

'Of course, if he *reminds* you of Dominic.'

'It's more than that.'

'Genevieve, I know you want Dominic to return in some way, but Brandon is, well, Brandon. You can see that, can't you?'

'It's his eyes. I can see it in his eyes.'

'After Dominic ...' She needed to choose her words carefully. 'After Dominic left, did you ever see anyone, a counsellor perhaps?'

'Oh, they tried. But I wouldn't go. You pay them a fortune to talk rubbish and they tell you all your problems are down to sexual repression.'

'I don't think it's quite like that. Maybe if you saw someone, they might help you accept—'

'Accept what? What are you saying?'

She should never have started the conversation. Looking at the pain in Genevieve's eyes, she could not say, *Accept that he died eight years ago on a Swiss mountain.* Instead she said, 'Accept that Brandon is Brandon, not Dominic.'

Even this was too brutal. Genevieve stood up and snatched the photo from Julia.

'I've made a mistake. I shouldn't have spoken to you. For some reason I thought you'd understand. I'd never have shown you the photograph otherwise. I don't show it to just anyone. I hate strangers gawping at him. That's why I don't keep pictures around the house. I showed you because I thought you'd believe me.'

'Genevieve, I'm sorry.' Julia stood up too.

'No. It's my mistake. Sorry to have disturbed you. It won't happen again.'

'Please, Genevieve.'

The door slammed and Julia was left staring at the white-painted wood, before she moved to the window and stared out onto the green bank rising up before the house. She'd done nothing wrong, had no reason to feel guilty. And yet her conscience troubled her. She could have done more, but what? Perhaps humour Genevieve a little. *Yes, I can see the likeness. How marvellous for you.* Or would that have been crueller in the long run? Genevieve really did need help. She'd speak to Ruth, next time she was in the garden.

Pearl's book could no longer hold her attention. Part of her wished she'd gone drinking with the boys. The weekend was three days away and she'd be in London from Friday to Sunday. On Monday, she'd start looking for a new place.

That night she dreamt of a thin teenage boy, sitting on her bed.

'Who are you?'

'I'm Dominic. I'm moving back in and you're moving out.'

The scary PhD student from her original house search came into the room and picked up Julia's packed suitcase.

'You'll be living with me now. Come,' he said.

'No,' Julia shouted. 'No. Where's Genevieve? Tell her I'm sorry.'

The front door banging woke Julia up. She switched on the bedside lamp, expecting to see the indent of a lanky teenage boy in her duvet. Noises came from the hall below. Some drunken shushes and a female giggle. Footsteps ascended the stairs. She heard Alan say, 'Night, mate.'

Then two sets of footsteps went towards Brandon's room. He didn't waste any time.

Chapter 17

2017 – Archway, London

Despite my troubled night on the sofa, Audrey manages to slip past me and I'm woken by the door shutting behind her. I sit up and stretch the knots out of my spine as I try to digest last night's events. The silent phone call spooked me more than the police visit. It can't have been a coincidence, coming straight after they left. I'd think it was Gideon trying to mess with my head, if I didn't know that his self-interest always comes first, even before his spite.

Thank God I'm going to Pearl's tonight. If I spend any longer rattling around in my own head, checking Garrick's phone every five minutes, freezing with fear each time my other one beeps, I'll end up losing my mind.

When Rudi answers the door to his and Pearl's Maida Vale town house, I immediately feel safer. It's the first time I've seen them since their return from America and my separation. He gives me a massive hug and leaves his arm around my shoulders as he leads me inside.

'The only thing I blame you for is sticking with him for so long,' he whispers in my ear.

I envy Pearl. Rudi's just so ... reasonable. He doesn't scream at her if she breaks a glass or tell her she's getting fat if she puts on two pounds. He buys her packets of Minstrels when she's feeling low and whisks their twins, Elsie and Lola, off to the Natural History Museum if she's frazzled. I don't fancy him, my envy is entirely benign. It's just a longing for the marriage I never had. And the girls adore him, as does Sam. He's closer to Rudi than his father, who he circles at a distance. Perhaps having discovered a joint enemy in me will draw them together. In the past, the only good thing my husband had to say about his son was that he *was* a son and not a daughter. He would have demanded another child if he'd been a girl. All through my pregnancy I was convinced I was carrying a girl. She was to be called Ariadne. We would be best friends and I would avoid all the mistakes Audrey made with me. But Sam turned out to be a boy and I just made different mistakes.

As we near the stairs Lola runs into the hall and clutches my legs. Elsie jumps from four steps up and wraps her arms around my neck. I fall backwards, and Rudi has to step in to stop me toppling over.

'Girls, are you trying to knock Auntie Jules out? You've only been allowed to stay up for a goodnight kiss.'

'Come and sleep in our room, Auntie Jules,' Elsie says.

'I'm not staying over this time,' I say.

'But we want to see you,' Lola says.

'You can make us pancakes for breakfast,' Elsie says.

'You could stay, Jules,' Rudi says.

'Yes, do stay. I should have said.' Pearl comes out of the lounge and tries to give me a hug but can't get close enough because of the girls. She prises Elsie's hands from my neck.

94

'Aw, Mum.'

'Time for bed, you two. You've seen Auntie Jules.'

'But she's not staying.'

'I'll come another time,' I say.

'Come and read us a story.'

'Bed,' Pearl says.

'Just a short one,' Lola pleads.

I look at Pearl. She shrugs her shoulders.

'Maybe I could manage a short one,' I say.

Elsie and Lola are six and still share a room. Their beds sit either side of a shared nightstand with matching lamps, yellow with a fringe. I sit on Elsie's bed with my back against the wall, a twin either side, leaning into me. They still have the clean sweet smell of small children. I open *The Gruffalo*. And though they've heard it a hundred times, they sit silent and engrossed, as if it's their first listening.

They remind me of Sam at that age, wide-eyed and excited about everything. Each bedtime story is an adventure. He used to sit with his knees tucked up under the duvet. 'Again, again,' he'd say, and I'd read for much longer than I'd intended. Then I'd tuck him in and kiss him on the head. 'I lubs you, Mummy,' he'd say. Now he's six inches taller than me and calls me a whore.

When I finish the story, Elsie demands another, though Lola's eyes are drooping.

'Next time,' I say.

'Please, Auntie Jules.'

'I'll come over again soon.'

I carry Lola to her bed and tuck her in as I used to do for Sam.

'Night, night,' she says softly, her eyes closed.

'Night, Lola. Night, Elsie.'

'Auntie Jules?' Elsie says.

'Yes?'

'You can come and live with us. You can share with me and Lola. We wouldn't mind, and you could read us a story every night.'

'That's very kind of you, Elsie.'

'Mum says you've nowhere to live.'

'I have a flat now.'

'But you argued with Uncle.'

'Everyone argues sometimes, even friends.'

'Will you make friends again soon? We want to see Sam.'

'We'll see – now go to sleep.'

I slump onto the sofa next to Pearl. She puts her arm over my shoulder. Rudi doesn't bother asking me if I want a drink – he just hands me an enormous goblet of red wine. 'Are you hungry? We've some Thai curry left.'

'I've no appetite.'

'Are you all right, sweetie?' Pearl asks.

'Of course she's all right,' Rudi says. 'She's just got rid of that arrogant shit.'

'Rudi!' Pearl says.

'I'm only speaking the truth.'

'What if they get back together?'

'Then this conversation never took place.' He fixes his eyes on me. 'You're not getting back together, are you, Jules?'

'No,' I say.

'See.'

'If you put it like that,' Pearl says. 'You've got to do what's best for you, Jules.'

'She already has,' Rudi says and screws up his face. 'I never liked him and neither did you, Pearl.'

Pearl opens her mouth to protest.

'It's all right, Pearl, I did realise,' I say. 'You've both been unbelievably patient.'

'Not as patient as you,' Rudi says.

'And Sam's a sweet boy,' offers Pearl.

Why has she tacked this on the end – overcompensation? Doesn't she like Sam either? Has he become too much like his father and I haven't noticed? Rudi seems to sense the direction of my thoughts.

'If Sam's taking this hard, I can speak to him. I've tickets for the Quinns game next week.'

'Is he still coming?'

'As far as I know.'

I look at Pearl. 'You know it was him who found us, saw us together.'

'I heard. Andre told me.' She grimaces. 'At that age you don't want to think of your parents having sex with each other. Let alone with your rugby coach.'

'You know, the few friends I've told almost slap me on the back. Wahey, a rugby coach. Well done.'

'It's the female equivalent of shagging an air hostess,' Rudi says.

'They wouldn't have been so congratulatory if they'd seen him.'

'No Jonathan Joseph then?' Pearl says.

I shake my head.

'Better luck next time.'

I clasp my wine glass in both hands. 'Our marriage was over years ago, but this ... I could cope with all of it, if it weren't for Sam. He hates me.'

'He'll come round,' Pearl says.

'Will he?'

Pearl rubs my back and Rudi refills my glass.

'And I've been getting weird messages.'

'From shithead?' Rudi asks.

'I don't think so.'

I feel a compulsion to tell someone, though I should really shut up.

'A body's been found near where I used to live on the Downs.'

'Where?' Pearl asks.

'The North Downs, near Guildford,' I say.

'I'd forgotten you used to live out that way.'

At the time, Pearl had been far too busy building a stellar career in the music industry and falling in love with Rudi to notice much.

'The police came to see me. They think it was one of my old housemates,' I say.

'Christ – I could have murdered a few of mine.' Rudi laughs. 'Do you remember that one who used to keep maggots in the fridge for his fishing?'

'Shut up. This is serious,' Pearl says.

I put my glass down so they can't see my hand shaking. 'It sounded like the body had been there for some time.'

'So, you did kill someone?' Rudi is still laughing.

'Shut up, Rudi,' Pearl says.

'We thought he'd just done a bunk,' I say.

'Some guy in Fairbridge Road did that. Owed us two hundred quid.'

'The thing is, his parents claimed he never contacted them after that and the year after he'd last been in touch, they paid a private investigator to come and speak to us. I didn't know anything.'

'Weren't the police involved back then?' Rudi asks.

'They thought what we did – that he'd done a bunk.'

'But what's to link him with this body?'

'I don't know. And now someone's been texting me about it.'

'It's that shithead trying to freak you out,' Rudi says. 'He's pissed off enough.'

'And spiteful enough,' Pearl adds.

'But the way they're worded. It's just not him. I know it.'

'If not him, then who?' Rudi says.

'The boy's parents?' suggests Pearl.

'How did they get my number?' I ask.

'You can find out anything these days, with the right sources.'

Rudi's a corporate lawyer, so knows what he's talking about.

'And then the police came.'

'Surely that's routine for them to come and ask questions, if you were sharing the house with him at the time,' Pearl says.

'I don't know,' I say. 'It's made me nervous. I keep thinking someone's watching me.'

'That's stress and paranoia.' She looks worried.

'Just because you're paranoid, it doesn't mean they aren't after you,' Rudi says.

'Thanks, Rudi. Not exactly helpful.'

'I have to trust a lawyer on that one, Pearl,' I say.

'This isn't what you need right now, Jules. Not with everything else that's going on. It'll make you ill again.' Her brow creases with concern.

'I'm fine, Pearl.'

'But all this stuff about being watched – it's like before. Why don't you stay with us tonight, Jules?'

'It's not like before, and I can't turn up to work in yesterday's clothes.'

'Borrow some of mine.'

'They'll never fit.'

'I'll find some that do.'

'Yes, stay,' Rudi says. 'Or Pearl will spend the whole night fretting and I'll get no sleep.'

'Thanks, you two,' I say.

A night in a house filled with people will chase away a few ghosts.

'I'll go and make up the bed,' Rudi says.

'He's so lovely,' I say to Pearl when he's gone.

'Oh, Jules, why did you ever marry that hateful man?'

'I can't remember,' I say.

But I do remember. It's the same reason that, despite everything, I want to be with him now.

Pearl clutches her wine with both hands and looks me straight in the face.

'What did happen in Guildford? You'd changed by the time you moved to London.'

'I grew up, that's all. You'd done all that before, when you left home at eighteen. I was just catching up.'

'You were different, Jules. Angry, volatile, even before—' She shakes her head. 'Don't you remember swearing at Audrey?'

100

I have a vision of a mug smashing into the kitchen wall. I can't remember the words.

'Audrey's enough to make anyone lose their patience.'

'And now you've moved back to Archway. I'd have thought that's the last place you'd want to be.'

'The flat's cheap.'

'Is that all? I wish you'd move over this way. Even stay with us for a while.'

It's more than tempting. But the cheer and harmony of their household only serves to remind me of my own desperate situation.

'It's kind, but it's easier where I am. If you want to help me ...'

'Do you need some money?'

I'd been preparing the question all evening. I need to get rid of my phone and buy a new one, eradicate all traces of those messages.

'How did you know?'

'You never turn up empty-handed,' she says.

'I wouldn't ask if I didn't have to, but ...' I don't know where to start.

'How much?' she asks.

'Four hundred pounds.'

'Four hundred?' Pearl looks incredulous. 'I thought you were going to ask for at least ten grand.'

She and Rudi probably spend more than four hundred pounds on their weekly date night. To her, it's a ludicrously small amount to worry about.

'What the hell's going on that you can't find four hundred pounds?'

'Don't ask, Pearl. And please don't tell anyone, ever. Not even Rudi.'

'I won't – but, Jules, I'm worried about you.'

She puts her arms around me. I push her away and have to press three fingers into my forehead to stop myself crying.

'Everything all right?' Rudi says when he comes back in.

'Jules is just tired,' Pearl says.

Rudi places a hand on my shoulder. 'It gets better, Jules. It really does.'

'I know.'

How did I end up here, lying to my oldest friend? I wish I could unwind time, go back to 1994 and stay on that train taking me to Guildford, arrive in Portsmouth Harbour and take the next ferry to France, then none of this would be happening. I would never have met Alan Johns or Gideon Risborough or Brandon Wells.

Chapter 18

1994 – Guildford

On Thursday, Julia learnt she'd be spending Friday night alone in Guildford. Pearl rang to say that she had last-minute tickets to a gig. Andre claimed to be too broke to go out both nights, so would only meet them on Saturday. In both cases, Julia suspected the real reason was a man. Why were her best friends intent on coupling up the moment she was single? The promise of Friday night in London had carried her through the week. Now the long evening stretched before her, with a batty landlady the only possible company. And as it turned out, even Genevieve had a more active social life than her. She was leaving the house just as Julia returned from work.

'I thought you were going to London,' she said as Julia approached.

'I'm taking it easy tonight,' Julia said.

Genevieve was dressed more conventionally than usual, radiating sophistication in a cream trouser suit and sage green silk scarf.

'A night in? I do envy you,' Genevieve said in a manner that conveyed she did no such thing. 'Edward's insisting on taking me to the theatre. One of those dreadful Russian plays where everyone's either young and thwarted or old and bitter. No wonder they embraced communism. The gulags must have seemed rather jolly after a week in a dacha.' She swept the scarf over one shoulder. 'Enjoy your evening and don't do anything I wouldn't.'

To be pitied and patronised by her landlady was the last straw. And though, rationally, Julia knew Pearl and Andre weren't responsible for her, and had a right to a love life, she still resented them.

Young and thwarted – Genevieve had hit the nail on the head. Julia would probably end up like one of those women in a Chekov play, old and withered, watching geese fly to Moscow.

Having no appetite, Julia opened the bottle of Chardonnay she'd bought on the way home and went straight to her room. She had never lacked company before. Now, alone in Guildford, she felt lonely and she needed to talk to someone. She fetched the cordless phone from the hall and dialled the one person she knew would always be in on a Friday night.

'Are you all right, Julia?' Audrey asked when she picked up.

'Fine,' she said.

'Only I don't usually hear from you on a Friday. Aren't you going out?'

Not Audrey as well.

'I thought I'd have a quiet night in.'

'You can do that when you're old. When I was your age, I was out every Friday and Saturday. Of course, we had dances back then, not these discotheques.' Julia was about to object to the word *discotheques*, then thought better of it. 'It's how

I met your father. The Apollo, 1965 – did I ever tell you about it?'

'Once or twice,' Julia said.

'And don't roll your eyes.'

'I didn't,' Julia protested.

'I can hear you down the phone,' Audrey said.

How did she do that? Julia had, in fact, just rolled her eyes.

'Though I don't suppose you can meet anyone in those places,' Audrey said. 'Far too noisy for anything like conversation.'

'I'm enjoying a little downtime.' Julia leant over to the side table and topped up her wine. 'And you weren't out every weekend at my age. You married my father at twenty-two, remember?'

'You're right. I still think of you as seventeen. But you should be out. I know the whole Christian thing was a low, but there are other men out there. I've told you, you can't sit around moping. Remember your Aunt Rena.'

'I'm going out tomorrow, Mum. And it's only been two months. I'm not exactly Miss Havisham.'

'You say that but Christian's not hanging about, even if you are. I saw Ellie the other day.'

Julia put her glass down. 'I don't want to hear about her.'

'You can't bury your head in the sand.'

'Please, Mum, don't.'

She turned to look out of the window. A tiny dot high up, a lark perhaps, hovered in the sky.

'She seemed embarrassed to see me,' Audrey continued. 'Guilt, I suppose. But I couldn't help noticing – I have to say, it's not very tasteful – didn't say that to Ellie, of course.'

Julia's attention returned to the phone.

'What's not very tasteful?'

'The ring – too flashy. A large solitaire diamond with sapphires, set in platinum,' Audrey said. 'Not my sort of thing at all, but it must have cost a pretty packet.'

'Ring?' Julia said.

'The engagement ring.'

Julia felt sick. 'Have they ...' She wasn't sure if she wanted to know the answer. 'Have they set a date?'

'Not yet. I did ask,' Audrey said. 'I hope you don't think me disloyal, but the village is too small to go around avoiding people and having feuds. She and Christian decided to wait. In my day it would have been *tout de suite*, but no one minds so much now. I'm guessing she'll want to lose the weight first.'

'She's got fat?'

Ellie had always been a little chubby. It would serve Christian right if she blew up like a tick.

'It's only natural,' Audrey said.

'For Ellie, I guess,' Julia sneered.

'You do know, don't you? I'd assumed Pearl or Andre would have told you.'

'Told me what?'

'Ellie's expecting. Why do you think they got engaged so quickly?'

Engaged and pregnant. Julia wasn't sure if she wanted to hang up or throw up.

'Oh dear. I wouldn't have sprung it on you like that if I'd thought you didn't know. You seemed to be taking it well,' Audrey said.

'She's definitely ... I mean, it's not a false alarm?'

'Lord no. She has quite a big bump – due in September.'

Right up until the day he and Ellie came to the house

together – *they were very sorry, they hadn't planned it, they hadn't meant to hurt her* – she and Christian had discussed children. How many, two; and names, Leonard and Hester. Now he and Ellie would be having those babies and using the names Julia had taken such care in choosing. And it was due in four months. They must have been seeing each other long before the few weeks they had admitted to. And now Christian was going to marry Ellie, when he wouldn't marry Julia. They should wait until they had a house, had established their careers, he had said. Late twenties, early thirties was the right time for children. He was twenty-three.

'Julia,' Audrey said. 'Julia.' More insistent this time.

'Yes.'

'Are you all right? I can tell you're not, but really you must have known this was coming.'

'I have to go, Mum.'

'Now, Julia, don't get into one of your moods.'

Julia hung up.

How could Christian carry on as if Julia had never existed? They'd known each other since they were eleven years old – more than half their lives. How could he not miss her?

The initial overwhelming pain, which had sunk to a gnawing sickness, now flooded back in a wave of anger and despair. Her whole body shook. Her breath was fast and shallow. She had been comforting herself that Christian would regret his choice. He'd soon find Ellie dull. She was so *ordinary*. Julia almost pitied her. News of the engagement and pregnancy shattered her protective shell of derision.

She should have finished with Christian after A levels, gone to a far-off city, slept with inappropriate men and smoked illegal substances. Instead she had stayed at home, supressing her ambition for a false dream of suburban domesticity.

The phone started ringing. Julia ignored it.

Had Pearl and Andre known and made excuses for Friday, so they wouldn't have to be the ones to tell her? Were they on the phone to Ellie, congratulating her and arranging a hen night? Isn't that what you did for newly engaged, expectant mothers – congratulate them?

Julia snatched her wine glass from the side table and flung it at the wall. It smashed into tiny shards, which scattered across the bed and into her hair.

A voice came from the landing. 'Is everything all right?'

Julia jumped. She'd thought she was alone.

'I just dropped a glass,' she said.

'Are you sure you're OK?'

Julia shook the glass from her clothes before she opened the door a fraction, hoping to block the view of wine dripping down the wall.

Brandon stood on the landing. His face changed from a smile to a frown. 'You're hurt.'

'No,' Julia said.

'You've got blood on your face.'

He reached towards her forehead and wiped it with his thumb. Julia saw the red stain on its tip as he withdrew it.

She put her hand to her head and realised it was bleeding.

'Wait a moment.' Brandon darted to the bathroom and returned with some tissue.

Julia checked her face in the mirror. A thin red streak ran down her forehead. Brandon made her sit on the bed and dabbed at the cut.

'You need some disinfectant on that,' he said. 'Want to tell me what this is all about?'

Julia shrugged.

'There's glass everywhere.'

'I was drinking some wine. It slipped out of my hand.'

Brandon looked at the wine still trickling down the wall. 'Tell you what,' he said. 'How about we clean this up then get out of here. Being stuck in on a Friday night – it's not natural. And I could kill for a drink.'

Chapter 19

2017 – Maida Vale, London

Ilie awake in Pearl's spare room, imagining the police crashing through the door with a search warrant. I've yet to bin the phones – the pain of wasting four hundred pounds or my subconscious demanding punishment? Pearl's money will help me buy a new one, but will that be enough to keep me safe?

The bed I'm in is enormous and only emphasises how alone I am. I think of Pearl and Rudi curled up together and the girls gently sleeping in their twin beds. Sometimes being with others just makes you lonelier.

Sleep's a long way off. I sit up and switch on the sidelight. There are no books in my room and— I don't know why I'm kidding myself, what I want is Garrick's phone. No new information comes through on the UK sites, but a video clip pops up on one of the New Zealand ones.

Wells' parents make plea to UK police.

I press play on the video beneath the headline.

A woman in middle age, tall and broad, appears. The captions says: *Mari Hewlett – Brandon Wells' sister.* Next to her is another man who, by his size and bulk, I guess to be

Brandon's brother, though it's difficult to discern a facial likeness. The man is in his fifties, jowls pulling at his cheeks. Would Brandon have aged like this?

'My brother was a sweet, quiet boy, who experienced much tragedy in his short life,' Mari Hewlett says. 'He went to Europe to try to escape his heartbreak in New Zealand. We never saw him again.'

Her voice becomes high and strangled. She buries her head on the shoulder of the man next to her, unable to continue.

A caption flashes up: *Austen Wells – Brandon's brother*.

'We are all inconsolable knowing Brandon will never come home and achieve all the things he wanted to achieve. Our sadness is mixed with frustration that it has taken so long to get answers and that our mother never lived to find out what happened to her son.'

A microphone is thrust forwards and a male voice asks, 'Are you angry your original inquiries weren't pursued?'

Mrs Hewlett manages to stop crying. 'We knew Brandon wouldn't just take off and never contact his family. He wasn't like that.' Her eyes slide right to someone off camera. She pauses. 'I can't say any more.'

Her brother puts his arm around her shoulder and they walk away from the camera.

'Mrs Hewlett,' the voice calls.

They continue walking.

'Do you suspect anyone?'

'Have the police given you a name?'

The camera cuts to outside Guildford police station.

DI Warren has found a smart suit and looks far more composed than when he appeared in my lounge.

'Is it true that Surrey Police ignored the Wells family's plea to find Brandon back in 1994?' a journalist with a New Zealand accent asks.

'We'll be reviewing the case. Our first priority is to find the perpetrator or perpetrators.'

'Do you have any leads?'

'We're pursuing several lines of inquiry and would appeal to anyone who knew Brandon at the time to come forward with any information, however irrelevant it may seem.'

Cut back to the studio.

The clip ends.

I never thought about Brandon's family. What they must have gone through and are still going through. I must be callous, devoid of empathy – or is it just self-preservation? I can't carry other people's grief as well as my own.

The ache caused by my separation from Sam, knowing him to be in good health, thirty miles away, cannot compare to Mrs Wells' agony at never knowing what happened to her son. I remember the time when we received a telephone call informing us that Sam had been involved in a coach crash while on a school trip. It was only minor, no serious injuries. Despite these assurances I was sick with fear. Sam's father told me not to be so stupid. My sickness didn't subside until Sam was home safe. He laughed at my fussing, his only wound a slight bruise to the cheek where a bag had fallen from the overhead rack and caught his face. Mrs Wells' son is dead. Genevieve never recovered her son's body.

It all boils down to missing sons, that one long summer that defined my life. Not the flirting and laughter and running across the Downs. Not my fling with Brandon. Not the house-mates I discarded or kept close. But the missing sons. I need to find a way back to Sam, to be his mother again.

He won't recognise the number for Garrick's phone. I ring him. It's nearly one o'clock, but he often stays up late. At first, I don't think he's going to pick up. The phone rings and rings and eventually he does.

'Hi.'

He sounds sleepy, not upset, not missing his mother. My mouth goes dry. I can't think what to say.

'Hello,' Sam says again.

I swallow. 'Sam, darling. It's Mum. I just want to—'

He hangs up.

Chapter 20

The Cross Bar in Guildford town centre was rapidly filling up with Friday-night trade and house music pumped through its sound system at an ear-splitting volume. Brandon was snaking his way through the crowd back to Julia, carrying a pint for himself and a large glass of Chardonnay for her. His bulk seemed too big for the room. In a bar more than a pub, his size overwhelmed his surroundings. He was better suited to the outdoors.

She'd been lucky enough to find them a table. Brandon placed the drinks down and looked around, his eyes lingering on a group of girls next to them, sharing a bottle of rosé. Their dresses, heels and make-up made Julia self-conscious of her uncombed hair and plain grey sweatshirt. Brandon was probably regretting asking her for a drink. If he was on the pull, he'd be better off alone.

Slurping on her wine, Julia realised she was already a little drunk. She didn't care. She'd get drunker, look a scruff and ruin Brandon's night. Ruin everyone's night. Why should they all have a good time, when she was so miserable?

Brandon dragged his eyes from the rosé girls back to Julia.

114

'So, what's wrong?' he asked.

He had to lean in close, to be heard over the music, and Julia caught the scent of tobacco on his breath.

'Nothing,' Julia said.

'That glass "slipped" with a lot of force,' he said.

'I don't want to talk about it.' Julia tried to speak and drink at the same time and wine slopped down her chin. She wiped it off with her sleeve. Brandon bent his head towards her.

'You can't fool me. I know the signs too well. What's his name?'

Julia's face crumpled. She had wanted to speak to Pearl and Andre. But they would be out with their boyfriends, not giving her a single thought. And Brandon, well, he was here, in front of her, willing to listen.

'Christian,' Julia said. 'His name is Christian.'

She told Brandon everything about the break-up, the engagement, the baby. Then about the baby, the engagement and the break-up. And throughout all the repetitions and contradictions – 'I hate him, I hope I never see him again', 'I just want him back' – Brandon said nothing and listened. Only when she mentioned for the seventh time that Christian had no right to dump her because he only passed A-level Maths with Julia's help, and that he and Ellie better not be planning to move into the new-build housing estate Julia had been researching, did Brandon pull his chair next to hers and say, 'It's rough. I know, I've been there.'

'Really?'

He'd struck her more as the love 'em and leave 'em type. The girl he'd brought home the other night, for instance, had never been mentioned, let alone seen again.

'I did the same as you – ran away. Only I came to the other side of the world, not just down a motorway.'

'That's what I should have done,' Julia said. 'Who was she, the girl in New Zealand?'

'Cara. Met her when I was sixteen. Thought we'd grow old together.'

'I didn't know,' Julia said.

'It's not something I go around advertising.'

'Did she find someone else?'

'It wasn't that. Her family didn't approve of me. They didn't think I was good enough. In the end, she listened to them.'

'I'm sorry,' she said.

'It gets better, you know.'

'When?'

'When you least expect it.'

'That should be about now,' Julia said. She laughed into her wine, injecting it with bubbles, which made her laugh some more.

'Being here, in a new place, meeting new people helps,' Brandon said. 'If I think about it, it still hurts. It's just I don't think about it as much as I used to. Not more than, say, fifty times a day.'

'Fifty would be an improvement,' Julia said.

'Hanging out with Alan helps, you too – having mates to talk to.'

Brandon must be unaware that neither she nor Alan liked him. Though that was changing on her part. Genevieve's constant eulogising had set her against him, that and his laddish attitude, which now seemed more of a front. Brandon was like her, alone and heartbroken in a new town.

'And what about the girl, from the other night?' Julia asked.

'What girl?' he said.

'I heard her come back to the house, that night you went out with Alan. Aren't you seeing her again?'

Brandon looked embarrassed. 'She just needed somewhere to crash,' he said. 'Nothing happened.'

Julia wasn't sure if she believed him. His gruff demeanour didn't sit well with this sudden coyness.

'I don't want to get tangled up with any romantic stuff at the moment,' he said. 'I just need to sort myself out, get my head straight and find a job. Genevieve's been a sweetheart about the rent—'

'You don't pay rent?' Julia said.

'It's just until I find work.'

Genevieve had been adamant on the subject of rent, two months down in advance and the rest paid on the first of the month, no ifs, no buts. Her hippy tendencies didn't extend to money. Only with Brandon it appeared they did. Something swirled to the surface of Julia's alcohol-befuddled consciousness.

He's like Dominic, it's like he's come back.

'You know about her son, don't you?' Julia said.

'She's got kids?'

The room started a slow spin around her, the lights streaking, the voices blurring into one. Julia tried to arrange her thoughts, but they refused to form an orderly queue.

'It's nothing,' she said.

Somehow her glass was full again. She didn't need more but drank anyway, a deliberate recklessness to obliterate the images of Christian and Ellie.

One of the rosé girls came over and started chatting to Brandon. She placed her hand on the back of his chair and leant over, her mouth so close to his ear it brushed his overgrown mop of hair. Julia wondered if she was the girl from the other week, the one Brandon had brought home, or if she'd simply wandered over on the off-chance. Their conversation was too low to hear above the music. Julia blinked to try to bring the bar back into focus. It only lasted a split second before her eyes drooped and suddenly Brandon was shaking her.

'Come on, let's get you home.'

He took her arm. Julia scraped her chair as she tried to get to her feet. Brandon hauled her up and she managed to stand and force herself bolt upright to stop the swaying.

'You look like a soldier, standing to attention,' Brandon said.

Julia started to giggle. Brandon laughed.

'Come on, Private Benjamin, home time.'

'I'm all right,' she said. 'I'll get a cab. You can go with thingy.'

She swirled her finger in the direction of the rosé drinkers. The girl who had been talking to Brandon saw her and scowled.

'Oops,' Julia said and lost her balance.

Brandon pushed her upright again.

'You'd better go and talk to her,' Julia said. 'Let her know we're not, y'know, whatever.'

'She'll keep,' Brandon said. 'Let's get you home.'

There were no cabs and they walked up the steep hill to Downsview Villa, Julia leaning on Brandon as he entertained her with tales of his travels across Europe, before arriving in Guildford.

'Florence is all right,' he said. 'But it lacks a Slug and Lettuce.'

'You're making fun of me cos I'm drunk,' she said.

'What makes you think that?'

118

'Let's be daring and go in the front door,' Julia said when they reached the house.

'Why is that daring?' Brandon asked.

'We're supposed to go round the side.'

'Since when?'

Julia tripped up the front doorstep and Brandon had to catch her.

'Shhhhh,' she said in an exaggerated manner.

'Come on.'

They went upstairs. Julia thought of her head on a cool pillow and a glass of cold water, but without knowing how, she ended up in Brandon's room.

'I reckon that Christian's insane to let you go,' Brandon said.

He kissed her and she kissed him back. And through all the drunkenness she felt a triumph. She wasn't going to be Miss Havisham, waiting around heartbroken for Christian or any man. She would make up for all the lost years of monogamy to a faithless coward. Brandon was funny, he'd travelled, he had ambition. Why had she ever thought Christian was the one?

Chapter 21

2017 – Central London

Coming into work from Maida Vale, I look far chicer and less formal than usual. The voluminous black shift dress and enormous shaggy cardigan cum coat that Pearl left out for me to wear would be large enough for both of us to fit into. I would have thought only someone as tall and thin as Pearl could dress in it without looking like a yeti, but it suits me.

Anya – our receptionist – even asks where I got the cardigan. 'Dover Street Market,' I say.

Pearl probably did get it there. I've never been in my life.

I ring my mobile company, claiming the phone's been lost and I need a new one. I'm still in contract and it's going to cost me three hundred and eighty pounds. Thank God for Pearl. I'm not sure what was more idiotic, thinking Sam would speak to me or using Garrick's phone to call him and creating a link between me and it – if Sam chooses to tell anyone. I removed and crushed both SIM cards beneath my heel on the way to the Tube. The handsets I threw over a metal barrier and onto a building site, in the hope they'd be smashed to pieces by a digger.

By the time I've finished ordering a new one, the cumulative sleep deprivation is taking its toll, making me light-headed. I start to giggle when Miranda talks about test scripts with her slight lisp – *tetht thwipts*.

'Are you OK?' She looks genuinely concerned.

'Yessh, thank you,' I say.

Jonathan breaks off from his call and comes over. 'Are the Russell figures all OK?'

He leans in close and sniffs, attributing my strange behaviour to alcohol. If only.

'I've saved them to the shared drive,' I say.

'Listen, Julia, if you're not feeling well perhaps you should have a rest, take it easy. Do you want to go home early?'

Miranda looks amazed and even Paulo's face states that this is a precaution too far. Jonathan has never before uttered these words, or any approximation of them.

'I'll be fine, Jonathan.'

Miranda and Paulo drift away and leave me to sift through my e-mails.

There's a conference call at ten-thirty. My only contribution is confirming my name at the start. Jonathan does all the talking.

I return to my desk and go back to planning the project's timelines. The coding will have to slip as the functional specs aren't complete.

A draught of air chills the office. I look up. A man in leathers has just come in, bringing the cold with him. He places a box on the front desk. Anya talks to him for a moment. My name is mentioned before he carries the package towards me.

'Julia Winter – could you sign for your phone please?'

I do so and watch him leave. Immediately, I want to search

for Brandon's name. The urge is so strong, I have to put the phone in the drawer, out of sight. I'll set it up and wipe the backup from my old one once Jonathan leaves his desk.

I get back to my work. But I feel the phone calling to me. I don't know how long I'll be able to resist searching for more information. I shouldn't have thrown the second phone away. I could have hidden it somewhere, behind a loose brick in a wall or in a tree trunk.

Someone, even more inconsiderate than the motorcycle courier, comes in. They don't close the door behind them and the wind blows papers across the floor. Two police officers are talking to Anya. The man leans on the desk, in the casual manner of someone ordering a pint in their local. The woman stands back and scans the office. I look down before she catches my eye.

'Can I help you?' I hear Anya ask.

I look up again. Anya flicks her fringe from her face.

'There's no Risborough.'

My hands freeze on the keyboard.

The man says something I can't hear.

'You mean Winter.'

He nods. Anya points in my direction. They walk towards me. My hands still hover above the keys.

'Julia Winter?' the woman says.

I stand up.

The whole office stops and looks at me.

'You are Julia Winter?'

'Yes,' I say.

The female officer steps forward.

'I am arresting you on suspicion of the murder of Brandon Wells. You do not have to say anything, but it may harm your defence if you do not mention when questioned something which you later rely on in court. Anything you do say may be given in evidence. Do you understand?'

No one moves. The office stands silent. Unaccountably, Miranda starts to cry.

Chapter 22

2001 – Kingston upon Thames

A warm glow ran through Julia as she crossed the perfume section of Bentalls department store in Kingston upon Thames, inhaling the sweet and spice of Chanel No 5, Opium, Rive Gauche and Anais Anais. To Julia such places were impossibly glamorous. Growing up, Julia's nearest town had a concrete shopping parade, with only graffiti to break up the grey. The lifts stank of urine and the phone boxes were permanently vandalised. As a treat, Audrey would take her to Rackhams in Birmingham, now a House of Fraser, where she would spend hours in the beauty department. Audrey was old-fashioned – you'd not find her without a dab of perfume, lipstick and some blusher, which she insisted on calling rouge.

To step into Rackhams, with its light and space, perfumes from France and handbags from Italy, to press a silk scarf to her cheek, was to step into another universe. After the shopping, Audrey would take Julia to the café, where she'd have rich chocolate cake submerged under a mountain of whipped cream.

Bentalls reminded Julia of her childhood, and that glamour existed outside of her life as a corporate ant and unsatisfactory wife. Her salary went into a joint account. But twice a year she was paid a bonus. The wage clerk was a woman a little older than Julia, called Amanda. She said it wasn't a problem if Julia wanted her bonus paid into a separate, single-name account and halted Julia's convoluted explanation by raising a finger to her lips. Their eyes met in a moment of silent solidarity – she understood.

The bonus had gone into the account on Friday. Today was Saturday. She wasn't going to buy much, just a deep red lipstick with a soft sheen, a new bottle of Oscar by Oscar de la Renta and a scarf. Really, she needed some new boots. Hers were twice repaired and no amount of polish could hide their shabby state. She hovered over a black patent leather pair, covetous of their sheen and Louis heel. But such boots drew too much attention.

Instead, she picked up a green cashmere scarf. Since her pregnancy, Julia's skin had become hypersensitive and the scarf's softness was exquisite. She held it to her face and shut her eyes.

'It's Julia, isn't it?' The woman standing before her was in her mid-twenties, wearing jeans and a grey T-shirt. Her oval face and almond-shaped eyes were familiar, though Julia couldn't place them.

'I'm sorry,' she said.

'You don't remember me,' the woman said. 'But you were very kind to me once, when I was in a bad place in my life.'

'I'm sorry, when was this?'

'Years ago, in Guildford.'

Julia took the scarf from her face. 'I don't remember,' she said and started to move away.

The woman was undeterred. 'I was stranded in the rain.

You gave me twenty pounds. I had nowhere to go. I was only a teenager.'

'I don't recall,' Julia said.

'I was pregnant.' She glanced at Julia's bump. 'It seemed like the end of the world.'

'You were pregnant?'

Julia's hand moved instinctively to protect her unborn child. 'So, you do remember me?'

She couldn't deny it now. 'Yes, you came to the house,' Julia said.

'That bastard. I was only seventeen when I met him and of course he said he was in love with me, until I got pregnant. He claimed it wasn't his – threw me out of the house, physically threw me. I didn't know where to turn. My mum didn't want to know. If it wasn't for you, I don't know what I'd have done.'

'It was only twenty pounds,' Julia said.

'It was the gesture. Someone actually cared. Though I did feel bad about leaving you there with him, knowing what he was like. He said you weren't his girlfriend. Was that true?'

'Yes.'

'Of course, you're far too smart to get involved with a shit like that. I was seventeen – that's my excuse. I know better now.'

'Did you have the baby?'

'No. It would have been stupid – no money, no partner. Got two now, though, and a nice bloke. What about you?'

'The same, I'm really lucky,' Julia said.

'Here, do you fancy a drink? A soft one obviously,' she said, looking at Julia's bump.

'I'd love to, but I have to get back.'

'Shame. I'll give you my number. It's Leanne, in case you've forgotten.'

Julia let her tap the number into her phone.

'Call me and we'll meet for coffee or something,' Leanne said.

'That would be great. Lovely to run into you. I'm glad everything turned out all right in the end.'

Julia dumped the scarf on the nearest display and hurried back to the car. She sat for a few moments without turning on the ignition. That girl, she'd been so young, only seventeen. If Julia found out more, would she regret it? Her finger hovered over the phone.

The baby kicked inside her. She took a deep breath and deleted Leanne from the contacts. She wouldn't come to Bentalls again.

Chapter 23

1994 – Guildford

Fingers of light spread from under the curtains and hot beer breath blew in snores across her cheeks. A hairy leg flopped across her body, pinning her to the bed. Julia noticed a dolphin tattoo on Brandon's buttock and grimaced. She pushed him off. He rolled onto his other side with no disruption to his snoring. Julia winced, a jagged pain shot from her eye to her temple. Surely a shard of glass must have lodged behind her eye and was burrowing into her brain for her to be in this much agony.

Swinging her feet to the floor jolted her stomach. She had to clamp her mouth shut to stop herself throwing up on the orange-brown carpet. She checked that Brandon hadn't moved before gathering her clothes and poking her head out of the room. It was too early for anyone else to be about. She crept to the bathroom, where she knelt next to the toilet and allowed herself to retch. She longed to lie down on her own bed and get some more sleep. But she was sticky, stank of stale booze and, now, vomit. Crawling into the shower, she let the hot water run across her skin, hoping the memories would be carried down the drain with the stench.

She and Christian had waited two and a half years before sleeping together. They'd discussed it, prepared for it, felt shy and nervous. Now she'd leapt into bed with Brandon, a man she barely knew and didn't really like, or even fancy. Last night, she'd thought of it as getting some sort of revenge on Christian. This morning, under the steam of the shower and apple-scented body wash, she realised he would never know, and if he did, he would despise her – *You won't believe how desperate Julia's become.*

The water couldn't wash away her shame, the squirming disgust she felt for herself. A result of Audrey's Fifties' morality trickling down a generation. Pearl would have laughed about it in the pub and moved on to the next man.

Stepping out of the shower, Julia pulled a towel around her, but let her hair fall loose and drip across her shoulders and down her back. She shouldn't get so stressed. Her anxiety was a result of the hangover, a long week and the shock of hearing about Christian and Ellie. After she'd slept and met up with Pearl and Andre, things would seem different.

She opened the bathroom door and jumped. Alan stood outside. He looked her up and down, amusement flickering around his mouth.

'Up early,' he said.

'I thought you were away for the weekend,' she said.

'Obviously not,' he said.

Julia stepped past him to go to her room. She could feel his eyes boring into her back.

Most of North London seemed to have chosen the Oxford Arms for their pre-clubbing drinks and Pearl and Andre were barely visible through the fug of cigarette smoke. They sat and listened patiently, downing pints and munching on peanuts, as Julia told them about her conversation with Audrey, and made sly allusions to getting drunk with Brandon.

It turned out they *had* known about Christian and Ellie but hadn't wanted to tell Julia over the phone. It was agreed that Ellie was a complete bitch and Christian a loser. Julia was right to move on. Going out and getting slaughtered with some guy had been a good move.

'It's about time,' Pearl said. 'I never could work out why you stuck so long with Christian, the Man at C&A,' Pearl said.

'He's not that bad,' Julia said.

'Never seen him out of polyester,' Andre said.

'And I don't know why you're defending him, Julia.'

'Habit.'

'A habit you need to break,' Pearl said. 'Get out there and have some fun.'

Maybe next time it would be fun – with someone else.

'So, tell me about this Brandon,' Pearl said.

'There's not much to tell.'

Pearl grinned at her. 'You're a terrible liar.'

Julia opened her mouth to protest then shut it again.

'Go on, Jules, I tell you everything.'

Julia screwed up her face. 'It's just so embarrassing. I don't even like him much. He's really not my type and—'

'Don't tell me you actually shagged him.'

'Well ...'

'You really are moving on,' Andre said.

'I don't know,' Julia said.

'What's he like? How did you meet?' Pearl asked.

'He's one of the guys in the house.'

'Julia, no!' Pearl looked as if she'd caught her finger in the door.

'You told me to get out there,' Julia said.

'Yes, *out* not *in*. Never, ever on your own doorstep.' She wagged her finger from side to side.

'Er ... Justin?' Julia said.

'Justin, exactly, I know what I'm talking about. Worst of both worlds, not getting laid at home and not being able to bring anyone back. A complete nightmare. Never shag your housemate, unless you're sure you're going to marry him. Otherwise you might as well wear a chastity belt until you move out. Bloody Justin. One drunken fling with him and I had to become a nun for the rest of the year.'

'It was on your birthday, in May. You only had a month of term left,' Julia said.

'The longest four weeks of my life.' Pearl waved her finger at Julia. 'You should learn from my mistakes. Schoolgirl error, Julia Winter, schoolgirl error.'

'Sorry, Miss,' Julia said.

'Pearl's right,' Andre said. 'You can meet someone in London, without what's-his-name hovering in the wings.'

'To be honest, I don't think he'll care. Seems to have a different woman every other night.'

'Never underestimate the male ego,' Pearl said. 'Just cos he doesn't want you, doesn't mean he's not expecting you to pine after him. Every guy I've ever been with thought I had a secret agenda to get him down the aisle. Ha! You should have seen the state of half of them.'

'So why did you go with them?' Julia asked.

'They usually pay for the taxi.'

Julia flicked a peanut at her.

'Ouch,' Pearl said, though it couldn't possibly have hurt.

'Seriously, Pearl, why?'

'Just cos they're ugly doesn't mean they're a crap lay. How was Brandon by the way?'

'Good deflection,' Andre said.

'We are talking about Julia tonight. My peccadillos are well documented.'

'He was OK,' Julia said.

'OK good or OK bad.'

'OK, I was too pissed to tell the difference.'

'Never mind. At least Christian won't be the last man you ever sleep with,' Andre said.

'That fantasy's over,' Julia said.

'You've met someone else now,' Pearl said. 'Christian's history.'

Julia realised Pearl was as inexperienced in love as Julia was in casual sex. A one-night stand with an unemployed carpenter couldn't erase her eight years with Christian. In fact, sleeping with Brandon had only made it worse. Pearl's world was bands, booze and boys, in that order. But it just wasn't Julia, even listening to Pearl's exploits was exhausting. Julia longed for weekends snuggled on the sofa with a takeaway, a couple of videos and a bottle of wine – her old life.

'I suppose Brandon's a start,' Julia said.

'Pearl's encouraging others because she has to live her love life vicariously, now she's married,' Andre said.

'Give it a rest, Dre,' Pearl said.

'They're moving in together,' Andre said to Julia in a stage whisper.

'*Might* be moving in together.'

'Is that so bad?' Julia asked.

132

Andre looked aghast. Pearl ignored him.

'I wouldn't mind living in Rudi's flat,' she said. 'I'm so fed up with Fairbridge Road. Rudi has a whole kitchen to himself and central heating that *works*. It's just he'll be expecting other stuff.'

Given their previous conversation, Julia's mind drifted to unappealing sexual proclivities, but Pearl's concerns were far graver.

'He might be expecting to get married and have kids or something.' Pearl wrinkled her nose.

'Is that so bad?' Julia asked.

Pearl leant over and squeezed Julia's knee.

'Sorry, darlin'. Wasn't thinking. Of course, it's great if you're ready.'

Julia imagined Ellie curled up on an enormous sofa with Christian rubbing her baby bump.

'Both of you have to be ready,' she said. 'I wouldn't mind, but it's Ellie. Ellie Martin. The most boring woman on the planet. You know she crochets, and colour codes her holiday photos.'

'That bad?' Pearl said.

'You say she's boring,' Andre said. 'But would you feel better if she was Courtney Love?'

'If Christian prefers her, how dull am I?'

'Darlin', you're an IT technician,' Pearl said.

'Software engineer,' Julia said.

'Who was living at home with her mum until a few weeks ago,' Andre said.

He and Pearl collapsed laughing.

'Well it's better than sorting through the mail and picking up somebody else's dry cleaning, Pearl, which is all a PA does, even if it is at a record company. And Andre – what do you actually do?'

Pearl and Andre were still laughing too much to respond.

'Even with my job, I'm not as dull as Ellie,' Julia said.

Andre composed himself sufficiently to say, 'No one's as dull as Ellie.'

'Audrey says that's what Christian likes about her. Apparently, I'm too volatile.'

'I'd never call you volatile,' Pearl said.

'Audrey's lovely, obviously,' Andre said. 'But she's talking out of her arse on this one. Christian likes Ellie cos he's a twat.'

'You know, Ellie barely spoke to me at school,' Julia said. 'Then one day she starts wanting us to hang out together. I'm an idiot. It wasn't me she wanted to hang out with.'

'All's fair in love and war,' Andre said.

'All is not bloody fair. She nicked my boyfriend. I'm gonna let her know – write her a letter. Have you still got mice in your place, Andre? I could send some droppings.'

'Whoa.' Pearl held up her palms and spoke slowly. 'Put the bunny back in the hutch.'

'She deserves it,' Julia said. 'Am I just meant to take it – let her get married and have babies and live happily ever after with *my* boyfriend?'

'Julia, you know we love you, so we're telling you for your own good, you'll just look psycho,' Pearl said. 'It might even give Ellie a thrill. Play it cool like you don't care.'

'I do care.'

'Don't let them know. And you've got this new bloke – Brandon, is it?' Andre said.

'He's not my new bloke.'

'He could be.'

'No, he couldn't. I want someone ...'

Perhaps it was the cider, or her general confusion, but apart from Christian, Julia wasn't sure what she did want.

'While you think about it, I'll get the drinks,' Pearl announced.

'You'll never get to the bar – it's five deep,' Andre said.

'I wasn't going to the bar.'

Pearl smiled and turned to the group of lads behind her.

'Hi, guys,' she said.

You had to admire Pearl, she didn't lack confidence. The boys were looking them over. Perhaps Andre and Julia would ruin Pearl's chances, or they'd only get a drink for her. But Pearl shouted, 'Two lagers and a cider, thanks.'

Pearl and Andre were right, she shouldn't be waiting around for Christian to realise his mistake. It wasn't going to happen. And if her future husband wasn't here, among this group of lads in Pearl Jam T-shirts, he might be in the next group or the one after that.

The fact that Pearl and Andre thought she had become dull was a warning. She didn't want to end up like Audrey, keeping house for a man, raising his children and yielding to his every preference without question, while he indulged in weekend golfing excursions and business trips, which always required the attendance of his latest attractive young secretary.

Julia would change, become someone new.

Andre nudged her elbow, making her spill her drink.

'Hey, no brooding. We're not doing maudlin tonight,' he said. 'Christian wasn't the right one for you. There are millions of guys out there.'

Julia watched the man in a Pearl Jam T-shirt opposite down his pint in one and belch proudly to his friends.

'Millions,' she said.

Chapter 24

So, the worst has happened. The discovery of Brandon Wells' body has led to here, to me sitting in a cell at Guildford police station, drumming my fingers on my second cup of coffee, waiting for my solicitor to arrive. I used my right to inform someone of my arrest to call Pearl. She burst into tears when I told her. Rudi grabbed the phone and shouted, 'Don't answer any questions, Jules. I'm sending someone.'

Does Sam know his mother's been arrested for murder? Will it confirm that he's right to hate me? Has Gideon been arrested too? Is he sitting in another room identical to this one, idly checking his fingernails for dirt, cool, unruffled, unconcerned? And what about Alan?

My mind's spiralling. What do the police know? What can they know? Their suspicions can run from here to the Antarctic and back, they can't prove anything. Then why am I here? Did someone see us? No, we would have been reported at the time. And we were careful to leave no clues. They've nothing more than suspicion, I tell myself, and remain unconvinced.

My solicitor arrives and I'm taken to the consultation room

and given another cup of coffee. I imagined all solicitors to be like Graham, who did the conveyancing on our house. He hailed from Basingstoke and had the nervous habit of continually pushing his glasses back to the bridge of his nose with his index finger. Shazia Haider has a Yorkshire accent, a no-nonsense attitude and a nose stud.

'Good to meet you, Julia,' she says.

Her smile doesn't reach her eyes, which scan me, taking my measure in moments. She sits down and places a file on the desk between us. I sense she's not come to tell me it's a mistake and I'm free to go. In all probability I'll be spending the night back in that a cell. I delay the moment she's going to have to tell me all this.

'How do you know Rudi?' I ask.

'From university.' Her face relaxes and, this time, the smile does reach her eyes. 'It seems a long time ago now. And of course, Rudi went over to corporate, the dark side.'

'I thought criminal law was the dark side.'

'The majority of his clients are far more morally compromised than mine. Sometimes Rudi sends one to me, for misdemeanours outside the boardroom. But we're not here for that.' Her smile fades. 'Tell me about Brandon Wells.'

A hulk of a lad, not much older than Sam is now. Drinking, so as not to admit he was lonely and homesick.

'The truth is, I'd not thought about Brandon for years, until the police came to see me,' I tell her.

Shazia nods, a cool, impassive gesture, merely conveying acknowledgement, not concurrence. I wonder if all her clients lie to her.

She spends some time reading through the notes she's been given and making ones of her own. I gaze aimlessly around the room we've been allocated, spartan, functional, grey walls and plastic chairs. I look down at my coffee. A cold film is forming across its surface.

Shazia finally looks up from her file. She places an elbow on the table and her hands under her chin.

'Why am I here?' I ask.

'Gideon and Alan have been arrested too. The police believe that the three of you killed Brandon to stop him getting hold of the money Mrs Pike had withdrawn from her bank account. You kept it for yourselves,' she says. 'As far as I can see all the evidence is circumstantial. Are you aware of anything concrete?'

'No.'

'My guess is that they'll try to get you to incriminate each other. They've little to go on, so far, if you all stick to the same story – that you know nothing about it. Do you think the others will do that?'

'They should do but ... I don't know if Rudi told you.'

'We didn't speak directly,' she says. 'Are you not on good terms with them? Any particular reason they'll blame you?'

I explain the situation.

Shazia looks to the ceiling and exhales.

'Not ideal,' she concedes. 'But it will be difficult to incriminate you without incriminating themselves. I know Gideon's solicitor. He'll advise him to take the same line as me. Is it likely he'll follow his advice?'

'Gideon will do what's best for Gideon. He won't say anything.'

'And Alan?'

'He'll do what Gideon tells him, but ...'

'But?'

138

'He's the most likely to change his story.'

An admission that there is an alternative narrative. Again, Shazia gives me that cool nod.

'Brandon left. No one knows when. But Warren and Akande are assuming someone in the house killed him,' I say.

'Assumptions won't get them far. The Crown Prosecution Service want facts,' Shazia says. 'And they've yet to produce any physical evidence. Is there anything else you need to tell me – anything incriminating the police could find out? I don't want any surprises.'

I think about the phones. Shazia notices my hesitation.

'Julia, this is a murder inquiry. The police won't be cutting corners.'

'Someone has been texting me about the case,' I say. 'I changed my mobile provider, got a new phone, number and SIM. But I hadn't got round ... I mean, it's backed up to my laptop.'

'What did these messages say?'

I tell her about the website links, the landline call – *better get your story straight* – the silent call after Warren and Akande came to see me.

'And you've no idea who could be sending the messages or making the calls?'

'I thought it might be one of Brandon's family, trying to freak me out.'

'What makes you think that? How would they get hold of your number?'

'They hired a private detective, back in the Nineties. Michael Lancaster. They could have done the same again?'

She writes down the name.

'I'll check him out. In the meantime, we'll tell the police

about the messages and calls. Is there anything relating to your phone you won't want them to find?'

'No. Nothing.'

I can't bring myself to tell her about the second phone. The same sense of shame that compels an alcoholic to tell medical staff they only drink a couple of glasses a night.

Shazia leans back in her chair and picks up the file. 'This isn't much to go on. Either there's more they're not telling us or they're waiting on tests. Is there anything else the detectives know or are likely to find out that could link you to this death? It's best if you're honest. There's a suggestion in the file that Brandon had a girlfriend in the house. Was that you?'

'No,' I say.

Shazia's sharp. She should have been a police officer. She waits a moment before saying, 'But?'

I close my eyes. How can some images fade after a couple of days and others remain so sharp? Decades later, I still see that blotchy dolphin tattoo and recall the exact orange-brown shade of the carpet.

'But we did have a one-night stand.'

'I see.'

'I denied it when the detectives first came to see me. I was embarrassed. It was meant to be a secret. But apparently, he told his friend and I'm pretty sure Lucy knew. She was the other lodger.'

'It's best if you're up front about this, or anything they can prove. It's better to admit to an unpleasant truth than to be caught lying. Is there anything else?'

'There's nothing,' I say.

I hear raised voices and bitter accusations, recall the sensation of hot blood soaking through my sleeve.

'Good. And remember, we don't have details of how Brandon was found, how he was buried, what he was or wasn't wearing,' Shazia says.

Her tone is casual, but she's giving me a warning. Don't mention anything you shouldn't know. If criminal solicitors only represented the innocent, they'd soon be short of work.

'Most people's memories would be foggy, more than two decades after the event,' she says. '"I don't remember" or "No comment" are acceptable answers. What you mustn't do is ramble or try to fill in gaps. You'll get drawn into admitting to seemingly insignificant things, which could be turned into major issues by the police and prosecution, if it goes to court, which I'm going to do my best to avoid.'

'I get it.'

'Warren and Akande are going to go in hard, try to fluster you, confuse and above all make you think that Gideon and Alan are blaming this on you – tempting you to make counter accusations that would actually reveal your involvement. Before you answer any question, breathe, think. "I don't remember" and "No comment". Are we clear?'

'Clear,' I say.

My future lies in keeping a pact made twenty-three years ago, with two men who hate me.

'We'll wait for forensics. See what they find.'

I don't like the way she says it, as if she's expecting something other than what I've told them. She puts her files in her bag and looks me straight in the eye.

'Do you know what joint enterprise is?' she asks.

'No.'

'In a murder case like this one, with more than one person suspected of involvement, it means that if there was common

141

knowledge or agreement on a course of action, which resulted in Brandon's death, all of you are held liable, regardless of who executed the plan. You need to understand this, Julia.'

Shazia waits for me to process her words.

'For instance,' she says, 'a woman lures a man to a secluded spot, with the offer of sex. But it's a trap. Two other men, rival gang members for instance, are waiting for him with knives. The man is stabbed to death. The woman is convicted of murder, despite never having laid a finger on him. Do you see what I'm getting at?'

I'm almost flattered that Shazia can view me as some sort of sex siren, irresistible to men, bending their will against their reason.

'That isn't what happened,' I say.

'Can you tell me what did happen?'

'I really don't know.'

It's the first time I've spoken the truth. How often have I gone over it in my mind – why it started, who did what and when? What Shazia is telling me is that none of this matters. Joint enterprise means we are all guilty.

Chapter 25

1994 – Guildford

Returning from London on Sunday evening, Julia wasn't even through the door of Downsview Villa when Genevieve called to her. Julia found her perched on the kitchen table, dressed in a purple print jumpsuit and matching scarf, its excess fabric swishing to her waist.

'How was your play?' Julia asked as she made herself a mug of tea.

'Dreadful.' She flung herself onto the bench with the air of a wronged woman. 'I do wish Edward wouldn't patronise me with light entertainment. I can't bear musicals. I'm a trained actress. I do look for a little more substance in plays.'

'As long as it's not Russian,' Julia said.

'Why shouldn't I enjoy a Russian play? It seems Edward isn't the only one who thinks I'm too empty-headed to watch a production without song and dance.'

'It's only you said—'

'I worked with Zeffirelli, you know, and with Polanski. *Macbeth*.' She sighed. 'Wonderful times. It was only a small part, and unfortunately none of my scenes made the final cut. But the experience was priceless. Halcyon days, Julia, halcyon.

You should enjoy being young. Not keep to your room. How was your night in, on Friday?'

'Good,' Julia said. 'Quiet.'

'Unlike Brandon's then,' Genevieve said. 'So loud, and yet another girl. Did you hear him come in?'

'No.'

Julia gulped her tea, so that the mug hid her face.

'I don't mind the girls – I mean he's young. But I do hope she's suitable and he's not being led astray by some floozy.'

She gave Julia a piercing look. Julia swilled back the last of her coffee.

'Did you see the girl?' Julia asked.

'No,' Genevieve said. 'But I know the type.'

Julia had no doubt that Genevieve knew the exact type. It takes one to know one.

'Perhaps you should speak to Brandon about this noise?' she said.

Genevieve looked affronted. 'No. I haven't had the chance,' she said. 'I've been very busy.'

Genevieve was never busy. That was part of the problem. She invented dramas to fill her time.

Julia left the kitchen and trudged upstairs, without waiting to hear any further complaints. Genevieve wouldn't be berating Brandon about the noise. That wasn't what had upset her. Behind her otherworldly abstraction and affectations, she was just an interfering old biddy, whose so-called maternal interest in Brandon was fooling no one but herself. Julia would rather age like her mother, prim and antiquated, than become this ridiculous woman. Guildford's answer to Blanche DuBois, though it was doubtful if she could be more of a caricature of delusional middle age than Genevieve.

144

Chapter 26

DI Warren's corpulence overspills the interview room's flimsy plastic chair. Both his seat and jowls wobble as he switches on the camera and states the time and date of the interview and those present.

Akande has swapped her trouser suit for a pencil skirt and bright lipstick. She appraises my new look, shaggy cardigan and shift dress, with mild disdain. Our dislike is instantly renewed, and so palpable Shazia senses it immediately. She shifts in her chair and gives me a look, *keep calm*.

I hug my coffee mug to my chest as Warren asks the same questions as when he came to the flat. When did I last see Brandon? Did I ever hear from him after I left the house? Did I know anything about the money? To which I give the same replies. And all the time Akande watches me with those sly cat eyes.

'There's another incident I'd like you to recall,' Warren says. 'Do you remember the police coming to the Guildford house a couple of weeks before Brandon left?'

'Before he left?'

'You've no recollection of DS Bellingham and DC Lewes coming to see you?'

I rub my temples. 'Sort of. I can't remember what they asked me or what I said. Genevieve was rattled.'

'Mrs Pike?' Akande leans forward. 'Jennifer Pike was upset by the police presence? It had nothing to do with her. Why would she be upset?'

'I can't remember the details.'

Even though this is being recorded, Akande writes something in her notebook, to make herself look important, no doubt.

'If you can't remember, we'll move on. I'm going to have to dig a little deeper now,' Warren says. 'I'd like you to tell me about the atmosphere in the house. Did you all get on, socialise together?'

'We went out occasionally,' I say. 'But I was in London most weekends. At the time, Gideon, Alan and Brandon were just guys I shared the house with.'

Akande's eyes narrow.

'Brandon was a bit more than that, wasn't he, Julia?'

I don't want to provoke her, but her dislike is so decided, appeasement seems wasted. Besides, it's not what they suspect. It's what they can prove.

'If you're referring to our fling ...'

'So you admit to it now?' Akande says.

'I was too embarrassed before. But yes, he was more than a housemate.'

'Tell me about this fling,' Akande says.

'There's nothing much to tell, a late night, too much wine. We were both embarrassed the next day.'

'You weren't seeking a relationship? I understand your fiancé had recently left you for another woman.'

A stab of pain shoots through my side. For some reason,

the remembrance of that first betrayal by Christian flares up, as raw and real as the day he left me for Ellie. Why here? Why now after so many years?

'Which is exactly why I wasn't looking for a relationship,' I tell Akande.

'And Brandon was OK with that?'

There's a name for girls like you.

'It meant nothing,' I say.

'Would it have upset you if Brandon had slept with other women?'

'He did sleep with other women, and no, it didn't bother me.'

'Not even Genevieve?' Akande looks straight at me. 'It must have been difficult, another woman being preferred, right under your nose too.'

'Really? Genevieve was old enough to be his mother.'

'Relationships do occur between younger men and older woman – you and Hugh Paxton for instance – as your son found out.'

I'm on my feet, leaning across the desk and somehow the coffee mug lies shattered across the floor.

'Sam has nothing to do with this,' I say.

Shazia places a hand on my arm. 'Sit down, Julia,' she says softly.

I stay standing, my face inches from Akande's.

Shazia pulls my sleeve. 'Julia.'

I sit back in my chair, my shoulder turned to the detectives.

'This has no bearing on the case,' Shazia says. 'DC Akande is simply trying to provoke my client.'

'It didn't take much,' Akande says. 'That's quite a temper you've got there, Ms Winter.'

'Enough, Angela,' Warren says. 'We'll take a break. Interview terminated.'

We're moved to a different room while the remains of the mug are swept away and the coffee mopped up. Shazia is furious.

'I warned you, Julia. You need to stay calm.'

'She had no right bringing Sam into this – none at all. It has nothing to do with him.'

'She has the right to ask you anything she wants, and if she gets a rise out of you, she'll keep doing it. Do you know what that looks like on camera?'

'I'm sorry.'

'Don't apologise to me – it's not my liberty at stake. You do want to see your son again, I presume,' she says. 'What if you react like that to a question about Brandon?'

'I won't,' I say.

'We want the CPS to drop the case and right now it's fifty-fifty. Maybe less, depending on what Gideon and Alan say. I can't help you if you won't help yourself.'

'Fifty-fifty? You said there's only circumstantial evidence.'

'They're either waiting on forensics, or more likely holding evidence back, hoping you'll contradict it. Tell me that's not about to happen.'

'I've told you, it's not.'

'Make sure it doesn't,' she says. 'We're resuming tomorrow. Maybe a night in the cells will serve as a reminder as to why you need to keep your temper under control. Artificial light and bad coffee will be your life for the next twenty years if you don't get your act together.'

She leaves and I'm taken to a cell. I know why thinking of

Christian hurt. Because his loss led here – going to Guildford, my fling with Brandon, what happened later with Gideon. It all stemmed from Christian leaving me for Ellie. They've been married for nearly twenty-five years, have three adult children and still live in Flaxley. While I'm here in a Guildford police station, on suspicion of murder.

Chapter 27

1994 – Guildford

Julia managed to avoid Brandon until Tuesday evening. She had entered the house via the side door and was coming through the garage when she heard raised voices from the kitchen. She opened the door to find Brandon standing in front of Genevieve's sister, Ruth, his arms crossed, his legs astride. He towered above her. Ruth stood with one hand on her hip and the other raised, a single finger pointing into Brandon's face.

'And don't you think—'

She stopped when Julia entered. Brandon glanced at her briefly, then looked away, a little ashamed, before taking the opportunity to push past Ruth into the hall. Moments later the front door slammed. Ruth dropped her pointing hand to her other hip.

'Did you know he doesn't pay rent?'

Ruth made it sound more like an accusation than a question.

'It's none of my business,' Julia said.

She thought Ruth was about to berate her for indifference, but her face relaxed and she said, 'I suppose not. It's not mine either really. Jenny should be old enough to look after herself. Only she's not. And that boy ...'

Ruth gave a sharp exhalation of annoyance. Up close Julia could see the likeness between the sisters, which was not obvious at a distance. Without the affected mannerisms, the hairpiece and the theatrical clothes, they weren't so dissimilar. Ruth had the same high, rounded cheekbones, the slight upturn in the nose and cleft chin, not unattractive, but ordinary when set in a short crop of curly hair and a burgundy body warmer.

'I'm sorry, I didn't mean to be rude,' Ruth said. 'It just makes me so angry. My ex-husband was just like that, could sniff out any weakness at fifty paces then move in to exploit it. And Jenny's always needed a bit of looking after, if you know what I mean.'

'I'm sorry,' Julia said.

She just wanted to get some food and escape to her bedroom. She pulled a loaf from the cupboard, only one thick crust remained. It would have to do. There were a couple of slices of pre-packed cheese to go with it and a squidgy tomato. She should have gone shopping.

'Genevieve's been lending him money too,' Ruth said.

Julia had a vague recollection of a conversation about money on Friday night. What was it Brandon had told her?

'Perhaps I should speak to Edward about it. What do you think?' Ruth asked.

'Maybe,' Julia said.

Her food looked minging. She threw the bread, cheese and tomato in the bin. She'd order a pizza.

'See you, Ruth,' she said and moved towards the door.

'Julia, would you do something for me?'

'What's that?' Julia asked cautiously.

'Keep an eye on Brandon and let me know if he's up to anything, especially if it's to do with money.'

'I can't spy on my housemates,' Julia said.

Ruth sighed. 'I know it's not fair to ask you. But if you knew what Jenny went through after Dominic was killed. She was never exactly grounded, always had some hare-brained scheme that was about to turn her life into one of permanent bliss – going to live in Athens, travelling to Bulawayo – no visa, no injections, no money. She came back from Laos penniless and half dead with malaria. Yet another man she was convinced was her soulmate. Downsview was our parents' house, left to us jointly. If it wasn't, she'd have given it away to one of her lovers. Edward's the only decent one. The rest were all the same – take, take, take. She thinks it's love, when it's just exploitation. She never learns and she's just so, well, fragile.'

Ruth looked at Julia, her eyes pleading with her. 'There were times after Dominic died, I thought she might do herself a mischief. Getting in lodgers was as much about keeping her occupied as the money. Do you see why I'm so concerned?'

'I guess so,' Julia said, reluctantly. She really didn't want to get involved.

'And quite apart from his scrounging, I don't want Jenny to get too attached to Brandon,' Ruth said. 'I mean, he'll be off back to New Zealand one of these days. She mustn't turn him into some sort of substitute for Dominic.'

Genevieve obviously hadn't repeated to Ruth her assertion that Dominic had come back to her in the form of Brandon. And Julia wasn't going to tell her. She didn't want to get drawn into their drama further than she already had.

'Maybe talk to Genevieve about it,' Julia said, trying to edge out of the door.

'She won't listen. Just like with the wretched pills. They'll be the death of her. I keep taking them off her and she keeps getting hold of more. God knows how.'

'I just can't see how I can help,' Julia said. 'Even if I knew she was giving him money, what could I do?'

Ruth turned her palms upwards in a gesture of despair.

'I'm at my wits' end. Maybe I'll call Ronald, our cousin. See what he has to say about this Brandon. Can I at least give you my phone number? Not to spy, but if Jenny's in any trouble.'

She scribbled it down and pushed it into Julia's hand. She was irritated that Ruth was forcing this onto her. None of this had anything to do with Julia.

And something else about Ruth's reaction troubled her, the comparison between Brandon and her ex-husband who could 'sniff out any weakness at fifty paces'. Brandon had barely had to do any work to uncover Julia's weaknesses. She'd laid it all before him, her fears and insecurity, detailed to the nth degree. But it hadn't been money he'd wanted from her – not even sex. What had it been – influence, traction, an assistant handling Genevieve? Whatever it was, he wasn't going to get it.

He was in bed when she left for work and out drinking when she came home. Avoiding him wouldn't be too difficult, especially if she flouted Genevieve's rule about using the side door. If she'd come in the front door today, she wouldn't have had to see him at all. She'd been foolish, naïve. It wouldn't happen again.

Her plans to avoid him fell flat the next morning.

Nearing midsummer, daylight lasted eighteen hours. The

153

thermometer was hitting the high twenties and Julia left not only her blinds, but her windows open too.

She had risen early and left the house before the others were awake. The air was cool and the streets empty. Fresh air filled her lungs and pushed out the nagging flashbacks to her night with Brandon and her worries that he would tell Alan, or even Genevieve, what they hadn't already guessed.

Julia had reached the bend in the road that turned steeply downhill and took her out of view of the house, when she heard footsteps running behind her. Not the rhythmic strides of a jogger but an uneven, stumbling gait. She turned to see Brandon, in scruffy shorts and a greying T-shirt that no longer covered his belly. He was panting heavily and starting to sweat. A man in his twenties shouldn't be so unfit. What would he be like in his forties or fifties? The image of their night together slid across Julia's vision. She shook her head in an attempt to drive it away. Why was Brandon here? He never got up this early.

If similarly uncomfortable thoughts troubled Brandon, they didn't show.

'I was hoping to catch up with you,' he said.

'Why?'

'Thought we could walk together. You go past the station, don't you?'

'Are you going somewhere?'

'London. Job interview.'

Julia felt relief. Genevieve's money was just a helping hand. Ruth was wrong. Brandon wasn't a manipulative freeloader, just a guy who wasn't going to look a gift horse in the mouth. It was the same as his night with Julia, they were young and single, and where was the harm? It was only what ninety-nine out of a hundred men would have done in his situation.

'Do you always get up this early?' Brandon asked. 'I don't know how you manage it.'

'You'll have to if you're working in London,' Julia said.

'I hadn't thought of that.'

'And didn't you just move from London?' she asked.

'Er ... yeah. It's nicer here. Greener.'

He was insane. Julia would kill for a job in London and live there in a shot. But she wasn't living rent-free.

'Would you care if I moved?' he asked.

'Makes no difference to me.'

She could tell he was looking at her, but her eyes were turned away and she couldn't see his expression.

'What did Ruth say about me, the other day?'

She wasn't getting into this with Brandon. The less she had to do with the house soap opera the better.

'Nothing,' she said.

He stopped walking. Julia carried on for a few strides before stopping too.

'The thing the other night,' Brandon said.

'Forget it,' Julia said.

He looked taken aback, then hurt. Had he expected her to beg to be his girlfriend – demand he take her out to dinner? She looked at him with his ancient shorts flapping around scabby knees, his belly poking out over the top like some fifty-year-old – and that cap, squashed over his head. Pearl was right, it was all about ego. He certainly didn't want her as a girlfriend. He just liked the idea of being a heartbreaker.

'Yeah, well, we'd both had too much to drink,' he said. 'The thing is ...' He still hadn't moved. 'It's best if you don't tell Genevieve.'

'Why would I tell Genevieve – or anyone?'

155

Was it anger that crossed his face?

'You might,' he said. 'Girls usually talk.'

'I thought it was boys who went bragging.'

Julia started walking again. He jogged to catch up and tapped her on the arm.

'Hey, I'm not like that,' he said.

'Good.'

'Look, I'm sorry if you think, well, I'm not sure what you think. I had a good time the other night. It doesn't have to be any more than that, does it?'

He'd pulled his hat over his eyes and she could only watch his lips move.

'No,' she said.

They'd reached the end of the road. The station was to the right and Julia's work to the left.

'I'll see you tonight,' she said. 'And good luck.'

'Eh?'

'With the interview.'

'Oh yeah,' he said.

He raised a hand in farewell. Julia picked up her pace. As she made a left-hand turn, she saw Brandon walking back up the road towards home. She pulled herself into a hedge, so she was almost hidden. He glanced her way, but she was sure he hadn't seen her. She should have guessed – his scruffy clothes, his surprise at her wishing him luck – he wasn't going to London at all. How could she have been so stupid as to think for a minute he was sincere? She'd not trust him again. She should never have trusted him in the first place. From now on, she'd be on her guard for Brandon Wells.

Chapter 28

I lie awake all night on my narrow cell bed until dawn arrives in the form of an electric light flickering to life. I sit up and rub my shoulders, sore from the unyielding mattress. Tea, cold toast and a microwaved full English are thrust into my room for breakfast. I manage the tea before a constable comes for me.

Shazia is waiting in the consultation room, her eyes bright and eager.

'Warren and Akande aren't looking too happy,' she says. 'Gideon and Alan must be sticking to the same story and they've not made me aware of any more evidence. They'll ask you some more questions, but keep you cool and remember what I told you, "I don't remember" and "No comment".'

The night in the cells has concentrated my thoughts. As Shazia said, electric dawns and cold, soggy toast will be my life if Akande has her way. I will remain impassive, I don't remember, no comment.

Akande's puffy eyes speak of sleep deprivation equal to mine. She must have been up late, combing through evidence,

157

finding proof of the absolute necessity of incarcerating me. Warren's pouchy eyes mean nothing – he always looks as if he's been pulled in from a late-night session down the pub. He goes through the formalities before saying, 'Can I take you back to something we discussed before?'

He sounds friendly, too friendly. I don't trust him.

'What's that?' I say.

'I explained previously that because of the location of Brandon's grave and his last known communication, on Saturday 27th August 1994, we concluded he was killed around that time.' He leans back in his chair with a satisfied air. 'There's also the fact that all his personal belongings disappeared, along with the forty-five thousand pounds in cash we know Mrs Pike withdrew from her account a week or so prior to that.'

'This is all circumstantial,' Shazia says.

Warren raises his hand to halt her. 'It's a little more than that.' He draws out a clear plastic folder with a photograph in it. 'I remember you saying you didn't have a camera at the time. Something you have in common with Gideon and Alan.' He flicks his eyebrows skywards to indicate scepticism. 'Fortunately, someone in the house not only had a camera, but was a bit of a hoarder too.'

He withdraws the photograph and places it in front of me.

It's Genevieve's lounge. Gideon, Alan and I are sitting on the sofa, smiling. Brandon leans on the arm, a beer can in hand, looking down on the group. I remember the beige sofa with its thick cushions, a dust magnet Genevieve managed to keep spotless. Solid teak side tables, ornamented with Aztec masks, Gambian carvings and Malaysian vases. The heavy lamp, which one of her 'gentlemen friends' brought back from

Morocco, is too large for the table it's perched on and looks as if it's about to topple over. Just in front of the sofa lies the cream and red rug with geometric patterns that sat at odds with the naturalistic designs from further afield. And against the wall stands a small oak bureau with desk tidy containing pens, pencils and a pair of scissors.

Often, I kid myself that I've not aged so much. The girl staring at me from the sofa tells a different tale. Her hair is naturally dark and glossy, her cheeks plump, her body lithe and strong. Her smile comes from a moment of glee, not tinged by regret of the past or fear of what's to come. Alan still has hair on his head rather than his face, and Gideon – Gideon is the least changed. He's only grown greyer and sterner, the pretence of amiability peeled away.

There we all sit, in our early twenties, not knowing that our best years were nearly behind us. In a few weeks Brandon would be dead and Gideon, Alan and I would spend the rest of our lives looking over our shoulders.

Since I left Guildford, guilt, anxiety and dread have been woven so deep within my thoughts their presence has gone unnoticed, until I see the photograph and have a sudden flash of who I used to be. The lightness of joy in everyday events, the anticipation of what adventures the future would bring. I would do anything to return and unpick the threads that led me to this interview room in this police station. Tears well up and roll down my cheeks, unchecked.

'Something amiss?' Warren asks.

'I was so young,' I say.

Akande rolls her eyes.

'What else do you notice?' Warren says.

I wipe my face with the back of my hand and lean over the

photo. It was taken at the far end of the lounge, opposite the French doors. The glare and our light summer clothes suggest the day must have been a hot one. Didn't we have a barbecue? I can't think of another time we all socialised together or sat in the lounge, which was usually off limits.

Lucy must have been behind the lens because she's not in the photo. It's not impossible that Genevieve took it, but Warren's comments about how the picture was obtained make me think it's Lucy. Surely no one would still be hanging on to any of Genevieve's photos. Hers must be the second shadow that falls across the floor in front of the sofa.

'I can't see anything strange,' I say.

'Here's another photograph,' Warren says. 'It was taken later, when Genevieve's estate was being valued.'

He pushes it across the table. I can see straight away what he's after.

In the second photograph, the light is cold and grey. It turned chilly that September. No one's crowded onto the sofa and the room looks dead and bare.

'Can you see the difference?' Warren asks.

'The room's empty,' I reply.

'And not just of people,' Akande says. Her look says she's not buying my feigned ignorance. 'Care to look at it again?'

She pushes it right under my nose. I push it back.

'I'm sorry. I'm very tired. I couldn't sleep in that cell. If I'm missing something—'

'If I'm missing something.' Akande copies the cadence of my speech with extra whine. 'Come on – my five-year-old could spot the difference.'

'Angela,' Warren says as a warning.

She leans back, crosses her arms and glowers at me.

I'm drunk with tiredness, the interview and pictures achieving what counting back from one thousand and imagining a relaxing walk along a sandy beach could not. If I put my head on the table now, I'd sleep for a week.

'My client's obviously exhausted,' Shazia says. 'If you could get to the point.'

'The point is, Ms Winter, that two items are missing.'

Warren moves his finger between two empty spaces on the photograph.

He says nothing, expecting me to fill the gaps. I'm not going to tell him which items are missing, despite Akande's assertion that a five-year-old would spot the discrepancy. Warren pulls the first photograph from me and positions it with the middle three fingers of his left hand. With his right he points a pen.

'This.' The pen lands on the marble-based lamp with ornate metal work winding around it, creeping up to a bottle green shade. 'And this.' The rug.

'I see,' I say.

'Do you?' Warren asks.

'No,' I reply.

'Oh please,' Akande says.

Warren throws her another look. 'This lamp may look exotic, but it wasn't a one-off. We've found matching models. And the rug is from IKEA.'

My throat tightens, my breath becomes quick and shallow. I know what he's going to say. Everyone in the room knows.

'The reason we're certain Brandon was murdered is because his skull was smashed in with a heavy object. Tiny fragments of gold leaf and chips of marble were driven into the bone. Both came from this make and model of lamp, which disappeared at the same time as Brandon. We didn't need microscopes for the next discovery. His body was found wrapped in bin bags and rolled up in a rug. This rug.' He taps the pen on it. 'It was heavily stained with blood.'

He pushes the photograph back towards me.

'I think you can tell me how it got there,' he says.

Chapter 29

1994 – Guildford

During the hot weather, work was a cruel imposition. Julia resented every second she spent shivering in the office air-con. She refused to wear a jumper on principle – it being summer.

On Wednesday, her boss spent most of the afternoon on the phone, squabbling with his wife, before leaving early to continue the argument in person.

'I'm not staying, if he's not,' Fraser said.

'Me neither,' said Bee.

Julia followed suit. Back home, she put on shorts and a T-shirt, took a bath towel and laid it on the lawn in the back garden. She decided against a bikini. Brandon might think it was for his benefit. She'd been effective in avoiding him, and he'd not sought her out. It was as she thought, an insignificant one-night stand. It meant nothing. In time, they'd become inured to one another, treat the whole situation in an adult manner. Not like Pearl and her former housemate, Justin. She lay back on the grass and watched the perfect sky above – not a cloud, not even a bird disturbed the solid blue.

'Want some wine?'

163

Julia lifted her head from the ground. Lucy was on the terrace, a bottle in hand.

'No, thanks,' Julia said.

There had been enough of that recently.

Lucy poured a glass for herself and joined Julia on the rug. She peeled off her T-shirt to reveal a sea green bikini. Her stomach was flat and dipped just below her ribs. Julia's should be like that. She used to run three times a week with Christian and do sit-ups on the lounge floor. Lack of exercise and too much booze had undone much of its effect. She was aware of the waistband of her shorts digging into her and, in general, her dresses were too tight and becoming uncomfortable. She needed to do something about it, go on a diet – tomorrow.

'I've got some news,' Lucy said.

Julia rolled onto her front and propped her head up on her hands.

'What?' she asked.

Lucy looked over Julia's shoulder.

'It will have to wait.'

Julia turned. Genevieve was coming down the steps towards them, a drink in her hand and a dreamy expression on her face. She was wearing capri pants and a flower print blouse. Before she even sat down, she said, 'I've had the most dreadful day.'

'What's happened?' Julia asked.

'Edward took me to Chichester,' she said with the melodrama of a rejected Ophelia.

'I didn't realise Chichester was such a distressing place,' Lucy said.

'Oh, it's lovely but the theatre. That performance. No. No. No. How can anyone expect me to pay for that?'

'I thought Edward paid,' Lucy said.

'That's not the point,' Genevieve snapped. 'It's not the play. It's the actors – well actually, the actresses. Any dumpy thing who can remember her lines seems to get a role these days. No glamour. No enunciation. Dreadful. Simply dreadful. I've thought about going back on the stage, but with my classical training I may not be in the current style.' She took a long sip of her drink and sighed. 'Really, I don't know why I go to the theatre these days. One production is as dreary as the next.'

Lucy was smirking into her drink.

'I guess it's like a second marriage,' Julia said. 'A triumph of hope over experience.'

'Really, Julia. You mustn't say such things,' Genevieve replied. 'A second marriage. The thought makes me shudder. A second marriage is a triumph of stupidity not hope.'

'Were you ever married, Genevieve?' Lucy asked.

'You mustn't ask me. I don't want to talk about it. The whole thing was just too ghastly.'

Genevieve put her drink down on the grass and seeing that neither Julia nor Lucy were going to ask, she continued.

'His name was Harold Pike – so very handsome, so charming, asking questions seemed unnecessary. I thought he was suave and sophisticated. He was just a spiv. We ended up living in a hovel in Notting Hill. Appalling. It wasn't rat-infested, but we did have mice. I was only seventeen, too stupid to realise there was a whole world out there – and we didn't even explore London.' Here Genevieve leant forward and lowered her voice to a whisper. 'And of course, he was totally incapable of fulfilling me sexually.'

Lucy could no longer hide her smirk. She looked at Julia who, feeling the corners of her mouth twitch, turned away.

'I'll always remember the day I realised it was over,'

Genevieve said, 'nineteen sixty-six, the day England won the World Cup. We didn't have a television and Harold had been to a friend's to watch the game. Of course, he came home drunk demanding his conjugal rights. Well, I knew what drunken sex meant and I told him straight, it wasn't happening. I found it distasteful. He told me it wasn't his job to fulfil my sexual requirements, it was his job to provide. I was there to meet his needs. I didn't call renting that filthy flat "providing". And I've loathed football ever since.'

'So, you wouldn't advise lying back and thinking of England?' Lucy said.

Julia couldn't stop her shoulders from shaking.

'What's that about England?' Genevieve said, looking around her, a little confused.

Julia managed to compose herself sufficiently to say, 'I'm starting to understand why you wouldn't marry again.'

'I would have married Auguste, but he wouldn't marry me. It was all his wife's fault. She deliberately got in our way.'

'How unreasonable!' Lucy said.

Julia avoided making eye contact. She wasn't going to be able to keep a straight face much longer. Genevieve downed the last of her drink, vodka most likely.

'The whole thing reminded me of that terrible music hall song Harold was always humming, about a woman waiting outside a church to get married, when she receives a note from her fiancé, "I'm afraid I can't marry you today, my wife won't let me."' Genevieve sang it in a tinkling little voice. 'Well, that was Auguste. He couldn't get away from his wife. And when I went to his house to have it out with her, Auguste was furious. He wouldn't speak to me after that. Even when Dominic came along.'

166

'That's the drawback with married men,' Lucy said. 'Those pesky little wives.'

Genevieve ignored her comment and, instead, looked down at her glass. 'I think I need a top-up.'

'She needs something,' Lucy said when Genevieve was out of earshot.

'Lucy, don't,' chided Julia.

'Come on, she's a fruitcake.'

'I feel sorry for her.'

'Me too. But there's only so much you can put up with. And all that rubbish about being a classically trained actress. Ruth said she used to work as a hostess in one of those dodgy Soho nightclubs they had in the Sixties. Hostess – you know what that means. Mandy Rice-Davies, that's all I'm saying. Genevieve's only complaint is she backed the wrong horse. Landed a small-time crook instead of a cabinet minister.'

'A hostess – really?'

'Uh-huh.'

Lucy gave a significant nod, then lay back on the rug and closed her eyes. Julia tipped her head to the sky. A couple of birds appeared as black spots in her perfect blue. Surely it must be too hot for them up there. Another shadow appeared across them. Julia looked up just in time to spot Alan staring at Lucy in her tiny bikini. He averted his gaze the moment he realised Julia had seen him.

He sat down on the grass, still in his work clothes.

'Did you know we're getting a new housemate?' he said.

'That's what I was going to tell you, Julia,' Lucy said. 'Have you met him, Alan?'

'How do you know it's a him?' he said.

Lucy pulled Genevieve's dreamy expression, focusing on the

middle distance, 'I feel the female energy in the house is overpowering. We need more Yang to the Yin.'

Julia giggled and even Alan had to smile.

'You're right, of course it's a bloke. I don't know anything else. Jenny's being mysterious.'

'Don't let her catch you calling her that,' Lucy said. 'And Genevieve's mysterious about everything. She thinks it makes her interesting.'

'He's probably another accountant,' Julia said. 'Sorry, Alan.'

Alan raised his head. 'This from a computer geek.'

'The geek shall inherit the earth,' Julia said.

'But not original puns, it seems.'

'Cut it out, you two,' Lucy said. 'It'll be good having someone else about the place.'

Alan looked as if she'd lost her mind. 'Why? More mess, less shower time, or just another bit of male flesh for Genevieve to drool over?'

'Jealous?' Julia said.

'Oh pur-leeese,' Alan said.

Julia took pleasure in finally having riled him, perhaps coming closer to the truth than she'd guessed. Alan feigned horror at Genevieve's advances, but was oddly proud of them, as if it made him more generally desirable. Ridiculous really, when the only attributes required were to be under thirty and male.

Lucy was obviously having the same thoughts. She smiled with fake sweetness.

'Look on the bright side, Alan – there'll be more of you to share the burden.'

'Lessen the load,' Julia added. 'We know how tiresome it is for you being a sex magnet.'

168

'You're not funny,' Alan said. 'You're just sad. And remind me who's single and who's not.' He stood up and marched towards the house.

'Remind me who's got a girlfriend who no one's ever met,' Lucy called after him.

Alan ignored her.

'He's so up himself,' she said when he was out of earshot.

'I thought that was just me,' Julia said.

'The next one better not be like him.'

'Or Brandon.'

Lucy raised her eyebrows. 'You didn't seem too against him the other night, I hear.'

'Who said that?'

'Alan.'

'He's making it up.'

'Brandon's all right actually,' Lucy said. 'We had a little heart to heart – underneath that macho shit, he's a nice guy.'

'Urgh, really?'

'And I think he likes you.'

'He likes all women.'

'No, I mean ... Never mind.'

'No, tell me.'

Lucy leant forward about to speak, then looked up.

'Hi, Brandon,' she said, in an unnecessarily loud voice.

'Hi,' Brandon called from the patio steps.

He came down into the garden with another guy. No doubt another best mate, who Brandon had met five minutes ago down the pub.

'We're about to head to The Ship to get better acquainted,' Brandon said. He stood back and let them view the stranger. 'Girls, meet your new housemate. This is Gideon.'

Chapter 30

2017 – Guildford Police Station

The interview room feels colder. Warren and Akande's eyes rest upon me as the lamp that crushed Brandon's skull and the rug in which his lifeless body was wrapped stare up at me from the photograph.

'I've no idea how these objects came to be with Brandon,' I say.

'Gideon and Alan are telling us a different story,' Akande says.

I can almost hear Alan, eager to blame me, repeating a story devised by Gideon. I want to scream – it wasn't me, it wasn't my fault, I couldn't stop it. Shazia is watching me. This is the tactic she warned me about – divide and conquer.

'If Gideon knows anything different, he's never told me,' I say.

Akande smiles. 'Gideon is only telling us what we already know. We don't need witnesses to place you at the scene of Brandon's death.'

'If you've further evidence, you need to inform me and my client,' Shazia says.

'We intend to,' Akande says.

Warren leans forward. 'Ms Winter, would you tell us your shoe size please?'

'What's that got to do with anything?'

'If you could just answer the question?'

There doesn't seem any point in refusing.

'I'm a size seven.'

Warren pushes forward the photo of us sitting in Genevieve's lounge. He taps his pen on it, where my foot touches the rug.

'Would it surprise you to know that we found a footprint on the rug we found wrapped around Brandon? It's not visible to the naked eye, but with lighting and the correct photography ...' He shows me the picture of the rug with the tread mark highlighted. 'It corresponds to a size seven Converse trainer. The same brand you're wearing in this photo.'

'I was living in the house – it's hardly surprising.'

'The footprint was in blood.'

I look at my blue suede trainers in the photograph, my favourite footwear at the time.

'Would you like to tell me how it got there, Ms Winter?'

'No comment.'

'Is that really the route you're going to take?' Akande says.

I look down to hide the antipathy, which must be written across my face.

'Is there anything to link this footprint specifically to my client's trainers?' Shazia asks. 'And can you state that, without question, the blood belongs to Brandon Wells? It's my understanding that a sample like this, exposed to the elements, wouldn't yield DNA. There's zero evidence linking my client to the crime.'

'Incorrect,' Akande says. 'Gideon and Alan link Ms Winter to the crime.'

'If they're saying anything different to me, they're lying,' I say.

'Gideon said you were angry with Brandon, for seeing other women.'

'I couldn't have cared less.'

'He says you're unable to control your temper, something you've already demonstrated to us. And that you actually threatened him with a knife during an argument.'

'Of course he's going to say things like that, because—'

'Julia,' Shazia says. 'I advise you not to respond further.' She turns to Warren and Akande. 'I'd like to talk to my client – alone.'

'Don't blow it now,' she says when the detectives have left the room. 'They're trying to turn you against one another. They'll be telling Alan and Gideon the same thing – Julia told us you did it. Julia said you had a grudge against Brandon. Really, it's a good sign. They've nothing concrete. Go back to "no comment" and you'll be out of here by the end of the day.'

On their return, Warren tries a different angle, while Akande leans back in her chair, restless and dissatisfied.

'We know Brandon liked you, but the feeling wasn't mutual. How did he react to being rebuffed?' Warren asks.

'He didn't,' I say.

'Did he attack you?'

'No.'

'Julia.' Warren attempts an avuncular tone. 'If there was some sort of fight or struggle, was there an element of self-defence?'

If they wanted me to plead self-defence, they shouldn't have told me about Brandon's skull being smashed.

I look at Shazia. She inclines her head.

'No comment,' I say.

Akande leans forward. 'What does your son think about your bed-hopping twenties?'

Anger twitches through to my fingers, but I'm not letting her rile me a second time. I look straight at her.

'No comment,' I say and enjoy watching her almost spitting with frustration.

'No comment' has switched the balance of power.

Realising they have little to go on, Warren terminates the interview and switches off the recording equipment.

'I assume my client can leave. You've no evidence that will stand up in court,' Shazia says.

Warren stares at Shazia, then me.

'We'll see,' he says before marching out of the room. Followed by Akande, who's too angry to look.

'You did well,' Shazia says once they've left. 'Especially after she mentioned your son.'

'Is that it?' I ask.

'Should be. All that "we'll see". They're sore losers,' Shazia says. 'I have to go. An aggravated assault. Hopefully we won't need to meet again.'

It feels unreal. This is to be my only punishment – fear, shame, a near miss? We were right all those years ago. No one can prove anything if we stick together. And even though the bonds between us have strained, they've not broken.

A uniformed officer comes in with yet another cup of coffee.

'Aren't they going to release me?' I ask her.

'No idea.'

'But I've been here ages.'

'Paperwork maybe,' she says.

The coffee looks revolting. I'll wait until I'm out and I can have a real drink. I walk around the room. What's the delay? Are Gideon and Alan to be released before me?

I'm still pacing the room when the door opens. The uniformed officer re-enters.

'You're to come with me,' she says.

I follow him along a corridor to the custody desk.

Warren is waiting there for me, accompanied by Akande, who makes no attempt to conceal her smile.

'Can I call someone to pick me up?'

Pearl would come, whatever the hour.

'I'm afraid not,' Warren says. 'New forensic evidence has been received. I've been advised by the Crown Prosecution Service to formally charge you with the murder of Brandon Wells.'

Chapter 31

1994 – Guildford

The sun blinded Julia. She had to use her hand to shield her eyes and still Gideon was just a silhouette. He was tall – not as tall as Brandon, a couple of inches shorter – and though square-shouldered, not nearly as broad. He wore light-coloured chinos and a white T-shirt.

'Would you like a drink, Gideon?' Lucy waggled her wine bottle.

'That would be—'

'Have a beer, Gideon,' Brandon said.

Brandon sat down and took two cans from the plastic bag he was carrying. Gideon sat opposite Julia, the sun still behind him, so she couldn't look at him properly. From what she could make out, he was a little older than the rest of them, perhaps twenty-eight or twenty-nine.

Alan reappeared on the terrace.

'Are you joining us?' Brandon asked.

More confident with the presence of two other men, Alan returned, still in his work clothes.

'This is Gideon.'

Brandon tipped his beer in Gideon's direction. Alan gave

him a formal handshake as he sat down. He looked out of place in his office attire – the rest of them wore summer clothes.

'Is that your BMW on the drive, the white one?' Alan asked.

'Yes.'

'Lucky you,' Alan said.

It was the only time Julia had seen Alan look genuinely impressed.

'Where were you living before?' Lucy asked.

'London,' he said.

'And you swapped it for here?' Julia was incredulous.

'You're the only one who thinks the streets of London are paved with gold, Julia,' Alan said. 'They're actually paved with shit.'

Julia watched Gideon smile as he sipped his pint.

'Not a fan of the place myself,' Brandon said. 'Too big, too noisy. You can't hear yourself think, and the rent's sky-high for some total dump.'

'Is that why you left so quickly – couldn't pay your rent?' Alan asked.

Brandon hesitated and looked annoyed. 'I didn't want to get sucked into a long tenancy.'

Alan also noticed the hesitation. Julia would leave him to wheedle out the details. He was good at that.

'Is that why you moved, Gideon?' Julia asked. 'Because London's too expensive?'

'I love London,' he said and smiled at her. 'But I was given a chance to work for my godfather. He hasn't any children and is looking for someone to take over his business in a few years. If I work for him now, hopefully that will be me.'

176

'Wow, your own company just handed to you on a plate, unbelievable,' Brandon said. 'What sort of firm is it?'

'We source nutritional supplements,' Gideon said.

'Vitamins and stuff?'

'More specialised than that. Things like green barley powder and algae.'

'What are you supplementing, whales?' Brandon asked.

Gideon managed a laugh.

'I bet the women are all the size of whales,' Alan said. 'Kidding themselves they're suffering from some nutritional imbalance, instead of gluttony.'

He glanced at Julia. She became aware of the slight bulge over her waistband.

'Who says they're all women?' she said.

'It's not about weight,' Gideon said.

'What is it about?' Lucy asked.

Gideon turned to her. Unlike Alan, who pointedly averted his eyes from Lucy's bikini-clad body, he was unruffled and looked at her with neither lust nor embarrassment.

'Our supplements are all nutrient dense, to counteract the deficiencies in the modern, processed diet,' he said.

'*Counteract the deficiencies in the modern, processed diet* – that sounds straight from an advertising blurb,' Alan said.

Gideon broke into a broad grin. 'Actually, it is.'

'Hang on,' Alan said. 'You don't believe in this rubbish any more than I do. It's just snake oil – right?'

Gideon crossed his legs and placed his elbows on his knees. 'The placebo effect is one of the strongest medicines known to science.' A smile still flittered about his lips.

'But you don't believe the supplements actually help people,' Brandon said.

'I believe they *could* help people.'

'Up for a trial?' Alan asked Julia, while staring at her midriff.

'Julia doesn't need anything, she looks great,' Gideon said.

Alan looked disappointed. Julia was starting to like Gideon.

'But if any of you want to try anything, I can get you some free samples,' Gideon said.

'Great,' Brandon said. 'I've always wanted to be covered in plankton and harpooned.'

'The harpooning could be arranged,' Alan said.

Brandon looked hurt.

'We don't just sell algae,' Gideon said before Brandon could reply.

'Yeah, well, I think you should have stayed in London,' Brandon said. 'It's the sort of craze that people fall for up there. But even people in London will realise it's a con in the end, and you'll be out of business. There won't be a firm to take over. No one's gonna keep buying, what was it, green barley? Wouldn't feed it to my horse.'

'You don't have a horse,' Alan said.

'I do back home.'

Alan couldn't think of a snide response and so turned his back to Brandon and looked at Gideon.

'How are you finding Genevieve?' he asked.

'Not that again,' Julia said.

She knew where this was leading. Alan pretended to be horrified, but, in fact, enjoyed repeating stories of Genevieve's nocturnal visits to his room.

'Not what?' Alan said.

'You always make such a big deal – Genevieve did this, Genevieve did that. I'm sure Gideon can make up his own mind.'

'Gideon?' Alan asked.

'She's a sweetheart, isn't she?' Gideon replied. 'Like your mother's best friend, who's known you since you were born.'

'You'll change your tune soon enough,' Alan said.

'Why?'

Alan darted a glance at Julia and took his time saying, 'She has a hunger for young flesh.'

'For God's sake. You make her sound like a vampire,' Lucy protested.

'If the cap fits ...'

'I didn't get that vibe,' Gideon said.

'I'm with Gideon,' Brandon said. 'She's just being sweet. Her son died a few years ago. He'd be about the same age as us. We're kind of substitutes.'

'Makes sense of all that fussing – she wanted to cook for me tonight, you know?' Gideon said.

'No, I didn't know.' Alan made it sound as if this were a personal slight on him.

'All this lusting after young flesh is Alan's overactive imagination,' Brandon said. 'Or wishful thinking.'

Alan rolled his eyes. 'Yeah, I'm some sort of gerontophile.'

'What do you think, Julia, Lucy?' Gideon asked. 'A woman's view.'

The way Genevieve talked about the boys made Julia uncomfortable. But she would sooner stick needles in her eye than admit Alan was right.

'She's just missing her son,' Julia said. 'It's a maternal thing.'

'Maternal, my arse,' said Alan.

'Has she been near your arse?' Julia asked.

Brandon sniggered loudly, and Gideon joined in, then stopped and looked at Alan. The light was behind Alan and his expression was lost, but the heat of his anger was almost tangible.

'Of course she hasn't,' Alan replied.

'It's all about the vibe you give off,' Gideon said. 'I think she knows what's what with me. You have to be firm with her.'

'I bet he was rock hard,' Brandon said.

Lucy snorted into her wine. And Julia couldn't stop her laugh.

'Shut up,' Alan said. 'I know she's been in your room late at night.'

His annoyance only amused her.

'Just a shoulder to cry on,' she said. 'Genevieve lacks female company. All her friends are male.'

'I bet they are.'

Julia ignored him. 'Lucy's hardly here and her sister's got no patience with her.'

'How do you know that?' Brandon asked.

'She told me herself. She ...' Julia stopped.

'She what?' Gideon asked.

Julia glanced at Brandon.

'Did she say something about me?' he asked.

It was best to say nothing, change the conversation. And yet, she was curious to know Brandon's side of the story.

'Ruth thinks you take advantage of Genevieve. Letting you stay for free.'

'You don't pay rent?' Alan asked.

'And giving you money,' Julia said.

'Services rendered?'

'Hang on a minute.' Brandon showed how serious this had become by letting go of his can and placing it on the grass.

180

'Hang on. Let's get this straight. It's just until I get a job, and I'll be paying her back.'

'Do you think Genevieve would let anyone else fall behind on their rent?' Alan asked.

'I had to pay two-month deposit and a month in advance,' Julia said.

'Me too,' Lucy said.

'You obviously look untrustworthy,' Alan said. 'I only paid one month. Gideon?'

'Nothing. Pay as I go.'

'That's not fair,' Julia said.

'None of it's fair, when he's living here for free,' Alan said.

'I'm going to pay her back. Anyway, it's different for me. I'm nearly family. My old man's best friends with one of her cousins.'

'That close?' Alan said.

'Fuck you,' Brandon said. 'At least I don't have to go around bragging about nearly making it in the sack with some woman ten years older than my mother.'

Alan sat up straight.

'I've got a girlfriend,' he said primly.

'Who no one's ever seen.'

'Because I don't want to bring her to this dump.'

Brandon looked hurt and puzzled. As far as he was concerned, Alan was his mate. His changed attitude was sharp, sudden and inexplicable. He didn't know, as Julia did, that Alan looked down on him. Now Gideon had turned up – a businessman, better educated and older – Alan no longer took the trouble to hide his contempt.

Lucy drank her wine and watched on in amusement, as if this were some spectator sport. Julia's amusement was mixed with a mild dose of guilt. She felt complicit in Alan's treatment of Brandon. She should never have mentioned what Ruth had told her. On the other hand, Alan would probably have used anything to attack Brandon. He'd done it to impress Gideon, to show he wasn't friend to some drunken scruffy oaf. Julia knew, because she had the same impulse.

What Gideon saw, she couldn't tell. He observed their squabble without changing expression and waited for a pause in their argument before asking, 'What about you two girls, anyone?'

He asked in a casual manner, not conveying any particular interest in their love lives.

'I've just started seeing someone,' Lucy said.

'And you, Julia?'

She stared at the grass, trying to think of a good answer. 'I've just come out of a long-term relationship,' she said. 'I'm not really looking.'

She tried to see Brandon's reaction from the corner of her eye. He was taking a swig from his can.

Gideon arched his back and stretched his arms to the sky. 'I was thinking of going into town, looking around, maybe go to the cinema,' he said. 'Is anyone joining me?'

'I wouldn't mind getting a drink,' Brandon said.

Alan looked at Brandon, then at Gideon. 'Suits me,' he said.

'Girls?' Brandon asked.

'Not me,' Lucy answered. 'I'm going to stay here and catch some rays.'

Julia didn't want to go with just the boys. 'I've a busy day tomorrow.'

'Your loss,' Brandon said.

Gideon was watching him, or more accurately, watching him watching Julia. Had something been said? Julia looked away.

'Have fun,' she said.

At around half past eleven, Julia heard them come home and exchange muffled guffaws and calls of 'night then'. No woman this time.

The house fell silent. She rolled onto her front and looked at the dark hump of the Downs directly opposite. She longed for home, her mother's house, somewhere safe, where she understood what tomorrow would bring. An unease she'd not felt since her first few nights in the house crept over her. Something was gnawing at her consciousness, and every time she drifted towards sleep it rose up, then dwindled the moment she turned her thoughts to it.

At three o'clock she switched her sidelight on and opened a book, but unable to concentrate on the pages, she decided to get up and make a mug of warm milk, Audrey's recipe for a good night's sleep.

Barefoot and wrapped in a cotton dressing gown, she padded down to the kitchen. She placed a saucepan of milk on the hob and sat, waiting at the kitchen table, staring at her reflection in the French windows. The door opened and a figure appeared behind her. She spun around. Gideon came into the kitchen, wearing just pyjama bottoms, his eyes putty from sleep. He gave her a weak smile.

'Didn't mean to startle you,' he said.

Julia still felt tense. His state of undress created a fake intimacy and she made a conscious effort not to look at his naked torso.

'I didn't realise anyone else was up,' she said.

'Me neither,' he said. 'Couldn't sleep?'

She shook her head. 'You?'

'Dehydrated. Too much lager with Brandon. My mouth's like the Sahara.'

He didn't sound drunk.

'Did you have a good time?' she asked.

'Not bad. We went to the cinema to see *The Crow*, then went for a few drinks at The Ship.'

'Any good?'

'The pub?'

'The film.'

'Not really my thing. I wanted to see *Bitter Moon* but was overruled.'

Julia smiled. 'Polanski? Genevieve would love it, but I can't see it being Brandon's type of thing.'

'I'd hazard a guess you're right.'

She noticed he'd yet to pour himself that glass of water.

'What do you like?' Gideon asked.

'Old film noir, like Hitchcock. I think my favourite modern director is Almodóvar.'

She didn't know why she said Almodóvar – she'd only watched one of his films and not from choice.

'*Women on the Verge of a Nervous Breakdown* was amazing.'

The pan of milk began to simmer. Julia went to the stove. She was turned away from him when he said, 'You should come next time, so I can have an ally on the film choice.'

'I think it'll take more than my recommendation to get Brandon to watch anything with subtitles and without guns.'

She stopped, suddenly self-conscious. If Brandon had told Gideon about their liaison, she'd look like a bitch, slagging

184

him off behind his back. Then again, what had he been saying about her?

Gideon went to the sink, filled his glass of water, downed it, then refilled it. Julia poured the milk into a mug and stirred in the sugar. Gideon watched her as he sipped his water.

'Is that a cure for insomnia?' he asked.

'There is no cure,' Julia said. 'Getting up and making a mug of warm milk is a distraction from the torture.'

'You don't sleep well?'

'No,' she said.

Not since she'd split up with Christian. She couldn't remember a bad night's sleep before that. Moving to Guildford had made it worse.

'I usually sleep like the dead,' Gideon said.

'Not tonight.'

'Except when I'm dehydrated. I guess I've got an exceptionally clear conscience.' He looked at her, waiting to be contradicted.

'Or a mind incapable of acknowledging guilt,' she said.

'Or that,' he said and yawned. He put his glass in the sink. 'See you tomorrow. And I'll check what's coming on at the cinema and work on Brandon about the joys of Almodóvar.'

'Night,' Julia said.

Gideon shut the door softly behind him. Julia strained to listen to his footfall, but he was silent as a cat.

She sat and drank her hot milk, pushing her hair out of her face. It had fallen out of its night-time plaits. She must look a mess, with her untamed hair and cheap cotton dressing gown. Perhaps Genevieve was onto something with her turbans and silk pyjamas, making bedtime into a fashion statement. Julia decided that she would at least get some new

185

pyjamas and a kimono-style dressing gown in silk. Well, viscose was more her price range – whatever, she would look more elegant about the house.

Why did she care about her appearance at this time of night? It was then she realised what had been nagging at the back of her mind. He was taller and older, his features more defined, but Gideon reminded her of Christian. Was it a good thing or a bad thing that she'd noticed another man? She was supposed to be escaping Christian, not falling for his facsimile. She wasn't going to make the same mistake with Gideon as she had with Brandon. Not unless you're sure you're going to marry the guy, Pearl had said.

She wanted to ring Pearl now, at half past three in the morning, and tell her. As it was, she finished her milk, rinsed the mug and returned to bed.

And anyway, she knew what Pearl would tell her. Gideon was nothing like Christian. Julia was seeing what she wanted to see.

186

Chapter 32

I'm being held at Her Majesty's Prison Bronzefield until my trial. On remand, the days are slow and the food inedible. My first night's incarceration reminded me of my first night in Guildford. The same hollow dejection I'd felt when my mother drove away, like a young child abandoned on a foreign shore. The girl placed in the cell with me only looked eighteen. Her scowl, the only reply I receive for my 'Hi'.

She scared me. I worried she was in here for violence, a little ironic considering the charges against me. Later, when the lights went out, the bed started to shake as she sobbed into her pillow.

I climbed out from the bunk.

'Hey,' I say and touch her arm. 'I know it's tough. Is this your first time away from home?'

The sobs increased.

'It's OK to be scared,' I say. 'Do you want to talk about it?'

She pushed the pillow off her head and turned to me.

'I miss my mum,' she said.

'Me too,' I told her. 'Me too.'

Grace – I learnt her name the next day – isn't a bad sort. She's had a few bad breaks and has been led astray. Her respect for me increases when she learns I've been charged with murder.

'You don't seem the type,' she says. 'He must have been a bastard.'

'I can't talk about it,' I say.

Ridding the world of a bastard and helping some of the longer-established women with their GCSE maths keeps me from being bullied.

Pearl visits as often as she can and always ends up bursting into tears. I haven't the heart to tell her not to come again because her visits make me feel worse. Andre managed to visit once and provided a welcome dose of gallows humour. Sam's not come. So, I'm left with Audrey. She's suitably formal for the occasion. A navy skirt with a light blue navy blouse. No perfume, no lipstick, just a swish of blusher – *rouge*. She surveys the room with mild bemusement. The unkempt state of some of the visitors is incomprehensible to her.

'They could at least *wash* their tracksuits,' she says.

I hush her. She doesn't have to live with these women whose loved ones she's eyeing with horror.

Rudi has directed Audrey to hire another of his university friends, Ralph Williams QC, to act in my defence.

'Who's paying for him, Mum?' I ask. 'Please say it's not Pearl, because I could never pay her back.'

'I'm paying, well your father, stepfather, is really. And there's no need to repay us.'

I clench my fists. 'Robert would never agree to part with that sort of money, not for me,' I say.

'Oh, he's agreed.' Audrey looks pleased with herself. 'I can be very persuasive.'

Something's not right.

'Mum, what's going on?'

'All right then. I told him I'd leave and damn well ask for a divorce if he wasn't prepared to support my daughter.'

'But you never ...' I try to find a tactful way to phrase it. Audrey saves me the trouble.

'I never stand up to him. I'm a Stepford wife.'

'That's not what I said.'

'No, Julia, for once you're right. I have never stood up to him. Put up with God knows what, but enough is enough. He can go on as many "golfing weekends" accompanied by one of his carousel of secretaries—'

'You know about that?'

'Really, Julia, do you think I'm stupid? Well, maybe I am, but not that stupid,' she says. 'Don't sit there with your mouth hanging open – it makes you look gormless.'

Dumbstruck would be closer. And it takes a few moments to follow Audrey's command and close my mouth.

'But you'd never actually leave him,' I say.

'Yes, I bloody well would,' she says.

Audrey has sworn more in the last minute than in the entire forty-seven years since my birth.

'He must believe you – a barrister,' I say. 'I don't even know how much they cost. But we're talking remortgaging the house, right?'

'Not necessary. We've plenty of savings. I've always been very frugal.'

'I was thinking about Gideon.'

'You need to think about yourself.'

'You believe I'm innocent then?'

'Irrelevant,' she says with a swish of her hand. 'I know you,

189

Julia, and I know you think I'm overly critical, but I've never thought you were a cruel or wicked person. And if you played any part in this – no, I don't want to know – but if you did, I'm sure he deserved it.'

'Wow, Mum.'

This is a new Audrey I've never seen before, defiant, bold and fierce in my defence.

She looks around the room before she leans towards me.

'You know, Julia, it might be a strange time to tell you something like this, but I realise it's something I should have said before. I really am very proud of you.'

Chapter 33

Monday had been a dog of a day at Morgan Boyd. Julia's boss had been in a foul temper, finding fault with everything.

His nit-picking meant she had to skip lunch and work late. Heavy clouds over Guildford made it much darker than it should have been at seven-thirty in July. And the moment she did step outside, it started raining, torrential summer rain that poured down so hard it rebounded off the pavement. By the time Julia arrived home she was drenched from head to toe and completely famished. Only then did she remember that all she had was a Lean n' Low lasagne and some limp broccoli, the first day of her new diet.

A light shone from the dining-room window, which was at the front of the house and overlooked the drive – one of Genevieve's private rooms. Julia had never been inside. The rain blurred the figures, but she could make out Genevieve, and a man whose bulk made her certain it was Brandon.

She couldn't be bothered to use the side door and Genevieve would never know. As she stepped into the hall, the warm rich smell of sweetness and spices hit her nostrils. Her stomach growled in response and she could hear laughter coming from the dining room.

'Dominic was just the same,' Genevieve was saying. 'Go on, have some more.'

'Don't mind if I do.'

It *was* Brandon.

For one moment, Julia considered knocking on the door, in hope of an invitation to join them. The lure of real food overriding her desire to avoid Brandon. What was it they were eating, duck?

While she hovered outside, the door opened and Genevieve came out. Surely her wretched state would move Genevieve to extend the offer of dinner.

'Goodness, Julia,' she said. 'Did you come in the front door? And on a day like this. You're soaked to the skin. Go and dry yourself off. You're dripping everywhere. The rug will be ruined. I suppose I'll have to mop all that water up now. Pudding will have to wait.'

'Sorry, Genevieve.'

'Humph.'

Julia trudged upstairs to the landing and when she heard Genevieve go into the kitchen, she shook herself like a dog drying its coat, hoping to leave as much water damage as possible.

In her room, she stripped off and wrapped herself in a towel. It was at times like this she missed being at home. Audrey, who lived in perpetual fear of her loved ones catching pneumonia, would have been up with a bowl of soup by now.

She dressed, wrapped her hair in a towel and went back downstairs to the sound of more laughter from the dining room. In the kitchen the warm spices mixed with much sweeter smells coming from the oven. Julia peered through the glass door. It looked like Tarte Tatin. She put her ready meal in the microwave. She couldn't be bothered with the broccoli. It pinged, just as Genevieve came in with a platter, carrying half a duck and a few roast vegetables. Genevieve barely ate, Brandon must have demolished the rest.

'I like a man with a good appetite,' she said. 'And it's so nice to have someone to cook for.'

Any hopes Julia had that Genevieve might offer her the leftovers were dashed by her reaching for a Tupperware box.

'There. That will be enough for Brandon's lunch tomorrow. I'm going out with Edward.'

He can make his own lunch. He's not eight years old, Julia wanted to say. Instead, she turned away and slid the lasagne onto her plate. It collapsed into a flaccid green and white mush, with a red watery film spreading out from underneath.

Meanwhile, Genevieve had removed the Tarte Tatin from the oven and retrieved a giant tub of ice cream from the freezer. She placed both on a tray and returned to the dining room.

Julia prodded the lasagne with her fork. Was there any cheese on it at all? She slung it into the bin, untouched, opened a bottle of wine and rang for a pizza, pepperoni with extra chilli, and some garlic bread – with cheese. The diet could wait.

Genevieve and Brandon were still in the dining room when the pizza delivery arrived. Lucy came in at the same time.

'Wanna share?' Julia said.

'Thanks, I'm starving.'

Lucy brought her own bottle of wine to Julia's room and

they sat on her bed and put the radio on. Julia poured from the already open bottle and Lucy put slices of pizza on plates for both of them. Food and company restored Julia to a better mood and she told Lucy about Genevieve's feast for Brandon with humour rather than bitterness.

'It's not the first time,' Lucy said. 'She did something with venison on Saturday, before he went out drinking.'

'Venison – is he aristocracy?'

'Her little prince,' Lucy said. 'At this rate, he won't fit into all his new clothes she's bought him.'

'Clothes?'

Lucy nodded and reached for another slice of garlic bread.

'They went out together – came back with armfuls of bags. Not any old tat either. Pringle jumpers. Paul Smith shirts.'

'How can he stand it?'

'What do you mean? He loves it. Would you object to someone buying you lots of beautiful clothes?'

'Depends. Imagine some old bloke doing that for you – what's expected in return?'

'Eww, do you think they've actually ... y'know?' Lucy said.

Julia didn't want to think about it. Brandon sleeping with her after he'd been with Genevieve. It made her feel ill.

'Maybe she *does* just miss her son,' Julia said.

'She'll be missing most of her savings soon. He's fleecing her.'

Lucy was the second person to tell her this. How had she ended up sleeping with this man?

'Ruth's worried about Genevieve,' Julia said. 'She thinks what you do – that he's taking advantage. But even she doesn't know how bad it is. Genevieve told me she thought Brandon was Dominic reincarnated or something.'

'She said something weird like that to me. I put it down to the Valium.'

'Ruth told me she's always taking Genevieve's pills away and she's always getting hold of more.'

'A good thing she still has vodka then,' Lucy said. 'It's not like she believes in real reincarnation, just her own brand of hippy shit – the universe sending you what you need.'

'More drunken ramblings than philosophical discourse,' Julia agreed.

'Was she an actual hippy, I mean in the Sixties or whenever? I can't imagine Genevieve in a muddy field with her tits out, can you?'

'I'd rather not,' Julia said. 'I think she'd believe anything that made her feel better. Ruth pretty much said that to me. And she's worried what Genevieve will do when Brandon leaves.'

'He'll never leave at this rate,' Lucy said.

'Maybe that's what it's all about.'

A sharp rap on the door startled them. They looked at each other in horror. They'd been too loud, too incautious.

'It's Gideon. Can I come in?'

Julia and Lucy laughed with relief.

'Yes,' Julia shouted.

'So, this is where the party's at,' he said.

He waved a bottle containing a luminous yellow-green liquid in one hand. In the other he carried three shot glasses.

'What on earth's that?' Lucy asked. 'It looks radioactive.'

'Chartreuse – my parents brought it back from France,' Gideon said. 'It's all I've got left and this is an emergency.'

'You had a bad day too?'

Julia shuffled along the bed and Lucy moved the pizza box, so that he could sit between them.

'Spent all day trying to get hold of this guy, Devon Garvey, stupid name, who took a huge delivery from us months ago but hasn't paid. Finally got through and he says, bold as brass, "I'm not paying – watcha gonna do about it?"'

'What are you going to do?' Julia asked.

'Not much we can do. It's more time and money than it's worth, pursuing it through the courts. My godfather went mental. Said it was my fault. He's the one who signed off on it.'

'Sounds like my boss,' Julia said. 'Here – there's garlic bread left. We polished off the pizza.'

She handed him the container.

'I'm all right,' Gideon said.

'Cool, more for me. Garlic bread and Chardonnay, a very underestimated combination.'

Gideon poured the Chartreuse into the tumblers.

'Down in one,' he said.

Lucy knocked hers back. 'Arrgggh,' she said and pulled a face. 'What the hell's in that? It tastes like fortified mouthwash.'

'Personally, I think Listerine has the edge on taste,' Gideon said.

'You're right. Give me another.'

Gideon obliged before turning to Julia.

'And what made your day so bad?'

She told him about her nightmare boss, getting drenched, and her unrequited longing for spiced duck. Then Lucy told him about Brandon's shopping trip.

'God, she's such a cliché. Surrey's answer to Norma Desmond,' Gideon said.

'Who's Norma Desmond?' Lucy asked.

Julia was about to ask the same thing, but was glad she hadn't when Gideon replied, 'Norma Desmond from *Sunset Boulevard*. One of the greatest films about Hollywood ever made. Julia will know it.'

'Of course,' she said. 'It starred, oh – what's her name?'

'Gloria Swanson,' Gideon said.

'That's it.'

'I mean, Genevieve even wears the turban,' Gideon said.

Julia laughed. Lucy looked perplexed, for which Julia would love her for ever.

'Norma Desmond is a faded Hollywood starlet,' Gideon explained. 'In middle age she becomes obsessed with a broke and much younger screenwriter. He moves into her mansion, she showers him with gifts. He goes along with it because he needs the money.'

'What happens?' Lucy asked.

'He tries to leave, and she shoots him dead.'

'Cheerful.'

'Yeah, well, tell that to Genevieve.'

'Or Brandon,' Julia said.

'Shhh.'

Lucy held her finger to her lips. She pointed to the door. They could hear the soft creak of floorboards underfoot. Then another knock at the door.

'It's Alan.'

Again, they laughed and invited him in.

There was no room on the bed and Alan sat on the floor with his back against the wall.

'Why's everyone squashed in here?' he asked.

And they went through the entire evening's events. Alan laughed. It was the first time Julia had seen him relaxed.

'Of course, she's modelled herself on Norma Desmond. I mean, who goes round in a fucking turban?' Alan said.

'Sikhs,' Lucy replied.

'I mean women.'

'Yeah, well, Brandon better stay for ever. Because if he doesn't ...' Gideon made a gun shape with his index and middle fingers and pulled the trigger with his thumb. 'Pow.'

Lucy spat out her pizza crust and Julia managed to spill wine on the duvet.

'And she used to be an actress,' Julia said. 'Or at least claimed to be. Worked with Zeffirelli and with Polanski in *Macbeth*, but her part ended up on the cutting-room floor. She said it was a valuable experience.'

'I bet her cameo wasn't the only thing that ended up on the floor,' Alan said.

Lucy snorted into her Chartreuse.

'And now she's the one chasing younger men. And with Brandon, it's working,' he continued.

'Did Genevieve tell you lot to use the side door when you first moved in?'

'Yeah,' Alan said.

Gideon and Lucy agreed.

'When I mentioned it to Brandon, he hadn't a clue what I was talking about.'

'More favouritism,' Lucy said.

'When was this?' Gideon asked.

Julia remembered it was when she had walked back from the Cross Bar with Brandon, drunk.

'Can't remember exactly,' she said.

They finished the garlic bread and wine, while Gideon entertained them with stories of his clients. The woman who'd ended up in hospital because she'd tried to exist on algae powder for a month. The man who wanted to sue because his sexual performance hadn't improved after taking every coffee with a scoop of green barley. They sat there laughing and drinking. For the first time they felt like friends rather than just housemates.

A knock silenced them. Brandon opened the door and leant on the frame.

'Mind if I join you?' he said.

The room fell silent. They all looked at each other, before Gideon stood up. 'We're all off to bed, mate.'

Brandon pulled himself upright, as if Gideon were squaring up to him. His eyes flicked around the room. He said nothing and turned away. Gideon looked back into the room and smirked and Alan started to laugh, which Brandon must have heard.

'You should all go now,' Julia said. 'I've work in the morning.'

She shooed them out, Lucy making a face and laughing as she passed out of the door.

It had been stupid, letting them talk about Brandon like that. How much had he heard? But then, what had they said that wasn't true?

She listened to the others use the bathroom and go to their rooms. Below her, Gideon was listening to the radio on low. The floorboards creaked and she heard someone move across the landing with unpractised stealth. She tensed and watched the door. The handle moved, a fraction of an inch. Then stopped. Julia stared at the door. The handle swung back to its original position. The footsteps retreated, creaking as they went. Julia breathed again.

She lay stiff and still on the bed. Soon after she heard lighter footsteps she knew to be Genevieve's coming up the stairs. Then the lightest tap on a door across the landing. It creaked open and shut behind her.

Chapter 34

2018 – Bronzefield

Ralph Williams, my barrister, comes to Bronzefield to discuss my defence. My first shock is when he tells me I'll not be giving evidence in court.

'I'd assume anyone who won't give evidence is guilty,' I say.

'The burden of proof lies with the prosecution,' he says in a clear Home Counties accent. 'It's up to the Crown to prove you *did* commit a crime, not for us to prove that you didn't.'

'The jury won't see it like that – I wouldn't.'

He stirs sugar into his coffee. 'It's a risk worth taking,' he says. 'I'm not prepared to put you in the witness box, especially as there's three of you. With multiple defendants, one invariably gives conflicting evidence to the others and raises doubts. And if one of you were to break down ...' He stops stirring his coffee and looks me straight in the eye. How much does he guess? 'If one of you were to break down, it would be disastrous for all three.'

'The truth is irrelevant?' I say.

'The truth doesn't always win trials.' He removes the stirrer from his cup. Black globules drip onto the table. 'Even if all of your testimonies confirm the others, there's the matter of likeability. If a jury finds you unsympathetic, well, I've seen them convict on weaker evidence than this.' He lifts the file half an inch.

I imagine Gideon would charm the jury, just as he did the magistrate, who expressed regret at not granting bail, the serious nature of the charge making it near impossible. Gideon portrayed himself as a businessman, responsible for the livelihood of many and, moreover, a selfless single father, dedicated to the upbringing of his only child.

I can picture the scene, Gideon in court, expressing the right amount of outrage to suggest it's barely credible that he, an upstanding citizen, could be accused of such a heinous crime. But the outrage would be tempered by concern, to show he fully respects the law and understands the necessity for such proceedings. I wonder if Sam was there to witness it. He's not responded to my request that he visit me on remand.

There'd be a repeat performance in the Crown Court. By the time of his summing up, the judge would probably recommend Gideon for inclusion in the New Year's honours list. I can see why there would be concerns about Alan. He would be either haughty or obsequious. Then I realise Ralph is *my* defence barrister. It's me he's thinking of. This takes a moment to sink in.

'Are you saying I'm unsympathetic?'

'No, no, no,' he says in the soothing tones usually reserved to assuage petulant children. 'All I'm saying is that the prosecution would undoubtedly portray you as such. You had a fling with Brandon and then dumped him.'

'That's not what happened,' I say.

'And your husband's currently divorcing you for having an

adulterous affair with your son's rugby coach – Hugh some-thing or other, was it? The jury won't warm to you.'

'I was single when I had the fling with Brandon. And Hugh, he was a mistake. One mistake after twenty years of unhappy marriage.'

'You abandoned your son.'

'*He* won't see *me*.'

'That's not going to secure you any more sympathy. The prosecution will portray you as a bad mother, who screws around behind her husband's back. A hard-nosed career woman, more concerned with climbing the corporate ladder than caring for her family.'

'How does any of that make me a murderer?' I ask.

'The jury are looking at your character as well as the alleged crime.'

'But ... but ...'

Ralph presses his hand on mine. '*I'm* not saying this about you, or that you're a bad person. What I'm saying is, that's the angle the prosecution will take.' He smiles at me. 'Don't look so deflated. There'll be no hatchet job, because, as I said, you're not going anywhere near the witness box.'

Ralph's character assassination feels like a physical assault. But why am I surprised? It's no more than Audrey's been telling me for years. Ralph even said 'career woman'. Apologies to Audrey, people do still use that term.

'What about Gideon and Alan? Will they be giving evidence?' I ask.

He shakes his head. 'I know their briefs, Helena Dryden and Arianne Baptiste – both pretty astute. We've agreed the same strategy. None of you will be giving evidence.'

'What if they change their minds?'

'They won't,' he says. 'However acrimonious the relationship between you, you're in this together. If the ship goes down, you're all going under.'

Chapter 35

1994 – Guildford

'Meet me in Sundowns at seven-thirty,' Lucy said.

Julia was sitting at her desk in Morgan Boyd Consulting. She picked up a pen and pad as if taking a professional call. Her boss watched her from the far end of the office.

'Of course, and may I ask where exactly that is, Mrs Howse?'

'Mrs Who? Oh yeah. It's the new cocktail place just off the high street. Linden's coming – it will be a laugh.'

'Linden?'

'Hot bloke I met last week. I'm sure his mates will be with him. See you later.'

The rest of the day dragged. Julia watched the clock's minute hand until the exact moment it hit half past five, before switching off her computer and rushing home. She was pleased Lucy had called. She wasn't going to London until Saturday and had spent most of the week on her own. On Thursday, the boys had gone to the pub again, without asking her – Brandon's doing, no doubt.

She threw on her only non-work dress, Converse trainers and applied a caramel-coloured lipstick she'd bought the previous week in London, and was about to leave when Brandon stopped her.

'Got a date?' he asked.

It was only six o'clock and his breath was heavy with alcohol.

'Just meeting Lucy, she wanted to try the new cocktail place,' she said.

'Sundowns, cool, see you there.'

'Er ...'

He'd already left the room.

Julia wished she had said she was going on a date. Now she couldn't think of a reason to tell him not to come.

'He didn't even wait for an answer, just assumed he'd been invited,' she told Lucy when she joined Julia in the hall.

'He likes you,' Lucy said.

'No, he doesn't. He just wants me to like him – male ego. That's why he lets ... Oh, hi, Genevieve.'

Genevieve sauntered in from the kitchen, wearing a long print skirt and white blouse.

'Why have you got your bags with you? You're not going out, are you?' she asked.

'It's Friday, Genevieve,' Lucy said.

'But I've spent all day preparing.'

'For what?'

'The barbecue,' Genevieve said.

'No one said anything to me about a barbecue.'

'It's a surprise.'

'It certainly is,' Lucy said. 'Why on earth are you doing a barbecue?'

Genevieve tilted her head and gave an unfriendly smile, which fell mostly upon Julia.

'It's been brought to my attention that certain members of the household are resentful of my making meals for Brandon.'

'Who told you that?' Julia asked.

'It's not important,' Genevieve said. 'I must say, I can't think why I shouldn't cook for him, seeing as he's family.' Lucy rolled her eyes at this. 'But some people will always be a little ungenerous. However, to show I bear no grudges, I'm cooking for all of you. And what's better than a barbecue on a summer's evening?'

'But I've made arrangements to meet someone in town,' Lucy said.

'Invite whoever you like, but I won't take no for an answer, Lucy.'

Julia made a little shake of her head. Lucy didn't see it.

'I suppose I'd catch Linden if I called now,' she said.

'Excellent,' Genevieve said. 'Gideon said it would be a good idea.'

'Gideon?' Julia said.

'He suggested it. Such a considerate young man. If I were twenty years younger. Ha ha.' She waggled her finger. 'Now, have to get on. Delia's a hard taskmaster when it comes to accompaniments.'

'Who the hell's Delia?' Lucy asked as Genevieve drifted back to the kitchen. '*If I were twenty years younger*,' she said when the door was shut. 'Or even if she wasn't. Poor Gideon – perhaps we should warn him.'

'I'm sure he can take care of himself,' Julia said.

'Talking of which. What do you think of Gideon? Hot, right?'

'He's all right.'

Julia didn't want to tell Lucy that he reminded her of

Christian. Or that they'd arranged a cinema date, if that's what it was. She'd barely seen him since the night of their shared insomnia.

'You're either blind or have a heart of stone. If it wasn't for Linden – and that may not work out—'

'But you live together. It's a bad idea,' Julia said a little too quickly.

'You're probably right,' Lucy said. 'Shame though, he really is ... Hi, guys.'

Gideon, Alan and Brandon were coming down the stairs. The hall really wasn't the best place to gossip.

'Was this barbecue your idea?' Julia asked Gideon.

'It will be too hot and crowded in town,' he said. 'And it keeps Genevieve happy.'

'It was supposed to be a girls' night out,' Lucy said.

'Ah, the lipstick, the dress,' Alan said, looking at Julia. 'Makes sense now.'

'I'm wearing the dress because we were going to a cocktail bar, *not* the pub,' Julia replied, half watching Brandon.

'Touchy,' Alan said.

'Come on, Alan, tonight's supposed to be bringing us all together,' said Gideon.

Genevieve reappeared. 'You're all here, fabulous. Look what I found, my old Polaroid.' She carried an ancient camera in her hand. 'Come into the lounge. You can all fit on the sofa.'

'Do we have to?' Alan said.

'Now, Alan, don't be a grouch,' Genevieve said.

Alan gave her an exasperated look but did as she asked.

They shuffled into the lounge, its parquet floor covered by a geometric-patterned rug. Above the fireplace hung a print of the Alps, which took up most of the chimney breast. Julia and Lucy saw it at the same time and exchanged puzzled glances. Wasn't it morbid to choose a picture of the mountains that killed her son? There were no pictures of Dominic. Julia remembered how jealously Genevieve had guarded the one photo of him she had seen, as if it were some sacred image, and only those truly worthy were granted a glimpse.

A small, open bureau held various bundles of correspondence as well as pens, pencils, envelopes and a large pair of scissors. The other surfaces, sideboards, mantelpiece and display tables were covered in vases, figurines and one rather hideous marble lamp, all swirls and gold leaf, far too large for the slender display table on which it stood.

'Squash up – you can all fit in,' Genevieve said as they sat on the sofa together. 'Now then, if I can only remember how to work this.' She fiddled with the camera's settings for a while.

'Here, let me,' Lucy said, taking the camera. 'Like this.' She pointed and clicked. The camera started to whir. 'Oh damn.'

'What is it?' Genevieve asked.

'It's out of film. You've got more, right?'

'They're may be some in the drawer upstairs,' Genevieve said. 'I'll go and check.'

Julia stood over Lucy as she shook the photograph and the figures seeped into life.

'It's not bad, I suppose,' Lucy said.

The camera does lie, Julia thought. Anyone viewing the snap would assume them to be friends. Somehow the photo had caught them looking relaxed, comfortable with one another, a happy band of housemates, instead of a random collection of individuals brought together by the need for a roof over their heads.

Brandon stood up. 'If I have to go to this barbecue—'

'You don't have to,' Alan said.

Brandon ignored him. 'I'm going to the pub to bring some friends back.' He stomped out.

Alan looked baffled. 'I didn't know he had any friends.'

The heat didn't dip with the dusk, nor as it darkened into night. Genevieve was in a flurry of activity Julia hadn't believed she was capable of, receiving food deliveries, making an array of colourful salads, placing lights and cushions around the garden. An industrious, organised woman who, having seen everyone was well fed, now sat, gin and tonic in hand, on her terrace, talking animatedly with Edward. She would not have looked out of place in any garden in Surrey. Even her choice of clothes bordered on the conventional and her general manner had been organised and rational. The food had been excellent, plates of marinated meat, chicken, pork and lamb, all perfectly cooked and seasoned, bowl upon bowl of salads and slaws, exotic mixes of fruit and grains unfamiliar to Julia.

It was a pity Genevieve didn't find a job. Julia was sure it would be more effective in nullifying her grief than vodka, pills and young men, like Brandon, who had brought an entourage of five girls and three boys back with him. None of whom he introduced to the rest of the house. Alan looked around him with disdain. As if he couldn't believe he'd lowered himself by participating in such a gathering. Gideon was the only one at ease. And somehow, Julia knew he would always fit in, whether at a cocktail bar, a rough boozer or a party full of strangers. He would have made a good spy, blending in, making friends.

The moment Linden arrived, Lucy ran over to him and they found a corner of the garden away from the rest, where they cuddled up, whispering in each other's ears between bursts of laughter. Julia sat with Gideon and Alan on the lawn. The grass was just long enough to clutch between her toes, having swapped her Converse for sandals.

She was watching Brandon. His behaviour troubled her. He was standing next to the barbecue, working his way through a plate of cold chops. His hair had grown into a thick, curly mop down to his shoulders. He looked like a grizzly bear, hunched over a kill. When she'd tried talking to him, earlier in the evening, he'd been uncommunicative and morose. Julia had seen him angry, but this was a different mood, not the work of a momentary irritation.

'What's wrong with him today?' Gideon asked, pointing the neck of his beer bottle in Brandon's direction.

'He's drunk,' Julia replied.

'So, what's new?' Alan said.

For some reason Julia felt responsible for Brandon. She was sure that, despite the gaggle of girls he'd brought to the barbecue, he was lonely. Ostracised by his housemates, mistrusted by Ruth – only Genevieve took an interest, and she was no substitute for a friend. Julia felt lost a mere two hundred miles from home, when Audrey, Pearl and Andre could all be reached within a few hours and she spoke to them on the phone most days. Brandon was thousands of miles from home and had no one and she'd never heard him make or receive a call. It couldn't be the cost of calling New Zealand, because Genevieve was sure to cover it.

Julia put her wine down on the grass and walked over to him. Her approach drew his attention from his food. He threw down a bone stripped of meat and wiped his mouth with his sleeve.

'Are you all right, Brandon?' she asked.

'Why wouldn't I be?'

'You're not with your friends.' She nodded at the girls.

'What's it got to do with you?' he said.

'I'm just a bit worried.'

He pushed his face forward, so that it was only a couple of inches from hers.

'That's very touching. And what about Gideon, are you worried about him too?'

'I don't follow,' Julia said.

He looked at her with contempt. 'I'm not in the mood today, Julia. I'm really not.'

He turned away from her. She stood where she was for a moment, unsure what to do. Brandon picked up another chop and started gnawing at it. Julia returned to Gideon and Alan, sitting on the grass.

Gideon was now telling Alan about his godfather's business, which Alan appeared to find engrossing, while Julia thought it beyond dull. She had no one to talk to – not that she cared so much. Guildford wasn't for ever. She had an interview for a job in Hounslow and if that didn't work out, another would come along. Tonight, she'd enjoy the beer, the warm evening and the food. Soon she'd leave and forget all of them. Except maybe Lucy. Perhaps she'd see Lucy after she left.

After switching to red wine, Julia felt a pleasant warmth run through her core. The barbecue was now dead ashes. The night was still warm and nearly everyone was drunk, laughing and shouting. Gideon was the exception. He was still sipping his first beer, Julia noticed, though not making a big deal of 'someone has to stay sober'.

Brandon finished his plate of chops and sat down with the

group he'd brought back from the pub. He fell into easy conversation with these near strangers and, again, Julia felt sad and a little ashamed that he was more comfortable with them than with his housemates. The girls were pretty and the boys friendly. No wonder he preferred them.

'Jealous?'

Julia hadn't realised Alan was watching her.

'Why would I be?'

'You tell me,' he said.

It was the second time he'd hinted at knowing something about her night with Brandon. Julia watched his face. Alan was guessing.

'If anyone's jealous, it's you,' Julia said. 'When was the last time a girl gave you any attention?'

'I've told you,' he said. 'I've got a girlfriend.'

'Who no one's ever met.'

'Cut it out, you two,' Gideon said.

Alan looked like he had a whole lot more to say, but Gideon gave him a meaningful stare and he refrained from commenting. Instead he downed his wine.

'This stuff's disgusting. I'm getting a lager. Gideon?'

'I'm all right.'

From his walk, Julia thought he was far drunker than she had realised. Not that it improved his mood.

'And what's his excuse for his girlfriend failing to materialise yet again?' Julia asked Gideon.

'She's at a festival, apparently,' he said.

'That's it. He's definitely made her up. Girls who go to festivals would never go out with someone like Alan.' Julia was thinking of Pearl.

'You could be right,' Gideon said. Then after a pause, 'And

213

you, Julia, you're horrified by Alan's celibacy, but you're single. I know you said you've just come out of a long-term relationship and being single's fine, if that's what you want, but you don't seem the sort.'

Julia wasn't sure if she should object to Gideon not thinking she was the sort, that she was some needy, clingy female, incomplete without a man. Or was it a vague compliment to an amiable nature and feminine charm? The wine and the slight unease caused by Brandon's strange mood made her thinking muddled. She didn't want to talk about the mess that was her love life, but she didn't want to seem aloof.

'It's complicated. I met Christian on the first day of secondary school. We started going out together when we were about fourteen.'

Gideon rested his head on his elbow and concentrated on her face. Then the whole tale came out. Her refusal to leave home while at university. Ellie's betrayal and Julia's longing for escape.

'And did you escape?' Gideon asked.

'I'm here now, aren't I?'

'That's not what I meant,' Gideon said.

'I'm getting there,' she said.

It was true. She still cried, but only two nights out of three, and she no longer framed every event by wondering what Christian and Ellie were doing at that moment.

'And Brandon?' Gideon said.

'What's he got to do with it?'

'I thought—'

'What's he said?'

'Nothing.'

Julia looked towards Brandon, still chatting away with his pub pals.

'I think he's unhappy,' she said. 'Have you noticed he never calls home?'

'I hadn't thought about it.'

'The only contact he seems to have is with girls he's pulled. He doesn't have any friends.'

'He's got Genevieve,' Gideon said.

'That hardly counts. We should be nicer to him.'

'You'll have a job persuading Alan.'

Gideon looked over his shoulder. Alan was coming back, a can of lager in each hand. Even if he hadn't been about to join them, Julia wouldn't have mentioned that Alan's current contempt for Brandon dated from Gideon's arrival. It was a weak analogy but it made her think of Christian, leaving her for Ellie. She was still looking at Brandon and hadn't noticed Gideon was observing her, until he put a hand on her shoulder.

'Are you all right?' he asked.

Alan was right next to them. She lightly pushed Gideon's hand away.

'I'm fine,' she said.

Alan planted his drinks down.

'What's going on?' he asked.

She now realised, her comment about Alan being jealous of Brandon must have struck closer than she knew. Of course he was jealous of Brandon, who was out every other night with a different girl, while Alan was in a fake relationship.

And what about Gideon? How easily she'd confessed to him the most painful details of her break-up with Christian, but she knew nothing about him. Did he have a girlfriend? He never mentioned one. Most of his time spent away from

215

the house was with his godfather, plotting their world takeover of nutritional supplements. Sometimes Julia thought Gideon showed her a preference, at others it seemed like general friendliness.

By now Julia was very drunk but didn't care. It was manageable drunk, not fall around and throw up drunk. The irritation she'd felt with Alan and Brandon dissipated as people drifted away from the party.

'I hope you've all had a delightful evening,' Genevieve announced from the terrace. 'I'm retiring now.'

'Night,' they called to her.

'I'm off too,' Lucy said. 'Going back with Linden.'

'That's the last we'll see of her till Saturday afternoon,' Alan said.

Julia glanced at Gideon. He looked on calmly with an expression of mild amusement. What did he think of them? Brandon oafish, Alan snide, Lucy slutty. You couldn't tell.

Brandon's friends had left, but he still wandered about the garden, beer in one hand, a cigarette in the other.

'Hadn't you better go up?' Alan said. 'Genevieve will be expecting you.'

'What the fuck is that supposed to mean?'

Alan was lying down and Brandon was on the other side of the garden.

'Well, all this was for you. Genevieve will be expecting something in return.'

'Alan,' Julia warned.

He ignored her. 'I mean, all the pretty girls have gone – you'll have to go for something more mature.'

Brandon was across the garden and standing over Alan in an instant.

'Fuck you,' he said.

Alan looked surprised and scared. Gideon jumped to a standing position.

'It was just a bit of fun,' he said, holding both palms out.

'I'm sick of his smart-arse comments. What makes you think you're so special?' Brandon prodded Alan with his toe.

'Don't kick me!' Alan scrambled to his feet.

'If I'd kicked you, you'd know about it.'

'Listen here.' Alan's voice was that of a whiny child.

'Guys, guys,' Gideon said. 'There's no need for this.'

'You're right about that,' Brandon replied.

'Look, I've got just the thing to mellow us out,' Gideon said.

'What's that?' Brandon's eyes were still fixed on Alan.

'Green barley isn't the only type of dried leaf I have in my possession.'

Julia stood up. 'You can't do that here,' she said.

'Somewhere else then.'

'There's only one place to go,' Brandon said. 'Up on the Downs.'

Chapter 36

Guildford Crown Court has none of the oak-panelled majesty associated with law courts in the common imagination. It bears more resemblance to a 1980's lecture theatre than the forbidding grandeur of the Old Bailey. With red patterned carpets and flip-down seats, its harsh lights work hard to compensate for the natural deficit, due to the room's high narrow windows. Gideon, Alan and I sit with a security guard in the dock, a glass cage from which we, the accused, can be observed at all times. No eye contact is made.

'Be upstanding,' the court clerk declaims.

His Honour Judge John Fleetwood looks like he was born in a courtroom. He is tall and lean, his walk is purposeful, his air resolute. He presides over the court, as poised and watchful as a heron over a pond, alert to the minutest ripple. The red sash and purple-sleeved robes of his office denote his pre-eminence, a rare dash of colour among the monochrome of lawyers.

On the other hand, the seven men and five women of the jury could have been randomly fetched from any shopping mall in the country. A lad on the front row, wearing a blue hoody and jeans, barely looks old enough to serve. A middle-aged woman wears a floral dress and bottle-green jacket, another about the same age is in loose slacks, a cream blouse and a pink scarf flicked over her shoulder. A younger man to the side has tattoos visible under his T-shirt. The only one formally dressed is a man of about forty in a grey suit and white shirt.

I'm wearing a fitted navy dress. Ralph told me I must be feminine but not sexy. There's little chance of either at forty-eight, and having spent the last six months on remand. I wonder how Judge Fleetwood views me. Ralph described him as 'fair'. Is that a euphemism for harsh?

Arriving in court is a relief, not just as a decisive conclusion to my time on remand, but to the last twenty-four years. I'll never have to wake in the night, shaking and drenched in sweat, fearing the worst. This is the worst. Brandon has been found, and Gideon, Alan and I are here, in court, on trial for his murder.

The court clerk reads out the charges. He sounds distant, underwater. My surroundings feel artificial and unreal. The room begins to blur around me. I've no idea if I'm guilty or not. To be convicted of murder, the accused needs to have shown malice aforethought, and I can't deny, by the end, I did want Brandon dead.

'Not guilty,' I say.

In the public gallery, a few rows of fold-down chairs, a man and woman flinch at my assertion of innocence. I recognise them from the New Zealand news clips. They are Mari Hewlett and Austen Wells, Brandon's brother and sister.

Audrey, Pearl and Andre sit together, their faces sombre. And Sam is also here. Though I've been longing to see him,

I wish he hadn't come. Ralph has warned me of the line the prosecution will take, as regards to my character: a harlot, a bad mother, a murderer. It will only remind Sam of what happened with Hugh and further convince him that his mother is a whore.

Perhaps he wants to see me jailed, to be rid of me for ever. We used to be close, laugh at silly in-jokes. I'd sneak money to him behind his father's back. Sam used to hate him. Now his loathing has switched to me. Is he close to his father now? Has he made Sam realise the value of looks and charm? Does he know the importance of making a good impression with the cut of his suit, the brand of watch, make of car?

So many parents would be proud of a son like Sam, academically gifted and excelling at sport. But my only wish for him is that he's nothing like his father.

The prosecution, Thomas Mapplethorpe and his junior, Alexandra South, sit behind Ralph and Helena Dryden, Gideon's barrister, and Arianne Baptiste, who is Alan's.

I wonder why Gideon chose her. He deliberates extensively over his every action. Hiring Helena will have an exact purpose, she's not just a competent barrister.

Thomas Mapplethorpe QC stands up and addresses the jury.

'Ladies and gentlemen.' He speaks slowly and with purpose. 'Brandon Wells was a young man from New Zealand, who came to England as part of an adventure. He wanted to travel the world. He was last seen in August 1994. Twenty-three years later his body was found on the North Downs, not four hundred yards from where he shared a house with the defendants, Gideon Risborough, Alan Johns and Julia Winter. His

220

skull had been smashed and he had sustained a serious wound or wounds before death.'

Mapplethorpe pauses to allow the jurors to digest his words.

'The defendants may appear to be upstanding members of the business and professional classes, but the prosecution will prove that together, for financial gain, the defendants took part in a cowardly attack, which led to Brandon's death. I would remind the jury that in such circumstances the law considers all three equally culpable, regardless of who struck the fatal blow that left Brandon's family with nearly a quarter of a century of doubt and fear. Brandon's mother unfortunately, or perhaps fortunately, never lived to discover his fate.'

Brandon's siblings squeeze each other's hands.

'Please do not be swayed by appearances or unsubstantiated supposition, but only by the facts and the facts alone. Facts that demonstrate, beyond reasonable doubt, the shocking events that led to Brandon's death. If, members of the jury, you do indeed find, as we believe you shall, that only one set of circumstances can explain how a young man met a brutal death, was rolled in a rug, wrapped in plastic and buried in an unmarked grave on a Surrey hillside, thousands of miles from his birthplace, the Crown would urge you to find all three defendants guilty of the charge of murder.'

Chapter 37

1994 – Guildford

Gideon hooked his elbow under Julia's arm and pulled her up the steep bank that led from the road to a small stile and up onto the open downland. The sun had long fallen below the horizon but a faint red glow lingered across the hill's ridge.

Julia wished she hadn't worn her sandals. The loose dirt slipped beneath her feet and she had difficulty keeping her balance, while the boys had no trouble, tramping across the grass in their boots and trainers. Gideon came and grabbed her hand. Relying on him made her feel like some helpless Victorian lady – all she needed was smelling salts. In the end, she took the sandals off and went barefoot. The ground was dry, the grass caressed her toes and the breeze made her feel lighter and alive. She skipped to keep up with the boys who were now nearing the ridge.

The town came into view below them. Somewhere down there, Lucy was embracing Linden. Julia didn't envy her, she wanted to be here, with the inky star-studded sky arching above her. It felt ancient and wild, a different world from the bustling town spread beneath them. Here, she felt more connected to her surroundings, giddy and high, long before Gideon rolled the first joint.

They found a patch of shorter grass on a spot over-looking the town and sat down in a circle, all animosity forgotten.

'Where did you get the grass?' Brandon asked.

'Contacts,' Gideon said and inhaled.

Julia had only smoked once before, some resin. She'd not liked it and hadn't bothered since. From Alan's spluttering as he smoked, she suspected he was also unused to it. Brandon, however, appeared to be a connoisseur.

'This is good stuff,' he said after his first drag. 'I'd go as far as to say excellent.'

Gideon nodded. 'Only the best,' he said.

Julia took a shallow puff, then a couple more. She felt the effects immediately. Her head started to spin and expand at the same time. Each muscle within her body twitched, she heard every blade of grass swish in the warm breeze. She lay on her back and watched the sky as the stars appeared, one by one.

'They're so beautiful, so far away,' she said.

She heard laughter. Had that been a stupid thing to say? She didn't care.

'Back home we'd drive out of town, until the only lights were the stars and moon,' Brandon said. 'You never get that here.'

'Do you miss it?' Julia asked.

Brandon rolled onto his side and propped his head on one hand.

'I don't think about it too much,' he said. 'Sometimes, you just have to get away and that's that.'

How had his relationship ended? Like hers – a broken engagement, a friendship betrayed?

'Sorry,' she said.

'What are you sorry for, Julia?' Alan asked.

She closed her eyes and felt the breeze brush her body. Every microscopic hair on her skin shivered beneath it.

'I'm sorry that Brandon had to leave everyone he loved and start again.'

'You didn't *have* to leave, did you, Brandon?' Alan asked.

Brandon had the joint and took a long inhalation, then an even longer exhalation.

'What does "have to" mean? No one put a gun to my head. But I couldn't stay. A bad situation – have you never done that – just left?'

An unfair question – Julia had already told him everything. He shouldn't make her retell it in front of the others. And only when Alan replied did she realise Brandon hadn't been asking her.

'I never had to leave anywhere. I chose to. But I can go back – it's only forty miles to Southsea.'

'What was that like growing up?' Brandon asked.

'Great,' Alan said. 'It's on the coast, the summers were fantastic – parties on the beach every night. We'd have a ghetto blaster and a fire, bowls of lethal rum punch, all the girls drunk, dancing around in tiny bikinis, a bit of spliff going around.'

'So why did you leave?' Brandon asked.

'Work,' Alan said.

Julia had barely heard Alan speak of anything without a heavy dose of sarcasm. The overwhelmingly positive description of his youth was alien to his nature. It was a fun-filled youth observed rather than experienced. The teenage years he'd wanted. Parties he'd heard other boys in sixth form laugh about on Monday mornings, or perhaps he'd watched from the promenade, as the bikini-clad girls danced round bowls of punch, before he returned home alone to his bedroom and a clutch of computer games.

Julia experienced a wave of sympathy for Alan. They weren't so different. Always shy and clumsy, she'd not have had friends at school if it hadn't been for Pearl and Andre. Christian was a blip, one that had now been adjusted. Girls at school would deliberately let her overhear their 'What is he doing going out with her?' comments. And one of Christian's friends once told him, 'Mate, you could do a lot better.' Well now he had done better, he had Ellie. Who would stick to the exact same shopping list from Tesco's every week, remember his sisters' birthdays and make homemade Christmas presents. Christian's parents would like her – they'd never been sure about Julia and their pretence ran thin.

'Why are you crying?' Brandon asked.

'I'm not.'

'You are.'

Julia touched her cheeks. They were wet with tears.

'You're wiped out,' Gideon said. He checked his watch. 'It's time to head back.'

The stars dimmed and the breeze was cooler. Gideon had to help Julia to her feet. Her legs wobbled beneath her and she leant on him as they tottered down the hill, no pride preventing her this time.

Alan and Brandon seemed as out of it as she was. Only Gideon appeared lucid.

'I'll get her upstairs,' Brandon said to Gideon, as they entered the house.

'I can manage,' Gideon said.

He placed her arm over his shoulder, helped her up the stairs and sat her on the bed, lifting her legs on top. He drew the curtains. She hated closed curtains – they made her feel boxed in.

'Sleep tight,' he said.

'Gideon,' she said.

'Yes.'

'You never told us about yourself, where you grew up, what you did as a teenager.'

'Another time,' he said. 'Go to sleep.'

One by one the doors shut, and the house returned to silence.

The dirt on her feet began to bother Julia. She should have washed them before coming to bed. She'd walked back barefoot. Where were her sandals? She'd left them on the Downs. The idea came to her to go back and get them but her heavy limbs anchored her to the bed. Her mind drifted back up the slopes, to the stars and the breeze. Her drift towards sleep was interrupted by a rap on the door.

'Julia.'

It was Brandon. She stayed silent and willed him to go away.

Another rap.

'Julia,' he repeated.

Then Gideon's voice. 'She'll be asleep.'

'Yeah, of course,' Brandon said.

'Best to leave her alone,' Gideon said.

Brandon's heavy tread retreated from her door. She heard

a door shut and waited, straining to listen for any movement. But Brandon did not return. And she had Gideon to thank for it.

Julia woke early, her mouth dry and her tongue swollen. She needed water. She crept to the bathroom without bothering to turn on the light. It was very late, or rather very early. The sky had just started to lighten. The water ran lukewarm from the tap and she stared out of the open window as she waited for it to cool.

The bathroom was at the rear of the house and overlooked the garden. Her stare was aimless, and it took a moment to register a figure at the back by the fence. It was Gideon, dressed only in a T-shirt and boxer shorts. He was on the phone. A strange time to make a phone call – it must be gone four in the morning, and why couldn't he talk in the house? And something else, other than the ridiculous hour, troubled her about the call.

The water was colder now. She filled her glass and returned to her room. The fan sent out a pleasant stream of cool air. She heard Gideon's door click below. Perhaps he had only gone outside so as not to disturb the rest of the house. Perhaps someone had rung him, though she'd not heard the phone.

She put it out of her mind and returned to bed.

Chapter 38

The prosecution's first witness is forensic scientist Dr Ambrose Urquhart. He has grey hair and a gaunt face, with deep lines that speak of having seen one too many corpses.

'Dr Urquhart,' Thomas Mapplethorpe says. 'Would you state your credentials and experience.'

In a soft Scottish accent, which certainly isn't from Glasgow where he studied, he tells the jury about his career, including working to identify victims of massacres from the Balkan conflict and many years working for Surrey Police, as well as being requested by other forces whenever his expertise is required. He has an understated confidence. If we walk free at the end of this trial, it won't be because he has overlooked or misrepresented the evidence. He calmly explains that the DNA has a one in a billion chance of not belonging to Brandon or a close relative. The dental records match those sent from Brandon's dentist in New Zealand.

Mapplethorpe nods along to each point Urquhart makes.

'Taking all these factors into account, Dr Urquhart, are you satisfied the body recovered from the North Downs does belong to Brandon Wells?'

'I am.'

'And given your extensive experience, how long would you say Brandon had been buried?'

Brandon. Mapplethorpe keeps repeating his first name, making him human, not a faceless statistic. He was a young man, who could have been your boyfriend, brother or son.

'One hundred per cent accuracy is impossible,' Urquhart says. 'But between twenty and twenty-five years.'

'So, between 1993 and 1998?' Mapplethorpe asks.

'That's correct.'

'And were you able to ascertain the cause of death?'

'Almost certainly it was due to massive head trauma. The skull was smashed.'

Mapplethorpe lets the jury wait a few moments for the importance of Urquhart's statement to sink in, before saying, 'Members of the jury, I would ask you to look at exhibits 3.1 to 3.3.'

The court clerk passes plastic folders containing the same photographs Warren and Akande showed me. A collective gasp escapes from the jury. One woman puts her hand to her mouth, another leans forward. Mutters run around the court. Mari Hewlett turns her face away, although the photographs are too distant for her to see. Her brother stares straight ahead, stern and stoic.

'I'm afraid this is going to be unpleasant, but I would ask you to take your time,' Mapplethorpe says.

The juror in the floral dress on the front row remains with one hand clamped across her mouth, holding the photographs in the other. The tattooed man clutches each picture for as long as possible, bringing them close to his face and twisting them to various angles.

Mapplethorpe adopts a serious tone. 'And what could cause such substantial injuries?'

'On examining the skull, I concluded that Mr Wells was lying on the floor and struck from above, at least twice, by a large object.'

Mapplethorpe appears to brace himself. 'If the jury will please observe photographs 3.4 to 3.9. Can you explain what we are seeing here please, Dr Urquhart?'

'The blows landed in a downward direction.' He makes a vertical strike with his arm and open palm. 'They split the left side of the skull. The right side is also fractured, injuries corresponding with the opposite side of the head striking a hard surface.'

'Such as a parquet floor?' Mapplethorpe says.

'Any hard surface.'

'Are you able to say what *did* cause these injuries, Dr Urquhart?'

'We found a tiny chip of marble, along with gold paint and metal fragments, crushed into the bone. These materials would have been integral to the weapon.'

'And has this object been identified?'

'Not the exact object,' Urquhart says. 'However, the police were able to provide me with photographic evidence of a lamp that was in Mrs Pike's living room around the time of Mr Wells' death.'

'I refer members of the jury to photographs 7.1 and 7.2,' Mapplethorpe says. 'I will be covering the photographic evidence with DI Warren shortly.'

Photographs of Genevieve's ugly marble lamp are passed to the jury. They receive them more calmly than the last.

'We were able to locate a replica lamp and analyse the

materials used in its construction,' Urquhart says. 'They matched those we found on the deceased.'

'From the materials found buried with Brandon, did you draw any other conclusions about his injuries?'

'No soft tissue remained, so it was impossible to speak of exact wounds. However, we know Brandon lost a lot of blood before his death.'

Mapplethorpe turns to the jury. 'This would be the evidence of the rug?' he asks.

'That's correct,' Urquhart confirms. 'It was a popular IKEA rug, far easier to track down than the lamp and yes, the same make and design as the one in the photograph provided by Surrey CID.'

'Please observe exhibits 4.1 to 4.4, showing a bloodstained rug.'

The woman on the front row looks ill. Though the blood is barely discernible from the dirt and original dark pattern.

'And you identified the blood as belonging to Brandon Wells?' Mapplethorpe says.

'We did.'

Words such as genetic fingerprinting and DNA profiling are so common today, they hardly require explanation. In 1994, we were completely ignorant of their existence.

'Brandon lost around two pints of blood,' Urquhart says. 'Not enough to be fatal in itself – that would depend on the actual injury. However, whatever the injury, it would certainly have required medical attention.'

Mapplethorpe looks upwards, away from Urquhart and the jury.

'And though you're unable to state the exact cause, could

you give the jury an indication of the sort of wounds that would typically result in such blood loss?'

'Typically, it would be the result of a serious laceration. Such as one caused by a knife or other sharp object.'

'It couldn't have come from the blows to the head?'

'The head injuries would have resulted in almost instant death. Once the heart stops beating, blood flow ceases. So, no, the blows to the head couldn't have resulted in the amount of blood we see on the rug.'

'Therefore, Brandon must have received a serious injury before the fatal blows to the head?'

'Yes,' Urquhart says.

The prosecution are not using the footprint evidence. Ralph would certainly spend hours attacking it as weak and inconclusive. Instead Mapplethorpe moves to evidence where the case is strong.

'We've established that the blood was Brandon's. You took DNA samples from the rug, which corresponded to all three defendants, did you not?' he asks.

'Actually, yes,' Urquhart says. 'It was unexpected after such a long period. But wrapping the body in plastic seems to have preserved more than we would have expected, whereas the victim can be identified though skeletal remains.'

He is rightly proud. Warren and Akande hadn't expected to find anything of forensic value from the grave that would link so directly to us. Their breathless excitement at the custody desk, Akande's undisguised glee, were the result of Urquhart's meticulous skills.

'We recovered samples of hair. Two correlated to Mr Risborough and Mr Johns. This was a microconidia DNA, less conclusive than full DNA. But Ms Winter's hair is more conclusive. It contains the root and therefore a full DNA match.'

'And why would Ms Winter's hair contain the root?'

'This would typically occur when plucking or pulling a hair, rather than simply shedding it.'

'Pulling a hair, such as in a struggle?'

Dr Urquhart won't be drawn beyond his remit. 'I'm not going to speculate as to that,' he says.

'But it could occur in a struggle?'

'It could,' he agrees.

'These samples were found where exactly?'

'Over the rug, and Brandon's clothes.'

'Given that the defendants shared a house, couldn't these hairs have been deposited over time as the defendants lived in the house?'

'It's possible,' he says. 'But there were a large number of hairs, particularly from Ms Winter and, significantly, hers were coated in blood. Brandon's blood.' The jury watch me more closely. 'And we found something else to link her to the crime,' Urquhart says.

'What was that?'

'The blood wasn't only from Brandon. We also obtained a small sample from Ms Winter spattered across Brandon's clothes.'

I can feel the gaze of the court upon me. I stare at the glass of water in front of me. I know the photographs being passed around the jury. Brandon's clothes. Magnified images of hair.

Ralph has assured me the case always swings towards the prosecution in the beginning. It's their witnesses, their version of events. I know the defence present their case later. But right now, I feel we've lost before we've started.

Chapter 39

Julia woke, unable to breathe, her duvet wrapped around her face and neck. She thrashed ineffectually, trying to release herself, before kicking it off the bed and onto the floor. The remnants of last night's dream clung to the edges of her consciousness. The Downs had been a living, sentient mass, moving towards the house, seeking her out, ready to engulf her and bury her deep beneath its sandy soil.

She was still wearing last night's dress, whose buttons had been pulled open by her thrashing about. Changing into her blue pyjamas instantly made her feel better, though her neck was stiff and her mind foggy. She drank the water next to her bed and went and opened the curtains.

The grey haze of a cool morning hung across the slope opposite. A lone bird, a gull, flapped from behind the house then swooped upwards towards the Downs. It was a long way from the sea, and she'd not seen one here before. Audrey told her, when she was young, gulls came inland during stormy weather, but the country was bathing in summer heat with only the faintest breeze. The gull had no reason to be so far from home. Perhaps it was lost.

234

There was a knock on the door. For a moment she thought of Brandon, but it was a light tap, one that was aware she might be asleep.

Julia put on her dressing gown. 'Come in,' she said.

The door opened slowly. It was Genevieve. She wore a thick towelling dressing gown, much like Julia's, one she'd not seen her in before. Genevieve's hair was pulled back from her forehead with a hairband and her face was dragged down by sleep, making the similarity between her and her sister more obvious. She looked less like a displaced West End actress and more like a harassed housewife.

'I've been awake since five,' Genevieve said. 'I thought I heard you cry out. Are you unwell?'

'Just a bad dream,' Julia said. 'I'm sorry if I woke you.'

Genevieve remained at the door. 'May I come in?' she asked.

Julia stood back. Genevieve entered and walked to the window, looking out across the Downs. The gull was back, squawking as it soared past the window, up over the roof and out of sight.

Julia placed the duvet back on the bed. She sat down. Genevieve returned from the window and sat next to her.

'I've been worrying, ever since the other Sunday.' Genevieve looked at Julia. 'I think I was a little harsh, in the things I said to you.'

It had been two weeks ago. It felt more like two months.

'It doesn't matter, Genevieve. I'm sorry too. I was overtired. I shouldn't have been so tetchy.'

'Only, I can't stop thinking about Brandon.' She gave a little smile. 'I want him to be happy.'

'Of course.'

'Don't want to stifle him.'

'No.'

'And I feel ... What I mean to say is that of course it would be wonderful if he had a girlfriend.' Again, she glanced at Julia, who didn't respond. 'But only if it's the right girl.'

'He's twenty-four,' Julia said.

'Exactly,' Genevieve said. 'The precise age when you're likely to make a bad decision. When you think you're an adult and know everything, but you don't. I married at nineteen.'

'You told me you were seventeen,' Julia said.

Genevieve waved her hand to bat away the question.

'Seventeen, nineteen, what's the difference? The point is, my mother and Ruth warned me against it. I wouldn't listen. And I should have done.'

'Why are you telling me this, Genevieve?'

It had been a mistake to let her in. She should have pretended to be asleep.

'I know you're a lovely girl, Julia. But Brandon is sensitive.'

Julia couldn't help her snort.

'He *is*, Julia,' she said. 'If you've failed to notice that, I really don't think you *are* right for each other.'

'Genevieve, we're both adults. And for the record, I'm not interested in being Brandon's girlfriend.'

'Does he know that?'

'He should do.'

'And Gideon?'

'What's he got to do with anything?'

'I can't help noticing you've been paying him a good deal of attention.'

'You're our landlady, Genevieve, that's all. You've no business interfering in our lives.'

'As I said, I try not to stifle him.' She sat upright. 'I did come in here with the intention of smoothing things over – you're not making it easy.'

Years of dealing with Audrey's passive-aggressive behaviour had taught Julia not only how to fight back but also when to fight. She had no interest in Brandon, or Gideon. The house was just somewhere to stay; if it became too much hassle, she'd move out.

'Genevieve,' she said, 'I can promise you, I have no intention of becoming Brandon's girlfriend. Or Gideon's for that matter.'

'That's really the assurance I was looking for.'

'I'll leave him to someone of your choosing.'

If Genevieve took this as a jibe, it didn't register in her response. 'I'm so glad we've had this little chat and everything's sorted out.'

Julia held her face in a smile and stood up. Genevieve copied her.

'I'll go and make some camomile tea,' Genevieve said. 'See if I can get back to sleep. Ruth took the pills my doctor gave me. She can be so bossy sometimes. Can I get you a cup?'

'I'm fine, thanks.'

Julia shut the door behind her and flopped onto the bed. She heard Genevieve descend the stairs.

It was still early, and Julia felt the pull of sleep. She remembered her dream, about the Downs engulfing Downsview Villa. And she was pleased to have the curtains open, to keep an eye on them.

Then another set of footsteps, slower and heavier, crossed the landing from the bathroom, before Brandon's door slammed shut. He must have heard the whole conversation.

Chapter 40

I become anxious when the usher calls for Detective Inspector Warren to appear before the court. Urquhart was detached and professional, conveying the facts without emotion. Warren's stare of open hostility towards the defendants' benches tells me he has a point to prove.

At lunch Ralph told me things were going well. Not something I'd have guessed from the jury's stern expressions.

'That forensic stuff was to impress the jury, to show the prosecution has a factual basis for their case,' he said.

Ralph had put forward that the hair could have come from a comb and the blood from a nosebleed. I'm not sure he's managed to convince himself of that, let alone the jury.

'They've proved the body belonged to Brandon Wells and he died from blows to the head. No one's disputing how he died, it's totally irrelevant. For a successful prosecution, they need to prove you did it.'

Warren states his name and places his hand on the Bible, his great jowls wobbling like an aged bull mastiff as he takes the oath. The jury won't find him as repugnant as I do. They will see his crumpled suit and wheezing breath as the result of being a harassed, underappreciated professional, meting out justice under trying circumstances and diminishing resources.

Mapplethorpe smiles at him.

'May I ask you how long you have been a member of Surrey Police, Detective Inspector Warren?'

'Nearly thirty years. Sixteen of those on CID, nine as DI.'

Mapplethorpe gives a reverential nod. 'And please would you tell the jury of your involvement in the case of Brandon Wells.'

'Certainly.' Warren straightens his jacket. 'We received information that a body had been found on the Downs, buried in a small patch of woodland, some way off the main path. It quickly became evident that the victim had suffered a violent death and a murder investigation was opened.'

'The first thing, in such a case, is to establish the victim's identity, is it not?' Mapplethorpe asks.

'Indeed. Forensics informed us that the body had been there for at least twenty years,' Warren says. 'We looked through missing persons but were struggling to find a match. Until we received a tip-off from the New Zealand police. Mr Patrick Wells, Brandon's father, kept up to date with UK news and that of Surrey in particular, via the internet. You see, he'd never given up trying to find out what happened to his son. Unfortunately, he's not been in good health and is unable to attend the trial. But it was he who alerted the New Zealand police force, who, in turn, alerted us. Once we had a name, identification was relatively straightforward.'

'And why was Brandon not searched for when he went

239

missing, back in the Nineties?' For a moment Mapplethorpe's tone slips a little, from respectful to accusatory.

'He was searched for, all right,' Warren says. 'But as a suspect in a theft, not as a murder victim.'

'I'll be returning to this aspect with one of your former colleagues, Luke Crane. For now, though, please take us through the chain of evidence that led to the arrests.'

Warren relaxes into his role. He must have attended many such trials.

'Brandon's body was found just a short walk from his last known address. We know he had told a friend he was going to the house to fetch some clothes and money, before returning that same day. Saturday 27th August. People have remembered the date, because it was the August bank holiday weekend. Brandon never returned and, as far as we know, no one ever saw him again. We also discovered that the occupants of the house at that time were the defendants, Gideon Risborough, Alan Johns and Julia Winter. Forensics linked their DNA to the crime scene. A large amount of money was missing. Money we know was withdrawn the week before, by Mrs Jennifer Pike, also known as Genevieve D'Auncey. This is the money Brandon was returning to retrieve after Mrs Pike's death. His room had been cleared of all his possessions, including his passport.'

Mapplethorpe examines his notes and nods to the court clerk before asking, 'The lamp and rug, discussed with Doctor Urquhart earlier, how did you link them specifically to the house, number 72 Downs Avenue?'

'We have photos of the property's living room, in which both the rug and lamp, and the defendants, are present.'

'Exhibit 1.1 and 1.2,' Mapplethorpe adds.

240

That fateful photograph of the three of us and Brandon, lounging on the sofa – the lamp and the rug on the periphery of the shot, innocent, harmless objects.

'The lamp circled is the one we believe was used to bludgeon Brandon to death. The rug, the one his body was wrapped in.'

The photo is passed to the jury.

'The second photograph was taken when the property was being valued, some weeks later. Both objects are missing. We believe only someone inside the house would have had access to these objects and could have cleared out Brandon's room.'

All the jurors look towards the defendants' benches.

'What else links the defendants to this crime, DI Warren?' Mapplethorpe asks.

'Ms Winter's blood-coated hairs indicate they were ripped from her head during a struggle between her and Brandon Wells,' Warren says. 'We know that he entertained romantic feelings towards Ms Winter, which were not reciprocated.'

The word 'romantic' does not gel with my memory of Brandon, lumbering around drunk and reeking of tobacco.

'The hairs prove Ms Winter's involvement,' Warren continues. 'But it's unthinkable that she overpowered a man of fifteen stone, disposed of the body and cleared the scene *without* the help and knowledge Mr Risborough and Mr Johns. Both of whom admit to having been at the property that weekend. And no one but the defendants had the opportunity to clear Brandon's room and/or could have known about the money.'

'And money was the defendants' primary motive?' Mapplethorpe asks.

'That was one factor. I believe there was a fair amount of

personal animosity involved. Brandon had told his friend everyone in the house hated him. He was returning to get money, collect his clothes and move out. But no one ever saw him again. Except his killers.'

'And did you find any financial activity linking the defendants to the missing cash.'

'A few months later, thirty thousand pounds was deposited in the account of SupaSupplements, the business owned by Gideon Risborough and for whom Alan Johns went to work immediately after they left Downsview Villa. Thirty thousand pounds corresponds to a two-thirds share of what we know to be missing. This is something that only came to light during the current investigation.

'Thank you, DI Warren.'

Mapplethorpe appears satisfied and concludes his questioning.

Gideon's barrister, Helena Dryden, purses her lips in place of a smile.

'DI Warren, you stated categorically that the thirty thousand pounds deposited in my client's business accounts was the money taken from Mrs Pike. But there's no actual proof of this, is there?'

'As I've said, the money corresponded to a two-thirds share, which supported our theory that the defendants were in on it together.'

'And because it supported your theory, you didn't look for another explanation?'

Warren looks heavenwards. 'Their claim that it was taken in cash, at trade shows, doesn't stand up. Other participants were taking three or four hundred pounds at each show maximum. The thousands Gideon Risborough and Alan

Johns took through SupaSupplements was unheard of. The explanation is wholly unsatisfactory.'

'It was deemed satisfactory when the police were first informed of the deposits into my client's account, over twenty years ago. A private detective approached the police with the details. It was considered too ludicrous to waste police time on.'

'That wasn't my decision. I wasn't even on the force then. Besides, with no body, what would have been the point?'

'For Christ's sake!' In the public gallery, Austen Wells is on his feet, glowering at Warren.

'Mr Wells,' the judge says. 'I understand this is very distressing for you, but I can't allow such interruptions in my court. Kindly remain seated.'

Austen's fists are clenched. For a moment, I think he's going to explode with rage. The whole court holds its breath. There's a moment's indecision before his sister grabs his arm and he lowers himself into his seat.

Dryden waits for the court to quieten, before continuing.

'By your own admission, there was no point. And only a quarter of a century after the money went missing are you claiming my client was responsible.'

'Priorities change. At no point in the original inquiry were we looking at a murder.'

I glance at Austen Wells. He's hunched up tight. I think he may shout out again but he turns his head. In doing so, he catches my eye. I'm frozen. I don't want to look at him but can't tear my eyes away. He stares back at me. I expected to see hatred. But there's a question – am I guilty?

Alan's barrister tears into the physical evidence. No conclusive proof that the hairs belonged to his client, no proof that any such hairs couldn't have arrived in Brandon's grave through everyday contact, around the house.

Ralph takes a different tack. 'You say no one else had access to the property or knew about the money, but that's not quite true, is it, DI Warren?'

'As far as I know it is,' he says.

'Then perhaps your inquiries should have been a little more extensive. Both Mrs Pike's boyfriend, Edward Farrington, and her sister, Mrs Ruth Fletcher, had keys to the property and knew about the money withdrawn from Mrs Pike's account. And given Mrs Fletcher's belief that Brandon Wells killed her sister, she had a strong motive to harm Brandon, wouldn't you say?'

'Mrs Fletcher was in her fifties at the time, as was Edward Farrington.'

'But it does disprove your statement that *no one* else had access, doesn't it?'

'I suppose, but Mrs Fletcher's blood-coated hairs weren't found in Brandon's grave.'

'DI Warren, you've already stated that Mr Wells had a romantic interest in my client, Ms Winter. Is that correct?'

'Yes.'

'Then is it beyond the realms of possibility that he obtained the hairs without her knowledge, from a comb for example, as some sort of token or keepsake?'

'It's possible but highly improbable.'

'But you cannot say with one hundred per cent certainty.'

'Ninety-nine point nine.'

'I'm sorry,' Ralph says. 'Where did you get that figure?'

'Well, I—'

'Made it up?'

'Used it to illustrate how far-fetched the idea is.'

'Isn't that for the jury to decide, DI Warren? It would be better if you stuck to established facts rather than invent statistics to advance your case. Thank you. No further questions.'

Chapter 41

1994 – Guildford

The sun had started to dapple the Downs opposite her bedroom window and Julia watched it rise fully until the entire hill was bathed in light. She'd been unable to fall back to sleep after Genevieve left. Brandon overhearing their conversation had left her uneasy. She checked the coast was clear and Genevieve was in her room before going downstairs to make some tea.

Gideon was at the kitchen table drinking coffee and eating toast. 'How are you feeling this morning?'

Julia had vague recollections of being put to bed, and hadn't Brandon knocked on her door?

'Not bad. I'm sorry if I was a pain last night,' she said.

'Not a problem, we've all done it. I thought you might be hungover.'

'No. I got up in the middle of the night and drank some water. I think that saved me.'

Gideon looked at her. For a moment a frown crossed his forehead, then it was gone.

'You got up – what time?' he asked.

'Not sure, to be honest. Around dawn, I think – why?'

'I was going to ask you to come to the cinema with me, but if you're too tired ...'

'I'm not, but I'm meeting friends in London at around three.'

Pearl and Andre had arranged to meet her in Camden. They were going to trawl the markets, eat noodles, sneak in a couple of pints. Then back to Pearl's house to chill out before getting ready for the evening back in Camden.

'I'm heading up there too. Do you fancy going early and seeing *Three Colours White* at The Prince Charles? We could catch the twelve-thirty showing. I doubt it will be showing down here.'

'Sounds good,' she said.

'Leave at eleven?'

'Great, it's just ...'

She thought of Brandon, knocking on her door in the night.

Gideon had half turned to walk away. 'Just what?' he asked.

Julia shut the kitchen door. 'Best not to mention it to anyone else.'

Gideon gave her a quizzical look, but said, 'Sure.'

Julia left the house first. Her bag contained only her purse, a paperback, black eyeliner, waterproof mascara, a change of top, a clean pair of knickers and a toothbrush. Gideon had agreed to leave five minutes later and catch her up at the station.

The train carriage was near empty, and they spread between four seats, facing each other.

'Have you seen any of Kieślowski's other work?' Gideon asked.

'Only *The Double Life of Veronique*, which was amazing. And *Three Colours Blue*, of course.'

Julia had little interest in arthouse cinema and had only seen these films thanks to Ellie, of all people, who claimed '*Blue*' to be the best film of the decade so far. *Why were people always blinded by Hollywood tripe?* Julia now realised it had been a play for Christian's attention. A ridiculous one, as Christian hated subtitles and his favourite director was Steven Spielberg.

Right now, he and Ellie were probably sprawled across the sofa, watching *Jurassic Park*. Still, one way or another it had taken Ellie another step towards her goal. And now Julia found herself dancing the same dance for Gideon. Why was she so desperate to impress him, when she wasn't even sure if she liked him? Was she even on a date? Gideon had made it seem so casual – *hey, look, we're both going to London and want to see a film* – they might just be two friends interested in the same thing. And who went on lunchtime dates when they had somewhere else to go afterwards?

'Are you all right?' Gideon asked. 'You look miles away.'

Julia realised she had been staring into space.

'I'm fine,' she said.

'You're not worried about Brandon, are you?'

'Has he said something?' she asked.

'I saw him trying to come into your room last night. After he thought everyone else had gone to bed.'

'I did hear something,' Julia said.

'It was a bit creepy. You were out of it. He must have known that.' Gideon put his head to one side and looked at Julia. 'He's got a thing about you, hasn't he?'

'Hmm,' Julia said and looked away.

'You should ask Genevieve to put a lock on the door.'

'That's a bit of an overreaction, isn't it?'

Gideon raised an eyebrow. 'Better to be safe. If he bothers you again—'

'It's OK. I'll talk to him.'

'Is he the reason you wanted us to leave separately?'

It was too complicated to tell him about Genevieve as well.

'Partly. People can jump to conclusions,' she said.

'Rightly, sometimes.'

His manner was nonchalant. Did his words mean more? Was this a date?

Gideon started talking about his plans for the evening. He was going over to his friend's house early, to help prepare for his thirtieth birthday bash. Julia didn't know anyone who was thirty, not socially at least. She'd forgotten Gideon was so much older. She'd only just finished the rounds of twenty-first parties. And again, it made her wonder why she cared if he liked her or not.

The film followed an unlikely plot: a man seeks revenge on his ex-wife by having her wrongly convicted for murder. Julia had brief thoughts about exacting a similar revenge on Christian. But she realised that, even if she had the means, she no longer cared enough. It still hurt to think of him with Ellie, and she would have been pleased to hear of their breaking up. But the raw anger, the active wish to enact revenge, had vanished. It was progress, of a sort.

Standing outside the cinema after the film and squinting in the sunlight, she felt awkward. She was still unsure about Gideon. What if he tried to kiss her? How would she respond?

Gideon looked at his watch. 'I'm going to have to hurry,'

he said. 'I'm meeting Jonny in twenty minutes. See you back at the house.'

He jogged off before Julia could say goodbye. So much for a kiss. Julia wandered through the street performers and endless snack options of Leicester Square. The date had been nothing more than two people going to see a film. She needed to get a grip.

'So, this Gideon fella, is he cute or what?' Andre asked.

'He's not bad-looking, I suppose,' Julia replied.

'Such enthusiasm,' Pearl said.

She had managed to bag them the best table in the pub, in the corner with a view across the market and Camden High Street. It was packed out – some generic grunge band was whining over the tiny speakers. They should really be outside on a day like this. Julia's pint of cider was nearly full. Pearl and Andre's were nearly finished, and they weren't their first.

'So, you don't fancy him?' Andre said.

'I'm not sure.'

'And Brandon?' Pearl asked.

'I was drunk – it doesn't count,' Julia said.

'Using that rule makes me a virgin,' Pearl said.

Julia couldn't help laughing. 'I'm being serious,' she said.

'So was I. What about you, Andre?'

'Drunken sex? Only with women.'

Both girls put their pints down.

'You've slept with women?'

'Only twice?'

'Who the hell were they?' Julia said.

'I thought me and Jules would be your first port of call,' Pearl said.

'Just a little experimentation. And can you imagine if it had been one of you?'

'Yuck,' Pearl said.

'Well, thanks very much,' Andre said with mock offence.

'You know what I mean. Too close to home and all that. More Julia's thing.'

'Hey – give it a rest,' Julia said.

Pearl was still laughing. 'I don't get you, Jules. All this self-loathing. All this shall I, shan't I? Have a fling, don't have a fling – it's just a bit of fun. You don't have to marry the guy.'

'Pearl's right,' Andre said. 'You've just escaped the dreaded Christian.' Julia didn't like to correct him and point out that Christian had escaped her. 'You don't want to leap out of the frying pan into the fire.'

'Run from a wolf to meet a bear,' Pearl said.

'From a Christian to a lion,' Andre added.

Julia wished she'd had more cider and found the satire on her love life as hilarious as Pearl and Andre. In truth, she was annoyed. Guildford was supposed be nothing more than a dormitory and her main life was meant to be in London. Instead, London had become the sideshow and her life was happening in Guildford, in a house with a batty old landlady and four other people with whom, apart from Lucy, she had little in common.

'But really, Jules,' Andre said. 'Don't get tied down on the rebound.'

'Gotta love a mixed metaphor,' Pearl said.

'Shut up, I'm being serious,' Andre said. 'Do you know how many people end up marrying someone they barely know – as a reaction to a break-up – and regret it? To show your ex you don't need him. When nothing says desperation like falling in love with the next guy you happen to run into.'

'Talking from experience?' Pearl said.

'You bet.'

'Who—' Julia began.

'We're not talking about me,' Andre said. 'We're talking about you. Have some fun. And forget Brandon and Gideon too. He sounds pretentious. Who's called Gideon in the twentieth century?'

'Says Andre,' Pearl said.

'I didn't choose my name.'

'Neither did he!'

Julia banged her fist on the table. 'Look, you're both getting carried away,' she said. 'I never said anything about being in love. I'm not sure I even like him.'

'But you went to the cinema with him,' Andre said.

'And he fended off this Brandon – that's quite sexy,' Pearl said.

'Yes but ...'

What was the but? Why didn't she like him? Because as soon as Pearl and Andre had started to insist she did, she realised she didn't. He was kind, thoughtful, cultured ... and yet ... and yet ...

'I'm bored of talking about both of them,' Julia said.

'Good, your round,' Pearl said.

'I'm not even halfway through this one.'

'Then keep up.'

'And we're going out tonight,' Julia protested.

'Training,' Pearl said and downed the last of her pint.

Julia sidled up to the bar. Who was she kidding? She wasn't Gideon's type. He would have the sort of girlfriend other men

252

envied. Not 'mate, you could do a lot better'. No, Gideon was just being friendly. He'd moved into a town where he knew no one. Alan was odd, Brandon hostile and Lucy never there. The mild interest from two men had gone to her head. She wasn't Pearl or Lucy. Even Brandon's attention had been more for convenience than due to any strong attraction. His apparent jealousy was merely the instinctive response of an alpha male guarding conquered territory.

Chapter 42

2018 – Guildford Crown Court

Former detective constable Luke Crane grows a full six inches as he takes the witness stand and swears in. He obviously enjoyed his job, retirement isn't suiting him and he's pleased to return to a courtroom.

'I remember the incident well,' Crane says at Mapplethorpe's prompting. 'I had only recently joined CID. On Monday 22nd August 1994, we received a call about the sudden death of a Mrs Jennifer Pike, also known as Genevieve D'Auncey, who was the landlady at 72 Downs Avenue, Guildford.' Crane turns to the jury. 'Police attend such deaths to ensure there are no suspicious circumstances.'

'And did Mrs Pike's death raise any concerns?' Mapplethorpe asks.

'None whatsoever.'

'And was Brandon Wells at the house on that occasion?'

'He was not,' Crane says. 'The other lodgers told me he had left the night before, following an argument with Mrs Pike.'

'That is the defendants, along with Lucy Moretti?'

'Miss Moretti was working away from home that week.'

'So, no one else was in the house, other than the three defendants?' Mapplethorpe asks.

'That's correct.'

'I see.' Mapplethorpe pauses as if this holds greater significance than the other information. Though I can't see how. 'And you returned to the house on Wednesday, a follow-up visit. Who was present on this occasion?'

'Again, just the three defendants. Lucy Moretti was working in Newcastle that week. Something confirmed by records kept by her then employer.'

'So to confirm one more time, the three defendants were the only occupants of the house on Wednesday before Brandon disappeared after telling his friend, Grant McCluskey, he was returning to the house to fetch his belongings?'

'Yes.'

'Thank you. No further questions, Mr Crane.'

Crane looks disappointed, he was enjoying giving testimony. He appears reinvigorated when he sees Ralph get to his feet.

'Mr Crane, am I correct in thinking that you established quite quickly that there was no third-party involvement in Mrs Pike's death, no suspicious circumstances?'

'Correct. This was later confirmed by the coroner.'

'My client, Julia Winter, found the body do you recall?'

'I do. She was young and very shaken. I didn't blame her for being upset. It's not something you ever get used to.'

'And yet, despite stating there were no suspicious circumstances, you returned to the property several times, searching Mrs Pike's belongings and questioning the housemates. Why was this necessary?' Ralph asks.

Crane sips his water and looks straight at Ralph.

'We had to make doubly sure nothing *was* amiss because Mrs Pike's sister was constantly on the phone to us. Ruth Fletcher knew the chief constable through her charitable work, and she insisted that Mrs Pike's death should be investigated further. She believed Brandon Wells had murdered her.'

Chapter 43

At Waterloo, Julia nursed her hangover with a can of Coke and a bacon sandwich. They settled her stomach and gave her just enough energy to plod up the hill at the other end and back to the house. A journey that seemed longer and steeper than last time. She must be getting old.

On entering the house, she half expected a summons from Genevieve, like the previous week, but the kitchen was empty. She'd make a cup of tea to take to her room. The kettle had just boiled when Brandon came in, as if he'd been waiting for her return.

'Where's Gideon?' he asked.

'Dunno,' Julia said.

'You didn't spend the weekend with him?'

'What? Of course not.'

'But you must have caught the same train.'

How could he know that?

'Are you watching me?'

'I knew you were both going to London and heard you leave around about the same time,' Brandon said.

257

'I saw him on the train, then went to meet my friends. That's all.'

She hoped this would end the conversation. Brandon had other ideas.

'You must think I'm stupid,' he said. 'Me the other week, Gideon this. There's a word for girls like you. You really don't care, do you?'

He took a step towards her. Julia held her ground.

'Am I supposed to?'

'I heard what you said to Genevieve.'

'You *have* been spying on me then,' Julia said.

'Just happened to be passing the door.'

'Like you just happened to be looking out of the window when I left yesterday? Or did you follow me to the station?'

Brandon didn't answer.

'Oh my God, you did.'

'Don't turn this on me. You're the one being a bitch.'

'Ahh,' Julia said and put on a toddler's voice. 'Are you going to run and tell Genevieve? Will she pat your head, tell you you've been a good boy and give you more money? You need to grow up.'

She grabbed her tea, sloshing half of it across the countertop.

'Wipe that up,' Brandon said.

'Fuck off!'

Julia stamped up the stairs and slammed her bedroom door behind her.

Brandon was an idiot. She shouldn't let him get to her. *He'd* wanted to sleep with *her* and now she was a slut.

She didn't want tea now. Instead she lay down and put the pillow over her head. Pearl had been right about 'not on your own doorstep'. She'd made a mess of her new start. On Monday, she'd look for somewhere else to live. The PhD students might still have space under their floorboards.

It was only six o'clock, but she was exhausted and fell into bed without undressing or even washing her face.

She was woken by someone shouting her name.

'Julia!'

Outside it was still just about light.

'Julia!'

Someone was calling her from downstairs. Genevieve? She had no idea of the time. Perhaps early evening. Whatever the hour, she needed more sleep. She decided to ignore whoever it was, turned over and put the pillow over her head.

'Julia!'

It was Genevieve. Her voice was sharp, insistent, a contrast to her usual languid tones. Julia peeled the pillow from her head and sat up. Genevieve wasn't going to go away. She went to the door and pulled it open an inch.

'Is everything all right, Genevieve?' she called.

A pause.

'Would you come downstairs?'

Julia wasn't in the mood for any more of Genevieve's engineered dramas. She walked to the bannisters and leant over.

'I'm very tired, Genevieve. Can it wait?'

'No, Julia,' Genevieve said. 'You have to come now. The police have asked to speak to you.'

Chapter 44

The court erupts into chatter at Crane's utterance of the word 'murder'. Ralph looks surprised, despite knowing this was coming. I can't help but glance at Brandon's siblings. Their lips are pursed, their hands still intertwined. Their brother was a thief and now a murderer.

Ralph waits for the chatter to cease, before continuing. 'Let me get this right: Ruth Fletcher actually called the police station and accused Brandon Wells of killing her sister, Mrs Pike?'

'She did,' Crane says. 'Repeatedly.'

'And what reason did Mrs Fletcher give for this belief?'

'She had Mrs Pike's savings account book. It showed that Mrs Pike had made three separate withdrawals of fifteen thousand pounds in cash over the three weeks prior to her death.' Crane's eyes wander towards the gallery and Brandon's siblings. 'On the day Mrs Pike took her own life, Mrs Fletcher had been in London, consulting a lawyer. She was trying to put measures in place to protect her sister.'

'Was the money ever recovered?' Ralph asks.

'No, and it was assumed Brandon Wells had stolen it.'

'Did you agree with Mrs Fletcher?'

All chatter, shuffling and coughing has died away. Luke Crane has the court's full attention.

'About the theft, I did agree with her, yes. The evidence was pretty damning. He'd taken off with all his belongings. Inquiries were made, and we accessed Mr Wells' bank account. It had thirty-seven pounds fifty-six pence in it.'

'Would you tell the court the date of the last transaction?' Ralph asks.

'If I may refer to my notes.' Crane pulls out a pair of glasses and spends a moment reading from the sheets of paper next to him. 'The last transaction was on Saturday 20th August. Twenty pounds were removed from a cashpoint in Ealing. We decided that Brandon didn't need any money, not with forty-five thousand pounds in cash. I believe that's what my senior colleague, who's no longer with us, told Mr Patrick Wells when he contacted us and reported Brandon missing.'

A stifled yelp emanates from one of Brandon's siblings. Judge Fleetwood's eye is quick to turn upon them. They are hugging one another, both their faces hidden in the other's shoulders. He considers them a moment. The yelp was almost certainly an involuntary reaction to their distress. Fleetwood makes no comment and nods at Ralph to continue.

'At the time there was no suspicion or evidence that harm had come to Brandon?' he asks.

'A man who has stolen forty-five thousand pounds is unlikely to hang around. The only suspicion was that of theft.'

Ralph pauses and looks down at his notes.

'Let me get this right: Brandon was seen alive after the date of Mrs Pike's death, by his friend Grant McCluskey? If the housemates including my client had the money, they had no need to kill for it – and if Brandon had it, why would he return?'

'As I said, I was not involved in any second investigation beyond Mrs Pike's death and the missing money,' Crane says.

'We've established that the three defendants were the only people sharing the house at the time. But others had access to the property, didn't they?' Ralph says.

'That's not something I have recorded,' Crane says.

'Mrs Ruth Fletcher had keys to the property. And given her belief that Brandon Wells killed her sister, she had a strong motive to harm Brandon, wouldn't you say?'

'I'm not here to speculate as to Brandon Wells' murderer. I'm in court to tell you what I saw at the time.'

'Quite so. Thank you, Mr Crane,' Ralph says.

Chapter 45

1994 – Guildford

Julia ran down the stairs, barefoot. Genevieve was in the hall, leaning on the bureau to steady herself.

'What do the police want?' Julia asked. 'Has something happened to Mum?'

'What's your mother to do with it? They're in the dining room and are insisting on speaking to everyone about Gideon.'

Julia relaxed a fraction.

'Gideon – why?'

'I don't know. He left a couple of hours ago. Go, Julia. Go and speak to them. I want them out of my house.'

Genevieve was shaking. Julia put her hand out to comfort her. Genevieve drew back.

'Please, Julia, just do what they ask, so they'll go and leave us alone.'

Catching sight of her face in the hall mirror, Julia saw that her mascara had smudged, and her hair was tangled. Not a good look for a Sunday evening. She rubbed under her eyes to try to remove the smudges and scraped her hair into a bun before knocking on the door.

'Come in,' a gruff voice said.

The dining room was out of bounds to Genevieve's lodgers. She'd never been inside before. It was as she had glimpsed it, containing a large mahogany table and sideboard, with a carriage clock and delicate china vases on it.

Two policemen occupied the room, neither in uniform. The older one, with iron-grey hair and wearing a charcoal-coloured suit and brown tie, sat at the table. The younger one, in dark trousers, light blue shirt and no jacket, was standing looking over the drive and across to the Downs beyond. He spun round as she came in, as if her entrance were unexpected, when he must have heard her outside.

Julia stood at the door, unsure what to do.

'Sit down please, Miss ...'

'Winter,' she said. 'Julia Winter.'

'I'm Detective Sergeant Bellingham and this is Detective Constable Lewes,' the older policeman said.

'Why ... er ... what?'

'I understand you had a pleasant party on Friday night and last night, by the looks of it.' He gave an insincere smile. 'A barbecue was it? It's the right time of year.' He rubbed the ring finger of his left hand with his thumb. 'Can you confirm what time you started and finished?'

Julia's mind was fogged by sleep and she failed to see the importance of the question.

'People started arriving around seven. I've no idea what time we finished.'

Bellingham took notes with his right hand and continued to rub the finger on his left.

'Were you all in the house and garden the whole time?'

'Apart from our walk – we went out onto the Downs.'

'Together – all of you?'

'Yes.'

'And you returned to the house together?'

'Yes.'

'But Mr Risborough left after that, didn't he?'

With this question, Lewes' attention shifted from the window to her.

'I wasn't aware that he did,' she said. 'But it's not like I keep an eye on him.'

'Really, you're not an item?' Bellingham asked.

'Absolutely not – who said that?'

'Just the impression I got. My apologies, your relationship with Mr Risborough isn't the focus of our inquires.'

Julia was tired, irritable at being woken up and wanted to go back to bed.

'What is your focus?' she said.

'Mr Risborough's movements.'

'I told you, he was with us the whole time.'

'Are you sure? You were drinking and taking other substances perhaps – it's easy to lose track.'

That was it. Gideon was a drug dealer, the supplements business a front, the grass only a sample of a huge stash. They would all be implicated. A sick panic clenched Julia's stomach and forced her awake and alert.

'I wasn't aware of Gideon leaving.'

'So, you're not one hundred per cent certain?'

'I've told you. What's this about?'

'We'll get around to that.' Bellingham leant back in his chair. 'I'd like to go over what happened later, when everyone returned to the house?'

'We all went to bed,' Julia said. 'Alone, before you ask.'

'I'll take your word for it,' Bellingham said. 'But Mr

Risborough's room is directly under yours. You didn't hear him get up?'

Until Bellingham said this, Julia hadn't remembered Gideon's phone call in the garden. She wasn't sure what time it had been and anyway, Bellingham was annoying her. She wasn't going to help. Especially if she was going to incriminate herself.

'I only woke up when Genevieve knocked on the door.'

'Fair enough,' Bellingham said. 'One other detail – does the name Devon Garvey mean anything to you?'

She had heard the name before but she couldn't place it.

'No,' she said.

'Are you sure? This is rather a serious issue.' Bellingham looked straight at Julia, appraising her reaction. 'At around 4 a.m. on Saturday morning a fire broke out at Mr Garvey's house in Ripley. The fire brigade suspect arson. Fortunately, they'd spent the night away to attend a family wedding. You see how serious this is?'

Not drugs, arson and an attempt at something worse?

'Yes, but—'

'Mr Garvey has been in a long-standing business dispute with Mr Risborough and his godfather. They claim he owes them nearly eight thousand pounds.'

Now she could place the name. Gideon had told them about Garvey that night they ate pizza together and drank Chartreuse.

'I've never heard of him,' she said.

'Taking into account the seriousness of the situation, I'll ask you one more time,' Bellingham said. 'Can you confirm Gideon was here throughout the evening?'

Technically Gideon hadn't left the house. Going into the

garden to make a phone call didn't count. It's not as if he'd screeched his car onto the drive and come in reeking of petrol. She thought back to the phone call. What was wrong with it? Not the time in the morning, nor that Gideon had been in his boxers and T-shirt. She dismissed it. It wasn't important. And Bellingham irritated her, this pompous middle-aged man, with his ill-fitting suit and light sweat patches under the arm. Gideon probably made him jealous. He was young, good-looking, could have lots of girlfriends, if he'd wanted. Unlike Bellingham, whose ringless finger, recently ringless if his body language was anything to go by – continually rubbing it with his thumb – probably went home to beans on toast and a cat.

'I've told you, as far as I know, Gideon was here all night. If this Garvey bloke hasn't paid Gideon, he probably owes money to lots of other people.'

'Other people didn't go to Mr Garvey's house and threaten him in front of his wife and children.'

Julia was going to speak again, then stopped. This didn't sound like Gideon. She couldn't imagine him angry or menacing. He had probably gone to the man's house to reason with him, and Garvey had exaggerated the encounter to the police.

'Why do you believe this man and not Gideon? He'd never do anything like that. You say it was a coincidence the family being away, but was it? He's in debt. He could have sent his family away and torched the place for the insurance.'

'You can leave the detective work to us, thank you, Miss,' Lewes said. 'All we want from you are the facts.'

'Which I've already given you. Has anyone said Gideon wasn't here all night?'

The two detectives looked at each other. Julia sensed their indecision.

'If there's nothing else, I'll go,' Julia said.

Bellingham gave a reluctant nod. Julia left and shut the door behind her.

Genevieve was sitting on the bottom stair, her hands clasped in a knot of anxiety. This time she allowed Julia to place a hand on her shoulder.

'What's the matter? You're not worried about Gideon are you? I think they're just making inquiries. He's not really a suspect or anything.'

'It's not that.' Genevieve's voice was faint and breathless. 'It's just, when they turned up here and showed me their identification, I thought ... I thought ...'

Genevieve's breaths came fast and shallow.

'Thought what, Genevieve?' Julia asked.

'I thought they'd come about Dominic. Like the last time. Oh, I couldn't bear it, not again.'

'I don't understand.'

'If they'd found his body – what then?' She spread her hands. 'He's alive. I know it. Whatever they told me. If he'd been killed, they would have found the body.'

Julia wanted to tell her the truth. That many, many people go missing in the mountains every year and their bodies are never found. Perhaps some of them do fake their own deaths and turn up years later at an Indian ashram. But most of them fall down a crevasse and are covered in snow and rock, making it too dangerous to search. If Dominic was still alive, he would have made his way home by now.

She looked at Genevieve. She was so thin, so fragile. It wasn't the time for tough love.

'This is just about Gideon. And no one's been hurt. Why don't you go and get some sleep – try to forget about it?'

Genevieve nodded but didn't move. Julia placed an arm around her and pulled her to her feet, then led her upstairs to her attic bedroom. She'd imagined Genevieve's bedroom to be some nineteenth-century boudoir, with silk scarves draped as a canopy above the bed, ornate mirrors and candlesticks. But it was plain, white being the predominant colour. A double bed was pushed under the slope of the eaves and most of what could have been standing room was taking up with a large oak wardrobe.

Julia coaxed Genevieve towards the bed, placed her down and removed her shoes. Genevieve lay down, obediently. Julia felt like a mother putting a young child to bed. She was about to pull the covers up when Genevieve said, 'Wait.'

She pushed herself onto her elbows and turned to the narrow side table, on which a lamp, a glass of water and a small bottle of pills stood. The bottle was already open. Genevieve took two small white pills and swallowed them with some water.

'Don't tell Ruth,' Genevieve said.

The bottle had no label and Julia wondered if it had been bought illegally.

'Try to get some sleep,' she said.

Genevieve closed her eyes and slid down under the duvet. 'Turn the lamp on, will you, Julia? I hate the dark.'

Julia switched it on. She watched Genevieve sink into the pillow and close her eyes before she crept down the attic-room stairs.

Where the hell was Gideon and how had he managed to drag all of them into this mess? She had enough to worry about with Brandon. The whole day had been a disaster.

She'd go to sleep and forget about it. She returned to bed, but she couldn't sleep. She lay looking out at the dark shadow of the Downs. Genevieve wasn't her responsibility. She was an adult, Audrey's age. She couldn't imagine her mother quivering under a duvet, reliant on sleeping pills. Genevieve should just pull herself together.

An hour later, she was still awake. Cursing herself for caring, she got up and went downstairs to the phone, clutching Ruth's number on a scrap of paper. She had started dialling when the dining-room door opened. Brandon came out.

'Who are you calling at this time of night?'

She put the phone down before it rang. 'None of your business.'

'Tell me.'

Julia turned to walk up the stairs. She wasn't making the call with Brandon standing over her. He blocked her path and snatched the paper from her hand.

'Hey,' Julia said. 'You've no right.'

'Why are you calling Ruth?'

'Are you the policeman now?'

He held the paper up, fingering it, as if the digits held some clue as to how he should act.

'I guess you're worried about Genevieve,' he said.

'She was really upset tonight. All of that stuff with the police reminded her of when they came to tell her Dominic had died. I had to put her to bed.'

'I'll go and check on her,' he said. 'No need to call Ruth.'

'I think she really needs someone from her family.'

'Ruth will take her pills away and make things worse.'

'How do you know?'

'Do you know how many times I've had to put her to bed?'

Julia didn't want to think about it. 'She shouldn't be taking those things. They don't even have a label.'

'It's more dangerous to stop suddenly – trust me, I've seen it.'

Julia looked at the phone. She had a good memory for numbers and didn't need the piece of paper to phone Ruth. Would Brandon physically stop her if she tried?

'I know you're trying to help Genevieve,' he said. 'But I know how to deal with her.'

Brandon wasn't going to move. Julia's courage failed her. She returned to her room. Brandon followed her up the stairs then continued up the next flight to Genevieve's room.

She couldn't believe that only a couple of nights ago, she'd been feeling sorry for Brandon. She should stand up to him. Get up now, go downstairs and call Ruth. But something about Brandon, looming over her, had frightened her. She imagined what would happen if he caught her a second time. For all his clumping about the house, he could move quietly when he wanted to. He'd managed to eavesdrop when she'd been telling Genevieve she'd never be his girlfriend. She dared herself to get up and phone Ruth. Instead, she pulled the duvet over her head like a child hiding from the monster in the wardrobe. It was none of her business. She could mention it to Ruth next time she saw her.

You're a coward, Julia Winter, she thought. You're a coward.

Chapter 46

Anyone entering courtroom one at Guildford Crown Court, without knowledge of the case, would assume Grant McCluskey was on trial. He fiddles with his cuffs and glances around the room, a film of sweat on his bald head reflecting the overhead lights.

Mapplethorpe softens his face and smiles, in an attempt to calm him.

'Would you please explain to the court your relationship with Brandon, Mr McCluskey?'

'We were school friends, from back home in New Zealand.'

His speaks in a loud but shaking voice, only a wisp of his New Zealand accent left in the occasional long vowel.

'And when did you first come to the UK?'

'In 1992.'

'And Brandon?'

'The year after.'

'He came to stay with you – is that correct?' Mapplethorpe asks.

'He wanted to sleep on the sofa for a few weeks until he got settled. He ended up staying several months, before he moved to Guildford. After that, he'd call sometimes or come over and we'd go out for a beer.'

'And when was the last time you saw Brandon?' Mapplethorpe asks.

McCluskey runs two fingers round the back of his collar, then rubs them together.

'It was the August bank holiday, Saturday, 1994,' he says. 'Brandon had been staying over at mine for a few days, said he'd fallen out with his landlady – not sure why. He was supposed to be picking his stuff up and coming back afterwards.'

'And did he?'

'No, I never saw or heard from him again,' McCluskey says. 'I rang the number he'd given me for the house a few times. No one answered. I wasn't worried – thought he'd changed his mind. The next thing I knew, the police turned up. They were looking for Brandon, said he'd stolen some money. Then it all made sense, him not coming back. I supposed he must have gone home.'

'And when did you become aware that wasn't the case?' Mapplethorpe asks.

'The next year. That would be 1995. I'd moved from Ealing to South London, Clapham. So, I guess Patrick, that's Brandon's father, didn't have my number. This guy turned up – a private detective.'

'This would be Michael Lancaster,' Mapplethorpe says to the jury.

'Yeah, well, Michael Lancaster said Brandon's family were worried. I thought they were making a fuss over nothing. Brandon's always done what he wanted. Hiring a private investigator seemed way over the top.' McCluskey pauses and takes a few breaths. 'My girlfriend was pregnant at the time, we were in the process of moving again, out to Essex this time. So, Brandon wouldn't have been able to contact me anyway, wouldn't have known where I was and, I must admit, I never thought about him, until last year, when the police turned up again.'

'Let's go back to 1994,' Mapplethorpe says. 'To reiterate, Brandon left your house on Saturday 27th August 1994. He said he was going to Guildford to pick a few things up and that's the last time we know that anyone saw him alive.'

'As far as I know.'

'Mr McCluskey, did Brandon ever tell you about the house, the other lodgers, whether they got on.'

'At first he loved it, said the landlady was like an auntie and made a big fuss of him and the place was amazing – a huge house with a lovely garden. He never got used to London, being from the country, and our house was pretty run down. The heating was constantly packing up and no one ever cleaned. You know what it's like in your twenties.'

'So, he was happy in Guildford?' Mapplethorpe asks.

'Yeah, until he got a crush on some girl in the house. He thought it was going to turn into something, but she gave him the cold shoulder. He never told me her name. He wasn't one to go on about his feelings, but I could tell he was pretty down. He'd had a bad break-up with a woman back home. I guess it reminded him of that. Like I said, he didn't say much. But I noticed he was drinking more. I mean, he always drank a lot. But when he came over, he'd be on the beer straight after lunch.'

At the time, I saw Brandon as someone who got up at noon and spent most of the day drunk. I barely credited him with being capable of deeper emotions. Looking back, I see a young man, lonely and depressed, gravitating towards Genevieve, as a mother figure, because no one else showed him any kindness.

'Did he mention anything about the other housemates?' Mapplethorpe asks.

'He said both the guys were wankers.' I resist the smile tugging at the corners of my mouth. 'They used to slag him off behind his back, because his auntie always favoured him, and then she started being weird and making him feel uncomfortable.'

'In what way?' Mapplethorpe puts on his most concerned face.

'She was a flake,' McCluskey says. 'Treated him as a replacement son, wanted to take care of him. He liked it at first. Then she became more intense, started touching him, just his arm and stuff, but he didn't think it was an entirely motherly interest anymore, if you know what I mean.'

'And you knew that Brandon was not paying rent?'

'No, but it doesn't surprise me.'

'Why not?' Mapplethorpe asks.

McCluskey's eyes flick towards the balcony and Brandon's family, then back to his cuffs.

'Mr McCluskey?' Mapplethorpe prompts.

McCluskey takes a deep breath. 'I hate to say it, but Brandon was always a bit of a freeloader. You'd be lucky if he got a round in. I know that pissed off the other lodgers. He'd heard them slagging him off. One of the reasons he wanted to move out,' McCluskey says. 'That last time he came over, he was in a bad way. Drinking too much, stoned the whole time. One of the guys I shared with, Andy, was moving in with his

275

girlfriend and I told Brandon he could have the room if he paid rent. Three months in advance, because I knew what he was like.'

'And he agreed?' Mapplethorpe asks.

'Said he'd have to go back to Guildford and pick up his stuff and get some money.'

'And that was the last time you saw him?'

'I never heard from him again,' McCluskey says.

'Thank you. No further questions.'

Ralph allows Mapplethorpe time to rearrange his papers before he stands up.

'Just a few questions, Mr McCluskey,' he says.

By now, McCluskey's less nervous and is able to look at the jury rather than his shirt cuffs.

'Would you say you were surprised about the original accusation of theft levelled at your friend?' Ralph asks.

Grant shuffles and darts another look at Brandon's siblings. 'Not really. He'd been in trouble before. One of the reasons he left New Zealand in the first place. And then again in London, he got involved with a married woman. She was wealthy, older, gave him presents, including cash. But she found out he was seeing other women, came to the house and demanded he hand it all back, threatened to tell her husband about him. That's when he went to his auntie's.'

'You mean Jennifer Pike?'

'Yes.'

'For the record' – Ralph addresses the jury – 'Mr Wells and Mrs Pike were not related. One more thing, Mr McCluskey, did Brandon ever mention Ruth Fletcher, Mrs Pike's sister?'

'Yeah. She was hassling him about not paying rent or something. I don't remember exactly.'

276

'Thank you, Mr McCluskey. No further questions.'

Neither Gideon's nor Alan's barrister have any questions. Ralph nods to me, to let me know it's all going to plan.

I shift in my seat, aware of Brandon's sister staring at me. 'He got a crush on some girl in the house ... but she gave him the cold shoulder.' Not how I remember it. But I'm in a court of law and can only defend myself in an allotted spot. Something my lawyer has advised me to decline. To them I shall remain heartless, shallow and, no doubt, guilty.

Chapter 47

1995 – Archway, London

Pearl had taken the lightshade with her before handing the room over to Julia, and the naked bulb made the drab room still drabber. Its harsh light cast a faint shadow across the careworn carpet as Julia moved about, tidying her few belongings, before checking one last time that the contents of the folder were correct and the envelope containing it addressed and sealed. Only when she had finished her tasks did she down half a bottle of vodka. People would realise, she hoped, that she'd got drunk to give her courage after she had made her decision, not before.

Outside, a dense fog, which had hung over the city all day, was pierced by fine drizzle. The streetlamps barely penetrated its gloom. Her final wish, a view across London, hadn't been granted. Then again, the fog could be her friend. Fewer people would be out in this weather, at this hour. Her only encounters on her walk up Archway Road were drunks, huddled in the murky corners of shop doorways, singing into their cans of Special Brew. Of course, Brandon was behind her at all times. His heavy tread upon the pavement, the slight wheeze from smokers' lungs. It would stop soon. When he got what he wanted.

The drizzle turned to rain, splashing on the pavements and driving into her face and eyes, blurring and blinding her in turn. Her dress was sodden. She'd chosen a pretty silk one, bought for a cousin's wedding – Audrey's upbringing guiding her to the last: *You have to look smart.*

The journey was further than she remembered. Her ballet pumps gave her no grip and the vodka unsteadied her. Still she kept to her purpose.

At the roundabout, she attempted to cross the road. It was impossible to see traffic in the gloom. She was halfway across one carriageway when her feet slid from beneath her and she sprawled across the tarmac. A screech of brakes and a lorry's headlights fell upon her. It blasted its horn.

'Are you trying to kill yourself?' the driver yelled from the window.

Julia got to her feet. The man was winding up the window, as quickly as he had unwound it. She ran the rest of the way across the road without looking back and carried on to Archway Road, up and up. Until she reached the narrow steps to the bridge. The fog was too thick to see the arch above.

Brandon had kept pace with her. Though he never revealed himself, she could hear his tread above the rain and traffic and every blurred outline of a man turned into a hulking ghost.

She toiled up the bridge's steps, slipping on every second one, before she finally arrived on top of the vast expanse, the fog preventing any visual reference. Her tired limbs and the faint rumble of traffic below were her only indication of its height.

As she started to climb the iron struts to the side, she heard footsteps coming from either end of the bridge. One heavy trudge she recognised, the others were accompanied by the chatter of young women, slightly muffled by the dense air.

Where had they come from? She needed to hurry. Her fingers slipped beneath the wet metal. She tried to stand up. She wobbled. Shouts. 'She's going to jump.'

Julia turned to see the two women. She didn't have to jump. She could just let go. Her fingers, only seconds ago so feeble, grasped tight and wouldn't release. She tried to relax her grip. It remained firm against her will.

Two sets of arms wrapped around her, dragged her backwards and brought her to the ground. Her head banged on the stone paving. One of the girls sat on top of her.

'I'll stay with her. Run and call an ambulance.'

The use of restraint was unnecessary. All Julia's strength had gone. Her ears were ringing from the knock to her head, which lolled to one side. For a moment the figure of a man appeared in the thin shard of light from one of the lamp posts, before being engulfed by the fog.

Chapter 48

1994 – Guildford

The atmosphere at Downsview Villa had changed over-night, from the easy camaraderie they'd shared on the Downs to something brittle, nervous and tense.

Julia had seen Gideon on the driveway getting into his BMW and heard him playing music in the room beneath hers but had yet to speak to him since the police came. Genevieve was similarly elusive and didn't leave her room. Julia was only aware of her presence because of the occasional glimpse of Ruth going up and down the stairs to the attic, her face set grim and stern.

Brandon had returned to his usual rise late, drink early routine and it was a surprise to find him in the kitchen with Gideon and Alan, sitting at the table when she came home. Alan looked agitated. Gideon's expression was unreadable.

Brandon turned from the table when Julia entered and came towards her, thrusting a mobile phone in her face before she was fully through the door.

'Do you like my new toy?' Brandon said.

Julia pushed the phone away. She was still angry with him,

for stopping her calling Ruth. She was even angrier with herself for letting him.

'Only city spivs and drug dealers have mobile phones,' she said.

'Are you suggesting owning a mobile phone is suspicious?'

He said it in a voice of mock outrage and tossed a glance at Gideon.

'Watch it,' Alan said.

His voice was strained and anxious, but Brandon wasn't listening and seemed to be enjoying himself.

There must be a specific reason for his being in the kitchen now, at six o'clock on a weekday evening, with Gideon and Alan.

'What's going on?' she asked.

Neither Gideon nor Alan replied.

'Where did you get that phone? Did Genevieve give it to you?'

'I don't rely on Genevieve for everything, you know. This was given to me by a mate.'

'You don't have any mates,' Alan said.

'Alan, you're breaking my heart,' Brandon said. 'I thought we were friends. Like me and Julia.'

He placed his arm across Julia's shoulders. He stank of beer and tobacco. She shrugged him off.

'Oh, don't want to be friends anymore?' Brandon said. 'Never mind, I've got a new friend.'

'Shut up,' Gideon said. His voice was barely above a whisper.

Brandon walked over to the table and leant on it, his face bent towards Gideon's.

'What was that, old chap?' he said, mimicking Gideon's accent.

'I said, shut up.'

'But Julia wants to hear about my new friend, don't you, Jules?' Brandon said.

'No, I don't.'

She tried to leave the kitchen, but he moved away from the table and blocked her path.

'Hey,' Gideon said.

'It's all right.' Brandon stood back and held his hands up in the air in surrender. 'I'm not touching her.'

Julia was nearly at the door when Brandon said, 'His name's Karl Brier, my new mate. It's *Karl Brier*. I think Gideon knows him.'

Julia caught Gideon's eye. There was a click of mutual comprehension, then she looked away and continued out of the room. She took the stairs two at a time. She was on the first landing when she saw Gideon come out of the kitchen and leave by the front door.

By the time she got to her room, he had driven away.

That split second of understanding between them, with the mobile phone and Brandon's delight in Gideon's discomfort, had made everything fall into place. Gideon had been alarmed when he'd found out she'd woken up the night they'd been to the Downs, the one the police had questioned her about. Was it because he suspected she'd seen him talking into a phone at the end of the garden? Because she remembered now what had been wrong, why something didn't fit. Gideon had been standing too far out of range to use the cordless house phone. It barely worked in the kitchen. Gideon had a mobile. Or used to have a mobile. One she'd never seen. One he'd used to make or receive a phone call early on Saturday morning. If she'd read the look between Brandon and Gideon correctly, it was the same phone Brandon held now. Had he found it hidden at the bottom of the garden, or had he gone into Gideon's room? Either way, it was clear the person Gideon had been speaking to was Karl Brier.

Gideon had been so insistent they stayed with him that evening. The police had to revise their suspicions because so many people had seen Gideon that night. He couldn't have torched Devon Garvey's place. But he could have phoned someone and told them to do it. Someone called Karl Brier.

Chapter 49

Considering nearly a quarter of a century has passed, the next witness is remarkably unchanged. Michael Lancaster remains solid and upright, his face line-free. He is confident before the court and knows to address the jury, not the barrister asking questions.

'I first heard of Brandon Wells in September 1995,' he says. 'When I received a call from a Mr Patrick Wells in New Zealand. He told me his son had been missing for more than a year. The police weren't interested. Mr Wells wanted to find him, but didn't know where to start.'

'And you agreed to help him?' Mapplethorpe asks.

Lancaster pulls a face, halfway between a grimace and a smile. 'In general, I'm dubious about missing person cases,' he says. 'But Brandon's struck me as genuine. I checked out what Mr Wells told me about the house, spoke to Grant McCluskey and set about finding the others. It wasn't like today where everyone is two clicks away on the internet. Back then you had to do your groundwork.'

He pulls at his jacket lapels, evincing a sense of pride in his professional proficiency.

'And what did you discover?' Mapplethorpe asks.

'I tracked them all down in the end.' Lancaster casts an eye across the defendants' bench. 'Alan Johns was aggressive and refused to answer any questions. Gideon Risborough was friendlier, though no more helpful and Ms Winter looked like she'd seen a ghost.'

The jury's attention turns to me. I try to maintain a neutral face as I recall the heavy footsteps that followed me through the streets of North London the year after I moved from Guildford.

Lancaster resumes. 'During my investigation, it became clear I was not the only one who had been trying to track down Ms Winter. Gideon Risborough was following her, and I think probably long before I did. He was watching her as she went to and from work, waiting outside her house.'

The shrinking shadow, the footsteps on empty streets – it wasn't a ghost or a manifestation of my guilt, it was Gideon who haunted me, drove me to that bridge over the A1. Right now, he's staring straight ahead. Others would see him as calm and impassive, but I notice his jaw is ever so slightly clenched.

'If Ms Winter went out, he used to knock on the door of the house she was sharing, pretend to be a friend and gain access. It's an easy trick to pull in multiple occupancy houses – no one ever quite knows who knows who,' Lancaster says. 'At the time, I wasn't sure. I put it down to infatuation.'

But it wasn't infatuation. Gideon was terrified I would crack, tell someone. Had he planned an accident for me? I was so close to doing his work for him. He must have been furious when those girls appeared and stopped me. I realise now the identity of the man who ran from the bridge. But not to be defeated, he constructed another plan to keep me silent and ensure no letter was ever sent to Patrick Wells.

'And Ms Winter – how long did you observe her before talking to her?' Mapplethorpe asks.

'A couple of days. She worked long hours in two jobs, didn't seem to have any friends. I felt a bit sorry for her. When I spoke to her, she looked terrified and scuttled into the house. About ten minutes later Gideon knocked at the door. It was the first time he'd entered the house when she'd been there. I don't think he realised that just as he was watching me, I was watching him. That behaviour did ring alarm bells. There was something holding those three together.'

The lad in the blue hoody on the front row of the jury nods his head.

'Apart from their rather odd behaviour, did anything else lead you to be suspicious?' Mapplethorpe asks.

'Firstly, there was the money. It just turned up – nearly thirty thousand pounds.'

'The money correlating to a two-thirds share in the sum taken from Mrs Pike,' Mapplethorpe says.

'Exactly. The police explanation for Brandon's disappearance was that he had stolen the cash withdrawn by Mrs Pike and run. As far as they were concerned, he was probably living the life of Riley on one of the Costas.' Lancaster clears his throat. 'But anyone walking around with forty-five thousand pounds' cash is vulnerable, even a strong young man like Brandon. There's two rules private investigators fall back on. One, *cherchez la femme*, and two, follow the money. Love and lust skew the most rational mind. In this case it turned out to be both.'

'Would you tell the court what you uncovered?' Mapplethorpe asks.

Lancaster clears his throat again. 'I managed to get hold of the accounts for Mr Risborough's company, SupaSupplements – that's the nutritional supplements company owned by Mr Risborough and for which Alan Johns still works. They'd attended an awful lot of trade fairs.'

'And that was unusual?' Mapplethorpe asks.

'It only started a few months after Brandon's disappearance. They were doing a roaring trade, all in cash. Over four months, thirty thousand pounds was passed through the company.'

'Couldn't that be legitimate?'

'Other companies attending these events made nowhere near as much money, despite their stands being much busier.'

'That's a shortfall of fifteen thousand pounds from the amount we know was taken from Mrs Pike,' Mapplethorpe says.

'I figured Ms Winter had the rest. Thirty thousand represented a two-thirds share for both Gideon Risborough and Alan Johns. I did report my findings to the police, but they weren't interested. By then it was two years since Brandon had disappeared and with no body it was difficult to interest anyone. Besides, private investigators are given short shrift. They've changed their tune since then though. It turns out I was right. Follow the money.'

Lancaster is looking pleased with himself when Mapplethorpe sits down. Gideon's barrister, Helena Dryden, wastes no time in her cross-examination.

'May I ask you, Mr Lancaster, how much Mr Patrick Wells paid you to investigate the disappearance of his son?'

'I don't recall exactly,' Lancaster says.

'Then let me remind you. In total it came to £19,482. In 1994 that was more than the average yearly salary.'

'I am a professional. I don't work for free.'

'That's evident,' Dryden says. 'Mr Wells was in New Zealand, entirely reliant on what you told him. All this sneaking around trawling through accounts and stalking young women at night—'

'Following,' Lancaster interjects.

'If that's what you choose to call it,' Dryden says. 'Tell me, what would have happened if you'd gone back to Mr Wells after a day or two and said, sorry, I can't help you, the police are in the best position to deal with this?'

'But I could help him.'

'We only have your word for it. Lots of surmises and guesswork but nothing concrete. No proof the money wasn't from trade shows.'

'No, but the facts suggest—'

Dryden cuts him off. 'Mr Lancaster. This is a court of law. We're not interested in suggestion. We're interested in evidence and cold hard facts.' She pauses and half turns to the jury. 'Be honest with yourself, and with the court please. If there were any corroborating evidence whatsoever, it would be here.' Dryden jabs a finger to the floor. 'In this courtroom, in front of the jury. Instead the supporting evidence is notable only by its absence.'

Lancaster looks to the judge, who shows no indication he's going to interrupt Dryden.

'You've presented nothing but the suspicions of a man who couldn't hack it as a real detective in CID.'

Lancaster grips the front of the witness stand and pulls himself so he's leaning over. 'That's simply not true,' he says.

Dryden looks down at her notes and back to Lancaster. 'You were asked to leave the CID, were you not?'

'No – it wasn't like that.'

'At the time of your resignation you were under investigation for misconduct,' Dryden says.

'A flawed investigation, my DI at the time—'

'Mishandling of evidence.' She waves a piece of paper in the air. 'It's not surprising your former colleagues gave you short shrift – your words, not mine, Mr Lancaster.'

'I was well respect—'

'Thank you, Mr Lancaster. No further questions.'

Lancaster is no longer looking so pleased with himself. He looks like he's been punched in the stomach, and is visibly distressed when he realises yet more questioning is to come.

Ralph stands up and looks at him kindly. 'Mr Lancaster, you talk of following the money, but at no stage during the Nineties did you find my client, Julia Winter, had come into any money, other than the wages from the jobs she needed to support herself.'

His tone is mild and moderate; still Lancaster eyes him warily.

'No, I didn't,' Lancaster says.

'In fact, working two jobs would indicate financial hardship not new-found wealth, wouldn't it?'

Lancaster lowers his head and doesn't speak for a moment. Eventually, he mumbles something.

'Sorry, Mr Lancaster, can you repeat that?'

'I said, yes.'

'I see,' Ralph says.

For a moment I think this is going to be his only question.

He pauses before casting his eyes down to his notes and looking up again.

'You've been a private investigator for nearly thirty years – is that correct?' he asks.

'Yes,' Lancaster says.

He's on his guard now, not sure from which angle the blow will land.

'And what sort of investigations do you normally carry out – you've already told us you don't normally take missing persons cases.'

Lancaster purses his lips. 'All sorts,' he says. 'Husbands and wives seeking proof of their other half's infidelity. Larger companies often ask for extra information about candidates for key positions. Debt recovery.' He gives a slight shrug.

'Ah, yes. Debt recovery,' Ralph says. He raises a sheet of paper. 'In fact, nearly eighty per cent of your work is for Longs Debt Recovery. Tracking down people who've fallen into arrears on hire purchase and other such agreements. Average amount of debt, seven hundred pounds and twenty-three pence. Although my learned colleagues implied your sole motivation is money and certainly you did take a considerable amount from Mr Patrick Wells.'

'*Earned* a considerable amount,' Lancaster says.

'My apologies. Although you *earned* a considerable sum, I don't agree that all your actions were prompted by greed, were they?'

'I do have my professional pride,' Lancaster says.

'And you continued your investigations into the defendants, and my client in particular, long after Mr Wells' payments ceased.'

Lancaster hesitates.

'You are under oath, Mr Lancaster,' Ralph says.

'I did take an interest in their lives,' Lancaster concedes.

He's a different man to the one questioned by Mapplethorpe. His swagger's gone; he's almost timid.

'Over the next twenty years, in fact.' Ralph looks directly at him. Lancaster is unable to maintain eye contact. 'It speaks of obsession more than interest.'

'Not an obsession,' Lancaster says. 'If work was slow, I'd look into what they were up to. That's how I found out about the money and Ms Winter's suicide attempt.'

No – not this, not now. Hissed words circle the court. I make myself look to Sam. He's gazing across at me. His expression is blank, with hate, shock, incomprehension – it's impossible to read. He shouldn't have had to hear it like this. I want to be with him now, explain, tell him everything's all right. He looks away. I close my eyes – this has to end. I have to speak to Sam.

Ralph continues to cross-examine Lancaster, but I can't register what they're saying. I can only think of Sam. What must he think of me? Are his father's claims of my instability and mental frailty gaining credence?

'I've been a fool. I should have realised there's a reason men don't marry women like you – because of the sort of mothers they'll make,' my husband told me. 'I'll keep it from Sam as long as I can, but one day I'll let him know, who or rather what his mother is.'

In Victorian times, a failed suicide meant jail. With my marriage, I imprisoned myself.

'... Ms Winter's phone number.'

What are they saying about my phone number? I must concentrate.

'Last year, you made calls to Ms Winter's phone on Wednesday 4th October at 11.12 a.m. lasting six seconds and again on Friday 6th October at 10.48 p.m., lasting eleven seconds,' Ralph says.

Lancaster's eyes dart around the courtroom. Mapplethorpe is looking to his junior.

'Mr Lancaster?' Ralph says.

'I did call her.'

'Can you tell us why you made this phone call, twenty-three years after your last direct contact with Ms Winter?'

Lancaster doesn't reply.

'It's dull in debt recovery, isn't it?' Ralph says. 'Following one person, who's unable to make a ten pounds weekly repayment to another. Making people in desperate circumstances more desperate.'

'Your honour,' Mapplethorpe says.

'My point, Mr Lancaster,' Ralph says without waiting for the judge to intercede, 'is that you became a private detective, fancying yourself in a heroic role, solving crimes too complex for PC Plod. Instead it's unendingly tedious. For your own amusement and because you have some fascination with Ms Winter, you concoct a complicated scenario in which three of Brandon Wells' housemates are his murderers. Over the years, as your paid work becomes more and more boring, you return to Brandon Wells, the one big case that will vindicate your worth and prove you're smarter than your former colleagues at Surrey Police. And one day, bingo – you hit the jackpot. By lucky chance you're right, Brandon was murdered. Emboldened, you begin to follow Ms Winter. I'll leave it to the jury's imaginations why you chose Ms Winter and not the two men. You try to frighten her with phone calls and implicate her in the crime by sending texts with links to the case.'

'That's just not true. I never sent any texts.'

'But you admit to the phone calls.'

'Yes.'

'Minutes after DI Warren and DS Akande left Ms Winter's flat, were you waiting outside, watching her?'

Lancaster looks to the judge to help him. Fleetwood shows no signs of intervening.

'If we were to triangulate the location of your phone over this period, where would we find it?'

Lancaster still doesn't reply.

'Please answer the question, Mr Lancaster, and, as a former police officer, I'm sure you don't need reminding of the serious view courts take of perjury.'

Lancaster tips his head forward and grimaces. 'I waited outside Ms Winter's work and sometimes outside her flat,' Lancaster says.

'What was the purpose of the calls?'

The woman in the floral dress is watching intently. Her eyes narrow.

'I'm not sure – I just wanted her to know that someone knew,' Lancaster replies.

The woman gives a dismissive shake of the head.

'And how long had you been following Ms Winter?'

'Since I heard about the body being found on the Downs. I guessed straight away it was Brandon. I wanted to observe her behaviour. And it *was* odd.'

'Not as odd as yours,' Ralph says. Blue hoody nods again. 'Following a woman around late at night, phone calls, texts—'

'It wasn't like that.' Lancaster looks to the judge and then the jury. 'I never sent those texts. They weren't on my phone, were they?'

'You were careless with the phone calls,' Ralph says. 'Did the other messages come from another phone you have since disposed of?'

'She was the one who got rid of her phone. I saw her. She bought it from a drug dealer. The police were too slow and never found it.'

Ralph raises his palms in a gesture of incredulity. 'I fear we're drifting further into the realms of fantasy, Mr Lancaster. My client works as an IT professional. She has no links to the criminal underworld. You, on the other hand, obtained her phone details and bank statements, almost certainly in an illegal manner – I can see you're not contradicting me – stalked, yes stalked my client late at night, then sent her threatening texts and followed them up by making wild accusations.'

'I did not send those texts,' Lancaster repeats.

'We're to believe there's another person out there, harassing my client about the events of twenty-four years ago? A little far-fetched, don't you think?'

Lancaster grips the bar in front of him, his head bowed. 'I know what it sounds like, but it's the truth.'

'May I suggest that in future you leave it to the professionals to find the truth,' Ralph says. 'It was the mishandling of evidence that led to your removal from the police force. How would your behaviour, trying to provoke a reaction, sending messages and threats, have been treated in CID? There's a reason your skills are only required for debt recovery. Thank you, Mr Lancaster. I have no further questions.'

Chapter 50

Another summer storm hit Guildford on Thursday evening as Julia walked home from work, the rain coming down in torrents. At least this time she was armed with an umbrella, so only her feet were soaked. As she neared home, she saw a girl at the top of the drive. She stood gazing at the house, in just a thin cotton summer dress, without an umbrella or even a coat. Julia considered ignoring her. Her sole wish was to get indoors and dry off. But the girl looked lost and very young, only a teenager. Julia walked up to her.

'Can I help you?' she asked.

The girl didn't seem to notice and continued to stare at the house. Julia tried again.

'Are you all right?'

This time the girl turned to her and gave a slight shake of the head. She had a long oval face with almond-shaped eyes.

'Why don't you come inside, out of the rain?' Julia said.

The girl took a tiny step forward, then stopped.

'It's OK,' Julia said.

She took the girl's hand and led her down the drive to the

side door, through the garage and into the kitchen. Gideon's light was on. Julia wondered if he'd seen her.

'I'll get you a towel,' Julia said.

Music was coming from Gideon's room as she ran upstairs to retrieve the towel. The girl hadn't moved and was still staring vacantly when Julia came back.

'Here.'

Julia wrapped the towel around her shoulders. The girl looked so young.

'Are you in some sort of trouble? Can I call someone for you?'

The movement of her head was so slight, Julia couldn't tell if it was a yes or a no.

'Do you want to use the phone?'

This time the girl signalled a definite no.

'I'm here to see Gideon,' she said.

'I think he's in – you should have knocked,' Julia said.

For the first time, the girl looked at Julia directly.

'I did knock.'

Her eyes looked empty and cold. Julia recoiled. She shouldn't have invited a stranger into the house, even if she was a lost teenage girl. She could be anyone.

'His music's on. Maybe he didn't hear you,' Julia said. 'I'll bang on the door.'

Once in the hall Julia hesitated. Maybe Gideon didn't want to be disturbed. He rarely played music. But then, what would she say to the girl? She decided Gideon could deal with her. And if he wouldn't, she'd give her an umbrella and ask her to leave.

Julia rapped on the door. The music's volume dropped and Gideon came out.

'What's up?' He was smiling and relaxed.

'There's someone here to see you,' Julia said. 'A girl. She looks a bit upset.'

Gideon's smile disappeared. 'Why did you let her in?'

'I couldn't leave her out there in the rain,' Julia said.

'Where is she?'

'The kitchen.'

He nearly knocked Julia over in his rush to get there. Julia steadied herself, then followed him as far as the door. The girl was still sitting on the bench, her dripping clothes forming a puddle of water on the floor.

'I told you not to come here, Leanne.' Gideon's voice was low and harsh.

'I didn't know where else to go.'

Leanne stopped and looked to Julia.

'Do you mind?' Gideon said. 'I need to discuss this in private.' He slammed the door shut.

Julia went to her room. Gideon had looked furious. And Leanne, Julia wasn't sure. She had a vacant quality. Perhaps she had mental health problems. Julia removed her sandals and dried her feet. The murmur of voices drifted up from below, though what they said was unintelligible.

About three minutes later, the side door banged and moments after that Gideon turned his music up to full volume. Julia watched from her window and saw Leanne walk up the drive alone. She looked as forlorn as before. At the top of the drive she turned to look back at the house, before heading away, down the hill.

Julia thought of her rejection by Christian. His cold response to her requests to speak to him, just one more time. 'I only want to talk,' she had said. His parents had stood fast at their front door and insisted he wasn't coming down. She had walked home in the rain that night, alone.

Taking some money from her purse and putting on her trainers, she ran downstairs, grabbing an umbrella from the stand by the front door. She wasn't using the tradesman's entrance today. She sprinted after Leanne, who had not gone far.

'Leanne,' she called.

The girl turned around. 'What do you want?' She looked alarmed and frightened.

'Just to help,' Julia said.

She handed her the umbrella along with a twenty-pound note and some loose change.

'There's a phone box on the corner of the next road,' Julia said. 'Call a cab.'

'But why ...'

Julia sprinted back to the house before she could hear the rest of the question.

This time she did use the side door. Gideon must have heard her, because he came into the kitchen at the same time she did.

'Why did you go after her?' he said. His body was stiff with anger.

'I wanted to give her an umbrella.'

Instinct told her not to mention the money. Gideon looked away for a moment, the anger replaced by an anxious expression.

'Look, you weren't to know this, Julia, and she can be very convincing, but please don't let that girl into the house again.'

'I'm sorry. She just looked so—'

'Sweet? Vulnerable? Like I said, she's very convincing, and it's not your fault. But in future ...'

'Of course,' Julia said.

'What did she say about me?' Gideon asked.

'Nothing.'

He looked satisfied. 'Anyway, I appreciate it,' he said and turned to leave.

'Who is she?' Julia asked.

He turned back and grimaced. 'We went out a couple of times, a while back,' he said.

'She's very young,' Julia said.

'It was a mistake. Nothing happened but now she's obsessed with me, turning up at my parents', my work. God knows how she got this address.'

'It sounds like she's ill.'

'She needs help.'

'Poor girl.'

'If you knew what she'd done, you wouldn't be feeling sorry for her.'

'What has she done?'

'I don't want to go into it, Julia. I've told her you're not my girlfriend and she seemed to believe me. So, you'll be OK. Tell me if you see her again.'

What did he mean – you'll be OK?

'Is she dangerous?' Julia asked.

Gideon took a moment to consider before answering. 'That business with the fire – I wasn't entirely honest with the police. It was Leanne.'

'You're not serious.'

'Deadly,' he said. 'She knew I was having problems with that guy and did it to impress me. Get my attention. She actually thought I'd be pleased, bragged about it. I didn't tell the police because I didn't want her to get in any trouble. She needs help, not prison. Besides, I couldn't prove I didn't put her up to it. And you've seen how sweet and innocent she can play. Who do you think the police would have believed?'

He was right. Leanne was little more than a schoolgirl. She certainly didn't look like an arsonist who'd set fire to houses, with the occupants asleep inside. If it hadn't been for those cold eyes, Julia wouldn't have believed it either.

'But what was all that business about, with Brandon and the phone. I thought—'

'Thought what?' Gideon said.

'That phone call you made in the garden, on the morning of the fire.'

'Karl Brier is a work colleague, nothing to do with Devon Garvey. And Brandon's acting like he's found a smoking gun. He'll be asking for money next.'

'Christ, what a mess,' Julia said.

'Tell me about it. Look, I'm sorry I was snappy with you,' Gideon said. 'She unnerves me. It's ridiculous. I'm a twenty-eight-year-old man, she's a teenage girl and I'm the one living in fear. Talk about the tyranny of the weak. Anyway, thanks for being understanding.'

'No problem.'

He turned to leave the room before twisting round at the door. 'And Julia?'

'Yes?'

'Please don't mention this to anyone,' he said. 'Anyone at all.'

'I won't,' she said.

Later, alone, Julia thought of her rejection by Christian.

Staring out of her bedroom window night after night. She hadn't turned up at Ellie's to scream, shout and threaten. But she had thought about it. Once she had got as far as Ellie's front door, before turning back. A paper-thin margin lay between despair and madness.

But shouting at someone and setting fire to their house were two different things. It was only luck the family hadn't been inside. They could have died. Even in her darkest moments, Julia had never wished Christian or Ellie physical harm. She could never harm anyone, let alone kill them.

Chapter 51

2017 – Dulwich, London

Hugh pulled Julia into the door of the wooden pavilion at the far end of the rugby pitch. The faint smell of sweat and bleach seeped from the changing room walls. Adrenaline and desire rushed down her spine and ran through to her fingertips – sensations that had been alien to her for so long. Julia didn't love Hugh, and hadn't found him especially attractive, initially. It was his admiration, and her longing to be wanted and yearned for, that had drawn her to him. As far as Julia knew, her husband had never found her attractive and had long ago stopped making any effort to hide his infidelity, his scant excuses for coming home late, the gift-wrapped perfume left around the house that Julia never received.

Hugh pressed her against the wall and kissed her. Her mind spiralled back to the nervous, delicious embraces she'd shared with her first boyfriend, Christian. She'd almost forgotten that sex was for pleasure, not an exercise in power. She never denied her husband. Refusal would be used against her as one more example of her failure as a wife. He knew this and used it to distress her, demanding sex when she'd been ill in bed all day or came home exhausted after an eighty-hour week. He had taken less pleasure in her discomfort since the start of his affair with Plain Jane. Julia should prostrate herself at the woman's feet and thank her.

Plain Jane's husband had done something lucrative in the City and had possessed sufficiently good manners to die a few years ago, leaving her with an enormous life insurance pay-out. With this money, and if Julia gave up the house and savings, maybe she'd be able to leave, without having an accident. Even this fear wouldn't have kept her in her marriage, if it hadn't been for Sam. Her inadequacies as a mother and mental instability could have denied her custody. Now Sam was nearly an adult, he could choose for himself.

Hugh pushed himself against her and she gasped with anticipation of release from her marriage as much as his touch.

She had always taken the easiest path, don't tell the police, do get married, don't get divorced, do pretend everything's fine. But the easiest path had led to the hardest life.

Julia kicked off her shoes and together they slid from their upright position onto the benches, only a few hours ago covered with muddy kit, now clean, dry and unyielding. Hugh pushed up her skirt. His enthusiasm was more alluring than his technique.

'God, Julia. You're incredible,' he panted in her ear. 'It's not that I don't love my wife—'

'Shut up about your wife,' she said.

'What about—'

'Just shut up.'

She silenced him with a kiss. She didn't want words. They crowded her every waking hour. Bad mother, failed wife. And most of all, coward. A coward. She had always been a coward.

She relaxed into Hugh's arms and wriggled beneath him, inhaling the excitement, danger and lust.

Something scraped on the floor.

'What's that?' Julia asked.

Hugh was making low grunting noises.

'Hugh.'

He wasn't listening. The overhead strip light flicked on. Sam was standing in front of them. Before Julia could speak, he switched the light off.

Julia shoved Hugh off her.

'Who was that?' he asked.

'Sam,' she said.

His face froze in horror. 'Jesus, no.'

Julia pulled her shoes on and rearranged her clothing as she dashed to the door. From the top of the steps she could see Sam. He was wandering aimlessly on a patch of green, not seeming to see where he went. Julia ran down the steps to him and grabbed his arm. He yanked it away.

'Don't touch me. Stay away from me.'

He was walking backwards, away from her.

'Sam.'

'All this time I was on your side,' he said. 'I thought it was him. Now I get it.'

'Sam, please, I can explain.'

Julia stepped towards him. His face twisted with hate.

'No. I told you, stay away from me. You're a whore. I hate you. I wish you were dead.'

Julia stepped back as if she'd been slapped. Sam turned and ran around the side of the building to the car park. She recovered and stumbled after him in her heels. The Range Rover was parked in the spot nearest the path.

Julia stopped at the edge of the car park. Sam jumped into the passenger seat on the far side of the car. He put his head into his hands and she could tell he was crying. Of course, his father had brought him here. This wasn't bad luck. This had been planned.

Leaning against the driver's side door, smiling and giving her a slow handclap stood her husband, Gideon.

Chapter 52

2018 – Guildford Crown Court

The court session breaks for lunch. I've no hunger but force half a sandwich down to maintain my blood sugar, otherwise I'm sure I'll faint. After I've finished, Ralph comes to see me. He looks at the coffee in front of me.

'Drink it,' he orders. 'You'll be needing the caffeine.'

I take a sip. It's scalding hot and I put it down again. This momentarily distracts me from the look on Ralph's face. His brow is lowered, his lips pursed.

'What is it?' I ask.

'I've some news, Julia, and it's not good.'

I wait.

'Gideon and Alan are going to testify,' he says.

'Why? You said if we all say nothing—'

'I know. It was Lancaster's testimony. Your husband thinks it was too favourable to you, and the trial's going against him. That thirty thousand looks suspicious and you're not linked to it. He wants to speak out, turn it around. Helena's advised him against it.'

'Trust him to think he knows better than his lawyer.'

Ralph rubs his fingers across the ghost of a five-o'clock shadow.

'There's something else?' I ask.

He nods. 'Sometimes in a case like this, where there are multiple defendants, the jury find it easier if they have one person to blame, a single guilty party to convict – it feels like justice has been served, even if they're not sure of the other defendants' innocence.' Ralph lowers his voice. 'Julia, do you know what a cut-throat defence is?'

A ringing starts in my ears. 'A cut-throat defence?' I repeat.

'It's when a defendant strengthens the prosecution case against the co-defendant to increase his chances of acquittal. Gideon and Alan are going to claim you killed Brandon, acting alone.'

This has nothing to do with Lancaster's testimony or how the case is going. Estranging me from my son and leaving me penniless wasn't enough. Gideon wants me jailed for life. This was planned with Alan long before the trial. It's the reason they have female barristers, so it doesn't look like a bunch of men ganging up on a defenceless woman and he's sprung it upon us, halfway through the trial, so we're underprepared.

'It's a risky strategy. The prosecution must be rubbing their hands,' Ralph says. 'I know Helena and Arianne have tried to talk both of them out of it. I get the impression Gideon's the dominant one in that relationship.'

'Gideon's the dominant one in every relationship,' I say.

'Your husband's a fool. One slip and you'll all end up being convicted. Whatever's happened between you two, he can't want his son to see his mother jailed.'

But he can. He does.

'He'll have fixed his story with Alan long ago,' I say.

'We can use that against him. Alan's livelihood depends on Gideon – he won't turn on him. And as for your husband, I'm taking it your split wasn't amicable.'

'It certainly wasn't a harmonious "let's put our son first" type break-up. And he didn't know that me and Brandon had a fling. I guess I'm sliding down the likeability scale,' I say. 'The scarlet woman.'

'Nevertheless, I'm going to have to put you in the witness box.'

'You said that was the worst thing I could do.'

'Things have changed,' Ralph says. 'I'm going to need to know about your marriage.'

I rub my eyes then rest my chin on my hands.

Unlike some women, I can't complain I didn't know what sort of man I was marrying. I knew exactly what he was, though I didn't care to put a name to it. It was myself I didn't know. I never acknowledged my feeble thinking and cowardice. Taking the easiest route out of any situation. What was it Andre used to say – running from a wolf into a bear? Each decision, each turn in the road, took me further from safety.

Sometimes, I would fantasise about Gideon's death. A business rival would burst into the office and shoot him. He'd be walking down a street late at night and knifed for his Rolex. He'd lose control of one of his beloved sports cars and hit a tree. Actually, that did happen. He was on the A3, it was dark and wet, and he was travelling at speed. He took a corner too fast, aquaplaned, flew off the road and smashed into an oak. The car was mangled beyond repair. Gideon walked away with barely a scratch.

'You're a very lucky woman,' the A & E nurse told me. 'I could easily be talking to Mr Risborough's widow right now.'

309

The good sister misinterpreted the look of horror her words invoked.

I think of Sam, sitting in the public gallery, watching.

'I can't put my son through this,' I say.

'Can you put him through seeing his mother go to jail? Because if you don't testify, I have a feeling things are going to go very badly for you.'

I test my coffee again – it's still too hot, but I drink it anyway, scalding my throat. Ralph watches me in silence. When I finish, I put the coffee down. Only then do I tell Ralph all about my marriage.

Chapter 53

1994 – Guildford

Julia's attempts at leaving the house in Guildford had stalled. The PhD students *were* still advertising, but she wasn't that desperate. What she really wanted was to find a new job and move to London. Brandon had stopped going to the pub and was permanently in the kitchen, drinking beer, and it was impossible to escape his drunken surliness. Gideon was greeted with false bonhomie.

'Don't suppose you fancy coming for a drink with me and my new mate, Karl Brier, do you?'

Gideon would bristle and say nothing. Julia felt all his agitation and had to give him respect for his self-control. Under Brandon's constant onslaught, she wouldn't have stayed silent to protect a girl, who she knew little deserved protection, and she felt his verbal assaults on Gideon more acutely than those aimed at herself.

'Off to London? I guess you might as well, as you've run through all the men in Guildford?' had been his adieu the previous Friday.

To avoid the kitchen, she'd taken to buying pre-packed sandwiches and eating them in her room. The only edible

311

ones from the local shop were cheese and pickle and tonight, she finally got sick of them, throwing the packet in the bin, before going to the bathroom to wash her hands. The window was open and she could hear voices on the patio below.

'It's none of your business,' Brandon was saying.

'It's very much my business,' Ruth said. 'Jenny is *my* sister and if you think I'm going to let some unemployed little toerag like you rip her off, you're very much mistaken. I know about the money.'

'It's a loan.'

'Two thousand pounds – how are you going to pay that back?'

'Genevieve's taken a shine to me. Where's the harm?'

'I know what you see, Brandon. A vulnerable middle-aged woman to be exploited. *Another* one.'

'What's that supposed to mean?'

'I've spoken to Ronald. You didn't just leave New Zealand to travel the world, did you now?' Ruth said.

'I've no idea what you're talking about.'

'And that sudden departure from London.'

'You know what,' Brandon said, 'I'm not having this conversation. It's Genevieve's money and if you don't like it, bad luck. There's nothing you can do.'

'I wouldn't be so sure about that,' Ruth said.

The kitchen door slammed shut, hard enough to make the floor vibrate.

Ruth stepped onto the terrace. Julia drew back from the window. She heard the click of a lighter and smelt cigarette smoke. Leaning forward again, she could see Ruth was sucking on her cigarette, her mouth set hard, staring into the middle distance.

312

Two thousand pounds. That couldn't be right. She'd thought it had been twenty pounds here and there. Surely even Genevieve wouldn't be so stupid.

It was none of Julia's business. She'd made the second round of interviews for the Hounslow job and if it wasn't exactly party central, at least it was on the Tube.

Living with Genevieve was proving to be as stifling as living with Audrey, only without the pressure valve of telling her to get lost when she became too annoying. Perhaps Dominic found Genevieve equally insufferable and *had* run away. Or maybe it hadn't been an accident. He'd cut the rope to free himself of Genevieve for ever. The moment the thought came into her head, Julia felt guilty. The death of her only child must have devastated Genevieve. It wasn't so surprising that her mind moulded another young man into the form of her lost son.

She came out of the bathroom. On the landing she could hear that Ruth had now taken up the argument with Genevieve. Julia couldn't make out the whole conversation. They hissed at each other under their breath, as if too well brought up to shout. She could make out the words 'Brandon', 'money' and, more than once, 'Julia'. Why was she being dragged into this?

She'd had enough. She wasn't supposed to be going out with Pearl until the following night but called her anyway.

'I can't take it anymore,' Julia told her.

'Don't blame you. Come up. I'm meeting Rudi, but you can come along.'

'He won't mind?'

'No. It's about time you met him.'

'So, things are going well again, between you two?'

'Not bad,' Pearl said. 'And, Jules, you know how pissed off

313

you were when we didn't tell you about Christian and Ellie's engagement?'

'And the pregnancy,' Julia added.

'That too. The thing is ...'

Julia closed her eyes. Nothing could be worse than learning of their impending marriage and child. Whatever it was, she could cope. Unless they'd split up. Was it possible? Perhaps the child wasn't Christian's.

'It's not as bad this time,' Pearl said. 'But they've moved into one of those townhouses along the canal at Oakham.'

Julia's dream home, the one she'd decorated a hundred times in her head, chosen the furniture and selected the plants for the garden. Was it a deliberate attempt by Christian to stamp on her feelings? Why else had they chosen one of those houses, when there were hundreds of other places they could go?

'You don't care anymore, do you, Jules? You shouldn't. You're too good to spend your life fussing over soft furnishings, which is what's going to happen to Ellie. And I need you here. I hardly saw you before you moved down.'

'It's fine,' Julia said. 'I'm fine.'

Why did it still hurt? She thought she'd moved on. Did she still love Christian, or was it the memory of love? Would she take him back if he asked? She pushed the question from her mind.

'I'll try to catch the quarter-past train. It'll be great to meet Rudi at last.'

Pearl was who she needed right now. It made her realise how shallow her friendships in the house were. Even with Lucy. She knew everything about Pearl, could guess what clothes she would buy and which men she liked and vice versa. They had a shared past of fun and tragedy. A few drunken nights out with strangers didn't turn them into friends.

She checked the time. There was still three-quarters of an hour. She wetted and combed her hair, pencilled on some eyeliner and changed into the cream dress Pearl said suited her, but Julia wasn't sure about. It didn't go with her Converse trainers but looked good with the black baseball boots. A weekend of escape lay ahead of her. No Gideon. No Brandon. No Genevieve.

As she came downstairs, she could hear Ruth and Genevieve still arguing in the kitchen. If she used the front door, she could avoid them. She crept across the hall, not quietly enough.

'You're not about to leave by the front are you, Julia?' Genevieve was at the kitchen door. 'I have asked you before to go around the side.'

'I heard you with Ruth. I didn't want to disturb you.'

'My sister has left, by the side door,' Genevieve said. 'It's good enough for her apparently.'

'I only—'

'This really is the last straw. I'm going to have to give you notice to leave.'

'You're not serious,' Julia said.

'A week's notice should be enough.'

The woman was unbelievable.

'You're throwing me out for using the front door?'

'Flouting a rather simple request. Symptomatic of your behaviour in general, I'm afraid to say.'

'Is this about Brandon?'

Genevieve pulled herself upright, and drawing on her imagined classical acting training, said, 'We did have words about him, Julia. Words you chose to ignore.'

'I've not been near him.'

'You've been spying on him.'

'*He* was spying on *me*.'

'And you've hurt his feelings.'

'Oh please – he's an adult.'

Genevieve gave her a look bordering on hatred.

'I'm not arguing about it. This is *my* house. And I'm disappointed you've chosen to treat it with so little respect.'

'Bollocks.'

'How dare you!'

'This has nothing to do with respect. It's to do with your fixation with Brandon. Well you can chuck me out, but he will get a girlfriend or move out or go back to New Zealand and then where will you be?'

'As I suspected,' Genevieve said, glowering at Julia. 'The green-eyed monster. You're just jealous.'

Julia's anger bubbled beyond boiling point. Learning about Christian and Ellie and now being ejected from the house by the woman she'd done her best to protect.

'You could go a long way without coming across a better case of projection. You're the one who's jealous,' she said. 'I could have Brandon with a click of my fingers. With all your money, dinners and gifts, you're nothing more to him than a meal ticket. Do you think he'd be interested in an old woman like you? He laughs at you behind your back – you do know that, don't you?'

Genevieve took a step back and used the doorframe to steady herself. 'I don't believe you,' she said.

Julia had never heard Brandon laugh at Genevieve, but

316

surely he did. And besides, Genevieve deserved her spite being thrown back at her.

'No, you always believe what you want to believe, like your son Dominic being alive.'

'He is!' Genevieve shouted. 'Get out. Get out at once.'

'Don't worry. I'm going.'

Julia stamped to the door and slammed it behind her.

Chapter 54

2018 – Guildford Crown Court

As he stands and takes his oath before the jury, Gideon plays with his wedding ring, which he hasn't worn for months. His voice quivers, as he swears to tell the whole truth and nothing but the truth. The jury will think the quiver is a sign of nerves. I know Gideon has gauged their expectations of how an innocent man should behave, indignant, but his vocal cords betraying anxiety. It's a convincing portrayal.

Helena Dryden gives him a benevolent smile, poor Gideon entangled in the treachery of others.

'Mr Risborough,' she says. 'We've heard about strained relationships between the housemates at 72 Downs Avenue and resentment at the preferential treatment shown to Brandon Wells by the landlady, Mrs Jennifer Pike. Is this how you remember your time there?'

Gideon looks to the jury. 'Not at all,' he says. 'I had very fond memories up until Mrs Pike's death. It's also where I met my future wife.' He smiles, looks at the ring, then lets the smile fade. God, he's good. 'Of course, we made fun of each other. Young men, sharing a house, going out drinking – that's what happens. And sure, we gave him some stick about the way Mrs Pike fussed over him. It was hilarious, a woman her age chasing after a younger man. It didn't mean anything. Just a bit of male banter, a bit of fun, and I know that's how Brandon saw it.'

The jury is watching Gideon. They don't notice Grant McCluskey, who's now seated in the public gallery, pursing his lips and shaking his head. Gideon sounds so reasonable, forgiving rather than patronising to those who, unlike me, haven't been told a thousand times they would understand if only they weren't so 'naïve', 'overemotional' and 'limited'.

'No animosity on your part then?' Dryden asks.

'None whatsoever.'

'And between Ms Winter and Brandon?'

'Frosty, to say the least. At the time I put it down to Jules being a bit of a snob.'

Gideon has never called me 'Jules'. He looks to his fingers and turns his wedding ring before looking up with a sad smile. 'She wasn't interested in a man who worked with his hands. She had more ambition than that. It wasn't until I heard Mr McCluskey speak just now that I learnt they'd had an affair and put two and two together.'

Dryden raises her eyebrows. 'In what way?' she asks.

'She tried to distance herself from him. I had no idea at the time she had her sights set on me. One night I caught Brandon trying to go into her room. I'd had to carry her there when she was blind drunk. I knew exactly what he was up to – had to warn him off. I didn't know back then that Brandon had previous encouragement.'

'Did you ever see Brandon and your wife arguing?'

'I *heard* them arguing. Jules would never tell me what it was about. And she was the one who told me Brandon had gone and cleared out all of his stuff.'

'Sorry, Mr Risborough. Could you repeat that? It was definitely your future wife, Julia Winter, who informed you Brandon had gone?'

'Yes, it was. On the bank holiday Saturday. That's when she told us, me and Alan. We had gone out for the day. There was a mini-festival in town and we went drinking afterwards. We didn't get home until late. Jules was still up. She told us Brandon had cleared out.'

'She waited up to tell you that?' Dryden's eyebrows shoot up again. 'And this is the Sunday we know that Brandon had told his friend, Grant McCluskey, that he was returning to the house. Is there anything else you can tell me about that weekend – anything odd or unusual?'

'There was the smell,' Gideon says. 'The house stank of bleach when we came home. It was coming from the lounge.'

'The lounge, where according to the photographed evidence of the lamp and the rug, we know Brandon Wells to have been killed?'

'Yes.'

'And how did Ms Winter account for this?'

'She said there'd been an infestation of flying ants and not to go in there because insect spray was toxic. But it didn't smell of insect spray, it smelt of bleach. We didn't use the lounge much. It was off limits when Mrs Pike was alive. We started using it a little, after her death.'

'And did you go into the lounge?'

'No. It stank from outside. I wasn't going in there. And

Jules' behaviour always was – how can I put it? – a little erratic.'

'Erratic.' Dryden repeats the word, as if it's synonymous with psychotic. 'Was there anything else peculiar?'

'Only that Jules looked so dreadful, a little unhinged. I thought she must be ill, but she said she was all right. I was tired, so I went to bed.'

'Did anything else occur out of the ordinary that night?' Dryden asks.

'It did,' Gideon says. 'I heard a car pull onto the drive. My room was on the ground floor and the headlamps came through my curtains and disturbed me. I could hear Jules' voice. I couldn't hear or see who was driving the car. It sat there for quite some time before driving off.'

'Did you ask Ms Winter about it the next day?'

'She moved out before I got a chance to talk to her. I noticed the rug in the lounge had gone.'

'The one in which we know Mr Wells' body was wrapped and buried.'

'Yes,' Gideon says.

'I see.' Dryden presses both palms on the bench in front of her and rocks forward before proceeding.

'Mr Risborough,' she says, 'I'll pre-empt Mr Mapplethorpe's and Mr Williams' questions, and ask why you never mentioned any of this in your police interview.'

'Jules is still my wife and I didn't want to be disloyal.' He looks to the ring once more. 'And to be honest, despite her erratic behaviour, I never thought she'd actually harm anyone. She's threatened me with a knife in the past, but I never thought she'd go ahead and stab me. I thought it was just a show of how angry she was.'

321

Dryden jumps a little, as if this is completely new information for her. 'Just a moment, Mr Risborough, Ms Winter threatened you with a knife?'

'She accused me of sleeping with other women. It was ridiculous.' Gideon lowers his head in faux embarrassment. 'She and I weren't having conjugal relations at the time. Even so, she was furious at the thought of it. Brandon was a young man, perhaps he had been seeing other women. Perhaps he was moving out and Julia—'

'Your honour, I must interrupt,' Ralph says. 'This is pure conjecture.'

'Agreed,' Judge Fleetwood says.

'Your honour.' Dryden nods, then turns back to Gideon. 'Had you, in fact, been conducting an affair?'

'Certainly not. She was the one with insatiable appetites. I put up with it for years, so as not to break up the family. It was my son who demanded we separate, after he saw her having sex with his rugby coach in the club changing rooms.'

Suppressed laughter ripples around the court. Dryden waits for it to subside. 'Mr Risborough, you were explaining why you decided to speak up now, about what happened in the house,' she says.

'My son needs me. I'm not leaving him on his own and going to jail for something Jules has done,' Gideon said. 'It's bad enough for him as it is, what with his mother moving to London and refusing to see him.'

Several members of the jury look over at me. I'm now worse than a murderer, I'm a bad mother.

'And so, to protect your son, you've decided to tell the truth. Despite your initial loyalty to your wife, your son comes first.'

'That's correct,' he says in fractured tones.

Gideon nods and puts a hand to his face, as if suppressing tears. The jury are muttering. Brandon's siblings switch their attention from Gideon to me. I can feel their gaze drilling into me.

I'm ready to convict myself.

Ralph stands up and adjusts his wig. He starts his cross-examination by looking a little startled. 'Mr Risborough, all this sudden, damning evidence against your estranged wife – the bleach, the car in the middle of the night, her violent temper – was never mentioned to the police.'

'I've explained my reasons. Look, I'm old-fashioned enough to believe in my marriage vows.'

We had a civil ceremony with the minimal wording necessary for legal requirements. No loving or cherishing. No till death do us part.

'So, your loyalty lay with your wife?' Ralph says.

'Yes.'

'Until it was time to save your own neck.'

Gideon looks affronted and distressed. 'I'm thinking about my son. Someone has to take care of him She walked out on him – on both of us.'

I cringe. Ralph's made an error with this line of questioning. The jury will side with the wronged husband. He changes tack. 'You pretend this is about loyalty, but what husband wouldn't feel aggrieved at his wife's infidelity? Who wouldn't want revenge? I understand you already have another partner, a Mrs Jane Middlefield.'

'I can't see why that's relevant.'

'You met Mrs Middlefield two years before the separation with Ms Winter.'

'Yes, but we never—'

'You regularly went to her house to help with DIY, the garden and' – Ralph pauses to give his last statement a comic note – 'unblocking her drains.'

Members of the jury smirk.

Gideon's jaw tenses. He can't tolerate being laughed at. 'I was being a good neighbour,' he says.

'Above and beyond, I'd say,' Ralph replies.

This raises a titter from a couple of men at the back of the jury.

'That'll do, Mr Williams,' Judge Fleetwood says.

'Apologies, your honour. Just a little "male banter".'

Gideon's breathing hard, trying to control his anger. He manages to conquer it and settle back into the role of the falsely accused. Did the jury gain a glimpse of what is apparent to me at all times, his simmering rage and his need to dominate every situation?

Ralph adopts a more benign attitude.

'Before your separation, would you consider yourself a good husband, attentive, caring?'

'I would,' Gideon says. 'I always put Julia and my son first.'

Ralph's rattled him. He's forgotten to call me 'Jules'.

'In what way did you demonstrate this caring?' Ralph asks.

'In every way I could.'

'Financially?'

Gideon hesitates a fraction. 'Yes.'

'You took care that your wife and son wanted for nothing before you bought a £180,000 car.'

Collectively, the jury sit up.

'I work hard. I deserve a little treat. Julia wanted for nothing.'

'And what car did Ms Winter drive?'

'She didn't need one.'

'Of course, there are plenty of buses for her to catch,' Ralph says.

'My cars were always available for her.'

'Cars, plural – of course they would have been, if you had ever insured your wife, but you never did.' Ralph adjusts his robes. 'Would you like to tell me why a woman earning eighty thousand pounds a year can't afford her own car?'

'She could afford it. Julia's profligate. That's why I—'

'Why you insisted on controlling all the finances? Her wages were paid into a joint account, which in reality, only you had access to. Isn't that correct?'

'I was saving her from herself. She was spend, spend, spend.'

'Spend, spend, spend?' Ralph turns to the jury. 'Remind me again, Mr Risborough, which one of you drives the Lamborghini.'

'It was second-hand,' Gideon protests before Dryden stands up.

'Your honour, I can't see the relevance to the case.'

'As Mr Lancaster told us, follow the money. This case revolves around the money both the defence and prosecution agree was taken from Mrs Pike's house around the time of her death. I am demonstrating that it is Mr Risborough who is obsessed with money and material possessions, not Ms Winter.'

'My client is hardly the first man to save up for his dream car,' Dryden says.

'Certainly not,' Ralph says. 'But it doesn't end there. A Range Rover, handmade suits, handmade shoes, a Rolex watch. In fact, the entire profits from SupaSupplements and a good proportion of my client's salary is spent on Mr Risborough.

Ms Winter is left to pay the bills, food, expenses for their son and the astronomic mortgage on the house Mr Risborough insisted they buy.'

'There's no proof which spouse—'

'And remortgaged *three* times. If anyone would kill for money it's not Ms Winter, it's Mr Risborough.'

'Julia could have spent her money as she liked,' Gideon says.

'Could she? Isn't it true that Ms Winter is frightened of you?'

'She has no reason to be. I've never so much as laid a finger on her.'

'Did you threaten to?'

'No – she threatened me.'

'But you have threatened other people, haven't you, Mr Risborough?' Ralph looks directly at Gideon. 'In 1994, less than three months before Brandon's disappearance, you received a police caution for threatening Devon Garvey.'

'The man owed me money.'

'So, we're back to money again, I see. It's really something that brings out aggression in you, isn't it? Subsequently, Mr Garvey's house was burnt down in an arson attack.'

Dryden's on her feet, but doesn't have a chance to object.

'That's enough, Mr Williams,' Judge Fleetwood says. 'No one was charged with that offence. The jury will ignore this last comment.'

'Apologies,' Ralph says.

'You also threatened a young girl, Leanne Grainger, didn't you?'

'Certainly not.'

'She states that you did.'

326

'A silly girl with an infatuation, desperate for attention.'

Gideon has regained some of his composure and his statement sounds genuine.

'Mr Risborough,' Ralph says, 'you are a man whose wife has been unfaithful. She is the main source of income and she left you. It would be a sweet revenge to blame this on her, with the help of your friend and employee, your co-defendant Alan Johns. Thirty thousand pounds came through your business after you left Downsview Villa, an incredible sum at the time for such a small concern. Whereas there is no financial link to Ms Winter. You strike me as the sort of man obsessed by money and material possessions. The sort who would do anything to get it.'

'That's not true.'

'Now that you're separated from Ms Winter, she makes a contribution to the house and the upkeep of your son,' Ralph says. 'Would you care to tell the court how much that is?'

'I can't say off the top of my head.'

'I'll remind you. It's three thousand pounds per month. Two thirds of her take-home salary.'

'It's not that much,' Gideon says.

'I have the figures here.' Ralph holds up a bank statement. 'And can you tell us why your wife is giving you so much, far beyond what is necessary?'

'Yes, I can,' Gideon says. 'It's guilt. She's trying to pay off her conscience. Trying to pay my son into forgetting he caught her having sex with his rugby coach in the club changing rooms.' Titters from the jury once more. 'And then she abandoned him – went off to live a single girl's life in North London.'

'It's difficult to live the full London experience when your remaining income barely covers your rent,' Ralph says. 'Isn't the real reason Ms Winter pays so much is not to pay off her conscience but to pay off you? She's scared of you.'

'That's completely untrue. I've never laid a finger on her.'

'You told her not to cross you when it came to money, didn't you?'

'No.'

'*You know what I'm capable of,* you said. What was that a reference to?'

'I never said that.'

'Did you mean Brandon?' Ralph asks.

'No.'

'Who then?'

'No one.'

Gideon looks to his defence team. Dryden stands up. 'Your honour,' she says. 'My client has answered the question.'

'Move on please, Mr Williams.'

'The story you've given the court, about your wife being in the house alone, then you returning and the place smelling of bleach. There's only Alan Johns to verify it. You've never mentioned it to the police, or anyone else, have you?'

'I've explained the reasons for my silence,' Gideon says.

'It's a very detailed story to remember from twenty-four years ago. Did you have reason to remember all the specifics, or is the entire tale a fabrication to incriminate your estranged wife? You could easily have transferred hairs from her comb to Brandon's grave.'

'That's preposterous.'

'Did you use the real story but substitute your own actions for that of Ms Winter? After all, it's very unlikely a nine-stone woman could have overpowered a fifteen-stone man, much less moved the body on her own. You yourself realised that, hence the need to invent the unknown collaborator. Someone who would drive to Guildford in the middle of the night to dispose of a body and become complicit in murder. Yet, despite being married to Ms Winter for nearly twenty years, you've not been able to provide a single name that could fit the missing piece of this particular jigsaw, have you?'

'She was always with a girl called Pearl and a homosexual called Andre.'

'Neither of whom had a car at the time. Did you know that?'

'They could have borrowed one. Or maybe it was her stepfather. They're not close but he wouldn't want her to go to jail.'

'He was on a working holiday in Spain.' One of many he took with various secretaries. I never thought I'd have a reason to thank him for it. 'Any more wild guesses, Mr Risborough? Anything even vaguely plausible?'

'She had a different man every week – it could have been one of them,' Gideon says.

'Ms Winter was promiscuous?'

'Very.'

'And, as we established earlier, a snob,' Ralph says.

'Yes.'

'And yet you went on to marry her. It seems a strange decision, given your low opinion. The truth of the matter is, Ms Winter was none of these things. These are lies you're telling the court to sully her name.'

'Not at all. I knew exactly what she was like. Julia Winter is a damaged person. I don't know what happened to her when she was young. It may have been her father's death, but she was highly emotional and unstable. When I heard she tried to kill herself I went to see her at her mother's. I was just trying to be friendly. She took it for something else. I should have said no, but I was young and back then she was a very attractive woman.' He raises his hands and shrugs in a *what's a guy supposed to do* sort of way. 'After that she latched on to me, then got herself pregnant.'

'All by herself – remarkable,' Ralph says.

Gideon ignores him. 'If we'd have split up, she almost certainly would have gained custody of our son. And I couldn't allow that. It was difficult enough to undo her influence when I was living with them in the same house. If she'd raised him alone, God knows what damage she'd have done.'

I look to Sam. He's staring at his father, his hands crushed together. Does he believe this? Is this the poison Gideon poured in his ear, month after month?

'So, you see, she was all the things I said and worse,' Gideon says. 'I was out of my depth. I used to think she couldn't help it. Now I think she was deliberately manipulative, Especially about the "accidental" pregnancy. I can't tell you the number of times I thought, if only I'd done this, or that. I knew I'd made my bed and I had to lie in it. But I never thought I'd end up in court, charged with a murder *she* committed.'

He jabs his finger in my direction – he looks wild, a man pushed to his limits and beyond by a woman he only ever wanted to help. In the jury box, the man in the grey suit jacket and woman in the floral dress look at me and shake their heads. Their minds are made up. Ralph did his best, but Gideon's too good. He's so plausible. To all but a few he's affable and charming. As he returns to the defendant's bench, he turns so that only I can see the triumphant sneer across his face.

'He's very clever, your husband,' is all Ralph says during the break.

We sit in silence and watch the seconds tick by until the next session. Ralph has warned me Dryden will spare me nothing. I'm a bad mother, a faithless wife, an avaricious woman. And Sam will be there to watch it all.

Chapter 55

1994 – Guildford

Returning to Guildford had never been less appealing. Julia lacked the patience and endurance for another week with Brandon and Genevieve. Yes, she had done Julia a favour, telling her she had to go, but it was a pity she didn't have anywhere else lined up. Pearl had said she could stay at hers until she found somewhere, but that would mean a two-hour commute, which, right at that moment, seemed more palatable than staying in the house. A sentiment reinforced by the sight of Brandon storming out of the front door as she came down the drive.

Coming through the side door, the bag that had been so light on Friday now felt heavy as she dragged it through the garage and into the kitchen.

'You missed all the drama,' Lucy said, when Julia came in.

Julia let the bag slide off her shoulder and onto the floor. 'What's going on?' she asked.

Alan sat next to Lucy, looking simultaneously amused and sneering.

'Who needs television, when you have Genevieve and

Brandon. They're both just a couple of drunks – birds of a feather. Pathetic really,' Alan said.

Julia turned to Lucy for an explanation.

'Brandon's leaving,' Lucy said. 'Apparently you're to blame.'

'Me – how did you work that out?'

Julia had enough problems of her own. The last thing she needed was to get dragged into Brandon's.

'Is it true Genevieve asked you to move out?' Lucy asked.

'She gave me notice on Friday.'

'That's what she told Brandon, like she was really proud and thought he'd be pleased. He was furious, said he was leaving and a lot of other things on top. Genevieve's distraught.'

'She'll get over it.'

'You're mistaking Genevieve for a rational human being,' Alan said.

'Brandon was vile to her,' Lucy said.

'She asked for it.' Alan's voice laced with glee.

'He shouldn't have said those things, even if he was provoked,' Lucy said. Julia felt a twinge of guilt about her own unguarded words on Friday. 'Brandon knows Genevieve's got a thing for him. He can't just announce he's leaving like that.'

'Is he supposed to ask her permission?' Alan said. 'And he did tell her before that he was thinking about it. But that's Genevieve – if she doesn't want to believe something, she won't.'

'How do you know all this?' Julia asked.

'They had a massive row, up in Genevieve's bedroom,' Lucy replied. 'It was so loud half the street must have heard. She was trying to get Brandon to stay – emotional blackmail, bribery. Said she'd got forty-five thousand pounds to give him.'

'That can't be right,' Julia said. 'Where would she get that sort of money?'

'Dominic's father sent it for Dominic. She was saving it for when he returns.' Lucy rolled her eyes. 'I don't think Brandon believed her. He got really angry and called her a sad old cow.'

Alan sniggered at this.

'He told her Dominic's dead,' Lucy continued. 'That he's never coming back, and she needs to check in to reality.'

'Harsh but true,' Alan said.

An echo of Julia's words on Friday. Hearing them repeated made her realise she owed Genevieve an apology. They'd both been angry. Perhaps neither of them had meant what they said.

'Maybe I should go up and speak to her,' Julia said.

'And say what? Dominic *is* dead,' Alan said. 'You'll only give her an audience for more histrionics. She does it for attention.'

'But I ...' Julia looked to Lucy.

'Best to leave it,' Lucy said. 'I doubt you'll get any sense out of her tonight. Talk to her tomorrow.'

Julia didn't need much persuading. She was tired, she had work in the morning, and she didn't relish the idea of spending hours listening to Genevieve's ramblings. A cup of tea, then bed was what she had in mind for the evening.

'I'll leave it then. I'm too tired anyway – need some sleep.'

'I'm going up now, too,' Lucy said. 'Flying to Newcastle tomorrow – the alarm's set for 5 a.m. Pity me.'

'Night then, ladies,' Alan said with uncharacteristic cheerfulness, the evening's entertainment having been exactly to his taste.

Julia listened at the bottom of the stairs that led to the

attic, to hear if Genevieve was crying. All was quiet. Lucy was right. She could speak to Genevieve tomorrow, when she'd calmed down. Julia was still leaving, but why go on bad terms? Her conscience told her forcing the reality of Dominic's death onto Genevieve had been cruel. Especially now she knew Brandon was also leaving, as Julia had predicted. She would speak to Genevieve the next time she saw her. It wasn't too late to apologise.

Chapter 56

2018 – Guildford Crown Court

Over the years, Alan's presence has seldom been a blessing, but watching his unfeigned nervousness, shifting from foot to foot, his eyes sweeping back and forth across the courtroom and drops of moisture forming on his top lip as he gabbles his oath, I'm glad he's here.

With prompting from his barrister, Arianne Baptiste, he repeats Gideon's story, nearly word for word and keeps looking across for approval. His delivery is as strained as Gideon's was fluid. The juror in the grey suit looks at him with a mixture of disdain and pity. Baptiste appears relieved when he's finished, before she casts an anxious glance in Ralph's direction.

Alan seems to shrink as Ralph stands.

'Mr Johns, you expect the jury to believe that after twenty-four years, both you and Mr Risborough recount exactly the same story, without prior rehearsal?' he asks. 'In nearly exactly the same words, *stank of bleach, she looked unhinged.* You've conferred and come up with this story together, haven't you?'

'No. It's the truth.'

Alan looks like a young child with chocolate cream smeared across his face, denying he's eaten the missing cake.

'You work for Mr Risborough, do you not?' Ralph asks.

'Yes, for nearly twenty-five years.'

'You joined his company, SupaSupplements, immediately after quitting the Downsview Villa house in Guildford, despite having a better-paid job at an accountancy firm?'

Alan looked to Gideon – perhaps they hadn't prepared for this line of questioning. He looks back to Ralph. 'I ... erm ...' He looks to Gideon once more. He's turned his face away. 'I didn't like accountancy.'

'A rather sudden decision,' Ralph says. 'You'd studied for years to reach your position.'

'Gideon's job was more interesting.'

'Gideon's job or Gideon?' Ralph asked.

'I don't know what you mean.'

Ralph raises his eyebrows. 'Really? You were a leading light in your accountancy firm, destined to be a partner. And you gave it all up to be the company dogsbody.'

'I wasn't the dogsbody. I was the corporate co-ordinator,' Alan says stiffly.

'Which entails?' Ralph asks.

'Liaising with customers and vendors, arranging venues. Ensuring Gideon is able to fully focus on increasing profits.'

'Booking rooms and chasing suppliers, but *not* a dogsbody,' Ralph says, archly. 'And you took a considerable pay cut to take this job, didn't you?'

'As I said, the work was more interesting.'

'Was your lack of concern about the pay because you knew you had a considerable amount of money coming your way – passing through the books as cash from trade shows – undetectable?'

'No, not at all. That's just not true.' Alan speaks to the judge.

His manner is petulant, like a schoolboy complaining to teacher. When it's clear Fleetwood sees no reason to intervene, he says, 'In fact, I'd forgotten the money until you mentioned it.'

'Are we to believe that as a qualified accountant you were unable to follow the argument laid before the court about the money?'

'No. I could, it's only ...'

Alan is straining not to look at Gideon again. He has to glue his eyes to the floor to prevent it.

'You're rather reliant on Mr Risborough, aren't you?' Ralph says. 'And I don't just mean at work.'

'Not at all.'

'You go on holiday together.'

'We're friends.'

'It's a bit of a one-way friendship though, isn't it, Mr Johns?'

'No.'

'Mrs Jane Middlefield, Mr Risborough's current girlfriend, weren't you romantically involved with her before your boss stepped into the frame?'

Alan can't stop himself this time. He looks at Gideon. 'I ... I ...'

Alan's barrister stands up. 'Your honour, this is hardly of relevance to the case.'

Reluctantly, Fleetwood swivels his gaze from Alan to Ralph. 'Your point, Mr Williams?'

'My point, your honour, is that most men would take

'exception to their friend stealing away their partner. And "take exception" is to put it mildly.'

'It wasn't like that,' Alan says.

Ralph turns back to Alan. 'What was it like, Mr Johns?'

'I liked Jane, but she was free to choose who she was with. I didn't own her.'

This is Alan Johns, who once dismissed the entire female population of Guildford as slags.

'And, of course, if she preferred Gideon ...' Alan continues.

'This is something Mr Risborough explained to you?'

'Yes. I mean no.'

'Just as he explained what a terrible, violent and deceitful woman his wife is?'

'I already knew that,' Alan says.

'Just as he had to explain your memory of an event twenty-four years ago, which you didn't mention to the police during your interview and recalled for the first time in this courtroom today.'

'No, not for the first time.'

'Why did you mention none of this in your police interview?'

'I ... he ... because ...'

'Because Gideon told you?'

Ralph waits for a reply. Alan looks around the court in hope of someone salvaging the situation. Gideon is staring at the royal coat of arms above the judge's head, as if Alan is completely unknown to him. Ralph lets Alan stand with his mouth flapping for some moments. Blue hoody looks amused. Ralph allows it to continue for a few moments before he says, 'Thank you, Mr Johns.'

Alan remains in the stand, his mouth open, but with no words coming out.

'Thank you, Mr Johns,' Judge Fleetwood repeats. 'You may leave the witness stand.'

Without looking up, Alan trudges back to our glass cage. Gideon continues to stare at the coat of arms above the judge.

Chapter 57

1994 – Guildford

The phone in the hall was ringing incessantly. Julia tried to ignore it. None of her friends or family rang on Mondays and she didn't want to run about the house acting as a human answerphone. The ringing stopped then started again. Each time she prayed for it to be the last and each time the ringing restarted. Either she answered it, or it would go on all evening. She hauled herself off her bed, went downstairs and picked up the receiver.

'Is that Julia? It's Ruth. I've been calling Jenny for hours. Is she not in?'

'I've just got home,' Julia said.

Not strictly true. She'd come home an hour ago and already eaten dinner. She hadn't tried to find Genevieve, wanting to delay the unpleasant business of having to apologise.

'Can you try to find her? I'm in London and it's important we speak.'

'I'll check her room.'

'I'll call back in five minutes,' Ruth said.

She wished she'd ignored the phone. Now she had to drag herself up to the attic, where she was sure Genevieve had a phone extension and could have answered if she'd wanted.

Julia tapped on the door. 'Genevieve.'

No reply. She tapped again, louder this time. Still no response. She was about to go downstairs when she felt a draught under the door, bringing with it an unpleasant sweet-sour aroma. Genevieve must have left her window open. Rain was forecast for later, she'd better close it. She pushed the door open. The room was chill, far colder than Julia would have thought possible in August. She saw Genevieve on the bed and gasped. The little sidelight was on and cast an ugly shadow across her face. Rigor mortis had pulled it into a tortured grimace. Julia stepped next to the bed and knelt beside her, pulling her sleeve over her nose to mask the smell. A rivulet of vomit ran from Genevieve's mouth and had seeped into the pillow – but her stomach had failed to expel enough to save her.

Some foolish memory of first-aid protocol made Julia reach forward to check for a pulse but she withdrew before making contact. The thought of touching Genevieve's waxy skin revolted her. What was the point? No one could be more dead.

Julia stayed by the bed, very still and numb with disbelief. She kept looking to Genevieve's face as if it were unreal – a trick of the light, she'd made a mistake. Each time the face appeared more gaunt and tortured.

The phone started ringing again. She had been right. Genevieve did have an extension in her room. It sat on the side table next to a glass and a pill bottle. The same one she'd seen last time, now empty. She sniffed the glass – vodka. Brandon's words and perhaps Julia's words had been too cruel. The pills and vodka, no longer enough to stop reality leaching into her life, had been used to end it. Had Julia done this to her? Would one kind word have saved her?

The stench was becoming unbearable. Julia felt her own stomach contract in revulsion. She wanted to leave the room.

The phone had stopped when she noticed an envelope, half concealed by the covers. Julia pulled it free. 'Brandon' was written on it in bold print. She pulled back the flap. It was stuffed with fifty-pound notes. Was this the forty-five thousand Ruth had spoken of? Had Genevieve been trying to bribe Brandon to stay? Julia placed it back on the bed and looked around the room.

Julia looked at her hands. She turned and intertwined her fingers in indecision. The phone started ringing again. She lifted the receiver and, immediately, slammed it back down. Brandon's name stared up at her from the envelope. She snatched it and stuffed it down the side of the bed, before picking up the receiver and dialling 999.

Chapter 58

2017 – Dulwich, London

Julia ran into her house.

'Sam,' she shouted.

He had to be in his room. She raced upstairs and banged on his bedroom door.

'Sam.'

No answer. She pushed the door open. The room was empty. She ran back downstairs and into the lounge.

Gideon was leaning against the sideboard, a tumbler of whisky in his hand. He stared and said nothing.

'I didn't realise you were back,' Julia said.

He took a sip of whisky. 'Sam's not here,' he said.

'I'll ring his mobile.'

'And what makes you think he'll answer?' He dragged his mouth into a sneer. 'Perhaps you failed to notice, but Sam seemed rather upset about stumbling upon you fucking his rugby coach.'

'How long have you known about me and Hugh?' Julia asked.

'Please, you're not being serious. Haven't I always known everything about you, Julia?'

He was right. He had always found out her secrets, meet-ups with Pearl and Andre, the yearly bonus paid to a separate account. Why had she thought she could get away with an affair? Maybe she hadn't. Maybe she'd wanted him to know. She hadn't exactly exercised discretion.

'You drove Sam there deliberately, to find us,' she said.

'Isn't it better he knows what his mother's really like? Though I must admit, I was surprised,' he said. 'I always had you down as frigid.'

'Look—'

'It's Sam I'm worried about. It can't be very pleasant seeing his mother at it. Most men's stomachs would turn at the sight, as it is.'

'So, you don't care yourself, about me and Hugh?'

He laughed. 'Good luck to the bloke. Rather him than me.'

'And you'll speak to Sam?'

'About what?'

'Us.'

Gideon rolled the whisky around the tumbler. 'And what exactly am I meant to tell him about us?'

'That what he saw was upsetting. But nothing's changed. We can live our separate lives. There's no need for us to be enemies.'

'I said, I don't care about you screwing someone else. I didn't say it was OK to humiliate me and embarrass our son.'

'You drove him there. You set the whole thing up.'

'Sam had left some kit at the clubhouse.' He smirked.

'Bullshit.'

'In the changing rooms, Julia. Always so classy. You know, if you'd been discreet ...'

'He's the first. The first in twenty years. Don't tell me you've never strayed. What about you and Jane?'

He ignored her statement. 'You'll have to move out,' he said. 'Sam will stay here. I won't humiliate you by asking him who he'd prefer to live with.'

She looked to the floor. Why hadn't Gideon died in that accident?

He put the glass down and picked up a jacket thrown across the sofa.

'I'm going out,' he said.

He walked towards the door. When he was just parallel to Julia, he grabbed her arm. He dug his fingers in so hard she cried out.

'You'll leave me the house and savings without a fuss. Do you understand?'

His grip tightened and she cried out in pain.

'Don't cross me when it comes to money.' His voice was barely above a whisper. 'You know what I'm capable of, don't you?'

He dug his fingers in harder. So hard, Julia thought she would faint.

'Yes,' she gasped.

He let go and headed for the front door. 'I've told Sam to go and stay at Alan's tonight. I'll be back around twelve. You better be gone by then.'

He shut the door behind him, with no more force than if he were heading for a day at the office.

Julia backed out of the lounge and sat on the hall stairs. In five hours, she had to be gone. Her arm was throbbing. She leant her head against the bannister. Gideon had outmanoeuvred her.

She would have to start her life again, without her son and with no money.

346

Chapter 59

I'm shaking so much at the thought of giving evidence, I think about backing out.

'Perhaps I should just plead guilty to manslaughter,' I tell Ralph in the break.

'The CPS would never accept it. The man's head was crushed,' he says. 'Stick to what we've agreed, or you'll be convicted of murder and Gideon will walk free.'

'If I told the jury what they did—'

'They wouldn't believe you. Not now. It's you or Gideon. Survival of the fittest, or most convincing.'

I've lost before I've started. Gideon's manoeuvres have been planned years in advance, I'm an amateur. But I'm also a mother. Sam is not going to have Gideon as his sole parent. Survival of the fittest – the ability to adapt. I've watched and learnt for enough years, an amateur maybe, but a knowledge-able one.

I take the religious oath. Audrey wouldn't forgive me if I did otherwise. I try to remember what Ralph told me: address the jury, state my recollections calmly, don't be tempted to embroider or fill in gaps. The simple explanation is the most plausible. Ralph pulls his gown to sit level on his shoulders. He looks at his notes for a moment. I take the opportunity to look across the court. Sam has returned to the public gallery. He's looks at me intently. I shouldn't stare at him, but I can't help it. He gives me the faintest nod.

Ralph shuffles his papers and coughs. 'Ms Winter, would you tell the court what you remember of the events surrounding your departure from Guildford.'

'It was very muddled,' I say. 'The whole thing was over-shadowed by Genevieve's suicide. I was the one who found her, you see. I couldn't get the image of her face out of my head. After that I was hardly at the house. I spent as much time as I could with my friends in London.'

'And the August bank holiday, 1994. Do you recall where you were?'

'Honestly, it's so long ago, I don't remember what I did that weekend. But I doubt I would have spent three days off work at the house. I think I only stayed there a few times after Genevieve's death. I gave my notice in at work. I wanted to get away.'

'And after you vacated Downsview Villa?'

'I took over a room from my friend, Pearl. It was in a shared house in Archway, London.'

'And did you find another job?'

'Not in software development, which I had been doing in Guildford. I was a receptionist by day and in the evening I worked in a pub.'

'Two jobs, so money was tight?'

'I had savings from when I was living at home with my

parents. But I didn't want to touch them. I hoped to get a better job and buy a flat someday.'

Ralph prepared me for this gentle preamble; it's meant to relax me, before we move on to more delicate matters.

'You say you wanted to forget everything associated with Downsview Villa, yet you reconnected with Gideon Risborough. How did that come about?'

'He visited me once in London.'

'What reason did he give?'

'He said he was in the area. The real reason was to warn me that a private investigator was asking questions about Brandon. That was the first time I knew his family were looking for him.'

'You had no idea in Guildford?'

'I knew he'd gone away. At the time it didn't seem particularly important. I assumed he'd moved on elsewhere – he was a backpacker.'

'Why do you think Mr Risborough wanted to talk to you about the private investigator?'

'Looking back, I can see he wanted to check on what I'd told Michael Lancaster, to make sure I'd not said anything that didn't tally with his version of events.'

'And when did you see Mr Risborough again?' Ralph asks.

'After I moved back in with my mother. I was unwell and couldn't work.'

Ralph stops and checks I'm ready for this, giving me an encouraging smile.

'This must be painful for you, but would you tell the jury why you were ill, and what happened? Was your suicide attempt down to guilt, as Mr Risborough maintains?'

Sam is watching. I can't raise my eyes. I shouldn't do this to my son.

'Genevieve's death hit me hard. Harder than I realised. I'd never seen a dead body before. Her face was horrifying, all twisted like she'd been frightened to death. I kept seeing it everywhere. I was exhausted through work and I felt I had no one to turn to.' I can feel Audrey's eyes upon me. 'I feel dreadful now, knowing how much it hurt my mother, but I tried to kill myself.'

I'm aware of the court's sudden stillness. Its eyes resting upon me, interpreting the slightest expression or hand gesture as a pointer to guilt or innocence.

'I was going to jump from Hornsey Lane Bridge. Fortunately, two women stopped me. My mother came to fetch me from the hospital and took me home.'

I can't tell the court that Gideon was there, on that bridge, silently wishing me success. Who would believe me?

'And it was while you were recuperating at your mother's that Mr Risborough contacted you again?' Ralph asks.

'At first, I didn't want to see him. He reminded me of everything that had happened. But then I thought it would be better to be with someone who understood what I'd been through and, to start with, he was kind.'

'And later?'

I look down. Please, Sam, leave the court.

'Ms Winter, I'm sorry, you need to answer the question.'

'Later I realised I'd made a mistake,' I say. 'I shouldn't have made any important decisions when I wasn't myself. Gideon wanted to get married and he encouraged me to go back into software development. I thought he was supportive of my career, when he only wanted someone to fund his lifestyle.

The money I'd saved for the flat we used to buy a house, far too big for what we needed, but Gideon insisted. My pay went to a joint account, but only he had a card. Then he found out from one of my colleagues that I received a yearly bonus, which used to be paid into a separate account. I've rarely seen him so angry. He insisted I close the account and made me show him all my payslips after that.'

'Why didn't you just leave?' Ralph asks.

'He said he'd take Sam away from me. No court would give custody to a fruitcake who'd already tried to kill herself once. Who never bonded with her child and spent as little time with him as possible. That wasn't true. I spent as much time as I could with Sam, but I had to work so hard. Sam and I were close until, well, until my mistake.' I look at Sam but can't hold his gaze. 'Also, I was scared of Gideon.'

Two jurors on the front row, a man and a woman, whisper something to each other.

'Was your husband ever violent?' Ralph asks.

'No.'

'Then why were you scared?'

'If you knew him, what he could be like, you'd understand. He'd never shout, or even raise his voice, he'd just say the most terrible things as if it was an everyday conversation. People always thought he was so charming. I think I'm the only person, apart from Alan, who knows what he's capable of.'

'Meaning?'

I've started shaking. I have to take some deep breaths to calm myself. 'Until the police came to my work and told me he was dead, I hadn't believed what Gideon told me about Brandon. I thought he'd been using it to add weight to his threats. But I *did* know he'd threatened both an ex-girlfriend and a man who owed him money.'

'So, Mr Risborough made specific threats to your safety and referenced Brandon's disappearance?'

'He said, "Don't cross me when it comes to money. Brandon didn't just disappear."'

'Thank you, Ms Winter. No further questions.'

Dryden stands up, her wig is slightly misaligned. I expect her to adjust it. She leaves it as it is, as if I'm not worth the effort.

'Ms Winter, we have only your word for this controlling behaviour by Mr Risborough, don't we?' she says. 'Who's to say you didn't equally enjoy the status of having such a large house and your husband having expensive cars and well-cut suits? Your version of events in Guildford are risible – you weren't there, you don't remember – how very convenient. And as for these threats, did you ever tell anyone, your mother, your best friend?'

'No.'

'May I ask why?'

'I was ashamed,' I say. 'From the outside I had the perfect life. A handsome husband and son, a massive house, a great job. Of course, people guessed something was wrong. All my clothes were from Primark. Other mums at school commented on my son's second-hand sports kit. We never had family holidays. But if anyone asked, I'd laugh it off.'

'Again, according to you. No one else recalls this pattern of behaviour. We have only your word for this, don't we?' Dryden says.

I try to think of a reply that won't give her the answer she wants.

'Ms Winter,' she repeats. 'We only have your word for this, don't we?'

'Yes,' I say.

'Just as we only have your word that you weren't at Downsview Villa on the bank holiday weekend in question, when Brandon disappeared. No one else can corroborate this version of events.'

'It was twenty-four years ago – why should anyone remember?'

'Your husband and Mr Johns remember it.'

'They cooked this up between them. Alan's always done whatever Gideon wanted, from the moment they met. It's pathetic, embarrassing. He was more interested in Gideon's opinion than his wife's – that's why they split up. I'm surprised he didn't admit to Brandon's murder, just to get Gideon off. He prob—'

'Ms Winter,' Judge Fleetwood interrupts. 'You will restrict yourself to answering the questions put to you. This is not a free-for-all.'

What did I say – too much, too little? How will the jury view it?

'Yes, your honour,' I say.

Dryden straightens herself to her full height, and exudes an air of stern amusement, as a teacher to a mischievous child.

'And if I may return to your claim that you were frightened of your husband, that's pure fabrication too, isn't it?' she asks.

'No,' I say.

'Please, Ms Winter, again you told no one.'

'I've explained why.'

'Perhaps you're unaware, but I've had the misfortune to deal with many cases of domestic violence,' Dryden says.

353

'Usually multiple instances have occurred, before the case comes before the court. The victim's family and colleagues see suspicious bruises. There are unexplained slips and falls leading to visits to A & E. Have your family or colleagues ever noticed such injuries?'

'No, I never said—'

'Visits to A & E?'

'I was trying—'

'Well, perhaps you could detail the catalogue of physical injuries inflicted upon you by your husband, before the court – Ms Winter?'

'He didn't hit me. It wasn't like that – it was always the threat.'

'So yet again, another totally unverifiable accusation. In truth, Mr Risborough has been an excellent husband. Many men wouldn't have married a woman in your position, living with your mother after a psychological breakdown and a suicide attempt.'

'So Gideon tells me, repeatedly.'

There's a second when Dryden looks taken aback by my bitterness, as if, until then, she'd not considered the possibility that anything I've said could be true. It's of little consequence, she is Gideon's defence lawyer and won't be turned from her task.

'He encouraged you in your career, even you admit that, and despite your claims of cruelty, never laid a finger on you. You had an adulterous affair with your son's rugby coach but you claim Mr Risborough is cruel. You abandon your son, but he is the bad father. You claim he's concocted a story to put you in prison, when for years he's protected you.'

I don't reply.

'And you had good reason to dislike Brandon. He was spoiling your chances with your future husband and you were overheard arguing with him. You were close to Mrs Pike and would surely have known about the money. My learned friend, Mr Williams, has made much of the difference in size between you and Brandon, but the blade of a knife can kill the strongest man. Two witnesses place you in the house on the day we know Brandon was to return. The house stank of bleach and you wouldn't allow anyone into the lounge. In the early hours of the morning a car arrives for you. We can guess its purpose. You are the only defendant whose DNA can be placed, definitively, at the crime scene – your hairs coated in blood found in Brandon's grave. Despite Mr Williams' attempt to obfuscate on this issue, the best explanation is the simplest. Your hair was at the crime scene because you were at the crime scene. No one else – not your husband, not Alan Johns – you.'

Chapter 60

1994 – Guildford

The paramedics pronounced life extinct at seven-thirty-nine that evening. Two uniformed police officers arrived to inspect the scene.

Julia, Gideon and Alan huddled around the kitchen table, drinking tea. Despite the August heat, Julia still felt the cold of Genevieve's bedroom run through her.

'Brandon was the last to see her,' Gideon said. 'Do you think he could have—'

'No,' Julia said.

'You seem very sure.'

She swivelled towards him. 'Don't you believe me?'

'It's just you and Brandon ...'

'Me and Brandon, what?' She glared at him. He returned the look with mild astonishment then turned away, as if it had been a throwaway comment and she'd overreacted. She hadn't. He was trying to say something, to implicate her.

'It pains me to say it,' Alan said. 'And not just because it means Julia's right, but Lucy heard Genevieve crying *after* Brandon left the house.'

'Oh my God,' Julia said. 'Someone will have to tell Lucy.'

'What's the point? She won't be able to do anything from – where is it?'

'Newcastle,' Julia said. 'And what about Ruth and Edward?'

The three of them had been ignoring the phone, which was ringing every five minutes.

'Leave it to the police,' Gideon said.

'And Brandon?' she ventured, wary of Gideon's response.

He and Alan looked at each other.

'I'm not going to shy away from telling him,' Alan said. 'I want to see his face, when he learns he's off the gravy train.'

Julia thought of the money. The gravy train was just pulling into the station. She was fatigued, shaky as well as cold now.

'I could do with a real drink – has anyone got some?' Julia asked.

'Even my Chartreuse is finished,' Gideon said. 'I could make us something to eat. Pasta?'

'I couldn't face it,' Julia said.

'Me neither,' Alan said.

'Just me then.' Gideon stood, went to the fridge, removed some vegetables and started slicing onions and garlic for the pasta sauce. Julia's belly ached with hunger, but the thought of eating repulsed her. Gideon had no such problem and wolfed down a bowl, then went back for more.

It was nearing dusk when they heard the heavy thunk down the stairs as the body was removed. Gideon carried on eating. Alan looked at Julia. He too was straining to hear each step and their eyes met in a rare moment of solidarity. By the time the police came downstairs it was dark.

'It's a pretty cut and dried case of suicide,' the constable said. 'As you found her, you'll be asked to give a statement,

Ms Winter, but we'll not be making further inquiries. And the bedroom's not being treated as a crime scene. So Mrs Pike's sister's free to come and collect anything she feels is of value. We'll be off then.'

The police presence had made Julia feel safe and she didn't want them to leave. Once they had shut the door the house seemed twice as dark, and far too large for three people. And though the police had ruled out foul play, she sensed danger. Genevieve's face, ghastly, contorted, floated before her. She understood why ancient peoples believed in daemons and possession.

'I'm not spending the night here,' she said.

Alan looked at her with contempt.

'You didn't find her,' Julia said.

'Where will you go?' Gideon asked.

'I'm sure Bee from work will let me stay. If not, Pearl will. Anywhere but here.'

Bee agreed to drive around and fetch her. Julia went to her room to collect pyjamas and clean clothes for the following day. The boys were still in the kitchen when she finished. She leant over the bannister.

'Sure you won't have some?' Gideon was saying.

'Couldn't eat a thing,' Alan said.

Perhaps he too wanted to spend the night elsewhere. Julia hovered on the landing a little longer, to ensure their conversation continued. When she was certain they weren't about to leave the kitchen, she crept up the stairs to Genevieve's room.

A dread rose within her on returning. She half expected to find Genevieve still lying there as she pushed open the door, but the room was empty and cold, despite the window having been closed. The duvet had been roughly pulled back across the bed, the pill bottle and glass removed.

Julia walked to the side table and switched on the light. She leant over and ran her hand along the gap between the bed and the wall. She repeated the action several times, becoming more frantic with each sweep. Finally, she pulled the bed back and checked underneath. It wasn't there. She looked under the mattress, threw the pillows to the floor, tore off the covers, shook and shook them again. The envelope had gone.

Chapter 61

2018 – Guildford Crown Court

Ralph is the only defence barrister to call witnesses other than their client. *If ever I can do anything for you*, she has said. Well now she can.

Leanne still has the appearance of a young and vulnerable girl. Her figure is slight, her voice high and tremulous. Through the forty-something woman, I can still see the slender teenager standing in the rain, looking up at the house.

'Mrs Grainger, would you tell the court the circumstances under which you came to know Gideon Risborough and his now wife Julia Winter.'

'I met Gideon at the shipping firm I worked for. I was an admin assistant. Gideon was my boyfriend. At least, I thought he was. He said that he was.'

'And when was this? How old were you?'

'I was seventeen, so it must have been 1994.'

'And how old was Mr Risborough?'

'Twenty-eight,' she says. The juror with the pink scarf shuffles in her seat and looks away from Leanne to Gideon. 'He asked me out. I was flattered. He seemed so much more sophisticated than the boys I knew. He didn't live at home.

He drove a white BMW. I'd just left school, you see, and those sort of things seemed important.'

'Was it a sexual relationship?' Ralph asks.

Leanne averts her eyes. 'Yes, it was. I thought I was in love and that he felt the same.'

'And how long did the relationship last?'

'About six months. Looking back, I can see I was naïve. He made me keep our relationship a secret. He often went away at weekends and was vague about where. When I asked if he was seeing other women, he said I was a silly, jealous school-girl. Then I fell pregnant.'

The juror wearing the pink scarf inhales sharply.

'And how did Mr Risborough react to the news?'

Leanne looks at Gideon. The first witness who isn't doing so for approval. Gideon angles his head away from her, and towards his defence team.

'He said it wasn't his and if I pestered him, I'd regret it.' Murmurs around the court. 'He told me to get an abortion. I wasn't brought up like that – our family didn't believe in it. Gideon didn't want to know. That was on a Thursday. I took Friday off, because I was so upset.'

'And despite the threats not to "pester" him, did you try to contact Mr Risborough again?'

'Over the following weekend I tried to call him, but he wouldn't answer my phone calls or come to the door of his flat. When I went to work on Monday morning I was taken into the boss's office. Three and a half thousand pounds had gone missing. They told me they weren't going to press charges, but I was expected to go without a fuss. They said it was lucky Gideon had spoken up for me and made excuses because I was so young. Otherwise they would have called the police.

I didn't have three and a half pounds, let alone three and a half thousand. No one listened.'

'So, the police were never involved?' Ralph asks.

'No.'

'And your parents?'

'There was only me and my mum. She was furious, called me a slut and threw me out.'

Leanne's breathing becomes uneven. Ralph gives her a moment to calm herself.

'So, you were seventeen, jobless and homeless. Did you take any further action to speak to Mr Risborough?'

'A friend let me stay at hers. The next week she rang the shipping firm. Gideon had left to work elsewhere. I know it sounds stupid, but at the time I thought it was a mistake – the business with the three and a half thousand pounds. I couldn't believe someone, who a few weeks earlier had told me he loved me, would deliberately frame me for theft. I remembered Gideon had talked about his godfather and how he had a supplements business in Guildford. Not many places sold algae in those days. It wasn't difficult to find. My same friend rang the office and tricked the owner into giving her his home address.'

'You travelled to Guildford, alone?'

'There was no one to go with me.'

'What happened when you reached the house?'

Leanne lifts her chin and stares at the defendants' bench.

'Gideon slammed the door in my face. It was pouring down with rain and I was standing there. I didn't know what to do, when Ms Winter came home.'

'Ms Winter was entirely unknown to you at the time?'

'Entirely. When she first spoke to me, I thought she might

be Gideon's girlfriend and tell me to leave, but she made me come in and gave me a towel to dry off with.'

'Did you make Ms Winter aware of your situation with regards to Mr Risborough?'

'No. I'm not sure if I would have done or not. But Gideon sent Ms Winter away, the moment he realised I was in the house. He was so angry. He threw me out of the house, *literally* threw me onto the ground. I grazed my knees. He said if I ever turned up at his home or place of work again, he'd make me regret it.'

'Was Ms Winter a witness to this?'

'I don't think so, but she did see me standing outside later. I wouldn't come in again, so she gave me an umbrella and money to get a cab. I'll always remember that. How kind she was, because it felt like the end of the world.'

'Did you have any dealings with Mr Risborough again?'

'I was too scared. I didn't go through with the pregnancy. I tried to put it all behind me.'

'It was the pregnancy that made him angry?'

'Well, more that he thought I'd ask him for money.'

'So, money disappeared, and Mr Risborough blamed you, his ex-girlfriend. He then went on to threaten you to ensure you made no financial demands?'

'That's correct,' Leanne says.

Ralph glances at the jury. 'A familiar scenario.' He turns back to face Leanne. 'I know this must have been difficult for you, Mrs Grainger. Thank you for your time.'

Chapter 62

1994 – Guildford

Julia returned to Downsview Villa early the next day. The house was empty. She couldn't imagine where Gideon and Alan would have gone on a bank holiday Saturday. Enjoying any entertainment seemed heartless. Still, their being gone was to Julia's advantage. She didn't believe the envelope could have gone missing so quickly. She had been in shock, panicked, made a mistake. For the second time since Genevieve's death, she returned to the room, checked the covers, pulled the bed back and searched the floor. It was nowhere to be seen.

The front door banged. Julia froze. She heard footsteps coming up the stairs. It must be Alan. Brandon always stamped, Lucy was away, and Gideon's room was on the ground floor. Alan's room was directly below Genevieve's. He'd hear the slightest creak of the floorboards. She waited, motionless. Alan was moving around, opening and shutting drawers. It seemed to take for ever before he left the room and went downstairs. Julia pushed the bed back to the wall and returned to her own room.

Anyone could have taken the envelope – one of the paramedics, the police, even Alan or Gideon. Both had left the kitchen at points during the previous evening. She couldn't

364

ask and couldn't tell, because she should never have moved the envelope. It may have been illegal, tampering with evidence or something. She hadn't planned on keeping the money. All she had wanted was to stop Brandon getting his hands on it.

When she came downstairs, Gideon and Alan were at the table, cradling beers. They turned around as Julia came in.

'Have you seen Brandon?' Gideon asked.

'No,' Julia replied. 'Do you think he knows?'

'Who would have told him?' Gideon said. 'The police said no third party was involved, but I can't help thinking Brandon's disappearance is suspicious.'

Suspicious, yes, just not in the way Gideon meant. Could Brandon have sneaked back and taken the money? Everyone had been busy, the house in disarray – it wasn't impossible.

'He's been acting strangely,' Gideon said. 'And his drinking's way out of hand.'

'He was always drunk by the time I got home,' Alan said. 'That night he argued with Genevieve, the bin was full of empty cans.'

'I wish I'd gone to speak to Genevieve, that night or even the next morning,' Julia said. 'She was probably still alive then. I never took all that melodrama seriously. I should have done.'

'You were her lodger, not her psychiatrist,' Gideon said. 'Ruth or Edward were better placed to do something.'

'Has anyone spoken to Ruth?' Julia asked.

Gideon and Alan shook their heads.

'I should go and see her. I didn't check on Genevieve. I'm not making the same mistake twice.'

Julia had never visited Ruth's house, but knew from Genevieve that it was on Watling Avenue, only ten minutes from

Downsview Villa and that it had 'by far the best rosebed on the street'.

Ruth was outside her house in front of a rose bush, secateurs in hand, lopping the heads off flowers in full bloom. She kept clipping, not noticing Julia until she came onto the lawn and stood right next to her. At first, Ruth looked at her without recognition, then she said, 'Oh, it's you.'

Her voice was flat, her face blank.

'I'm so sorry,' Julia said.

'Sorry won't bring Jenny back,' Ruth said.

Did Ruth blame Julia? She'd asked her to look out for Genevieve, to keep Brandon from hurting her. She'd failed and much worse than that.

'Is there anything, *anything* I can do for you?'

'No. Thank you,' Ruth said.

Did she know Julia had argued with Genevieve and said such terrible things?

'Do you want me to leave, Ruth?'

'I want ...' She trailed off and looked back to her plants. 'I want to know what Brandon said to her. I know he's behind this. The police told me they argued – but what about? I can't believe it was suicide. She wouldn't ...'

You delusional old cow. Dominic's dead and he's not coming back. Would Ruth benefit from knowing any of this?

Ruth composed herself and began lopping at the plants again.

'Brandon did something to her – I don't know how. Genevieve took out forty-five thousand pounds over the last few weeks. Was it to give to him?'

'Is that what she told you?'

'No. I found the cash had been withdrawn and put two

366

and two together. How did he get that much money out of her – blackmail?'

'A blackmailer wouldn't kill his victim. It defeats the object.'

'What then?' Ruth asked.

To bribe Brandon to stay with her, because she was a sad, desperate woman.

'I don't know,' Julia said. 'Do you have the money?'

'It's disappeared, along with Brandon. I told the police. They're looking into the theft but won't consider Genevieve's death as anything other than suicide. Accidental death at the most. The physical evidence ...' Ruth's voice became strained. 'The physical evidence doesn't correlate with a homicide. What do they know?'

Julia thought of Brandon, his great bulk, his workman's hands. If he'd wanted Genevieve dead, there would have been bruising, blood and broken bones, not a cunning recreation of a suicide. She saw the room again. Genevieve had been lying under her duvet, the room ordered, the sidelight turned on. Brandon hadn't killed Genevieve.

'Had Genevieve ever tried before to ... you know?' Julia couldn't decide how to phrase it. 'Had she tried to hurt herself?'

The secateurs fell to the ground. Ruth put her head in her hands and started to sob.

'I never understood my sister. We had the same parents, the same upbringing. She had everything. Why ... why was she so bloody stupid?'

Julia stepped towards her and put her arms around her. Ruth's head fell onto Julia's shoulder.

'I'm sorry. I'm so sorry,' Ruth said.

'It's fine. It's totally normal.'

'I blame myself.'

'You mustn't.'

'Over and over, I told her about Brandon – what type of boy he was,' Ruth said. 'She wouldn't listen. In the end, I said it was up to her. But I wasn't going to pick up the pieces yet again. She was on her own. I didn't mean it. I was angry. I thought if I let her stew a bit, I'd make her see sense. If only I'd gone around to see her, patched things up.' Ruth raised her head. 'She drove me mad. But I miss her so much already. I wish you'd known her when she was younger. She was such fun with all her flights of fancy. And people found her eccentricity enchanting. Only after Dominic died, it wasn't enchanting, it was unnerving, morbid. That's when she started drinking and taking those pills. I tried to get her off them, without success. And people no longer found her charming. At best they pitied her. If only they'd recovered Dominic's body. She could never accept he was dead, you see.'

But Genevieve had finally accepted it. And it resulted in her own death.

Ruth pulled away from Julia, picked up the secateurs and wiped her face.

'It was kind of you to come to see me,' she said. 'And, actually, there is something you can do for me.'

'Anything,' Julia said.

'You must tell me the second Brandon gets back. Even if Jenny did take her own life, in my eyes, he's still a murderer.'

Chapter 63

Genevieve's sister Ruth has changed little since the Nineties. Her hair is a little greyer, her back a little more bent, and, out of her gardening clothes, she cuts a smarter figure, but otherwise she's the same. Just before she enters the witness box, she turns directly and deliberately towards me, an odd expression on her face, one I can't decipher. Why look at me, not Gideon or Alan?

She takes the religious oath and waits for Helena Dryden to question her. She is the last and calmest witness. Her attitude is that of someone about to chat to a neighbour across the garden fence, rather than be examined by a hostile barrister in Crown Court. Because Helena Dryden *is* hostile now. The cut-throat defence means that evidence that once supported Gideon's innocence now weakens it.

'Mrs Fletcher, after the death of your sister, Mrs Pike, you looked after the house, didn't you?' Dryden takes the slightly patronising tone usually reserved for the very old or very young.

'I did,' Ruth says.

'And I believe, even before her death, you took care of certain matters for her.'

369

'As soon as I learnt she was letting rooms, I made an inventory. There were some quite nice, quite *valuable* pieces around the place. I wanted to keep an eye on them. Jenny was hopeless with anything practical.'

'Is the inventory still in your possession?' Dryden asks.

'Of course not,' Ruth says. 'It was over twenty years ago. I'm not one of those hoarders you see on television – can't get into the house for old newspapers and disused cereal packets.'

Pink scarf woman smiles at this assertion.

'So, your recollection as to which pieces were and weren't on the inventory at that time is purely from memory?' Dryden says, scanning her notes.

'There's nothing wrong with my memory,' Ruth says.

Dryden looks up in mock surprise. 'Really?' she says. 'Because when the police originally showed you the rug and lamp, Mrs Fletcher, you claimed not to recognise them, not to *remember* them. But later, you changed your mind.'

'Out of context, I didn't recognise them,' Ruth says. 'Naturally, I remembered when I saw them in the photograph of Jenny's lounge. I think Edward, one of her gentlemen friends, bought her that lamp. He's dead now, so I can't ask him.'

Ruth is much older than any of the jury, and really does come across like someone's rambling great-aunt.

'Can you say without a doubt and from memory that both the lamp and rug were on your inventory?' Dryden asks.

'I remember nothing was missing on that first look around the house after the lodgers left. And the lamp and the rug would have been on the inventory.' Ruth pauses and looks at me again with a slight smile. 'Of course, that was before ... Maybe I should have done another inventory.'

The next obvious question is why should Ruth have wanted a second inventory? But barristers don't like asking a question when they're uncertain of the answer. Dryden looks disconcerted, unsure. Ruth is waiting, her head to one side, a smile on her lips. Dryden decides not to take the bait.

'But we established this is all from memory,' she says. 'The records no longer exist.'

'I just told you that, dear, less than a minute ago,' Ruth says. 'It strikes me you're the one who's having difficulties with their memory.'

Judge Fleetwood cuts short the stifled laughter around the court by looking up and searching for the culprits.

'Thank you,' Dryden says. 'Nothing more.'

She sits down and looks at Alan's barrister. I can't see what passes between them.

Ralph spends a moment adjusting his papers, before addressing Ruth.

'Mrs Fletcher, you worked as a bookkeeper for many years, is that correct?'

'After my husband left, I had two daughters to support, so I had no choice,' she says.

'And in your retirement, you've chosen to volunteer and have continued to keep books for several local charities?'

'Yes.'

'So, you've kept your mind pretty sharp?'

'I still finish the *Times*' cryptic crossword every day.'

Ralph smiles. 'I've no doubt,' he says. 'The prosecution and, latterly, Mr Risborough and Mr Johns maintain that the lamp used to kill Brandon, and the rug in which he was wrapped, went missing when the lodgers left the house. Your evidence

371

contradicts that; you say the lodgers left *prior* to the disappearance of the objects.'

'They did.'

'Thus precluding my client from carrying out an attack in the manner so suddenly suggested by the two other defendants.' He gestures to the dock. 'And we've already seen that the forensic evidence is inconclusive. And just for the record, you've no personal interest in the defendants or have any reason to protect them.'

'Lord, no!' Ruth says.

'You never thought about them, until the police came to see you?'

'I did think about them. They were there when Jenny died. Julia found the body. It must have been awful for her. But I've had no contact with them since. I'm sure they'd all rather forget about it.'

'So, you are stating, categorically, that the defendants had left the house before the lamp and the rug the prosecution allege were used in the murder disappeared. Nothing was missing in that inventory take.'

'Not on that first inventory, no.' Ruth pauses and looks at me again. 'Of course, that was before ... Now I know I should have done a second inventory.'

Ralph hesitates. Like Dryden, he is cautious. He can't guess the response of the question begging to be asked. He glances down, clears his throat and takes a moment before saying, 'Before what, Mrs Fletcher? Was there a reason for you to do a second inventory?'

'If I'd been in a better state of mind, I should have realised they'd returned to the house. Because I saw them all again nearly a month later, at the bottom of Downsview Avenue.'

'But you told the police you never saw them in the house again,' Ralph says.

'I didn't see them *in* the house, but I did see the three of them at the end of the street, about a month later, as I said. They were in a white BMW, heading towards Downsview Villa.'

That's something she can't have seen. Why is she lying? Is Dryden right about her? Am I about to be convicted because of the ramblings of some batty old lady? Do they check witnesses for dementia?

'Let me get this right, a month after they all claim to have left the house, you saw a white BMW, a car we know Gideon Risborough to have been driving at that time, on Downsview Way, and inside you saw the three defendants.'

'When I said three of them, I wasn't referring to all defendants – only two of them, Gideon and Alan. The third person in the car was Brandon Wells.'

Gasps from the public gallery. Brandon's brother and sister sit bolt upright. Judge Fleetwood goes so far as to remove his chin from resting on his hand and he leans forward. Alan flicks his eyes to Gideon, whose fists are clenched as he stares at Ruth. The jurors look at one another, confused. Mapplethorpe mutters something to Dryden. Ralph is serene.

'So contrary to the assertion of Mr Risborough and Mr Johns, Brandon must have been alive and well on the Saturday 27th August bank holiday, the day they've insinuated my client took his life. You are certain it was after this date?'

'Yes, 22nd September.'

'You remember the exact date?'

'It was the day of Jenny's inquest,' Ruth says. 'They ruled it was suicide. I was walking home when I saw them.'

'So, a date you'll never forget. Can you think why the two defendants would implicate Ms Winter?'

'Your honour.' Dryden stands up. 'Mrs Fletcher is not here to answer for my client.'

'Indeed,' Judge Fleetwood says. 'Mrs Fletcher, kindly refrain from answering that question.'

Ralph inclines his head towards Fleetwood before continuing. 'Mrs Fletcher, you don't strike me as a woman prone to flights of fancy. You've stated that you remember the day clearly because it was just after your sister's inquest. Now, can you confirm that you had a good view of the occupants of the BMW?'

'Yes.'

'Would you reiterate who was in the car please?'

'Certainly. Gideon Risborough, Alan Johns and Brandon Wells.'

'And my client, Ms Winter, most definitely was not in the car.'

'Not unless she was in the boot.' This elicits a nervous smile from the woman in the pink scarf. 'No, it was just the three lads. Julia, Ms Winter, wasn't with them.'

'For the record, can you confirm once more that you've had no contact with any of the defendants in the intervening years?' Ralph asks.

'None, whatsoever.'

'Thank you, Mrs Fletcher, you've been most helpful.'

Before Ralph can sit down, Dryden's on her feet in a flutter of papers, which float from her desk and her junior has to scurry on the floor, picking them up as Dryden addresses Judge Fleetwood.

'Your honour, I'd like to re-examine the witness,' she says.

'Yes, Ms Dryden. I expect you do,' he replies. 'If you would remain in the stand, Mrs Fletcher.'

I tense in my seat. Ruth's lie is about to unravel.

'These sudden revelations, Mrs Fletcher, after twenty-four years, can you tell us the reason for it?'

'It wasn't sudden, dear,' Ruth says. Her stance is relaxed, but her eyes are animated. 'No one asked me, until just now, and I have sworn to tell the *whole* truth.'

Dryden doesn't know how to handle a witness contradicting her case, who is neither openly combative nor intimidated.

Several members of the jury nod. Dryden tries a different angle.

'Let me get this right, Mrs Fletcher,' she says. 'You saw Brandon Wells, the man you accused of murdering your sister, the one the police were seeking for theft, in a car with Gideon Risborough and Alan Wells and you told no one, didn't call the police. Would you please explain to the court why?'

Ruth sighs. 'It's a bit embarrassing really,' she says. 'The problem was I'd called the police before, claiming to have seen Brandon. It was to kick their backsides into gear, because they were doing nothing, as far as I could tell. They started getting quite sharp with me. In the end my friend, the chief constable, who I knew from my charity work, called me, off the record, and told me to stop. Or I'd be charged with wasting police time.'

'He can verify this?'

'Unfortunately, he's long dead, but there may be detectives from that time who remember taking my calls.'

Ralph half stands. 'Former detective Crane said as much in his testimony,' he says.

Dryden doesn't acknowledge him.

'Go on,' she says to Ruth.

'And then, you see, I felt such a fool when I *did* spot him. I was the typical girl who cried wolf.'

'And this was definitely after the bank holiday, after Mrs Pike had died?'

'It was the day of the inquest, 22nd September 1994,' Ruth says.

'Can you tell the court why you never mentioned this before, during your questioning by the police?'

'There's a very simple answer – no one asked.'

This raises another smile from the woman in the pink scarf.

'You're aware your testimony directly contradicts that of Mr Risborough and Mr Johns, both of whom last recall seeing Brandon in early August?'

'Is that what they said? They must have forgotten,' Ruth says.

'Mrs Fletcher.' Dryden sounds exasperated. 'You are seventy-four – is that correct?'

'Yes.'

'Hmm,' Dryden says. 'Given that three people's lives and liberty rest on your testimony and given the events were twenty-four years ago, would you like to reconsider?'

'No thank you. I know what I saw.'

'You haven't merged the memory, of seeing the three young men another time, with walking home from your sister's inquest?'

'No, I haven't.' Ruth's eyes focus in on Dryden. 'I'm sorry if my testimony doesn't suit your client's version of events. But I saw what I saw and I've no reason to lie. The lamp and rug disappeared after I saw those three back in Guildford.'

Ruth telling her lie to Ralph was a stroke of luck, letting

it settle in the jury's mind before Dryden had a chance to pull it apart.

'You must realise, Mrs Fletcher, that sudden changes in court, to the version given to the police, cause suspicion.'

'It's not a change, it's an addition and I said, if anyone had *asked* me, I would have told them.'

'You're aware of the penalties for perjury, Mrs Fletcher?'

'You're calling me a liar?'

'I'm making you aware of the risks you run sticking to your version as absolute fact. In a case of murder it's very unwise. After twenty-four years and given your age—'

'Gladstone served as prime minster until he was eighty-four and you think I'd forget the day of the coroner's inquest into my sister's death. Having to hear all the details, how unhappy she had been, how fragile she was – the vodka, the pills, the vomit clogging her lungs. No, my love, I'd have to be well into my dotage before I forget those things.'

The jury sit forward.

'I see you're sticking to your version of events. But you will agree that is your version and no one can verify it.'

'If you say so, dear,' Ruth says.

'Thank you, Mrs Fletcher,' she says and sits down.

Gideon is glaring at Ruth through the glass of the dock. She doesn't notice him. Ralph looks at me. His gaze is calm and steady. Has he realised Ruth is lying?

Ralph looks more serene than ever as he stands before the jury in his summing up. He is superb.

'Only two of the defendants are known to have come into a large sum of money after Mrs Pike's death. Only two were seen by Mrs Ruth Fletcher in the company of Brandon Wells, nearly a month after Mr Risborough and Mr Johns claim Ms Winter killed him. The same two who sought to blame my client for a crime she cannot possibly have committed. They thought they'd committed the perfect murder, killing a man no one would miss for many months, taking his money and channelling it through their business and finally, planting evidence against Ms Winter, so that should anything go wrong she would be blamed. Unfortunately for Mr Risborough and Mr Johns, Mrs Fletcher spotted them on a day and date she would never forget, and their avaricious and vindictive plan fell to pieces. Gideon Risborough and Alan Johns killed Brandon Wells and have maligned my client not just to clear their names, but for reasons of personal spite. I urge the jury to look at the evidence, which overwhelmingly points to my client simply to have been in the wrong place and married to the wrong man. You must find her not guilty.'

Chapter 64

1994 – Guildford

Genevieve had been dead less than forty-eight hours when Julia and the other lodgers started taking liberties with her home. Julia came in the front door, which they'd all started using, and from the hall she could see that Gideon and Alan were in the lounge, feet up on the coffee table watching the TV news. Neither of them noticed her come in.

She climbed the stairs and paused a moment, before going into Brandon's room. His clothes were strewn across the floor, which was no indication of whether he'd return. His possessions were of so little value that even without forty-five thousand pounds they'd hardly be worth retrieving.

Julia opened the wardrobe. It was empty, except for a backpack slung on the floor. She knelt down and checked its compartments. She didn't think Brandon would leave the money so casually but checked anyway. The main compartment was empty, but something was in one of the pockets. Rummaging around, she found a packet of tobacco and a cigarette lighter. She pulled the backpack out of the wardrobe to examine it properly. It caught on something. Julia yanked it. One of its straps was caught in the join between the wardrobe floor and its back panel. The backpack contained nothing more. Julia returned to the wardrobe. There was a definite gap at the back. She poked her fingers through it and managed to grasp something flat and rectangular and pull it out. It was Brandon's passport. He would have to come back now.

'What are you doing?'

Julia jumped up. Gideon stood in the doorway.

'I was checking Brandon's things. To see if he was coming back.'

'I already looked,' Gideon said. 'I can't see why he'd bother returning for any of this.' He indicated the small heap of greying sweatshirts and jeans on the floor.

'He'll bother returning for this.'

Julia held out the passport. Gideon looked confused for a moment.

'Where did he hide it?' Gideon asked.

Julia showed him the wardrobe panels. Gideon examined the gap, then sat back, put his leg inside and kicked three times, until the panel came loose.

'What are you looking for?' Julia asked.

'Nothing,' Gideon said.

Did he know about the money? It seemed unlikely. Then she remembered the phone.

'He's probably taken it with him,' Julia said.

'Taken what with him?' Gideon asked.

'The mobile phone.'

Gideon turned to her, anger and shock on his face. 'What do you know about that?' he asked.

'Nothing. I just thought—'

'That whole phone thing was Brandon thinking he's smart.

It doesn't prove anything about Devon Garvey. Do you understand?'

'Yes,' Julia said.

'As long as we're clear,' he said. 'And I'll take that.'

He snatched the passport from her.

'You can't keep it,' she said.

'It's just to make sure we do get to see Brandon before he goes anywhere.'

It felt wrong, taking Brandon's passport. Whatever the morality, Brandon had broken no laws. Even if he had taken the money, it had been a gift.

'If he wants to leave, we should let him,' Julia said. 'It's definitely best if he doesn't meet Ruth.'

'All the same ...' Gideon put the passport in his pocket and patted it. 'I'll take care of it.' He replaced the panel. 'Brandon will have to come and see me now.'

Chapter 65

The foreman, the man in the grey suit, stands.

'On the charge of murder, do you find the defendant, Alan Johns, guilty or not guilty?' the clerk asks.

'Guilty.'

Mutters.

'On the charge of murder, do you find the defendant, Gideon Risborough, guilty or not guilty?'

'Guilty.'

A shout of 'Yes!' from Brandon's brother.

'On the charge of murder, do you find the defendant, Julia Winter, guilty or not guilty?'

'Not guilty.'

I nearly faint.

Gideon lunges for me. 'You bloody bitch.'

The security man is too fast. He grabs Gideon around the waist and drags him back. Two policemen come and handcuff him.

'It was her,' he shouts. 'She stabbed him, she killed him.'

He struggles against his restraints, his poise and calm superiority all in shreds. The jury look shocked. In the public

382

gallery Brandon's siblings watch as Gideon is dragged from the back of the court. I cannot believe that this is possibly the last time I will ever have to see my husband.

I stand here, not sure what to do. I look to the public gallery. Audrey is weeping into Sam's arms. Pearl is crying too, but smiling at the same time. Andre blows me kisses.

Ralph comes over. 'There's some forms to fill in, but you're free to go,' he tells me.

I'm confused and disorientated, more so than if I'd been imprisoned. I don't know who I am anymore, where I work, where I live.

'We should leave by a back entrance to avoid the press,' Ralph says. 'I kept it from you, because you're under enough pressure, but I've been fielding endless enquiries into selling your story, should you be acquitted.'

Since my arrest, there's not been a single moment when someone else hasn't decided where I am and what I do. Standing in a corridor, I'm bemused with no idea where to go.

Arms wrap around me. It's Audrey, Pearl and Andre, all in tears.

'Why did you never tell me, Julia – what he was like?' Mum says. 'I blame myself.'

'I knew something was wrong,' Pearl said. 'Why did you never say?'

'I've let you down, Julia,' Audrey says.

'No,' I say. 'You're both amazing.'

And suddenly I'm in tears too. We're in a huddle so tight, I don't notice him at first. It's when I break away from Audrey and Pearl that Sam puts his arms around me. He's grown in the year since I've not seen him. A man, not a boy, and nothing like his father.

As I'm holding him, I open my eyes and see Ruth leaving the court. She turns and just for a second catches my eye, then she's gone.

Chapter 66

1994 – Guildford

'It's too creepy. I'm not coming back,' Lucy said, when Julia told her about Genevieve.

She had only rung to see if Julia was willing to go on a blind date with one of Linden's friends.

Julia felt lost. Pearl was on holiday in Puglia with Rudi. Andre hadn't returned her calls and she couldn't face telling Audrey. All that tutting and *I knew it would end in tears*. Though even Audrey couldn't have foreseen such a delicious disaster.

After her conversation with Lucy, Julia returned to the lounge and stretched out on the sofa with a large bar of Fruit & Nut. She broke a chunk off, placed it on her tongue and let the warm sweetness spread through her mouth. A spasm of guilt seized her, when she thought how much more she was enjoying the house without Genevieve. Despite the macabre events, the atmosphere was more relaxed. Genevieve's notice to leave was void and Brandon had gone. It was more the kind of place she'd envisaged sharing, when she first came to Guildford.

Of course, they would have to move out eventually, though

385

Ruth had yet to mention it. Julia would probably leave Guildford and find a new job. Even be brave, like Pearl, and risk a few years of squalor to find a more exciting career. Morgan Boyd Consulting wasn't where she wanted to be.

For Julia, Guildford had been a false start in her new life, but it was only the delay of six months. There was plenty of time to change course. There'd be no reason to see Gideon and Alan again. Lucy had already agreed to stay in touch and was considering moving to London as well.

The Commonwealth Games was showing on the television; she watched people running around the track without taking much notice and put her feet up on the coffee table.

When the lounge door swung open, she looked up, expecting to see Gideon or Alan.

'Having fun?'

Brandon was leaning against the doorframe.

'What are you doing here?' Julia asked.

'I live here, remember?' he said.

He ambled over to her. His clothes were the same ones he'd been wearing the last time she saw him, as he stormed out of the house following that final argument with Genevieve. He reeked of sweat and stale beer.

'It's just, we've been worried where you were, Brandon.'

'Sweet of you to care.'

He stood between her and the door and didn't look as if he were moving any time soon.

'Can I get you something – tea?' Julia asked.

'Tea – really? You want to talk about anything else – Genevieve, perhaps?'

'You heard?'

'I heard.'

He stepped closer to her.

'Where is it, Julia?' he said.

She looked to the patio doors for an escape – they were locked.

'Gideon's got your passport,' she said.

Brandon stepped closer still. He couldn't have washed for days. The stench was revolting. Julia wanted to gag. He jabbed her shoulder with his forefinger.

'Where's my money?'

Julia hesitated a fraction too long to make a denial credible. 'I ... I don't know,' she said.

'But you do know about it?'

She nodded.

'And what – you just left it where it was?'

The truth was probably her best defence right now.

'I pushed it down the side of the bed. It was me who found Genevieve, you see. I didn't know what to do with the money, so I hid it. And when I came back, it had gone.'

'You expect me to believe that? Does Gideon have it as well as the passport?'

'No – I don't know.'

'Are you two a couple now?'

'No,' Julia said.

'A little threesome with Alan then?'

'Brandon.' She spoke softly. If she were calm and reasonable, perhaps he would be too. 'It's nothing like that. We just share a house.'

'The same way you and me share a house? But you think you're too good for me now he's around. I've seen the way you look at him.'

'I'm moving out soon. I doubt I'll see him again.'

She began to edge away from him.

'After he arrived you started to ignore me. Pretended it had never happened. You whine about how your fiancé went off with another woman but how do you treat people?'

She took another step back.

'It was a mistake, wasn't it, that night? I mean, we were never going to be boyfriend and girlfriend,' Julia said.

'Not with you sniffing round every man you come into contact with, like some bitch on heat. The second Gideon turned up, you were all over him.'

'That's not true.'

She was frightened now. Every word she spoke stoked Brandon's anger. He was leaning over her and her back was against the wall. She had nowhere to go.

'I'm not wasting my time worrying over a little slut like you,' he said. 'But I'm not leaving without my money. You and Gideon have come up with this together. Well, he's not here now. So, you need to tell me where it is. What does he want in return – the phone?'

He grabbed her hair and yanked her head back. It cracked against the wall. A sick pain ran through her neck to her stomach.

'I don't know, really, Brandon,' she said.

'Where – is – it?'

His face was an inch from hers. The stench of his breath was unbearable. She tried to twist away. He pulled her hair back farther, his weight against hers, so she couldn't move her body, only her arms. His free hand travelled to her throat and he began to press. Julia tore at his hands with her nails. His grip only tightened and he moved his elbows to pin her arms low against the wall.

'Tell me,' he said.

Her heart banged against her chest. Her scream was stifled by the pressure applied to her neck. He was going to kill her. He'd find the money and disappear. She twisted and kicked. His weight didn't move. She couldn't breathe, couldn't raise her arms – Brandon still pinned them low to the wall. She scratched around the small bureau next to her. Paper, a pen, a ruler, then something cold and hard. Scissors. She grasped them, swung her hand as hard as she could. Adrenaline gave her strength. The points pierced the soft flesh under his rib.

Brandon released the pressure on her neck though he remained leaning over her. He looked more surprised than hurt. Julia wriggled and pushed him away. He fell back. She held one hand on her throat. The other was warm and wet. She looked down to see it thick with blood. Brandon clutched his side.

He looked at the scissors. 'You bitch—'

He lurched forward, releasing his hand from his side. Blood gushed from his wound and he fell to his knees.

Julia dropped the scissors. She was still struggling for breath. Blood burbled up through the gash in Brandon's side and she thought she was going to faint.

'Call me an ambulance.'

Julia fell on the sofa. She couldn't breathe. She couldn't move.

'Call me an ambulance!' he screamed.

Julia remained paralysed. The door opened.

'What the hell?' It was Alan.

Gideon pushed past him.

'That bitch stabbed me,' Brandon said.

Gideon was next to Julia on the sofa. He took her hands from her throat and examined it. 'Did he hurt you?'

'Fuck her,' Brandon said. 'I'm bleeding to death here. Call me an ambulance.'

Alan moved to the door.

'Wait,' Gideon said. 'I need to think.'

'I'm bleeding out,' Brandon cried.

Alan hovered at the door.

'Get me an ambulance now. Or I'll tell everyone about the phone.'

Alan moved to the door.

'And that you took my money,' Brandon said.

Alan stopped and looked at Gideon. 'We have to get him to hospital.'

Julia tried to stand. Gideon pulled her back onto the sofa.

'Think,' he said. 'You could go to prison for this.'

'It was self-defence,' she said.

'He's bleeding. You've barely a mark on you.'

She looked down at her sleeve drenched with Brandon's blood.

'Get me a fucking ambulance,' he wailed.

'We can't let him ...'

Julia stopped. Gideon was already striding across the room. She knew what he was going to do, before she had time to react. He picked up the heavy marble lamp, raised it high and smashed it onto Brandon's head. The vibrations seemed to last for a whole minute, rippling through Julia in wave after wave. No one spoke. Brandon's head lay split in two, dark sludge oozing onto the floor. The flow of blood from the wound in his torso slowed. Gideon brought the lamp down again with a sickening crunch. Brandon's leg twitched one more time, before the blood from his wound ceased and he lay inert.

It wasn't real. It couldn't be real – just slapstick, comedy violence, Tom and Jerry. Julia started to laugh. And once she started, she couldn't stop.

'Shut up,' Alan said.

She kept laughing.

'Will you shut up?' Alan said. 'What's wrong with her?'

She was unable to stop, her whole body was shaking with laughter. Alan grabbed her arms and shook her.

'Shut the fuck up!'

She looked a Brandon. The blood had seeped from his body and spread across the rug. He was dead. Not Tom and Jerry. Dead. Her laughter transformed into sobs.

'What have you done, Gideon?'

'I think you mean, what have we done.'

'I didn't ... I never.'

'You never what – stabbed him?'

She looked to Alan. 'We have to call the police.'

Alan looked scared. 'She's right, Gideon.'

He drew back before Gideon had even turned to him.

'And why would we do that?'

'What else are we going to do?'

'Get rid of him.'

'We can't.'

'Do you think you're going to come out of this well, Alan? Are you going to blame it all on me?'

Alan was looking at the marble lamp, still clutched in Gideon's hands.

'No ... no, I wasn't, but ...'

'If you ever breathe a word of this, to anyone—'

'I won't.'

'I'm going to need more proof than just your word, Alan.'

'What do you mean?'

'You're going to help me get rid of him. Then you're in it as much as me – you too, Julia.'

Julia was shaking too much to speak. Alan was still looking at the lamp.

'Of course. Of course I'll do it.'

'Good,' Gideon said.

'We can't,' Julia managed to say. 'We can't.'

'Take her upstairs and put her in the shower,' Gideon told Alan.

'I'm not dealing with her,' Alan said.

'You'd rather deal with this?' Gideon asked.

Alan looked down at the bloodied mess on the living-room floor.

'Jesus,' he said.

'Then get her upstairs.'

'I'm not going,' Julia said.

But she had no strength left to resist. He pulled her to her feet and dragged her upstairs. She hadn't the strength to stand, as he pushed her into the shower fully clothed, and she slid down the side into a foetal position on the floor as he turned on the cold water.

'Clean yourself up,' he said.

She sat slumped and let the shower run over her.

'We have to call the police,' she said.

'No, Julia. We do not,' he said.

'There's a phone in Genevieve's room. Gideon wouldn't hear you.'

Hope flashed across Alan's face, then faded. 'You know what

would happen if I did that. You know what would happen to both of us.'

She was still in her clothes when Gideon came upstairs. He turned the water to warm, then stripped her naked, without ceremony, and put her clothes into a bin liner. He washed her hair with Alan's shampoo, rinsed her down, then turned the shower off and wrapped her in a towel.

'You need to rest,' he said.

'But Brandon ...'

'I'll deal with Brandon.'

He placed her on the bed.

'Swallow this,' he said.

It was one of Genevieve's little pills.

'That's what killed her,' Julia said.

'It's only one. You need some rest.'

She put her hand in front of her mouth. Gideon pushed it apart and forced the pill between her lips.

'Swallow.'

She moved the pill around her mouth and under her tongue. Gideon looked at her.

'I said, swallow.'

He knew. She swallowed.

'Now lie down.'

He rose and closed the curtains before returning to the bed and sitting beside her.

'I'll wait until you fall asleep,' he said.

He didn't have to wait long. Drained of adrenaline, her body gave little resistance to the pull of the drug.

'Julia, you need to get up.'

Someone was nudging her arm.

She dragged her eyes open. It was dark.

'Is it the police?' she asked.

She was pulled to an upright position. The lamp came on. Gideon was looking into her eyes.

'You need to wake up,' he said.

'Where's Brandon?' she asked.

'In the lounge.'

'Is he ...'

Is he dead? The blood, the smash to his skull, his leg ceasing to twitch. Of course he was dead. But perhaps she was confused. It had only been a fight and she'd dreamt the rest. She looked to Gideon's face for a clue. It revealed nothing.

'You need to get dressed,' he said. 'We have to move him tonight.'

The clock radio said 1.13 a.m. Gideon helped her dress.

'Wear your trainers,' he said.

The night was moonless. Once on the Downs they would be safe. Only crossing the street presented a problem. One insomniac, one adulterer sneaking home, would have them put in jail. But no one came to witness their laborious progress. The weight of Brandon, folded in a rug and wrapped in plastic bin liners, was nearly too heavy, even with three of them. Julia was of little help, the sleeping pill had robbed her muscles of strength.

Alan wouldn't look her in the eye during the hour and many rests it took to haul Brandon up the hill. Gideon had come there earlier in the evening and chosen the spot in a small copse, far enough off the path for the disturbed earth to go unnoticed. He had left three shovels and set up three torches.

'You're going to have to dig too, Julia,' Gideon said. 'We need to finish by dawn.'

'We can't do this,' she said.

'You want to go to prison? Come out an old woman, with no friends or family'?

She didn't reply. Gideon threw her a shovel. 'Dig.'

Her first and second strike sent shudders through her body. But with each blow she became stronger. Her shoulders and back ached, but they belonged to another person, the old Julia who hadn't killed someone. This Julia ignored pain, she was an automaton and kept digging. Shovel after shovel of earth piled high. Only Alan's occasional 'Is it deep enough?' interrupted their labour.

Eventually Gideon agreed that yes, it was deep enough.

Gideon and Alan pulled the plastic towards the hole and rolled Brandon into it.

'It'll be light soon. We need to work fast filling it in,' he said.

Julia looked into the hole. The black plastic was barely visible in the dark.

'We should say something,' she said.

'Like what?'

'I don't know. A prayer?'

'Don't be fucking stupid,' Gideon said.

Later, stumbling down the hill, filthy and too exhausted to even lift the shovels dragging behind them, they looked up to see a red glow starting to stretch along the ridge above. Dawn was breaking.

'Hurry up,' he said.

At the bottom of the hill, she managed to haul herself over the stile, only to tumble down the slope on the other side and fall face down in the road, her fingernails bloodstained, her mouth and nose clogged with dirt. She could have fallen asleep there and then, not caring if she were seen.

A hand reached under her armpit and hauled her to her feet.

'Keep moving.'

What was the point in moving or any attempt at concealment? He wouldn't lie buried for ever. Someday, maybe tomorrow, maybe next week or next year, someone would find him.

Julia looked up at Downsview Villa. For a moment she thought she saw a light glint at the top of the house in Genevieve's room. She looked again, and it was gone. The wisp of a shadow moving across the window. Impossible. It must have been the reflection of some distant headlamp and her own imagination. Genevieve was dead. Brandon was dead. The bedroom was empty.

Chapter 67

1995 – Flaxley, Worcestershire

Audrey's chicken and sweetcorn soup had gone cold. Julia wondered if she could throw it out of the window of her childhood bedroom and onto the rose bushes below, without being noticed. She wasn't sure. The wind might simply blow it onto the window underneath hers and how would she explain that to Audrey? If she attempted to throw it down the toilet, Audrey would hear. Julia wasn't allowed to go to the bathroom alone, even though all the razors had been removed. So, Julia sat and stared at the soup she'd had little desire to eat warm, let alone stone cold.

Homemade soup was Audrey's cure-all. From broken bones to broken hearts, chicken and sweetcorn, leak and potato or carrot and coriander was the remedy. Julia couldn't face any more liquids. Perhaps Audrey denied her solids in the belief that even blunt dinner knives would prove too much of a temptation. She needn't have worried – blood turned Julia's stomach. When she woke at night, shaking, her nightdress warm and wet, her first thought was that it was soaked in blood. Only when she switched on the light did she realise it was sweat.

Audrey didn't know, couldn't fathom why her daughter had tried to throw herself from a North London bridge. And Julia could never tell, not her mother, not Pearl, not anyone. But they would find out soon, when the Wells received their letter.

Audrey came in and took the tray, placing it on the chest of drawers, without noticing the full bowl of soup.

'Now where is it?' She looked around, picked up a comb and started to tug at Julia's hair. Julia pushed her away.

'What are you doing?' she asked, irritated.

'It's a real tangle,' Audrey said.

'I can do it myself,' Julia said. 'I'm not an invalid.'

Audrey watched her, assessing the comb's lethal potential and whisking it away the moment Julia had finished.

'Now, Julia. I don't want you to get overexcited, but you have a visitor,' she said.

'Pearl or Andre?'

'Neither,' Audrey said, a little breathless. 'But I think you'll be pleased to see him.'

Gideon came in and went and sat on the bed next to Julia, taking her hand. She wanted to pull it away but wouldn't in front of Audrey.

'Tea, Gideon?' Audrey asked.

'Please, Mrs Hathersley.'

Audrey scurried from the room.

'You should have come to me, Julia,' Gideon said.

Julia removed her hand from his. 'I couldn't.'

'You'd rather tell a stranger?'

'I didn't tell anyone.'

'Not completely true.'

He pulled an envelope from his jacket, its address written in Julia's hand. To Mr and Mrs Wells, c/o Michael Lancaster.

'How did you—?'

'Does it matter? It was simple enough. I was passing your house and knocked on the door to be let in. I must say, I was shocked and disappointed by what I found when I went to your room. What were you thinking?'

'They have to know,' Julia said.

'And the money, Julia, what a waste.'

'You don't understand. I think about it all the time and I've no one to talk to. It's getting worse.' She rapped the side of her head with her knuckles.

'You can speak to me,' Gideon said.

'You're not here.'

'I could be,' he said. 'I could be here all the time. Taking care of you, making sure this never happens again.' Did he mean her suicide attempt or the envelope? 'It was me who protected you from Brandon, remember? I did it all for you.'

Before Julia could reply, Audrey returned with the tea and a plate of biscuits.

'I'm glad you've come,' Audrey said. 'I've not seen Julia so animated since she's been here. You can't imagine how worried I've been about her. If that silly Genevieve woman wanted to kill herself, she should have swam out to sea, or something. For Julia to find her was dreadful. You'd never seen a dead body before, had you, not even your grandmother's. I wouldn't let you come to the funeral parlour. Even though they made her look so nice, just like she was sleeping. God knows what state that Genevieve's body was in.'

Julia flinched.

'I'm sorry, darling,' Audrey said. 'But I wish I'd followed my instincts and refused to let you move into that house. I always had a bad feeling about it. I'll never stop worrying about you, never.'

She started to weep. It was one of the few times Julia had seen her mother cry. She felt embarrassed for her.

'Don't worry, Mrs Hathersley,' Gideon said. He put his tea down and took Julia's hand again. 'She's going to be just fine. I'm going to be taking care of her from now on.'

Chapter 68

2019 – Guildford

Winter has passed, but spring has yet to arrive. Wet squalls batter Pearl's Mini as I trundle down the A3 towards Guildford.

Ruth lives in the same house I visited over a quarter of a century ago, two streets away from Downsview Villa. The front garden is dull and sodden. Later in the year, when the roses bloom, it will look spectacular.

It's a Tuesday morning. I'm not working right now as I don't need the money. I wasn't going to sell my story to the papers, but Ralph said it was the best way to get the press to leave me alone. Also, it has meant I can repay Audrey for my legal costs and have some left over. I sold the oversized house in Dulwich, which I always hated, and bought a three-bedroom flat in Tufnell Park. Sam lives with me. He's taking a year out before university, working in a bar. Audrey comes to stay. And I see Pearl all the time and, occasionally, Andre.

I ring the bell. Ruth answers almost immediately. I'm sure the burgundy body warmer she's wearing is the same one I remember from all those years ago.

'I've been expecting you,' she says.

'I wasn't sure if I should come.'

'It's good to see you,' she says. 'A free woman.'

She leads me to her lounge.

'Sit down, I'll make some tea.'

There's nothing of Genevieve's eclectic global collection of *objets* in Ruth's lounge. Everything is plain and functional. Ruth returns with two mugs of hot tea.

'You don't take sugar?' she asks.

'No.'

'I knew you wouldn't. Jenny wouldn't even have milk, let alone sugar. Makes you fat, she said, ruins your complexion. She always had a wedge of lemon instead. I used to keep them ready sliced in my freezer for when she came. I still do.' She puts her mug on the table. 'I'll always miss her.'

Ruth stares into the middle distance. Such a contrast between those sisters – but a deep, deep bond.

'Ruth,' I say.

'Why did I lie in court?' she says without looking at me.

I hadn't expected her to be so blunt.

She smiles. 'I was going to repeat what I told the police. That nothing was missing from the house, when you left.'

'But even that wasn't true,' I say.

'He deserved it – Brandon. He as good as murdered Jenny. I would have done it myself if you three hadn't. I knew what you'd done. I came around to find a few of Jenny's things. I saw you moving him. I didn't know exactly what had happened, but it must have been his fault. By the way, you did a shocking job of cleaning the lounge. It took me two days of scrubbing to get the blood off.'

402

'You knew all the time? I thought ...'

'What?'

'When we came down from the hill, I saw a figure move across Genevieve's window. I thought it was a ghost.'

'Really, Julia. I never took you to be so fanciful. That's exactly the sort of thing Jenny would have come out with. There's no such thing as ghosts. Just overactive imaginations.'

'Was it you who sent the text?'

'Yes. Sorry about that. I thought I was helping you. I found you on some software company website. They said you'd moved on. I told them I was an old friend and needed to get in touch. They gave me your number without asking many questions. Really, some people's privacy policies are terribly lax. Still, it got you what you needed, to be ready for when the police came – I thought you might not get the Surrey news. I didn't want you to be caught unprepared and end up in prison. You should have got a medal for ridding the world of that maggot.'

I do deserve prison. Brandon didn't have to die. I don't say so.

'But you changed your evidence. You told the court Gideon and Alan came back to the house with Brandon.'

'I wanted you all to get off. Of course, I didn't know how things would turn out. Didn't know you ended up marrying Gideon. And I would have tried to keep you all out of prison, until I learnt what sort of man he was. I spoke to Leanne in the sandwich shop down the road from the court. She told me everything.'

'You know it would invalidate the trial, if they found out witnesses were conferring.'

'I've no intention of telling anyone, except you,' Ruth says.

'That Gideon sounds just like my ex. Controlling, grasping. And Alan – so slimy.' She shudders.

'Did Gideon really remind you of your ex?'

'Just like him – spent my money, even money put aside for the children, their school uniforms and things like that.'

'What happened to him?'

She looks at me, a vacant expression on her face.

'Oh him,' she says. 'He disappeared, years ago. No idea where he could have gone.'

And her eyes stray to the Downs, their tops just visible through the front window.

I drive the few streets to the foot of the Downs. A steep path takes me through the long, wet grass. By the time I reach the crest of the hill, my jeans are dirty and sodden. The wind whips around my head, my hair blinding me. It's been twenty-five years since I was last here. The view has barely changed. And I have not changed as I should.

I've been a coward all of my life, taking the easiest route that presented itself. Leaving home, marrying Gideon, staying with him. After Brandon's death, I should have been strong – done what I knew to be right and gone to the police. Even if I had served time for manslaughter, I would have been free by the age of thirty. Free to marry or not marry. To choose my career. But I took the easier path and paid the price. And not just me – Audrey, Pearl and Sam.

I kneel down and touch the muddy soil. *He disappeared years ago,* Ruth said of her husband. I wonder how many more bodies are buried beneath the Downs.

I slip and slide down the slope, through the wet grass and over the stile at the bottom. I brush the worst of the dirt from my jeans and climb into the car. Debris from overhanging trees is strewn across the windscreen. I clear it with the wipers, drive to the end of the road and head for the A3. I don't look back.